THE MASTERFUL MANIPULATION OF GEORGE COVE

GERRY CRYER

BROVARY
LIMITED

Cover and book design by Swan & Horn
www.swanandhorn.co.uk
Printed by Createspace

For more information, visit:

www.gerrycryer.com

DEDICATION

This book is dedicated to two people.
To both of you I say a deep and sincere thank you.
SY created the inspiration, time and space for me to
start writing, while AS gave me the love,
purpose and reason to finish.

Эта книга посвященная двум людям,
которые преданные друг другу.
СВ, Ты вдохновляешь меня,
помогаешь найти место и время
в моей жизни,
чтоб начать писать,
АС, ты подарила мне любовь,
цель и причину довести это до конца.

ACKNOWLEDGEMENTS

There have been many who have helped
me get this far. They have helped by giving me
encouragement, advice, reading and editing.

As always, there are too many to name, but I will
pull out some for special mention. These are
Maria Hampshire, Tina Blackaby,
Greg Hancock and Terry Adams.

PROLOGUE

The phonecall came out of the blue. It was a pleasant distraction and for that reason appreciated.

'Is that you, George?'

'Yes.'

'It's Aleksandra,' the voice said. 'Please, George, can I come and see you? Will you find a room for me, somewhere to stay?'

He was taken aback. It was at least ten years since they had spoken and many more since they had last met. He heard in her voice both urgency and concern.

'Of course. Of course you can, Aleksandra, and you must stay with me. Is there a problem? When are you planning to be here?'

'I was hoping we could meet in a week's time. Will that be okay?'

'Of course,' he said and began to worry, hoping she was not unwell. 'You'll stay with me and I'll meet you at the airport.' He didn't wait for a reply but continued. 'Boryspil can be such a barren place. It will be so good to see you again.'

The prospect of seeing her again excited him. He tried to remember how long it was since they'd last met. Certainly he had not seen her since the disaster at Chernobyl. He still shuddered at the thought of that time and how closely he had been involved with it all.

One afternoon, a week later, he was standing at the airport arrivals gate, looking out for Aleksandra. Even in her late sixties, she was as easy to recognise as she had been when he last saw her over twenty years ago. She still had the classic looks and elegance that had always been her hallmark; not for her travelling in jeans and sneakers.

'Aleksandra, you look wonderful and as beautiful as ever. A princess if ever I saw one,' he said as he clasped her hands and kissed her on both cheeks. He was relieved that she looked so well.

'As ever, George your skill at flattery is totally undiminished.'

He smiled. 'I'll take that as a compliment, Professor Aleksandra Ponomarenko.'

George picked up her luggage and as they walked towards the carpark, Aleksandra looked all around her.

'Kiev is much changed in thirty years.'

'Is it that long since you were last here?' She nodded. 'You're right. It has. Even Paul McCartney came here for a concert. He was finally *Back in the USSR* although the weather was awful. It rained all day and all night. He would have felt quite at home.'

In animated chatter they meandered arm in arm across the open carpark to George's old Russian car.

'What do you want to do while you're here? Sightseeing and the tourist bit, or just relax and rest?'

'Just some R&R please, George. Let's just sit in the sun, relax, and chat about old times. Is that okay with you?'

'Sure. That sounds good,' George said as he started up the car for the drive to his home in Brovary, a rural suburb on the city outskirts. His was one of the older houses in the area, set in an acre of land, with lawn, shrubs and woodland heading to a small stream; possibly a minor bureaucrat's *dacha* at one time. Inside, it was decorated oddly, a mix of modern English furniture and the fussy Russian influence of too many ornaments,

George drove carefully, scanning every other car behind and in front of him. 'The roads are no safer now than on my first day here,' he said.

Although keen to ask her the reason for her trip, he was reticent. The Aleksandra he knew rarely did anything on a whim, but with the flight and all her preparations it had been a busy day for her and she was tired. So back at the house he held back his inquisitiveness; they had supper, then relaxed and retired early.

Aleksandra slept very deeply and the next morning, already a beautiful summer's day, she found George sitting on the sunny patio overlooking the garden, drinking coffee. He looked up from his newspaper and saw her.

'Sleep well? What plans do you have for today?' he asked. 'Want a coffee and some breakfast first?'

'Yes please, George,' she said. 'Are you free all day? There's a lot we need to talk about. There's a lot I need to tell you.'

'Of course I am. I've cleared the whole day to look after you. Shall we go into Kiev and play tourist?' he replied.

He looked at Aleksandra who now looked pensive and nervous.

'You've got to tell me, Aleksandra – is everything okay?'

'Let's just sit, please, and you can pour me a coffee. I need to tell you your life story.'

'*My* life story? I think I know all of that. What can you add, Aleksandra?" he quipped. 'Is it s ome scandal you've uncovered? I'm clean!' George was amused, but Aleksandra did not break a smile. She began talking in measured tones.

'I'm sorry, George, but actually you know very little, and it's about time someone told you. You see, almost the whole of your life has been manipulated in ways you cannot imagine. Since you were young, everything you've achieved was scripted in advance – even Chernobyl, and you need to know I was part of the team that managed the "process"; I've carried that guilt for too long. So please, sit with me a while longer. Tolerate your old supervisor from Oxford just one more time, and please try to pay more attention than you did all those years ago!'

Her attempt at humour was weak. Long ago he had put Chernobyl behind him, filing it in a box that was never to be opened. He had put it far, far behind him and he really didn't want to talk about the terrible events that had totally changed his life, but if Aleksandra had something *new* to say, he simply had to know. He was deeply intrigued, and despite already feeling uncomfortable, he had to know more.

'Okay. So when did it all start?'

Aleksandra settled back into her chair. 'For me,' she said, 'the earliest I know is what happened in 1967.'

PART I

1967–1973

THE BEGINNING: A DISPOSITION OF ASSETS

CHAPTER I

1967

It had been more than five years since 13 August 1961, when Berlin had become an enclave. Bill Familiant had kept cuttings in a file ever since. It was now a very large file. Today he was again sitting at his large mahogany desk in a sparsely decorated office rereading the news of that day from *The Times* broadsheet spread across his desk. But he didn't really need a newspaper to remind him of the events, or their impact and the aftermath.

Also on the desk were six green-covered government folders. The result of five years' work. The final shortlist of applicants.

He tilted back on his chair and swung his long legs onto the desk, presenting the soles of his highly shone black, lace-up shoes to anyone who entered his room; not that anyone other than Miss Shaw was expected. His waistcoat rose up as he put his hands behind his head and closed his eyes in deep contemplation. Unusually, he thought, not one of the applicants had ever applied for the job and, in fact, not one of them even knew there was a job, but soon they would. A wry, thin-lipped smile crossed his gaunt face.

The news of that day in 1961 had made this project more real and more urgent. He had seen it coming, while others had hoped it wouldn't. He had prepared, while others had considered. This project, the project to which he had devoted his life, would be a project that could last a long time. How long? Maybe five or ten years? Maybe a generation or two? His eyes and his mind flicked back to the newspaper headlines. Yes, this was important. It was very important. He may not be alive to see the end of it, the dénouement, but he would make sure that there would be an end; and that it would be a successful end. He would make sure that this evil of communism was crushed. It had to be, and all his life from that point had been focused on freeing Berlin, freeing

Europe, and freeing the world. He thought about that – the Free World. It was a phrase that summed up his purpose and his rationale.

Familiant was not Foreign and Commonwealth Office, nor was he MI5 or MI6. He didn't have offices in Whitehall or Curzon Street, but he did have influence, and he did have resources – both government and private – and he would make this work. His was a new world of economic sabotage. He had seen how Japan and Germany had lost the battles of arms but were already starting to win the economic war, and he was determined that Russia and their Eastern bloc allies would not do the same. He was going to make sure that they didn't win this war.

He stood up and started his familiar routine pacing around the room. It was a regular path that took him past the glass doors of the bookcase with their shelves full of files and papers, but few books. He walked past the heavy wooden door and the light switches, which worked intermittently, past the portrait of the Queen, where he always stopped as a mark of respect, onwards around and past the desk to glance out of the large sash windows onto workers and early commuters below. This is for you, he thought as he looked down at them.

His tall, thin, languid frame carried his dark pinstripe suit like a model or guardsman, neither of which he was. His background and education were suitable for a military career and overt demonstration of strength, but his style and choice was fixed to the life of subversion. He still wore his jacket in the office. He had not taken to the American fashion of working in shirt sleeves. To him, to be modern meant going without a waistcoat. He cleaned his glasses on the silk of his blue tie and leaned forward against the desk to stretch his back. Squash was not the game for someone of his height but he struggled through at least one game every week. He ran his hand through his Brylcreemed hair. It was slightly longer than it had been ten years before but it was still short; no concessions to the liberal ways sweeping in from California and the American West Coast. Familiant was a naturally conservative person.

He returned to the folders. Of all the candidates, two stood out and he was sure that if they had been asked, they would have applied. The sifting and sorting had been ongoing for almost three years. *How old would they have been when this all started?* he thought. *Barely teenagers.* It hadn't been easy to start recruiting for talented people of such young ages. Would their potential be fulfilled? Could he find the stars, or did that matter? After all, he would be behind them, a hidden hand guiding them, pushing them unseen to positions where they would do his work.

Familiant was not married. He had once reflected whether a wife would be useful to his career but had decided it would be an unnecessary encumbrance. Of course, a wife would be essential to see his genetic stock progress but through this project he would see even that ambition fulfilled. His 'children' would carry his views into new generations more than any progeny ever could, and he would be a better father than most. He would nurture and cherish his children like no other. They would succeed and take his values, ethics and principles forward. He did not need a wife for that. So, two candidates had shone out of the pack and he wanted to read their files just one more time. To be sure. After all, today was decision day.

First was George Cove. He was now sixteen. His father was from Yorkshire and his mother Scottish. Well at least there would be no profligate expenditure, he thought as a brief smile formed. He hummed as he read. In his own ear he heard himself pitch perfect, but in fact a low toneless drone filled the room as his morning tea appeared silently on his desk, served by the ever-attentive Miss Shaw. Familiant looked up. Where did the Government find this endless supply of selfless secretaries? And were they really all unmarried? It was a passing thought that didn't last too long as he returned to his reading. The low hum continued, words hardly mouthed. '*Nessun Dorma! Nessun Dorma! Tu pure, o, Principessa.*'

He returned his attention back to Cove: 'an outstanding linguist and a minor rebel at a minor public school' he read ... a *minor* public school? He supposed that it didn't matter too much because they at least had a similar ethos to the major ones. He read on: 'a competent sportsman and socially very adept'. But what else was it that made him different? He was bright enough, of course, but there were many bright ones, many of them far more intelligent, but his language skills made a difference; they made him stand out. So what was it about his background that made him different or special? Cove's father, Allan Cove, born and educated in Yorkshire, had been a captain in the British Army at the end of the Second World War and among the first into Belsen on the clean-up mission. That must have given him some character and backbone. His mother must have been tough, too – she lost her parents at the age of fifteen in a bombing raid. So Cove's genes were good, he reminded himself, but would he get on with the second candidate to be chosen? That was crucially important.

Familiant opened a second file. Anna Kowalski. She was older than Cove, but by less than a year. Her father was Polish and had come to the Britain during the war to fly Spitfires. He had been lucky to survive the ordeal. Not many did, Familiant reflected. Well, luck would also play its part in what these two youngsters would had to face. Her mother was English, and, like Cove, also from Yorkshire. No more than an interesting coincidence. Anna, was feisty and confident and determined to become an engineer. Unusual for a girl at that time.

Even so, Familiant again reflected on just why they were so special. What was it that made them his first choices? Plain old intuition, perhaps. Sometimes in life, he thought, there is value in intuition, just as sometimes fate plays its part. However much good one tries to create, fate can always trump good intent. Fate has a power of its own that takes us forward. And so, he thought, however much I analyse and try to reach a rational conclusion, sometimes it is intuition that drives me forward. He knew that, but still it sat uneasily with him, the most rational of people. Was this, he wondered, a plan based on wishful thinking and hope, or was it a meticulous programme with the purpose of undermining the evil of communism? Could he allow the sentimentality of fate and intuition to make this decision for him – this, the most important of all his decisions? If these two 'assets' were wrong, the first part of his grand design – his destiny – would fail.

There were other operations, too, to consider. He was looking at issues with Japan, China and even at home in Britain. After all, there was this Labour Prime Minister, Harold Wilson. Damn – another Yorkshireman! Maybe he had known Cove's father or Kowalski's mother? Another interesting, but fleeting thought, but this operation with Cove and Kowalski was the jewel in his crown and he had to be sure of his assets. All he had to do was give the process his approval.

He looked again at the detailed assessments laid out on the desk in front of him, and realised this involved more than sentiment – this was a real *cause*. These were his first two; the first of 'his team'. He reached for the ink pen on his desk, turned to the front page of each file in turn, and wrote in large letters: APPROVED.

He waited for the ink to dry and sat back with a satisfied look. All that was needed now were a couple of telephone calls, one to Professor Candish at Oxford, and the other to the Head Master of a public school near London, and his plan would be set in motion here.

CHAPTER II

NOVEMBER 1970

George Cove sat in his small, typically untidy student room in Jesus College, Oxford, having just returned from seeing his tutor, Professor Julia Candish, and – had he known it – even that was quite remarkable. The transition from school to university had been far less difficult than he had thought possible. In fact, getting into Oxford had been easier than he could ever have imagined. His final terms at school had been presaged by each Master who taught him, urging him not to be over-optimistic about his chances of going to Oxford.

'Cove,' Stapleton, the school's Head of Languages, had said politely, 'Oxford may be just one step too far. You really ought to be thinking more in terms of Bristol or Leeds, and even they may be a squeeze. It's fine to be able to speak these languages but you need to read all the literature as well, and we have to face the fact that you have not been as diligent as you could have been. You know we have to forecast your results and I've had to say that we all feel you're not much better than three Bs. And that will not get you into Oxford. You do understand that, don't you?'

George had listened to this homily from this man whom he hardly respected. He had heard this speech many times before, and not one of them had changed his attitude or, more importantly, diminished his own self-confidence. This latest well-meant effort to drive him to increased effort had not fazed George; nor did it encourage him to greater effort. Three Bs it may be, but Oxford needed him. It's my destiny, and Oxford's, he thought. We are meant to be as one. When it came to filling in the forms, Oxford and Jesus College were his top choice.

He was called for an interview in late November. Even getting the interview had been a surprise to Stapleton, causing him to mutter his way through a morning in the common room. The train from Paddington was slow, and George, dressed more like a country squire than a middle-class boy, daydreamed his way to the 'city of dreaming spires'. He knew his head should have been full of Stapleton's recent words of encouragement and the Russian literature quotes he'd crammed in the night before, but instead all he could do was stare aimlessly out of the window.

Oxford was colder than London and he was grateful for the dark blue Burberry overcoat. When he reached Jesus College, he found it to be more imposing than he had imagined, but then again, he thought, it's just another building and this interview is just another day in my life. Nerves were not a problem that George Cove had ever suffered from. He was confident – verging on arrogant –just one of the traits that upset Stapleton.

'Confidence is no substitute for diligence,' he had often said in class, always looking at George.

'The meek might inherit the earth,' George had once replied, 'but they never get the mineral rights.' That had landed him a double detention.

'*Privet, kak dela*?' Professor Julia Candish had asked as she welcomed him into the interview room. Hello, how are you? They spent an hour in gentle conversation in Russian, with Candish explaining some of the differences in dialect between Leningrad and Moscow. She tested him by speaking to him in Ukrainian, a language similar in many ways to Russian but not used everywhere. Romanian, a more romantic language, was one he hardly knew, but Candish tested him on it all the same.

The offer letter arrived at the school a few weeks later.

'Two Es!' exhaled Stapleton.

He didn't understand why they were setting the standard so low for George. He had more talented students who knew their literature and who were more diligent and more intelligent. He had given those students the best references and yet only one had an offer of three As, and the other two had nothing at all. But somehow Cove had been granted an almost free pass into Oxford. On his return to school he had quizzed Cove about his interview and was still none the wiser. As Cove lay back on his bed even now, he could imagine Stapleton's reaction.

Candish's assessment was similar. 'Bill,' she had said in a phonecall later that day, 'he undoubtedly has a special talent and will learn the Slavic languages to a high level of fluency, but as to an Oxford degree … I'm not sure. Are you sure you want us to take him?'

'Julia, yes please. We have a special task for him and we need to start him on his journey now. Will you be his tutor?'

'If that's what you want,' the professor said, keen to understand but knowing from past experience that she was unlikely to get much back from Familiant. 'But, it would be highly irregular, if not impossible, for me to tutor in a *male* college. I'm not sure it's been done before. I'm not sure it's even possible.'

'It's not just what *I* want, Julia, it's what *we* want. I need you to make sure he gets the education we require for the task ahead. Make it possible. I'm sure it will be far easier for you to tutor him in a male college than to get him into a *female* college! I will speak to the Vice Chancellor and the Master of Jesus if that would help.'

Sitting in her book-lined Oxford study, Julia nodded her agreement and acceptance of Familiant's will. George Cove knew none of this, and Professor Candish made sure that only she and the College Master, under threats of all sorts of government secrecy acts, were the only ones who did.

This was George's first term and he had already noticed the special attention he was receiving. He had always been attractive to women – well, girls actually, he corrected himself – and his first sexual experience was now a distant four years ago. Technically both he and Lynne Bennett had been underage, but that had never been a consideration for either of them. It had all been too exciting and too exhilarating to even consider any of the laws of the land. He had taken a bus and a train to visit her on an afternoon during the summer holidays. That term at school there had been fondling at summer parties, made dark by heavy living-room curtains. Cider, beer and Mateus rosé had been the drinks invariably supplied by fretting parents.

There had been little chance to get much further than undoing a few blouse buttons and trying to slip a hand inside. Over the weeks, Lynne had moved from resistance, to acceptance, and then encouragement. That afternoon nothing had been explicitly agreed.

'Why don't you come round and see me? Everyone will be out and we can turn the music up loud. I have the new Mothers' album.'

But the agreement was tacit. They had gone up to her room and the record was spinning as they lay on the bed. How it started George couldn't now remember. Probably he'd managed to undo the buttons on her blouse so that it was open, and probably soon after that he managed to push her bra up to expose her small breasts. He closed his eyes to remember them. They were the first breasts he had ever seen for real, and definitely the first he had ever touched or held. He had seen voluptuous breasts in *Health and Efficiency*, the naturist magazine, which had been handed around the school dorm, but these were different. They didn't sag and they were, well, they were pert. Why, he thought, couldn't all breasts stay like that for ever?

How they had moved from there to his first full sexual experience, he now couldn't recall. He only remembered that it was clumsy, with some embarrassment afterwards. But, like riding a bike, his and their competence had increased, and had there been a proficiency exam, he would have passed well before he was seventeen. He had met Lynne a few more times during the summer, had more sex, and then they drifted apart. They were part of the new hippy generation, the generation that led to Woodstock and the Isle of Wight festival, and they had absorbed the culture without any understanding of the principles. Their sex was simply part of their shared education.

The year with Francesca had been when he first experienced something that he felt was love, realising sexual activity could be more than a drive for procreation. Their lovemaking had a tenderness that had been missing from those first few times with Lynne.

And now in Oxford, opening his eyes just a little, he looked around his room. Maybe that's it, he thought. Maybe his professor, who was, after all, a good-looking woman for her age, fancied him. Maybe he was going to be asked for sexual favours in exchange for tuition. He would watch out for that. He'd never had sex with anyone older than him – let alone at least twenty, maybe even thirty, years older. He realised he had no idea how old she was. Yes, that would be an interesting tutorial.

Anna Kowalski's entry to Oxford had been more straightforward and had required far less intervention from Familiant. She was diligent and hard working. There weren't many girls who reached the necessary academic standards and showed such interest in engineering. All that was required was a gentle prod to make sure the University's natural prejudice against a grammar-school girl didn't hold her back.

Familiant thought it slightly odd that it was the school and *not* the gender that had been the biggest obstacle she had to overcome. She managed to obtain three A grades at A-level with little effort or discomfort, and went up to University in the first week of October. She was more than just a little bit apprehensive.

Oxford's architecture was on a scale she had never seen before. Her interest in engineering had been awakened at a very early age, as she had sat waiting in Huddersfield train station for her father to return from a trip to Poland. The trains filled the platform of the Victorian station with white plumes of smoke and steam that reached high up into the vaulted glass ceiling. She had been only five or six years old, and she remembered wondering why the ceiling hadn't fallen down on her head.

Across the cobbled road from her home was a path leading to a bridge that spanned the railway. She used to spend hours there, waiting for the steam locomotives pulling their carriages to some far-off place. She would run across the bridge to be right above the track carrying the belching locomotive so she could be covered in and breathe the steamy smoke. She loved the power of the trains and dreamed someday of riding the footplate herself.

Then there was the closed and covered market in the middle of the town, a bustling palace of people hunting for the best value. She remembered the huge – well at least they were to a five-year-old – table of loose eggs, and spending hours with her granny trying to find ones with double yolks. It was a game they continued back in the kitchen of her house in Green Park, where they kept a tally of their success. Anna was sure they always did better than any other shopper. It was through the tallying of the eggs with her granny that she learnt all her numbers and how to add and subtract. When she went to her first school she could already manage with ease all the simple arithmetic, way beyond the ability of all the others.

Frilly dolls and girly games were not for her – at least not then. She had her bike and was as much interested in taking it apart to put it back together again as riding it. Of course, that meant she was turned away and shunned by other children in her school. The girls didn't understand her lack of interest in dolls and the boys resented that she excelled at things in which they were supposed to be master. They didn't enjoy being beaten by a girl.

But solitude had given her strength and purpose, and she had shown this as she had grown to become beautiful in a Slavic way. Sharper angles to her face than her Yorkshire friends and an independent streak of defiance were tempered only by her desire, deep down, to be one of them. She chose her partners on *her* terms. Many of them had tried to court her and lure her into sex with offers that, at best, involved the back-row seats in the cinema. All were rejected.

Instead, she planned how and where at the age of seventeen she would give away her virginity. It was to be with a much older man who, she thought, would at least have experience; far better than her and her novice partner both groping about without knowledge. This man wasn't to become her lover; once he had fulfilled the purpose she had in mind, he was never to be in her life again. Today, she thought, he might be leaning on a bar in Leeds or Bradford, or even better London or Plymouth – both faraway places. Later, he would be bragging to his friends about how he deflowered a seventeen-year-old Polish girl. Let him, she thought, but he would not be in her life.

She took a mid-week train to Leeds and went into the Station Hotel, via the ladies room where she applied heavy make-up to make her look older. Then she headed to the bar. She watched carefully before choosing her partner for the night. Mid-twenties, she guessed, and probably a sales representative. Perfect. Feigning poor English and speaking mostly in Polish, she sat next to him and tried to explain that she had little money and nowhere to stay that night. He bought her a port and lemon, offered her scampi bar snacks that were easily refused, and then another port and lemon. She refused the third, saying she had to leave, but he insisted that if she really had nowhere to stay she could use the couch in his hotel room, only three floors above. Should they go up there now? She looked tired. So they did.

They had to sneak round corners as they knew the hotel would have strict rules. She giggled a little, trying to show she had drunk more than she should, but coming from a Polish family she had probably drunk more than he could ever manage. She would survive her family celebrations far better than he would! If only he really knew. Through her giggles his ardour increased and, quickly, in his room, he tried to kiss her. She did not resist, and shortly she was no longer a virgin. At five in the morning, in the dark of the room and the cover of the night, she dressed and slipped away.

She had become a woman. She was preparing herself for a new life – soon, she hoped, in Oxford. She didn't know this man and no one else would ever know about this night – except of course for Familiant, because he knew everything about the two young people on his shortlist.

Her early Oxford days were uneventful. She performed well in her tutorials and was liked by her professors. She settled into her rooms but did not make many friends. One morning, while Anna was going about her studies, and George was idling, doing nothing more than lying on his bed, a meeting about them was being held in Familiant's office in London.

'Julia, tell me about George. How is he doing in his first term?'

Professor Candish considered the question for a moment. 'I'm not sure I can say much about his academic abilities. He is an infrequent visitor to many lectures. However, socially, with his very British good looks, fair hair and cheeky blue eyes, he is still a real hit, particularly in the female colleges! If we don't act quickly, Anna may be outside and beyond his range.'

'And, Douglas?' Familiant asked turning to Douglas Beck, Professor of Engineering at Oxford University. 'How is Anna?'

'A perfect student,' was the short and sure answer.

'So, Julia. Douglas. What do we think? Is it time to bring them together?'

Julia Candish looked across at her colleague from Oxford. They shared a glance and then both gave a short nod of agreement.

'Yes, Bill. I think it's time we did that. If we don't act now then we may be far too late.'

'Then very soon I will again call everyone together and we can make a plan. Thank you both,' and with that, Familiant brought that gathering to an end.

CHAPTER III

JANUARY 1971

The meeting was in Familiant's office. The tea, as always, was served by Miss Shaw who had added Jaffa Cakes to the usual selection of plain and chocolate biscuits. How are you supposed to dunk those? Familiant thought, but he saw his guests were quick to eat them and didn't worry about the niceties of dunking. Did Miss Shaw have her own intelligence network? Every guest to his office seemed to get the food they wanted. It was just a passing thought while waiting for Julia and Douglas to finish their conversation on what Familiant assumed was some Oxford business.

It surprised Familiant that the final two members of this informal and unofficial group should also seem to be so deep in conversation. Aleksandra Ponomarenko and Lord Richard Ridley were unlikely companions. Of course, if he had not seen the skills and influence they could bring, and so brought them to the team, then it was unlikely they ever would ever have met.

Aleksandra Ponomarenko was a Byelorussian who had come to England with her parents, as a thirteen-year-old, soon after the end of the war. Familiant knew how it had been arranged and what information and knowledge her father had brought with him, but there were always secrets that even Familiant was unwilling to share. Aleksandra was here because of her own skills and her deep knowledge of life behind the Iron Curtain based on her own personal experiences and studies.

Based at the LSE – the London School of Economics – she had become a leading analyst and authority on Soviet economics. On this side of the Iron Curtain there was probably no one with greater insight or understanding into the world of five-year centralised Soviet planning than she did. Her skill was not just that she was an outstandingly good economist; she was also a political analyst who had connections and access, and she was allowed to travel.

In fact, so important was she to the governments of the West that she had to be hidden.

Hiding her had been Familiant's idea some ten years earlier. That was when they had first met, but the brilliance had been how he'd hidden her skills from the Soviets. To complete her work he needed her to be able to travel and be available to her contacts. But if she had been hidden too deeply, then travel would be restricted and her lustre diminished. Familiant had hidden her in open view of everyone, therefore, as an average and junior research assistant at the London School of Economics.

There she published a few rather uninspiring papers, often written by Familiant's team, that neither caught anyone's eye nor marked her as one to watch. Instead it freed her for her real work and allowed her to live a more normal life, attending conferences as just another middle-rated academic. Sadly, Familiant thought, she rather dressed the part, with a cheaper choice of clothes than her slim body deserved and a mousey haircut of academic featurelessness that hid her natural beauty. One day, he thought, she would be seen for what she was and then maybe he could countenance another project of a slightly more personal nature.

In fact, it was through Aleksandra that Cove had first been brought within the net of his search. In Germany in 1946 there were three occupying armies: the British, the Americans and the Russian. Often they had to meet to resolve local difficulties and protocols. As soldiers, they had pride and they had to demonstrate hospitality to each other in time-honoured ways.

Often trips into the Russian sector, with Russian hospitality and too much vodka, left every British soldier with a sore head the next day; and so, before such trips, the young British officers, many hardly out of university, were stood in a line by their Commander and lectured on the need to stay upright – at least until they were back in their cars. Then they were fed a large spoonful of foul-tasting olive oil 'to line your stomachs and uphold British reputations'. They hoped the Russians felt as bad on their reciprocal trips, after a night of single malt whiskey, but they doubted it.

It was on one of these sorties that a young British captain, Allan

Cove, was approached by a Russian Captain, perhaps two decades older than him. This was Pavel Ponomarenko – Aleksandra's father. Their meetings were at first no more than routine. Later, as they became more cordial, and it became clearer to Cove that there was a wider agenda. Ponomarenko was a soldier *second*, with no more interest in being in Germany than Captain Cove; his first and major role was as an economist. He had participated in the central planning committee and he understood not just the structure but also the detail of the Soviet state. He knew the personalities, he knew their weaknesses, he knew their foibles; and, more importantly, he wanted out.

Cove was coached through Pavel's extraction from the East by unnamed officers of the British Special Operations Executive. But there were conditions. Pavel would only come if his family, were also smuggled away from their home in a small town south of Minsk, the capital of Byelorussia, as they would be in danger of retaliation and retribution. Their journey to freedom took them from the heart of the Russian empire, through Lithuania, Latvia, Estonia and the Baltic, on to Stockholm, across to Scotland, and finally down to London. It was a terrifying ten days for Aleksandra and her mother, but it culminated in safety and reunion with her father, whom they hadn't seen for four years, and that was how Aleksandra arrived in England. Aleksandra owed her skill as an economist to her father, her resilience to her mother, and her life to George Cove's father. If Aleksandra had been brought up as a rough-and-tumble street fighter, then Lord Richard Ridley was a scion of the establishment and a dashing sabre man of the one-on-one duel. Schooled at Eton, he came from inherited money, had been Cambridge-educated, trained in the City, ennobled, and on the death of his father some twenty years ago, promoted to Chairman of Wollacott – a leading London bank – and a dozen other major companies. His type was known to all, but *he* was unknown except to a few.

He was connected through every layer of British society from personal contacts, many of whom were the sons of his father's friends, through to the proverbial man on the street in the now defunct Clapham omnibus, who bought the products his companies made. These connections turned him from simply rich to wealthy. As the interest and dividends just kept arriving, he couldn't spend it fast enough to reduce his wealth.

Now in his mid-fifties, and seemingly as round as he was tall, Lord Ridley was a trader and a financier; and Russia needed trade and finance. This, Familiant supposed, was the basis of the conversation between them now. Aleksandra would be acquiring more information to make new connections to help her join up more dots, to make better predictions, so that, among others, Familiant could make better decisions.

The interruption by Miss Shaw with the tea had been timely. They concluded with agreement on the immediate way forward and the only question left was when precisely the right time was for George and Anna to meet. What did they want out of such a meeting? Did they want them to be social friends or lovers? The possibility of marriage had been discussed, but quickly rejected; other relationships might become necessary as the plan progressed.

'Friendships are awfully fickle at university these days, from what I see,' Beck suggested while running his hand though a full but unruly mop of white hair. 'To keep them together, maybe they need to have a – what should I call it? – more fulfilling relationship.' His nervous tone suggested a rather prudish view by the standards of the day, but with an acceptance of the realities of life and the needs of the project.

'Of course,' Familiant interrupted. 'We will have to break them apart at the right time. We can't have them getting sentimental and soppy over each other. Otherwise all this effort will be wasted.'

Picking up the theme, Lord Ridley continued.

'If we need them to stay close after all this is over then we need to make sure that they have common and shared passions, but we also need to make sure that the breakup leaves them as friends. From my little experience a long time ago with Lady Tara Lindstedt, that's not always so easy. I have to say that she was not a very happy person.'

He smiled with the assumption that this scandal was well

known and the lesson he was proffering was well and easily understood.

Familiant mused on the indiscretion. Well, he thought, I suppose he's said little more than what was in the papers of the day. At that time there hadn't been the kind of lurid details that would accompany a similar action in the tabloids today. He tried to remember the short court report. What was it? Criminal damage caused by a Tara Lindstedt with a pot of light blue paint poured over a black Bentley belonging to a young Lord Ridley?

Familiant brought the meeting to a halt.

'I don't think we all need to hear all of the details of what has to be planned. Can we leave the task of getting them together you two, Julia and Douglas? After all, we have already put their pastoral care into your hands for the next couple of years. Can you deal with it for us? I am sure you will let me know when and how, and – how shall I put this delicately – the key parts of what you have planned are "consummated". Meanwhile, let us all think about the wider context.'

Further nods of approval followed around the table, and one more step had been achieved.

The professors Candish and Beck travelled back together on the Oxford train and discussed the next steps and actions to be taken. They both understood the importance of their task and the delicate nature of what was required. To bring two people together was easy enough, to make sure they became lovers more difficult, but to build a bond so strong that they would become life-long friends was almost impossible.

The problem was almost intractable for two academic minds, untutored in affairs of the heart. This wasn't their specialism. They only dallied with the pastoral care of the students; their responsibility was to feed the mind and not the soul. No wonder, Candish thought, Familiant hadn't wanted a long discussion. She wondered if he had cut the conversation short because he was unable to relate to the task. As the train pulled into a cloudy and overcast Oxford Station they had come to a conclusion and developed a plan. But they needed help, and this required clearance from Familiant. For that, they would have to wait until they were back in their rooms in Oxford.

It was later that night that Familiant took the phonecall from Professor Candish and he considered their request; it made perfect sense. The next step would make or break the project, and he understood exactly what had to be done, but it had to be handled most sensitively. This plan did mean one more person would become involved, and he knew that one more person who knew about the plan and its purpose, was one more security risk. A secret is never a secret if more than one person knows about it. It had to be someone who could read their minds and understand their needs, and who was already in the team. But who? Familiant reached for his phone.

'Miss Shaw, could you see if Aleksandra could join me for dinner tonight?'

'I see the problem, Bill,' Aleksandra said later across the table from Familiant. 'I had wondered what Julia and Douglas would come up with. And I see your problem. What can I do?'

Familiant had spent the afterno on pondering that same question. The skills required were clear. Whatever other skills they brought, introducing anyone else was a risk. Could he afford to take such risks so early? Also he – or for that matter she – also needed to be a good counsellor and advisor to his children. The security requirements were already specified but did they need to know the whole story? Probably not, he thought. Familiant spelt out these new parameters to Aleksandra.

'The bigger issue, *Sashunia*,' he said, 'is what else they can do for us.'

The use of the affectionate diminutive of her name surprised her. Although they had had many dinners together like this, never before had he called her by any familiar name. She hesitated as if brooding over his question, but now her mind was elsewhere.

Familiant was only ten or so years older than her and she had always looked on him as an uncle and friend, but *Sashunia*? She looked carefully across the table. Why *Sashunia*? Why now? She looked into his eyes across the table and there was no discernible change. He gave nothing away for free and Aleksandra pulled herself back to the core question.

'Bill, what if we had someone who could also read their minds and intentions? What if they also knew the Eastern Bloc politically? Would that help us?'

He considered what she said.

'Interesting, but Aleksandra, you will get to know them and understand their intentions, hopes and aspirations so well. Do we really need anyone else in on the secret? You are the person we need. I'm not sure we want anyone else right now.'

Aleksandra contemplated his words. This was so much like Familiant, she thought. Nothing could ever be simple, and he had to be in control. He needed to manipulate and move the pieces around his own personal chess board, but was this really him, or was it because of the importance he placed on the project? Was there even any difference between Familiant and the project? She had known him for over ten years and he had always been driven and focused on the outcome.

The more she listened to him now, the more she responded to his enthusiasm and commitment. His drive mirrored her passion, and she had been a willing and supportive advocate of the project from the very start. Unlike Familiant, however, she had not thought through where and how it would move forward, but now there were real people involved. George and Anna. She had never met them, but already they had become part of her life.

'You have a plan, Bill. You've worked something out and just want to test me with it. You don't listen to my ideas; you just want me to agree with you!'

Aleksandra didn't quite know why she started to taunt him. Was it because he had called her *Sashunia*? She had not spoken to him like that before and it felt unnatural and awkward.

A hint of a smile. 'Of course, *Sashunia*, I want all of your skills brought to this matter. I would never want you to be just a yes woman, but you are right; I do have an inkling of an idea. Did you know that Cove's father and Anna's mother are nearly the same age and both were brought up in Yorkshire? I wonder if they've ever met? Wouldn't it be interesting if they knew each other? Or if they were related?'

Familiant sat back in his chair contemplating first his words, and then which of the many fine grappas on the menu he would have as a *digestivo*.

'You couldn't make that work, Bill?' she asked. Or was it a statement? 'Of course if it was true, then they would certainly share something that would keep them together. But don't go down that road. It's very unseemly. What else do you have in mind? How would you do it? What do you need?'

'We need someone in Poland or Ukraine,' he replied. 'When is that conference you are going to at Chernobyl? The energy conference is in Kiev, right? Close to that new nuclear station they are building. By the way, when will that be finished?'

As ever, Familiant's grasp of her everyday life astonished Aleksandra.

'The conference, as you know full well, is next year, and the reactors are due to be finished in around five or six years; nineteen seventy-six or seven.'

'Are you writing a paper for it?' Familiant barely looked up from the drinks menu.

'No.'

'I think you should.'

This wasn't a statement, it was an order, and Aleksandra riled at its directness. One moment *Sashunia*, and the next I'm staff again.

'And,' he continued, 'you may need some help from a bright Oxford engineering undergraduate.'

Familiant looked up momentarily to check that Aleksandra had fully grasped his idea. She had, and so he returned to his grappa selection and Aleksandra's thoughts turned again to Familiant. She still didn't know him, but she trusted him. Yes, she trusted him –almost with her life.

CHAPTER IV

MAY 1971

George had taken to Oxford life and Oxford had taken to him. Well, not all of Oxford. A social animal at his best, he was living the high life. Friends made in the few weeks that constituted a term at Oxford had been met again at balls and parties around London. George had already risen a few rungs up the social ladder. His personal life had become enhanced with an almost never-ending stream of beautiful girls to date or, as his grandfather used to say, to walk out with. He had rejected the term 'girlfriend' and replaced it with 'companion', which he felt more accurately described the relationships he was trying to build.

But of all his social coterie, he was spending more and more time with one special companion. Jamila Mnatzakanova was a beautiful and almost statuesque postgraduate history student from Azerbaijan. He enjoyed the attention of the slightly older woman, even if it was only by three years.

They each had their own rooms, and though very much against the rules of their colleges, had managed to spend many evenings and then latterly, nights together. Jamila had an infectious laugh, a winning smile and a strength of character he enjoyed. She and George spoke together in Russian and made love with a Slavic intensity. They had become one of the social couples in Oxford.

While he seemed to know nearly everyone in Oxford worth knowing, sadly this did not include many of the academic staff. He was an infrequent visitor to lectures, although he did try his best, hangover permitting, to attend tutorials. These he enjoyed due to what he believed was the extra attention being paid to him by Professor Candish, which he was sure, of course, was really due to his sexual attractiveness. So when she asked him to stay on after a tutorial and 'share some tea with her' it was easy to agree.

'George. I'm sure you have a huge talent but I need to see more of it.' George spluttered over his tea as he heard what he thought was an obvious innuendo. Was this to be his day? His optimism was quickly deflated as Professor Candish continued.

'You are a most talented linguist. A natural. You have absorbed dialects and slang, but that isn't sufficient to get you the sort of degree you want, if in fact you'll get any degree at all. You play at the *dilettante*, but we didn't bring you here to enhance your social skills. We need to find something to test you, to stimulate and stretch those idle brain cells of yours into life. Literature clearly isn't going to make that happen. We need to find something more real for you, with real and living people.'

Candish looked up at George to see if her words were having an effect. Timing now was crucial. There would, of course, be other opportunities and times but, in discussions with Professor Beck, they had fixed on this as the best – and most likely successful – route forward. His eyes were certainly fixed on her, but she was unsure what she saw. Her cheeks flushed when she realised. He wasn't concentrating on the words; he was concentrating on her. His eyes were focused on her breasts, then her legs and back to her breasts. So be it. She had never thought of herself as a *Mata Hari*, but if a little sexual overtone was required to convince him, then that was what it would be. And to be honest, she thought, slightly adjusting the buttons on her blouse, she enjoyed his physical attention. She looked at him and fleetingly wondered what it would be like to seduce a student, and in particular George. Would Familiant ever make that request of her? She blushed slightly at the thought and moved on.

'I have two things in mind for you, George. We need to broaden your regional language skills a little. Your Russian is superb, but as a diversion I think you should also learn a little Polish this year. You'll find that easy, and next year we'll add Ukrainian. They're not in the syllabus so it would mean you having to come to extra tutorials with me…' she hesitated. 'Although it would be better if you could also find a natural Polish speaker to practise with. And here is the second thought: we should drop literature totally from your workload.'

At this, George started to show some real interest in what

the professor was saying. Literature was eight hours of lectures a week that now he wouldn't have to attend. Of course, he didn't go to many of them anyway, but at least he could feel less guilty about it now. He reflected on that for a moment. He didn't actually feel much guilt about missing the lectures, but to leave with no degree would not be a good idea. He had already settled for a third class and had never had any real aspirations to a first or even a second. To get those you needed to miss all the social events and work instead, and that, he thought, was hardly what university was all about. He didn't notice that Professor Candish had started speaking again.

'Of course, we can't just let you do nothing here. I would like you to think about taking up politics and economics. I have discussed this with the Master and we can change your Tripos to a different degree.'

The Master had expressed grave reservations. However, another phonecall from his old college friend, Familiant, had made his decision easier and finally it had been agreed. Changing Tripos was one thing, but changing the syllabus for a particular student, and hence the examinations, was very unusual. Professor Candish had struggled with the protocol and etiquette before she had approval from the Senate by explaining to the Vice Chancellor, the academic head of the University, as much as Familiant allowed her. And she had to do it in such a way that gave away none of the real rationale. Then, more sensitively, the Vice Chancellor had to explain to the heads of both Economics and Politics why an undergraduate was going to be supervised by a female researcher from the LSE. That tested all his skills as a lawyer and advocate.

A new and expanded Tripos was not what Cove wanted to hear. This now sounded like more – not less – work, but Candish pressed on. She leaned slightly forward, spoke more softly and, as George was to remember later, she took both his hands in hers. She didn't, but the older academic was doing her best to woo and romance a young undergraduate.

'George, your talents are unique and we don't have the skills here to bring them to the fore. In addition to my undivided attention to your progress, I want you to accept an additional supervisor who will be joining the university next year as research associate.'

George's mood dropped even more. More work. Another supervisor. Finding the time to meet one was bad enough, but now he had to fit in two.

'If we don't do this, George, soon we may have to face other problems around your degree. You do understand, don't you?'

He recognised the subtle threat couched as a question. He recognised the subtlety and knew he was now cornered.

'I would like you to meet her tomorrow and let's see if you can get along?'

At least it's a female, thought George. Well that might lessen the blow.

'When would you like me here and does she have a name?'

'Let's say four-thirty for tea here, in my rooms, and her name is Aleksandra Ponomarenko.'

At the same time, Professor Beck was having tea with Anna Kowalski. Her academic performance could not be faulted. If anything, she was overzealous and had started to develop a reputation for being excessively focused and socially clumsy, which, if they knew her better, they would understand was ill-deserved. She was going to be successful and she wasn't going to let any of the frippery of Oxford get in her way.

'Anna,' Professor Beck started, 'outstanding work this past year. You have certainly come to the fore and been noticed. I wonder, could I ask a favour of you?'

Like Cove sitting across in Oxford in a different college, this was not what she had expected when the request to meet with her professor had been delivered to her rooms by a college porter. Like most people when called in to see the Beak – one example of the slang she had quickly come to learn – she had assumed it was for a reprimand. She had spent the previous night trying to work out what action or omission had given cause for one, and could find none. That wasn't helpful and only increased her worry. Who had she offended, or who had complained? It reflected her core insecurity. She was a loner and she was female, and those didn't fit well here, but, she thought, if talent and perseverance meant anything, then she would succeed.

'May I?' Professor Beck broke into her thoughts.

'May you what?' she answered, slightly confused, having already lost the thread in their conversation.

'May I ask a favour of you?'

'Of course.'

'We have a new research associate coming up to the university and she's a bit of an economist or something. Don't quite understand her work. It's all a bit qualitative for me. I much prefer the things we can build and kick.'

It wasn't at all true, but for the purposes of this request it was a good piece of bumbling and acting.

'She is writing a paper for some conference later this year. Something to do with energy and the new nuclear reactor being built at Chernobyl. She will need some support on the engineering side and I thought, as you originally come from that part of the world, you might like to help her. What do you say? It will look good on the old CV someday.'

This was not what she had expected and Anna was taken aback. Why her? There must be more talented students. What about all those postgraduates in the labs? They would jump at this opportunity. But what was the expression? *Never look a gift horse in the mouth.* Her part of the world was Poland, and she was really only English by default. She could see why Beck didn't teach geography. *Chernobyl is in the Ukraine,* she thought, but if he could overlook these minor discrepancies then she would as well.

'Absolutely, Professor. I would be delighted. When? What do I do next?' The words fairly tumbled out in her sudden and obvious enthusiasm.

'That is wonderful, Anna. She will be in Oxford tomorrow, when you can meet her and work through how you are going to work together and what needs to happen. Now let me just say, Anna, that this must not interfere with your other work. This will not get you a degree. Do you understand?'

Anna nodded with her thoughts elsewhere.

'Then it is agreed. Let's say you should be here at ten-thirty for coffee in my rooms, and her name is Aleksandra Ponomarenko.'

Aleksandra Ponomarenko was already in Oxford as George and Anna were accepting their invitations. She was reading the files given to her by Familiant and decided they were two very different people who required two different approaches. George, she thought, had to see the excitement, the thrill and how it would take him to new and more exciting places. He had to be sold in his heart. Anna, the engineer and pragmatist, had to see it as an intellectual challenge and be sold in her head. Yet over time, one had to add his head to his heart, and the other her heart to what her head told her. Why did Familiant make her life so difficult? Or was it that he was the one who made it interesting?

The meeting with Anna was first and, as she expected, it was the easiest. She explained about the conference and the need for some technical support with her paper on the workings of the nuclear plant that was being built, the infrastructure of roads, and the personnel needed to support it. In return, she would teach Anna some economics, which she felt would be beneficial to her studies.

To pull at Anna's heart, Aleksandra told her the story of the journey that had led to her being in Oxford that day.

'Aleksandra Ponomarenko, known to her closest friends – of whom,' she added quietly, 'there were very few – as *Sashunia*, arrived in England just after the war as a thirteen-year-old. Fluent in Russian, she spoke no English.'

Aleksandra reminisced about Minsk and Byelorussia, the summers, the flowers and the driving, bitter cold of the winter snow. She talked of those awful ten days when she and her mother had made their way to Stockholm and then England, where they knew no one, and couldn't speak the language of anyone they met, but she also remembered the joy of again being with her father after their four-year separation, and the tears of happiness when at last they hugged. From the day she had arrived in her new country, she had studied hard and learnt English, although she still had a 'Russian' accent that made her different.

As she was talking, she thought she remembered and understood the same loneliness and exclusion noted in Anna's file, because she, too, was different. She felt she understood Anna better than she would George. Anna had been different and had fought just as Aleksandra had fought, and both had achieved. George, however, had drifted through his life with good looks, charm and an unusual gift for words and language. He had been blessed, and life had been easy. Now Familiant was making it even easier.

She looked deep into Anna's eyes. 'I studied as my father watched over me, ensuring not a minute was being wasted. First, he made sure that I learnt English to match my native Russian. It was so much easier for me than my mother, who wasn't surrounded each day at school by the chattering of classmates.'

She explained how they had arrived in England late in May and the next full term of school was three-and-a-half months away. In this time she had learnt enough English to join a class of nine-year-olds. Almost twice their size, she had found it a humiliating experience, but over the year she had moved closer into her own age group. It was hard for the school as well. Aleksandra had been a talented mathematician and the simple sums given to the nine-year-olds offered her no challenge at all. Her maths class had to be set separately.

By the end of the year, she was on a two-year course finishing in the national examination of O' level exams. The brightest children in the school would take up to ten subjects. Aleksandra was among these, but because of her poor English she was only able to take the maths and, of course, the subject in which she excelled – Russian. Again she remembered the exclusion and the need to be part of the school. She wanted to be like her new friends, and feel the same excitement of waiting for exam results. She wanted to feel the pressure and be the same as the rest, but in those early days, she never did feel quite the same and that feeling had stayed with her forever. It had driven her on ever since.

At the times when others were struggling with dissections of frogs' legs or translating Greek, Aleksandra was improving her English, and she committed herself with a passion. So when she started on her A-level exams – she had reached near fluency in English. She loved the English language but she shunned the study of its literature because she didn't want to have to compare it with the Russian masters she so adored. So, instead, she read newspapers and found her real love – economics. With her three chosen subjects of mathematics, economics and Russian, she started on a course that finished with a first-class economics degree from the London School of Economics.

Aleksandra had joined *The Economist*, a weekly magazine, and was writing under her own by-line. Her editor complimented her, saying she was incisive and perceptive and had a real understanding of Soviet thought. She saw both the strategic issues and the immediate imperatives. She could interpret, understand and predict. This was where her story with Anna finished.

'Why did you go back to the LSE?' Anna asked.

'They made me an offer which I thought meant I could do more of the things I really wanted to. I could still write for *The Economist*, but also do proper research.'

She didn't add that it was at this time when she first came to the attention of Bill Familiant, who recruited her when she was twenty-five. Recruiting her was not difficult, for, despite her background, her economics had told her that the rigid dogma of the five-year plan and the centralisation of planning could lead to nothing other than deeper misery for the people she loved so deeply. Unlike Familiant, hers was not an ideological dislike of communism and its demand of loyalty to a dogma, nor of the brutality that enforced the dogma; it was a practical humanitarian concern for those who lived under these regimes. She could not accept the lack of food, the hardship in the winter and the suffering that stretched from Leningrad to Odessa, and from Minsk to Lugansk. These were still her people and she was going to help them. Familiant saw she wasn't just an economist. She had become a strong and insightful political analyst.

Anna sat rapt as Aleksandra spoke and told her life story. Anna knew what she meant and she felt an immediate connection and understanding. She wanted to be like Aleksandra, and after years of fumbling around she felt she had found a role model she could admire and respect. Anna wanted a background like Aleksandra's. Although she was English, she was really Polish. She spoke Polish as well as she did English, but she didn't know who her relatives were and she had never seen them. She wanted a personal story and she wanted a heritage. She wanted to help Aleksandra. As she was running with these thoughts she didn't hear Aleksandra say, 'And of course you will be named on the paper as co-author.'

Even if she had heard, it wouldn't have mattered. She was sold and was already thinking through where to locate and access the technical sources she would need and which professors she would have to consult. She was sure Professor Beck would help with that. After all, he had almost insisted that she should do this.

Aleksandra now had to turn her thoughts to George. She was dreading that meeting. Talking to Anna had been so easy. They were two of a kind with the same motivations. George was a different type. He had no reason to want her as a supervisor.

For once, George was early and was in Professor Candish's room just before four-thirty. Candish was at her desk working while George poured them both some tea. A knock sounded and the porter popped his head round the door.

'Professor, you have a guest, an Alexander Pora...' His voice tailed off as he struggled and mumbled his way through the Russian name. Aleksandra was right behind him. She pushed past and outstretched her hand.

'Hi, I'm Aleksandra. You must be Professor Candish. I have heard so much about you. It is a pleasure to meet at last.'

They had long ago agreed that the subterfuge of ignorance of each other was an essential part of this play.

'And you must be George Cove? So we are here to decide if I will take you on as your supervisor.'

The shock was visible on George's face. He thought he was here to decide if he wanted her as a supervisor and not the other way round.

Aleksandra switched to Russian speaking at a pace which demanded every ounce of his concentration. She explained the basis of the five-year centralised planning, and the move from a rural farming society into an industrialised country with a preponderance of heavy industry. She explained how the satellite countries such as the Ukraine were being used as industrial heartlands. It was an incisive summary covering the role of the Council of Ministers, the Politburo, Gosplan and the likely outcome of Brezhnev's new policies. George often had to interrupt to get explanations of words he didn't know, mainly economic terms.

Candish sat at her desk, half listening and half watching, as she thumbed through some papers. She was trying to assess whether Cove was moving in their direction, and if she would have to interrupt and nudge him. But she had never seen him so animated and engrossed. Was it the challenge of the language, the power of the subject. or Aleksandra's enthusiasm for a subject that she was passionate about? Aleksandra finally finished talking and took a sip of the tea that George had poured.

'Now, Mr Cove, may I have your analysis? You now have some data and facts. I assume you read the newspapers. You're at Oxford because you have some brains. What do you think are the prospects for the Soviet economy for the next five years?'

He was being examined and he knew it. He hadn't expected a viva. Up to this point in his life he hadn't sat any examination that had meant anything to him. Everything had been on his terms. He had decided where he went and what he would do. He was the centre of his world and he determined his destiny, yet here was someone who challenged that notion. Here was someone who was going to decide if he could join her club. It was not going to happen like that because George was in control and he decided what happened in his life. A streak of competitiveness surfaced. She had set him a challenge. If he backed out and said 'no' now and walked away, then she would win and he would lose. He didn't like losing. He wasn't going to allow that to happen.

Although he didn't really read the newspapers, he had occasionally listened to some friends' talk of the evil of communism, and Aleksandra's analysis had been so sharp and insightful that it seemed easy to draw some conclusions. George started by trying to mimic her Byelorussian accent.

'I'm here to learn, so it is hard to draw any conclusions that you would find anywhere near as perceptive as your analysis. That I hope to do when I have finished the tuition.'

He looked at her, flashing what he thought was his best, most winning smile. Better to compliment her early, he thought. Maybe his charm, if not his economics would win out? But he got nothing back but a slightly raised eyebrow. Maybe I will have to be sharper on the economics after all? She's not going to be impressed with the charisma, he thought.

'Okay, where do I start? You have talked about centralised planning, and how in 1965 there was a move to free up production into a more economic value-based system, and that has led to increased output. However, as I understand it, despite these reforms, central planning still rules, corruption is increasing, the military is still spending heavily and workers are suppressed by the KGB and state police. It doesn't look good.'

Aleksandra watched him carefully and then replied, 'That is a fair summary, but I think we need to work on the conclusions. "It doesn't look good" is hardly discerning. Your Russian is good, but your Byelorussian accent is awful.'

She reached down into her bag and drew out a sheet of paper.

'Mr Cove, I would be grateful if you would read these articles.' She gave the sheet to George. 'We will meet next Tuesday at three in the afternoon. I have already checked with Professor Candish and you are not timetabled then.'

She turned to the professor. 'Can I share your rooms until I am sorted here?'

Julia nodded. 'Thank you, Mr Cove. I think that will be all until next week. We might just make some sort of economist out of you.'

George looked around. He was being dismissed as Professor Candish started a conversation with Aleksandra, and so he left.

George stood to leave, and Julia and Aleksandra sat looking at each other. The door closed and each exhaled a deep sigh. Julia Candish spoke first.

'That was a bit rough on him, but you played the part perfectly. He is not used to being talked to like that, especially by a woman.'

'Yes, Julia, I agree. It was difficult, but I have had practice.' Aleksandra smiled. 'Maybe you already know women from my homeland really rule the roost. When a Byelorussian woman stands at the door with her hands on her hips, the men cower. It is not a pretty sight. The men are such drunkards and so pathetic, we have learnt how to make them do as we want. They drink too much vodka. The system has taken away all their pride and now it's in their genes. We may be able to change many things through this project, but I'm not sure we will ever really get our men back, as real men, not at least for many years yet. George is young and still faux, a *dilettante* and vaporous. So much like the men back home.'

Julia wasn't sure she fully understood. Still single, she had wedded her career but was not without the occasional lover who had been drawn mainly from the academic life in which she felt most comfortable. Mainly they were gentle relationships with little shouting, few lows and even fewer highs. She had drifted into them and then just as easily out. Maybe, she thought, she missed the passion and the emotion. She wondered what it must be like to feel so angry or so much in love.

'Will he do what you ask? Will he read the articles and turn up next week? What do you think, Aleksandra?'

'Oh, he will do what we ask. The bigger question is will he fall in love with Anna and will she fall for him? That is what we need to work on next.'

CHAPTER V

OCTOBER 1971

Despite its size, the Bodleian Library at Oxford could be small if two people were both researching similar subjects. George and Anna bumped into each other there, saying hello as they collected articles and books. They acknowledged each other, and George's eyes had followed her, admiring her shapely legs, as she walked away. For the first time, unlike Anna, he was actually interested in an academic subject, so his attention to her was passing and cursory. It took him much longer than it took Anna to find the articles and books on Aleksandra's list. Being in the library was such a strange, almost unique experience, that he didn't know what to do. Eventually he had to seek help from the librarian. After trying to understand his requests, she tried to refer George to the Head of the Slavonic Department in the Bodleian Library, Mr Walker.

'I am sorry, you don't understand,' George said. 'My request is nothing so complicated that I need his help. I just need someone to show me how the filing system works. You see, I don't come here very often.'

The librarian looked at him and nodded knowingly. *A Blue or a Champagne Charlie?* she wondered. *I suppose one visit per degree was okay.* She took George's list and helped him with the first search. Anna, of course, had none of those problems.

George found his papers, books and articles, stuffed them into his bag and left, fully intending to start on them straight away, only to meet Jamila on the library steps.

'George,' she said. 'Coming for coffee? What are we doing tonight?' He looked at her and saw again how beautiful she was. He was tempted. He knew how the evening would end and it was tempting to be entwined with Jamila's body. He looked at his case.

'Just a quick coffee, then. I have work to do and I have made a promise.'

After only two weeks' supervision, George had quickly agreed to Aleksandra's suggestion to increase their meetings to twice a week. George had shown a level of diligence like never before, and Aleksandra saw an immediate improvement in his analytical skills. They spoke only in Russian and his confidence grew, and he started to tease her by again mimicking her accent, but now with increased effectiveness. He was soon passable as a Byelorussian.

'George, your accent is much improved,' she said. 'Soon we might even have you passing as Muscovite or from Leningrad.'

Her meetings with Anna were still once a week. She was given the areas of interest and she researched them well, giving Aleksandra the data they needed. The paper was coming together. They were also building a personal relationship and more than once had met for a coffee at a local café. They talked about life in the East and the changes they both wanted to see.

'Anna,' Aleksandra said at one of their coffee meetings, 'it will be difficult with your background, but if it can be arranged, would you like to come with me to the conference? After all, you are a named contributor. It is only proper that you should be there as well.'

Anna had thought about this, but dismissed it just as quickly. She already understood that she would never see Poland. But was this hope? The Ukraine wasn't home, but it was close.

'Can it be arranged? I mean, how?'

'I can make no promises, but I will try, but to be at the conference you will need to be able to speak some Russian. You only speak Polish?'

'Yes, only Polish,' Anna said. 'In fact, there are a number of Russian documents I want to read and I am struggling to get them translated. I should learn Russian.'

The conversation had gone as Aleksandra had hoped. She could now arrange for George and Anna to meet but it would still have to be managed carefully.

CHAPTER VI

JANUARY 1972

They were all gathered again in Familiant's office to review progress. The professors from Oxford sat next to each other at the end of the desk to Familiant's right, a little like twins who knew each other's inner thoughts. Lord Ridley sat opposite Familiant, with Aleksandra to his right. Miss Shaw poured the tea and Aleksandra handed around a plate of biscuits as Julia spoke.

'Academically, Cove has improved dramatically. Now there is a real possibility, if he continues the improvement, that he might get a good degree with even the outside prospect of a first. Also, his relationship with Jamila is in decline. He spends more time on work and she is starting to resent his diminished interest in her. She likes to be seen at all the best social events, and George is spending more time on his work with Aleksandra. She has been seen out quite often now with a Rugby blue.'

'Kieran Kensella. Might play for Ireland someday soon,' said Familiant.

And then Professor Beck reported that Miss Kowalski, insisting on the formality, was still fully on track for a first, and Aleksandra added that her contribution to her paper was outstanding.

'She will soon develop and build a formidable academic reputation. She is adding economics to her undoubtedly high-class engineering background, but now,' said Aleksandra, 'we need them to become lovers. They will meet for the first time next week. I have arranged that.'

'Not quite, Aleksandra,' Familiant interrupted. 'Actually, they have met already, in the Bodleian Library, about two months ago.' He looked down at his file. 'In fact, just over two months ago. But, of course, they didn't know each other. Tell us your plan, if you would.'

Like many successful plans, simplicity was at its core and after Aleksandra had explained her intentions agreement was swift. Two weeks later, while Aleksandra and George were finishing a tutorial on Marxist Economics, there was a knock at the door. Anna pushed her way in without waiting for a reply.

'Sorry. I didn't know you were busy. I thought you said four?'

'No worries, Anna, we were just finishing. Weren't we?' she said, looking at George. 'I will see you again on Thursday.'

George was waiting for an introduction, but Anna seemed not to notice him. With no introduction, he gathered his books together, pulled himself out of the deep armchair and said, 'Yes. On Thursday.'

He glanced at Anna who was already heading into his place. He thought about saying *Hi* but resisted, and as he headed to the door he nodded what was both a greeting and farewell in the general direction of both of them. He closed the door clumsily and loudly, which Aleksandra and Anna both noticed.

That was George and Anna's first proper meeting.

'That one is a bit of a minor celebrity but is at last starting to work and stop his socialising. George Cove. Brilliant linguist. Slavic languages. Mainly Russian dialects, but he needs to broaden his knowledge a bit. We might make a scholar out of him some day. Switched Tripos and I am supervising him with modern Soviet economics.'

Both to instil the air of nonchalance and because of her fear of how it was being received, Aleksandra had barely looked up as she painted this quick-pen picture of George.

'Don't worry, though, Anna. He's not your sort. He is far too impractical for you. He's full of romantic words and dreams. I doubt he knows how to even change a light bulb. He needs to get his feet on the ground a bit, and,' Aleksandra leaned forward to intimate she was about to break a confidence, which she was, 'he already has too many girlfriends for his own good. You'd hate to come second to any of them.'

The barb was well set and Anna's concentration on their meeting had gone. Come second to some of those airheads, she thought. I'll be damned!

George was irritated too. The impoliteness of not being introduced to one of Aleksandra's students he could stomach, but that one seemed to have a special place. She could wander in and, because she had arrived suddenly, then his time was up. Aleksandra and her tutorials had become special to him. It wasn't because there was a sexual attraction. He still thought Professor Candish looked at him longingly, but he appreciated – no, it was far more than appreciation; he *knew* somehow that Aleksandra Ponomarenko had saved him from a mundane and ordinary life. She had awakened a spirit and a drive in him. He didn't like being usurped. He was jealous.

Worse, however, was that Anna – if that was her name – was, well, rather attractive. He thought he had met her before but couldn't place where. If he could remember maybe he could manage to be there again. He tried to pull together a picture of her in his mind, but it wouldn't form. What use was that? If she wore different clothes it was distinctly possible that he wouldn't recognise her, but if she talked and he heard her voice again he would know her, even with his eyes shut. What had she said? *Sorry. Didn't know you were busy. I thought you said four o'clock?*

The words spun in his head. It wasn't the words themselves but the voice he heard. Not a shrill, accented English voice, but it was a Slavic voice speaking English words, deeper in tone, with overtones far more beautiful and captivating than any he had heard before. The sound of her voice alone, he thought, could send a man into raptures. The hook was also well set.

At the next tutorial, after he first met Anna, George asked Aleksandra, 'Who was that who came to see you the other day?'

'Oh, you mean Anna Kowalski? She is helping me with technical details for my paper for the energy conference,' Aleksandra said, trying to seem nonchalant and as indifferent as she could, although she had rehearsed for this moment ever since she had made the introduction. Thank God he had said something because she had been unsure how otherwise she was going to move it forward. She had talked this moment through with Familiant, who needed to know how every step was progressing. She had described the meeting to him almost verbatim.

'Don't worry,' he had said. 'He will move. Men are natural

predators and he will want to stalk his prey. If you will excuse the analogy, he will want to circle for a time to ensure there is enough meat to feed on before he kills.'

'I am not sure I will excuse the analogy, Bill. It is awful, but I do understand.'

She could almost hear him at the other end of the phone sitting with a slightly self-satisfied grin, knowing that he had again raised an unnecessary emotion in her. Surely he could have found a hundred other analogies. Familiant was extraordinarily clever and highly articulate and… The thoughts tailed off as another idea came to her. He was also a supreme manipulator. He had meant to stir an emotion. He was causing her to start feeling something for him. It didn't matter if the emotion was positive or negative. But if there was an emotion, then there was a relationship which went beyond their professional bond. She thought for a moment. *He knows I will understand what he has done. He has heard my reaction. What else does he want from me?*

She had to tune back in again quickly as she heard Familiant say, 'Your bigger problem will be Anna. You may think you have her hooked, but like most Slavic women, resilience and stubbornness often get confused. If she ever once says "no", there will be no way back, even if everything around her changes. Be careful there. You will only have one chance or it's a big fight back to what we want. *Dosvidaniya, Sashunia.*' And the phone went dead.

And now he says goodbye to me in Russian, she thought, and uses my familiar name. Damn you too, Familiant.

She turned back to George. 'Actually, maybe you two could help each other. There are some documents on the progress of the Chernobyl reactors and they are written in Russian. Anna needs to get them translated for me and she also needs to improve her Russian skills. I hope she will be coming to the conference with me. Also, it would be a good insight for you to understand the technical infrastructure of the new power plants and the effort and costs of building them – it would really significantly help your energy economics understanding.

'And aren't you also supposed to be learning some Polish? She speaks it fluently. Her father was Polish; they spoke it all the time at home. She will be here tomorrow evening to go through some new reports on the progress of Chernobyl. Why don't you drop in afterwards for a sherry? Say nine?' Again it was much less of a request and more of an instruction.

The timing had been carefully thought out. Aleksandra knew that Cove would have arranged either to be with some girl or other, probably Jamila, or at some party after supper with copious amounts of wine from the College cellar. She was breaking into his schedule. Maybe this was becoming his new passion, but he could just as easily still say no; and now a girl was involved. How interested was he? George was thinking much the same.

'Yes, nine will be fine. I'd enjoy that.'

It was nine o'clock and Aleksandra and Anna were deep in a technical review of the expected and latest power output estimates from Chernobyl. Two reactors were to be on-line in 1976 and two more five years later. There was a knock at the door. They both looked towards it but nothing happened.

'Perfect manners,' said Aleksandra. Another knock sounded. 'Come in, George.'

George pulled up a chair around the coffee table as Aleksandra took three glasses and a decanter off a sideboard. Placing the glasses on the table, she handed the decanter to George who poured each of them a sherry. 'So, George, this is Anna and Anna, this is George. Let me explain where we are and what we have to do.'

As Aleksandra talked to them about the targets, objectives and logistics that would produce the paper for the conference, she was thinking about the few words spoken to Anna casually before George had arrived. She had reminded him how he could help her and that he needed to learn a little Polish and she finished with a simple throw-away line.

'And of course he's dating that Azerbaijani girl, Jamila Mnatzakanova. Do you know her?' Anna shook her head. 'No, well maybe not. Of course, she was the one that wrote that paper on the Warsaw Ghetto suggesting that some Jews were complicit with the Nazis.'

At that moment Anna hated Jamila passionately, even though she hadn't yet met her, and hoped with all of her heart she never would. Although she was not strongly built, Anna knew she would have to hit her. These were her people and that Mnatzakanova woman had no right to say those things. What did she know? A mere Azerbaijani and probably Turkish by origin at that. Not even a real Russian, and definitely nothing Polish about her.

This part of the plan had been Familiant at his best, thought Aleksandra.

'To bring them together we have to create a common enemy,' he had said, 'and who better than that Jamila girl? It is just perfect.'

They talked of their tasks and by ten they were finished.

'So, I think we are done,' Aleksandra said. 'Everyone happy with what we have to do? Good. Let's meet again next week. Probably slightly earlier? I will drop a note to each of you,' she said, clearly indicating that all was over and it was time to leave.

George was interested in what had been said, but had taken only a few rather pathetic notes as he looked at Anna, wondering if she would be a good lover. There was her voice too. An angel couldn't speak more sweetly. But Aleksandra had not allowed them much time to chat and kept the 'meeting' very much on business. He was ready waiting for this moment as they left Aleksandra's rooms. Now he would have his chance to talk to Anna alone as they headed back through the quad and onto the streets of Oxford. Would she like a quick drink before she went home? Maybe if he was lucky he could manage to persuade her to come to his rooms. It was unlikely that she would let him into hers, he thought.

They stood and walked towards the door, collecting their papers into portable piles. As he opened the door to let Anna through, Aleksandra asked absentmindedly, 'George, can you spare me a quick moment, please? Bye, Anna.'

George turned at Aleksandra's words, and then turned back

to see Anna drift down the corridor. If Aleksandra was quick then he could still catch up with her.

'Of course,' he replied, and turned back into the room leaving the door ajar.

'Close the door and sit. I won't keep you long,' said Aleksandra.

Both Anna and hope had gone.

George heard none of what was said as he thought of how he would catch up with Anna now. He would have to wait until the next get-together. Until then, he had some translation to finish and that wouldn't be as easy as normal because of the number of technical terms that were being used. It would require some research and much time. He was unsure how long he could wait to see Anna again.

CHAPTER VII

MARCH 1972

The week that passed until their next meeting seemed endless to George. He had become used to having what he wanted and now he wanted Anna. Her voice was still as mesmerising to him as it was the first time he had heard her speak those few words. During that week, he had another tutorial and Aleksandra had given him some background economic pieces around the Chernobyl paper. Anna spent the week working, but was also tracking down the paper by this Jamila woman. She was not just angry, but increasingly despised her.

After two days she found it. It wasn't as difficult a search as she had expected, and each time she read it just increased her ire. Of course, these feelings were not surprising as Familiant had both written the paper, drawing on his own Modern History degree and a great deal of imagination, and had it placed in the library. A week later, at their next meeting, Aleksandra was berating George for not bringing with him the economics papers.

'I told you, George, that Anna needed them and you were to bring them with you today.'

George couldn't remember such an explicit request.

'If we don't do what we say we're going to do, then we will get nowhere.'

'I have them in my rooms. I didn't know that you wanted them here tonight, I am sorry, Aleksandra,' George said.

'Then, Anna, you will just have to go back with George to his rooms and collect them tonight. We will finish here and you two go. George, you have wasted our time!' Aleksandra huffed as she turned to her other work.

While George hated being shown up in front of Anna, he looked up to say thank you to a God he didn't believe in. The walk back to George's room wasn't long and the conversation between them was initially friendly, but not intimate. George still resented

Aleksandra for her harsh words, but he couldn't get over the joy of being instructed by her to walk her back to his rooms. The air was warm and the streets quiet, and the tensions eased.

Anna started to talk about the paper for Aleksandra and George tried to quiz Anna all about herself. At first she said little, but as they walked he found a style of conversation and subjects which started to amuse her. George tried to persuade Anna to stop with him for a drink on the way, but she declined.

At one point, as they had turned a corner, Anna ran her hand down his back. At its simplest, it was to guide him, but George thought it seemed much more a sign of affection. He had felt a tingle, and the hairs on the back of his neck had risen. He had turned to look at her. Suddenly she seemed not just pretty, but beautiful. He had not seen her as beautiful before, but that sudden sign of tenderness had somehow affected him in ways he didn't understand.

He tried to put the thought behind him as he led the way back to his rooms, but in that he failed. He could feel her light touch all the way.

As they came up the stairs to his corridor, George and Anna were laughing. George was doing a tour de force of mimicking various Russian dialects as he told some simple harmless jokes in the guise of teaching Anna some basic vocabulary. But while George and Anna were walking back to his rooms, Jamila was waiting outside his door.

Earlier that evening, as Jamila had left the dinner hall, the college porter had delivered a note to her. Signed by a 'dearest friend' and handwritten, it explained that George was now having an affair with an undergraduate, and for the past term after each tutorial they had slipped back to his rooms. He had been lying to Jamila all this time. They would be back around eight-thirty. Familiant had found the note hard to write. His style was much too formal and his handwriting almost indecipherable. Miss Shaw had come to his rescue with both the style and script.

The shock on George's face when he saw Jamila was palpable. Could this be his worst nightmare?

'So is this the slut? You have been cheating on me with that slut?' rasped Jamila.

'Who is this?' demanded Anna.

'Jamila Mnatzakanova—, ' he waved an introduction, 'Anna Kowalski. I think we should go into the rooms.'

He really didn't want this conversation in public. He knew it might get very heated.

For all his *sang froid*, this was going to test George to the limits of his charm. He opened the door and it took only a short time for the argument and shouting to break into Russian and Polish. He was being excluded. It was between the women, and he was the subject of the debate. Anna was shouting about her people and what really happened in Warsaw during the war, and Jamila was convinced that Anna and George had been sleeping together for months. There were two women shouting at each other in different languages, neither knowing exactly what each was saying, but understanding exactly what they meant. That neither woman seemed to understand the other just added to the general level of confusion and chaos, but body language and the volume of the argument left nothing to the imagination about their intentions.

George observed them as the intensity of the swearing increased and the threat of violence rose nearer and nearer the surface. He was detached and calm. Trying to break them up would be dangerous, and he was rather enjoying watching the show of shared jealousies, and then it dawned in him. Anna was defending him now. She cared; and in her defence of him she showed she cared very deeply for him. She could have said to Jamila, 'Just have him – because he's not worth the effort', but she didn't. She was his companion and she was fighting for what was hers. With that realisation, he stepped in and shouted,

'Enough! Jamila get out of here. Whatever you think, Anna and I have only known each other for three weeks and we haven't been doing any of what you suggest. But let me tell you this. I really think we're about to and I hope we will be for a very long time to come. Go!'

With that, he opened the door pushed the screaming Jamila out, then closed and locked the door. He turned and held a shaking Anna closely to him. They stayed like that until he could feel her start to breathe more slowly and calmly. He looked into her eyes, still red from crying, and stroked some hair from her face. As he let her go, he took her hand and they walked to the bedroom, where they stayed until the next morning.

CHAPTER VIII

SEPTEMBER 1972

Familiant read the reports with a satisfied smile. George and Anna spent much of the summer together and were lovers, but – better for Familiant – they were working well together. George had shown greater academic skills and talents than even he had hoped for. This phase had nearly come to a conclusion.

Familiant now turned to Aleksandra's visit to Kiev and the energy conference. Her paper was a quality piece of work; in itself a dissertation worthy of a Master's Degree. Well, it should be with all the effort that had gone into it. The offer of Anna attending the conference had never been real. Aleksandra had explained to her that the people she knew at the Foreign Office really weren't that senior and they couldn't do anything about getting a visa, although in truth no one had actually tried. The offer of the visit was for no other reason than to inflame her increasing Polish nationalism even further.

Anna's disappointment was mitigated as she realised that it meant she would now be staying with George rather than going away, and by adding Anna and George as co-authors, they had started to gain credibility while Aleksandra's profile was lowered. That was good.

It was never easy to get anyone behind the Iron Curtain. Aleksandra had been accredited with a British delegation comprising academics and industrialists. She had been to Moscow and Leningrad before with only a few minor problems, apart from maybe one covert attempt to 'turn her'. Getting to Kiev was just another bureaucratic nightmare to be overcome, and this time she had to be routed through Moscow. She was to be in Kiev for just under six days, one of which would involve a trip to Chernobyl, no more than a hundred kilometres to the north, but only to have a cursory view of progress. No one would be allowed anywhere near the inside of the construction.

This was her first time in Kiev, split as it was by the river Dnieper, one of Europe's great water ways, running from Russia to Byelorussia before arriving at the Black Sea. Aleksandra's hotel was, like most of the resident population, on the west bank. Kiev was an ancient city and the hub of many great empires of the past, from Khazars, Lithuanians, Rus, Polish and German. Now, of course, it was an important satellite of the great Soviet empire.

Aleksandra had hoped for but never really expected any great contact with the Eastern Bloc delegations and she was not, therefore, too disappointed to discover that the segregation was almost complete. The only real chance of contact was at the conference break-outs when delegates mingled as best they could despite the attempts of State police to monitor and maintain political and philosophical integrity.

Her paper was received with critical acclaim just before the break on the morning of the third day. As she left the podium, delegates gathered round to shake her hand and ask more questions. Among these was a strikingly beautiful Russian woman whom Aleksandra judged to be in her early thirties. Aleksandra could tell her nationality immediately, by both her features and her clothes, but it was more difficult to judge her age. If her life had been as hard as that of many others, she could have been in her twenties, but the natural beauty of Russians always seemed to defy age.

'I am Vera Safarova and I work at the Kiev University. *Kak vashi dela?*' she asked. 'I have wanted to meet you personally for a very long time.'

'Aleksandra. *U menya vsyo khorosho.*' Aleksandra replied that she was well, and their conversation continued in Russian. She felt there was a kinship, an immediate warmth and a connection between them that somehow seemed to transcend their status as academic colleagues. It was a warmth that she couldn't place.

'I was impressed by your paper and I have read others. Maybe we can talk some more?'

'I am not sure how that will be possible,' said Aleksandra. 'The authorities here don't actually make that terribly easy!'

'Well, I think we should try. We have a lot to discuss; at least, I would like you to have a copy of some of my work. It covers many similar areas, but of course without the same depth as your research.'

Aleksandra accepted the hard-bound book that looked just like the thesis she'd written for her doctorate. It was titled a Master's Dissertation by Vera Safarova. Other delegates surrounded Aleksandra, and Vera drifted into the shadows. Aleksandra tried to track her over the heads of other delegates trying to get her views or impress her with their own, but Vera was gone. She wanted to spend more time with her, but the opportunity had passed.

It was back at the hotel that she picked up Vera's work and flicked through the pages. Its content was nothing special or unusual. It was mainly a collation of data and information on nuclear power station construction in Europe, which Aleksandra knew about well, together with some vague conclusions that showed only little insight.

Aleksandra was about to put it down and think more about supper when she saw that two extra pages had been inserted. There were three pages numbered eighty-four. She studied them. She was here to learn about Soviet thoughts and intentions and try to understand their attitudes. She was not a spy, but the extra page eighty-fours had placed her in a new and unusual position.

The first described how on 24th May 1968, a K27 Soviet nuclear submarine had a reactor failure and partial meltdown leading to the deaths of nine submariners and more than eighty other injuries. The second page was a list of nuclear accidents in the Soviet Union, the most recent of which was in Kiev itself in 1970. Aleksandra knew a great deal about the nuclear industry and she knew that this information was not commonly available. This was surely what Vera had wanted to talk about. Reluctantly Aleksandra became a Western spy; she wasn't trained as one, she didn't want to be one, and she didn't know what to do next.

She sank down into a chair to think. She was scared and angry that Vera had picked her out. Why me? she thought.

There are maybe a hundred western delegates here she could have chosen to hand the book to. So why *me*? She thought of standing on the river's bridge and throwing the whole book away, but then she might be spotted. If she just left it in her room then it could be found because certainly the maid worked for the state police or at least informed for them. Logic said she had to do something positive. To leave the pages in the dissertation didn't seem right. The book without its extra pages was not a risk. She had a penknife with her, so working as closely as she could to the spine, she ran the sharp penknife point down the pages and extracted both. She looked at what remained and was happy that, without a detailed examination, the removal of these pages was not obvious. The book could now safely be left with all her other papers.

What was she to do with the two sheets sitting on the table in front of her? Aleksandra knew she had a good memory, but it was not photographic. Maybe she could reverse the process that Vera had used and insert them into one of her books, but that would mean taking the binding apart, and she didn't know how or where to get them rebound. Just asking would make her obvious to someone's spying eyes. If she knew the right sort of spying eyes, she thought, she could just hand them to someone else; a proper spy for Great Britain. Maybe that was a possibility. Maybe someone here was also a British spy?

There was a knock on the door and Aleksandra froze. She had information she shouldn't have. Why should two pieces of paper so quickly and so suddenly change her demeanour? It was the consequences of having them that frightened her: imprisonment and never seeing anyone she knew again. Pain, maybe, and maybe even Vera's life was in her hands. She had to open the door. Procrastination would not change anything. She put the two loose sheets among her own papers. If they were going to search her room they would find everything anyway, but it was best not to leave them open to casual prying eyes.

'Good evening, Aleksandra.'

It was just another member of her delegation. She had noticed him briefly at Heathrow, and then again occasionally as they made their way to Kiev.

'My name is Graham Walder. A very fine presentation and paper, I thought. May I come in?'

Aleksandra suddenly realised that she had hardly opened the door. She was peeping around the door frame and blocking his way.

'We haven't met properly. It seems so odd, doesn't it? We have to travel all the way from England to say hello. I saw you at the airport, of course, but that doesn't really count, does it?'

Although a rhetorical question, Aleksandra felt the need to agree with a nod of her head. This is the last thing I need right now, she thought. I am about to be arrested by the secret police; they must have been watching when Vera gave me the book, and here now is a slightly overweight Englishman in my room, hoping, no doubt, for cheap and quick holiday sex. She had no real alternative other than to open the door and let him in. Walder strode into the room. Instead of sitting, he wandered around rather aimlessly.

'Graham? You said your name was Graham?' Aleksandra asked. 'How can I help you?'

'I rather thought you might be able to spare a little of your time to go over parts of your paper. It was absolutely fascinating. Maybe we could have dinner tonight?'

Aleksandra's heart sank a little. This really was the very last thing she wanted. With all her other problems, now she had to repel the advances of a sex-crazed Englishman in Kiev. She would tell him politely but firmly to shove off, and was just about to do so when he said, 'I'm sure we've met before. It was probably at some conference or other. Maybe it was Cambridge?'

She had never been to Cambridge for a conference and her face showed the boredom of being chatted up by someone she didn't want to talk to. But he went on.

'I am sure it was that old professor who set it up. Now what was his name? Damned if I can remember properly. What was it? Familiar or Family? Now I remember – Familiant. Professor Familiant. Doddery old sod he was, as well.'

Hearing his name alerted all the antennae. Was it coincidence? It couldn't be, but it must.

'I'm sure you were there as well. No? Well, I must be mistaken. Now what about some supper and you can allay me of all those concerns you raised today at the conference? Don't suppose they will let us out, but the rations here are okay. Meet in the bar at seven?'

He turned and left as Aleksandra spluttered a 'Yes' with an accompanying nod. Walder had obviously been told that using Familiant's name would ensure she would agree to meet with him. It must be Familiant's doing, but was it a trap? Ever since the James Bond films had started, Aleksandra knew like everyone else about spies and spying. Now, if that had been Sean Connery and not Graham Walder who had knocked on the door, she could imagine what sort of night she would have in store. Maybe, she thought, Sean Connery wouldn't have even waited for dinner to ravish her, but it was Graham Walder, and it was supper, and she had learnt from bitter experience not to trust anyone.

She could think of nowhere good to hide the pages, so she thought it was best just to carry them with her as she went down to the hotel bar. What else could she do? She pushed open the door to the bar and looked around. Walder was there with another couple of men from the British delegation and they had quickly taken up and adapted the Russian habit of vodka with pickles as a side order. Walder saw her, said something to his friends, and walked across the bar to meet her.

'Let's get a drink and sit here,' he said, pointing at an empty table. 'Vodka?'

'*Da.*'

The chat was technical and Aleksandra was bored. She had the papers in her bag and they, not Walder, were occupying her thoughts.

Suddenly, he said, 'That old professor. I quite liked him, actually. Always humming opera, as I remember. An aria from Turnadot. *Nessun Dorma.* Aleksandra, I think you know you can trust me? Earlier you met Vera and I hope you enjoyed reading her dissertation. I would like to read it myself before I leave. Would that be possible?'

Aleksandra looked carefully at him, totally unsure what to do next or what to stay. If nothing else he was direct. She needed to buy time.

'Of course. I'm not sure what I did with it. I haven't even looked at it properly yet. Let me see if I can I find it, and we can catch up on it tomorrow.'

She went back to her room to think. The issues were clear and the choice was simple. Was he real? Was he who he said he was? Was he working for Familiant? If not, then he was the opposition and then all the rules changed, but how could she determine which? Not only did he seem to know Familiant, but he knew he often hummed an out-of-tune *Nessun Dorma*. And although Walder might not know what it was all about, he knew something Aleksandra didn't – he knew Vera Safarova was going to approach her. Of course, maybe Vera had been Walder's real focus and Aleksandra was being used simply as a courier. Was Walder privy to Familiant's big project of which Aleksandra was so key? Which side was he on? Was he a good guy or one of the baddies? Whatever she did she was at risk.

She hardly slept as she went through all the alternatives and their likely outcomes. Not one of them made her happy. The next day, she sat at breakfast, hardly able to eat. She had been taken further than she ever wanted to be taken, but she had reached her decision. She was always going to return to England before the formal end of the conference and so today was going to be her last day in Kiev.

Through most of the continuing proceedings she sat in a daze, hardly taking in what was being said, while still fending off those who wanted to talk to her. Her plane back to Moscow was at six-thirty that evening, which meant being at the airport at four-thirty and catching a taxi at three. She had confirmed all these details at the hotel in the morning as she checked out.

Just before three she went to search out Walder. She found him in the lobby, reading.

'Graham, how good to see you. I am just about to leave and I have read the dissertation. It's good. I thought you might want it.' She handed it over. 'Can you send it back to me at Oxford when you have finished reading? Sorry I can't stay. Take care, got to run.'

With that hasty outburst, she turned and almost ran to the main lobby. Her plan was to give him as little time as possible to arrange an arrest or even question her himself. That was the best she could manage. She would only feel safe when she was back in Britain. It would be a long time until that happened and, worse, she had to go through Moscow. Who was Walder working for? She would soon find out.

She spent the night either flying or waiting at Moscow airport. There, in the lounge, she drank a couple of vodkas. She wouldn't allow herself to drink too much, so it was fewer than she wanted or felt she needed, but she needed to keep her wits about her. She had never noticed how suspicious everyone looked. Even the paranoid have enemies, she remembered.

Finally, her flight to London – and safety – was called.

She avoided the eye of immigration officer who checked her passport surely more carefully than before. Was he about to stop her? Was there anywhere to run? There wasn't a British embassy in Moscow so who would visit her in jail? Would it be a show trial before being dismissed to the cold north of Siberia?

Aleksandra was convinced that her anxiety showed in every line of her face, but she worked hard to conceal the shaking of her hands as she took back her passport.

The roar of the engines throwing her back into her seat as they took off only gave her some relief as she set off to complete the last leg of the journey back home. It was only as the wheels of the plane touched the ground at Heathrow Airport that she felt calm and safe. The tension eased on her face and her body relaxed. It was now early morning.

What her body wanted to do was to go home, shower and sleep. What she did instead was find the taxi rank and go straight into central London to Familiant's office. Miss Shaw was surprised, not just by her unannounced arrival, but also the luggage. She could sense the anger on Aleksandra's face. She flew past Miss Shaw, trailing her luggage, shouting, 'I assume he's in'. Without waiting for an answer, she pushed open Familiant's door.

Familiant was just thinking that Aleksandra should be back from Kiev later today when she burst into his room.

'Do you know Graham Walder, and did you send him to meet me?' The rage in her voice was only just below the surface.

'*Sashunia*, how wonderful to see you. You look a tad flustered,' Familiant said, closing the file on his desk, returning the pen to its lid, and getting up to meet his guest.

'Do you know Graham Walder, and did you send him to meet me?' Aleksandra again demanded.

'Of course I did. I hope you managed to pass over what he asked for?' His voice was calm and measured; Familiant was not rising to her anger.

'No, I didn't. You bastard. Why didn't you tell me?'

'My dear *Sashunia*, should I ask you first what you did with Vera's dissertation, or answer why I didn't tell you?'

Familiant looked calm and relaxed as he tried to guide Aleksandra to an easy chair. She was steaming with anger and reluctant to be led, but nevertheless sat unwillingly. He sat opposite her with a small coffee table between them.

'Miss Shaw!' Just as he called she came in with a tray full of tea and biscuits.

'Why I didn't you tell me?' There was still a very chilling edge to Aleksandra's voice.

'Quite simply because you wouldn't have gone to the conference, or if you did you would have been so worried you would have given yourself away quickly. So, what did you do with the dissertation from Vera?'

'I gave it to Walder, of course.'

Familiant looked just a little perplexed.

'I thought you said that you didn't?'

'I am not trained; nobody can be trained for that. You had no right!'

'*Sashunia*, I have—'

Before he could finish Aleksandra snarled back. 'Please do not call me that. I am Aleksandra.'

Familiant's eyebrow raised on his normally impassive face. 'Aleksandra, let's take a step down. Would you like me to tell you about Vera Safarova?'

'Please do.' She was starting to feel just a little calmer, but being Russian, was still far more than Familiant was willing to confront.

'Well, let's first have some tea,' Familiant started to pour Aleksandra a cup. 'So why don't I tell you a little about Vera Safarova? You know she can help us. Like you, she is Byelorussian. She has been in Kiev for most of her life. She is a talented nuclear scientist. The document you read and may still have is a poor example of her capability – or so we think, and from what we understand it does not fully reflect her role and the knowledge she has of the Soviet nuclear programmes, especially at Chernobyl. You do agree Vera can help us? Of course you do. Was it a terrible surprise meeting her?'

Familiant hardly waited for Aleksandra to reply as he continued. 'You need to know something important, so I now really need to take you back into a little bit of Ukrainian folklore.'

Aleksandra looked a little confused. It was so unlike Familiant to weave a story. He was usually so much more direct. She had calmed and she sipped at her tea.

'Stay with me, Aleksandra. This is important.'

Familiant had seen the look on her face.

'It starts in the ninth century when two Byzantine brothers from Thessaloniki started a Christian campaign in the Slavic countries. There had been so many changes and the Ukrainians in particular had been subjected to so many different rulers that they always strove for an independence of sorts. It is strong in their character; it is part of their make-up. Their culture has always been at risk.

'In December 1845, a certain Mykola Kostomarov founded a secret society with some Christian principles of freedom at its core to free the Slavic countries. So, going back in history, it was right, he thought, that their group should be called after those two monks who nine centuries earlier had similar objectives. So they called themselves the Brotherhood of Saints Cyril and Methodius, or in Ukrainian *Kirillo-Mefodievskogo brat stvo*.

'Unfortunately, the authorities of the day weren't overly impressed and most of the members – around a hundred of them probably – were arrested a couple of years after its formation. But while they were together, they talked of a federation of free Slavic people, although not so free as we might today, because they saw Kiev as the centre of all Slavic nations and not just Ukraine. Well, it's all gone and it is really just a passing footnote in history. Except that we believe there are a number of intellectuals on the Ukraine, Byelorussia and Polish axis that feel the same today as the Brotherhood did over a century ago.

'This group does not enjoy the hegemony of the Soviet Union, with Russia at its core, and is committed to return its lands to self-determination to embrace again their language and culture. Of course, in any country that is invaded and overrun there will always remain resistance, however deep and suppressed. Now that voice is beginning to be heard, and we believe the Brotherhood of Saints Cyril and Methodius has been reformed.

'Vera is our first proper contact with the new Brotherhood. We need to support their development because, through them, we will increase our chance of achieving our goals. We share the same goals as them. Let's be clear. We do not think that they are in any sense a formal group that ever meets. This is all underground and highly fragmented and unstructured. Our first real knowledge of their existence was about six years ago; and our project was, in part, constructed to be a contact with them. So, in part, we – you, me, George and Anna – are all part of the Brotherhood of Saints Cyril and Methodius.'

If stunned and astonished had a look then that is what was reflected that moment on Aleksandra's face. She said nothing but reached into her bag and took out two sheets of paper and handed them to Familiant.

'I gave Walder the dissertation but not the two extra pages. I cut them out first. Here they are.'

'Thank you, *Sashunia.*' Aleksandra smiled. Well, maybe he can call me by my favourite name, she thought. 'What happens now?' she asked.

'Well, of course, we do need to get some verification of these,' he said waving the sheets, 'though that won't be too easy, but we can check parts, and if they check out, we have the start of what I hope is the end. We will need Cove and Kowalski mobilised soon. We are moving into the next phase. Now, would you like some more tea?'.

CHAPTER IX

OCTOBER 1972

In Oxford, none of what had happened in Kiev was known. George and Anna had moved into a flat together and lay in bed planning the day of study.

'Do you think all went well with Aleksandra? I do hope so. After all, it has our names on it as well,' said Anna as she headed to the bathroom for her shower.

George watched her naked form. He was transfixed by her beauty. Despite his new found commitment to academic work and the ease with which he had forsaken his social life, going to bed early or even waking before nine in the morning was still a challenge for him. Anna was slowly changing that, and so here she was, just after eight o'clock, trying to engage him in conversation. She wasn't overly successful as he muttered some obscenity before rolling over to go back to sleep.

Aleksandra's contract at Oxford had been extended by another year, so the tutorials with George and Anna were to continue, although without the pressure of a paper to write. Anna had shown no signs that her general performance was on the decline and George, buoyed up by his new-found interest in his studies and the challenge of keeping up academically with Anna, was also in line for a proper degree. Professor Candish was surprised with this turnaround as she had not seen his capabilities when she first interviewed him. It made her wonder how many other potentially great students she had missed, but then again, George had had the most intensive of supervision which was denied most of her other students. Living with Anna had given him the chance to learn and practise Polish, too; another great plus.

The team met in Familiant's office and it was decided that the pair should be left under Aleksandra's supervision to complete their degrees. All had been fully briefed on the trip to Kiev and the existence of the Brotherhood. Vera's documents had checked out.

'We have two new campaigns to plan now,' said Familiant. 'First, we need to know where are we going to place Cove and Kowalski after their degrees, and part of that decision is whether we want them to stay together.'

Aleksandra flinched a little. She had become more than a tutor. Now she was a friend, and the thought of tearing them apart upset her. She kept reminding herself that the bigger issue was about millions of her countrymen and women who were being persecuted. She let the point slip by without interruption.

'Second, how can we coordinate our effort with the Brotherhood and provide them with all the support they require? Of course, our plan for the second will drive the first. Agreed?' There was a collective nod.

'Good. Your views, please?'

The meeting went on for over another hour, and tasks were discussed and actions agreed.

Familiant sat in his office afterwards and pondered. He had already formed his own ideas but the timescale for the decision was not on top of him just yet and he was grateful for the extra input from a group with so much intellect. Flicking the intercom switch on his desk, Familiant said, 'Miss Shaw, Lord Ridley and I wish to meet soon. Check with his secretary, if you will. Thank you.'

Lunch with Lord Richard Ridley was at his club just off Pall Mall. Familiant stopped off at Trumper in Jermyn Street on his way for his weekly haircut. His father, like his father before him, had gone their there every week too.

'There are only three barbers of any note in London,' his father had said. 'The three Ts – Trumper, Truefitt, and Taylor – and we use Trumper.' Since then, this was where Familiant had his hair cut.

'And a shave today, sir?'

Familiant thought for a moment. The hot towels and the scrape of the cut-throat for wet shave was a special joy. But he didn't have enough time.

'Maybe next week, but thank you, Reeve.'

He took the time in the chair to think about his next meeting. Reeve finished and Familiant set off down to St James'. If Trumper hadn't changed much in a generation or two then nor had this particular London gentlemen's club. The porters must have aged and retired, but the current ones all look like they had been there forever, stuck at some venerable age. They knew every member, or so it seemed, and they understood every preference, even knowing when to wake an older member who was relaxing after his lunch, but most importantly of all, they understood discretion. They knew where to place members for that very discrete conversation and they knew how to forget the occasional snippet of overheard conversation, and so it was today. Familiant and Lord Ridley were placed at a quiet corner table. Each ordered a lightly poached salmon with a green salad. Ridley chose a crisp Pouilly-Fumé, and lunch was congenial as they covered all the pleasantries.

Coffee and cigars were served in the lounge. Despite being able to afford the best Havana, Ridley always carried and smoked his square Villiger Export mild Grossformat made in Switzerland. He offered the packet to Familiant, who declined. If ever I was going to smoke, he thought, surely a good Cuban would be better, but each to their own. However, he did have areas in which he had his own unique preferences (his Nonino grappa, for instance.) He wondered how blessed Orazio Nonino, whose name the wine still carried, must be. If I believed in God, he thought, I'm sure that Orazio would be making grappa for him right now. He made a note to pilgrimage to Ronchi di Percoto, in the Friuli region of northern Italy to pay a proper homage. Ridley ordered his customary Armagnac.

'So,' said Lord Ridley, 'where next? You have some ideas?'

Familiant took a sip of his grappa, savoured the taste and replied, 'Quite so, quite so, but before that, let me ask you to tell me about your commercial connections in the region.'

'Of course. Russia is the centre of everything and Moscow the centre of that. There is little autonomy for any of Poland, Byelorussia or Ukraine. I mean, we should remind ourselves that the Ukraine really is *Ukrainskaya Sovetskaya Sotsialisticheskaya*

Respublika or the Ukrainian Soviet Socialist Republic. Let's not go over all the history, but it's probably the second largest population in the Soviet Union. But whatever the situation with local politics, trade has always found a way to carry on. Think of the Second World War. Sweden sold iron ore right through the war to Hitler and some say that both GM and Ford traded with the Third Reich – not just before but *during* the war.

'Trade with Russia has a long history going back to the sixteenth century with the Muscovy Company, or originally The Company of Merchant Adventurers, with English traders looking for the Northeast passage to China, but the Truman Doctrine at the end of the war basically tried to remove all trade and finance from Russia. The USA wanted free trade and Russia was scared that opening up for trade would cause their people to see the benefits of the West and erode, or even worse, remove the power of state and the totalitarian regime they operate. Let's put it this way: today dear old Leonid Brezhnev would rather fight a Siberian tiger than see that happen.

'In the fifties we had Khrushchev's thaw. Actually, I always had a little bit of a soft spot for the old codger. I liked the showman in him. Anyway, that eased some of the worst excesses of the regime by, for example, reducing the Gulag population by almost seventy-five per cent. It did change life in Russia. However, we shouldn't forget that he was still an iron hand. We saw that when he put down the uprising in Hungary in 1956 with Russian troops.'

Lord Ridley stopped to draw on his cigar. He looked upwards for a moment and thought about his next words.

'And you know,' he said, leaning forward, 'Khrushchev was trying to reform agriculture and the party mechanism and he also tried to rein back on military spending. He was never a liberal western economist but he was starting reforms. In sixty-four, when Brezhnev and his cronies – and that includes that bastard Kosygin, I really don't trust him at all – took over, things got a bit more stable but certainly no more liberal. I mean, for all the things he did, Khrushchev was a bit wacky and unstable;

banging his shoe on the table at the UN in 1960. Great theatre, though. But they were also tough, and the way they put down the Prague Spring in sixty-eight was ruthless, and now we have the Brezhnev Doctrine. Basically they can intervene in any country that is not on the "correct" path of socialism. So in short, Moscow has Poland, Byelorussia and Ukraine by the economic balls, and how do they enforce it? They do it by shipping Russians into those countries under the pretext of manning the industrial development. Warsaw, Minsk and Kiev are Russian. Don't ever believe they aren't. By the way, do you think the Brotherhood had anything to do with Prague?'

Familiant shrugged. It wasn't that he wasn't telling; he just didn't know. 'The history lesson is interesting, Richard, but where does this take us?'

'I'm sorry, Bill, but I think this is really important to understand what has happened and how trade has developed,' Lord Ridley said. He sat deep in the high-backed leather chair. As his eyes closed slightly, his hands came together in front of his chin as if he was about to pray.

'Trade has been inhibited and almost stopped. The Russians do, however, need hard currency to buy technologies for the refurbishment of their industry. Their other problem is quality. There is a story that all the tractors they export have to be serviced before they are sold. Their biggest source of currency is gold and oil. But their main trade is with the satellite states and increasingly with the third world to extend their political influence. It's a bit like the two ski guides and their Saint Bernard dogs with the brandy casks under their chins.'

That reminded Lord Ridley to pause and take a sip of his Armagnac.

'They walk up the mountain selling tots to each other and when they reach the top they have both sold everything, both are drunk but neither is rich. But trade is trade and we all do business with them. We are making trade finance available and getting good rates, at least two hundred basis points above the market. They have a demand and we have a supply and a businessman abhors a vacuum as much as any physicist. We trade and don't worry about that. You won't see much on the Wollacott Bank balance sheet, but we are a major player and lubricate many of those deals. Did you know, by the way, that New Zealand is a leading player here? They have maintained strong political links and have had a Bilateral Trade Agreement since 1963 with reciprocal "Most Favourable Nation" status. If they ever elect that Labour man Kirk as Prime Minister all that may get even cosier, because he is likely to change their foreign policy and have even closer links. You see, for them, it's all about power struggles in Asia and they want to be friends if Russia wins that area, and we can use that link to trade through New Zealand.'

'Okay. Got that,' said Familiant. 'But what are their prospects going forward?'

'Hard to tell, really,' Ridley said. 'There's a lot at play here. If nothing major changes then they will grow more slowly and we must assume that Brezhnev won't have it that easy, but he's getting old and who knows, with their bureaucracies and politics, who will take over. Aleksandra may have a view on that. Hard cash will be an issue and we can force their hand on that a little. But what about us, you might ask? Growth and productivity in Britain is very low compared to Europe. These unions are supported by the Trotskyites. We may have our own problems soon. We may be dealing with Russians much closer to home.'

'I know.' Familiant nodded. 'It doesn't look too cosy. I have my eyes on that, but let's put that to the side for the moment. Let's talk about Cove. I would like you to do something there.'

'If I can. Is it easy?'

'Of course,' said Familiant. 'Now let me tell you what I have in mind.'

CHAPTER X

MAY 1973

The year in Oxford was focused on exams which, when finished, moved into the May College Balls. As usual, May Day was celebrated at six in the morning on Magdalen Bridge with crowds listening to the choir singing Hymnus Eucharisticus from the top of the Magdalen Tower, and again, as every year, there were the usual large numbers spilling out from parties that had started many hours earlier. Champagne bottles were more empty than full.

George and Anna had come straight from the Jesus ball. He was dressed in white tie and Anna in a beautiful, bare-shouldered, wispy, sky-blue ball gown. George was happy. His exams had gone well and he felt confident with the most beautiful of companions on his arm. He was so happy that it took all Anna's powers of persuasion to stop him joining a few others jumping from the bridge into the river.

It was a coincidence when two letters arrived at their home on the day the exam results were posted; they were left unopened while they went to the Senate to get their results. From the moment they woke until they reached the Senate steps, they felt trepidation, more about the class of degree than about failing, but they soon saw they had both received the Firsts they'd worked for.

George decided that a letter to Stapleton was in order and began composing in his head even while he and Anna danced a jig of joy on the Senate steps. They lunched and punted on the river and, as the sun set, drifted home arm in arm, and in love. As they walked, George tried to remember who he had been when he had arrived and where he was now in his life. He was impressed by all he'd achieved.

Meanwhile, professors Candish and Beck were sharing a sherry. Their most direct involvement in the project had come to an end. Candish was pleased she hadn't had to intervene with

Cove's results. He had earned his First honourably – without her. That pleased her immensely.

'What do you think, Julia? Do you think Kowalski will accept our offer and stay or will she want to follow Cove to London?'

Julia was sure. 'She'll stay. The chance to work towards her doctorate and continue working with Aleksandra will be the greater pull. After all, London's not that far away.'

'Making Aleksandra's appointment here permanent will be good for the university. We've benefited very much from all this. Two first scholars, a doctoral candidate and a really good research assistant who may well become a Fellow someday.'

'Agreed, Douglas. We have benefited.' Julia lifted her glass towards Douglas who nodded.

Meanwhile, George and Anna were opening their letters without considering the coincidence of them arriving on the same day. Anna exhaled first.

'It's from Professor Beck. I've been invited to apply for a postgraduate place, then move on to a doctorate, working with Aleksandra as my supervisor. It's wonderful, George. What should I say?'

'You should do what you want to do. Do what will make you happy. What do you want to do?'

George wasn't sure what else to say. He was delighted for her but he'd never thought of staying in Oxford so if she accepted and they wanted to be together then he'd have to stay. They couldn't be separated, could they? Maybe an academic life for him wouldn't be too bad?

'What's in your letter?' Anna asked, hoping it was good news. She couldn't face the prospect of dealing with bad news when she felt so happy. She knew she would accept the Oxford offer but she didn't know how she was going to face being apart from George. He was bound to go and get a job somewhere in London, probably in an accounting firm, and become boring. Did that happen to all the beautiful people?

She reread her letter to make sure it was real and didn't notice that George had gone almost white as he was reading his.

She looked up. 'What's the matter, darling?'

'I've been… well, it looks like I've been offered a job.'

'You didn't tell me you'd been applying for jobs. I thought we'd talk about that first.' Anna did not just look upset – she was.

'I didn't! I mean I haven't applied for any job. Honestly, *lapushka*. Here, read it.'

Anna took the letter. It was from a Lord Richard Ridley, Chairman of the Wollacott Bank. She read it out loud.

Dear Mr Cove,

We have been following your career closely and believe that the talents you have shown while obtaining your First Class degree could now best be developed here at Wollacott.

We would like to make you an offer of employment and I would be grateful if you would contact my secretary, Jane Sutton, so that we can discuss and, I trust, finalise the terms of your imminent employment.

Yours, etc.,

Lord Richard Ridley—Chairman

Anna noticed an indecipherable squiggle above the name. She was unsure what to say. Why hadn't George said anything about applying for jobs? But she held back her anger.

'This is marvellous! How wonderful for you.' Then, 'What's wrong?' as she saw the concern on his face.

'Give me the letter again, please. See here. Look what it says here: "while obtaining your First Class degree". This is a hoax, darling. We only found out today.'

'But everyone knew you were going to get a first. Maybe they were just being confident in your abilities. You must phone them. You really must.'

'If you say so, but tonight we will only celebrate your news until this is cleared up. Yes? I will call them tomorrow, but even if it's for real, do we want to be in different places? We are together in this, aren't we, darling?'

George didn't know what to think. He wanted it to be real but he also desperately wanted to stay close and be with Anna. He would have to resolve his thoughts. It was just over seven weeks to his twenty-second birthday and he had already thought that this birthday would be a perfect time to propose to Anna. Maybe he could delay that until her birthday in September?

The next morning, as usual, Anna was early to wake and encouraged George to phone the number in London immediately. She, too, wanted this to be resolved quickly. She couldn't think about herself until George knew if it was a hoax or genuine. He dialled the number on the letterhead. It rang twice.

'Good morning, Woollcott's.'

'I'd like to speak to the Chairman's secretary please. Jane Sutton.'

'Certainly. Please hold the line, sir.'

'Lord Ridley's office. Jane Sutton here. I am Lord Ridley's personal assistant. How can I help you?'

Anna could sense the increasing trepidation in George's voice. She knew he thought that the conversation was never going to happen and that probably the number was false. She knew that he hadn't really prepared himself for a conversation going this far.

'Oh, yes. This is George Cove. I have a letter in front of me purporting to be from Lord Ridley. I just wanted to make sure it was genuine.'

Anna flinched. Not the best line, George, she thought. George was listening intently now for the answer.

'Oh, yes, Mr Cove. How kind of you to phone back so quickly. Lord Ridley was hoping you would call. Can we arrange a date as soon as possible before he goes away for the summer? How is your diary looking? Can we say next Tuesday, eleven-thirty, and lunch at one in the board room in our office? You have the address?'

'Oh yes. Next Tuesday will be fine. I have the address, thank you. It's on the letter.'

Anna saw the look on his face. It was real. They could celebrate and they could both be happy. George sat down. The Chairman of Wollacott. The board room. What was happening? Whatever it was, it sure as hell sounded like good news!

Lord Ridley replaced the phone. Miss Sutton had just phoned through to say that he was meeting Mr Cove for lunch next week. She wanted to confirm the venue. She had been briefed thoroughly that the meeting with Cove was a priority. She had typed the original letter and placed it an envelope, but had been instructed not to put it in the post. A courier would collect it and that had been three weeks ago.

'So, Bill, are you sure he is good for us? You're not landing me with a turkey are you?' Familiant was sitting opposite Lord Ridley in his offices just off Cheapside in the City of London.

'No, no, Richard. Remember that is just what Julia said when she interviewed him. He will be a great asset for the bank. Just convince him the bank will be a great asset for him.'

George was unsure of what was happening and he needed the answers to some questions. He had been through them with Anna and they were clear in his mind, but nevertheless he went through them again on the train down to London.

The train arrived at Paddington and it was a long hike across London to Cheapside. The Underground was never pleasant. Cheapside was the start of the 'City' and led down from St Paul's Cathedral to the Bank of England. George followed the directions he had checked before he left: Out of St Paul's station and down Cheapside. On the left is an alley which opens out into Gutter Lane. Walk down to the end and there on the right is Wollacott Bank.

George took a deep breath, checked the time – ten minutes early – pushed the door and strode purposefully into the reception area.

'Good morning. George Cove to see Lord Ridley.'

The receptionist looked at him slightly wearily. Most of the Chairman's visitors arrived in chauffeur-driven cars, were more the Chairman's age than in their early twenties, and certainly didn't carry an *A to Z of London* in their left hand. But still she phoned his office.

'Jane – a George Cove to meet the Chairman?'

George could hear from her intonation, her voice rising a half tone at the end of the sentence, that she was asking a question.

'Oh. Okay. Will do.' She hung up.

'Mr Cove, if you could take a seat? Miss Sutton will be down soon to meet you.' She pointed at a low comfortable-looking sofa in the reception. There was a copy of the pink *Financial Times* on the table in front of him. Not a paper he normally read but he thought it was better to be seen reading that than anything else. He heard the clink of high heels on the floor before he saw the long legs. His eyes were level with her knees. He looked up.

'Good morning. You must be George Cove. I am Jane Sutton, the Chairman's personal assistant. It is a real pleasure to meet you.'

The long legs weren't a disappointment as an introduction for the rest of Jane Sutton. Thin, and at least five foot seven, George thought, with long blonde hair pulled back and tied with a bright red hairband. She wore what George thought must be the female equivalent of a pinstripe suit and the open-necked white blouse framed a beautiful long neck. George was at a loss for what to say.

'The only thing I know about Sutton is a place in south London and a flower seed company.'

Even as he said it he wished he hadn't. How crass could you get? Why didn't he ask about the share price or the oil crisis which was starting to become an issue? Places or seeds!

'Well, Daddy does have an interest.'

'Sorry?' said George.

'In Sutton Seeds. Daddy does have an interest.'

'Oh, then I guess buying you flowers won't be very special. It will have to be chocolates.'

This is getting worse, he thought. Well, at least best to get the nerves out of the way now before he met the Chairman.

'Oh, I don't know. Maybe you should get me both flowers and chocolates. Thank you.'

To George's relief, the lift doors opened and Miss Sutton led the way out. How could he feel so trapped with a beautiful secretary? If the Chairman's secretary could do this to him, he thought, what chance did he have with the Chairman?

'Lord Ridley, George Cove is here to meet you.'

'Thank you, Miss Sutton,' said Lord Ridley. George noted the formality. *Miss Sutton* and not Jane.

'George, come on in.' George was now confused. Lord Ridley or Lord Richard? He would try Lord Richard and hope he didn't offend. No doubt he would soon find out.

'Thank you Lord Richard.' No reaction. One hurdle jumped.

'Come and sit down over here,' said Lord Ridley pointing to the corner of the office. For the first time, George took in how large and sumptuous the office was. This wasn't an office; it was almost a house, larger probably than all the living space he shared with Anna and one piece of this furniture probably cost more than everything in their home. No pretence to any modern design, this was classic, luxurious and lavish; desk, book cases and the side tables all carved from a light oak and sitting on a carpet in dark red with a deep pile. Suddenly he thought of Miss Sutton lying naked on that carpet, looking longingly up at him. Put those thoughts away, or at least think of Anna. George walked in and sat down where Lord Ridley was pointing. He sat and waited for something to happen. He felt it wasn't for him to start this conversation.

'I know Aleksandra quite well,' Lord Ridley said. At least that explained some of the riddle, thought George. Had she spilt the beans on his grade? If she had, they must know each other quite well. Lovers? George filed that for later.

'She speaks most highly of you, as do others I have spoken to.'

Who might these others be? thought George.

'Let me get right to the point. No doubt you know about Wollacott but you may not know about the full range and scope of our operations and the interest we have built up in a range of companies. By the way, I hope you will be able to stay for lunch. I have arranged for you to meet a couple of my directors.'

George nodded. After all, he thought, that was why he was here. If he had realised lunch was in doubt he would have had a bigger breakfast.

'We need to strengthen our role in the USSR and in particular in the satellite states such as Ukraine, Byelorussia and Poland. I need to build a unit focusing on that area. It will not be easy and it will be a long-term project. In short, I want you to head our local thrust into that region. Let me tell you it will not be easy nor will it be straightforward and, given the state of affairs between the West and USSR, there will be a small amount of danger, but really not too much if you behave appropriately and stay within our rules. Well, George, what do you say?' Lord Ridley sat back in his chair, obviously expecting a response.

'I really don't know what to say. Of course I am interested, otherwise I wouldn't be here. But I suppose I would need to know a lot more and think about it.'

'I'm sorry, George, but I clearly didn't make myself clear. I can't tell you any more. This is the world of commercial secrets. If it's money you're worried about, then don't. You'll be a very wealthy young man if you're successful, which I'm sure you will be. You will have to live in the Ukraine for at least three years, although you will of course be able to come back here frequently. You have to decide now, George. If it's yes, we sign our contract and go to lunch; if it's no, we say goodbye and I thank you for your time.'

Lord Ridley knew it was a bold play but he and Familiant had talked it through at length. Despite all his new-found academic focus, deep down George was still a buccaneer and the thought of being very wealthy would excite him. They were confident.

George stuttered. He didn't know what to say. 'Can you leave me alone for five minutes, please, to think through what you have said?'

'Of course; stay here. I have things to do.' Lord Ridley stood and headed to the door. It reopened and Miss Sutton popped her head round.

'Can I get you anything?'

George wanted to be flippant in reply but he didn't have time for that. 'No thanks. I'm fine. Thank you.'

He had five minutes. It was strange, George thought, that

you could live your life so comfortably with all the time to think and make decisions and then suddenly it was all compressed into five minutes. It must be like that when you have a car accident. One moment you're a successful, happy sportsman and then, in one flash and a bang, it's all changed. Or you go to the doctors with a cough and end up in hospital with cancer. Does everyone have these life-changing events compressed into five minutes? He wondered if anyone could really be prepared for them. Whatever decision he made now would change his life forever. Blast and damn you, Lord Richard Ridley and your bloody bank.

'Well?' said Lord Ridley as he returned. 'And your decision is?'

I only have one chance to say yes. I can always keep thinking right up to the time I sign anything, thought George, and I can always talk it through with Anna and change my mind. Surely he could do that?

'If I say yes, then what happens?'

'Say yes and you will find out,' said Lord Ridley.

He was cornered. George wanted to say yes but he also wanted Anna. Could they keep it together while he was away all this time? Well, of course they could! Lord Ridley said he would get back to England frequently and, anyway, she would be working on her doctorate. He was only twenty-two. They could get engaged next year and then marry when he was twenty-five, and by that time he would be rich and that would be a far better basis for starting married life. If they were destined to be together then the fates would ensure that would happen.

Maybe it would work and they could stay together and she could even come and visit him? And what of the job prospects here? Well, the economy looked okay but there was clearly a downwards pressure and things could change just as quickly and get worse. He would need money from somewhere and that would probably cause them to be in different cities. Oxford to London or Oxford to the Ukraine. What was the difference?

'Yes. My answer is yes,' George said with both fear and excitement. *Oh what have I just done?* he thought. *I could say 'no' and then nothing would change.*

'Yes,' he reiterated.

'Good. Well done. Now here is the contract. Sign and I will tell you all you need to know.'

'I have said yes, but I should at least read it, shouldn't I?' said George with a little more confidence now. Maybe he had bought some time.

'Of course. Here.' Lord Ridley handed over a single sheet.

It doesn't look overlong, thought George. Damn, I wish I had read law. He took it and started reading.

'I, George Cove, etc. etc. Party of the first part … report directly to and only to the Chairman or persons nominated by him…' He read on. Wow, what was this? 'Confidentiality and secrecy, absolute… Salary £12,700 per annum.' *What?* 'Start immediately.'

'It says an *immediate* start. I still have things to do,' said George.

'That is right, an immediate start, but we will not need your services full-time for a couple of months except for the odd day here and there. But we do need to make sure you are bound by the confidentiality from this moment and so we need you to start immediately, and that means from the very minute you sign. We will, of course, start your pay from now as well,' said Lord Ridley, smiling.

Pay, thought George, what does it say about that?

'Excuse me,' said George, 'has there been a typing mistake on this salary?' Maybe, he thought, it should be £2,700 which – if it was right – would be rather miserly. He had heard of some graduates being offered nearly £3,500, but that wasn't wealthy.

'No, George, as I said, I intend to make you a wealthy young man, but you must give me everything.'

'It says nothing about what my duties will be. Shouldn't it be somewhere in the contract?' George was fishing here. He didn't actually know.

'You are right. It doesn't. You will do whatever I ask you to do. Be assured, George, we are a very reputable firm and I will never ask you to do anything illegal. The contract would be void if I did.'

Lord Ridley hardly blinked as he handed his pen to George. George looked at the pen. He looked at the contract and he signed.

'Excellent,' said Lord Ridley, holding out his hand which George shook. 'Now lunch and then you will be briefed this afternoon. I'm afraid we will need you to stay in London this evening and you can return to Oxford tomorrow.'

Much to George's surprise, immediate clearly meant immediate. He would have to let Anna know and tell her the news. He was still unsure how she would take it, let alone how he would tell her.

'Oh, and Miss Sutton finishes work at six. She says both roses and chocolates. – and *La Gavroche*. She will meet you there at eight.' And with that, Lord Ridley turned and headed to the door with George racing behind to catch up.

As they passed Jane's desk she looked up at George, smiled and said, 'Eight?'

'Yes, eight.' George turned to see Lord Ridley racing away. Looking back as he accelerated down the corridor to catch up with Lord Ridley, he added, 'Eight at *La Gavroche*.' He had no idea what that was, a restaurant presumably, nor where it was.

Lunch was in the directors' dining room and was, for George, uneventful. He was introduced to a number of 'grey suits' without catching too many names or roles.

The discussion between them related to the British economy; the prospects for the country, George discovered, were not too good. For George it was a blur as he tried to take in what had just happened to him. He wasn't actually able to say much about it over lunch, nor ask the advice of the collected wisdom, because as they had walked along the portrait-plastered halls, Lord Ridley had said 'George, your confidentiality agreement has already come into force. Please say nothing to these people about our contract. You are just here as my guest as a promising student from Oxford who has just been awarded a first. This afternoon you will be driven to our company flat in Great Smith Street where you will be briefed on your job role. That will be given by Nikolay, who is the only other person at the bank, other than myself, to whom you can talk. Now, young man, let's see what you're made of.'

It was just after one-thirty when the uniformed driver ushered George into the waiting car. They drove away past St Paul's Cathedral, along the Strand, past Nelson's Column and Trafalgar Square, down Whitehall to Parliament Square. George looked to his right as they passed Downing Street and wondered whether Prime Minister Heath was working there right now or was at the Houses of Parliament ahead of him. *I suppose my problems are nothing compared to his*, George thought. After a right turn onto Victoria Street and a quick left, the car drew up in front of a library.

Up three large stone steps from the pavement, a large wooden door opened and a tall, lean man in a white T-shirt and blue denim jeans stepped out as the driver opened the car door for George to get out.

'*Privet*. I am Nikolay but my friends call me Coss. You should also. You must be George. I have been looking forward to meeting you.'

'*Privet*, Nikolay. *Kak dela*?' replied George, stepping out of the car.

'I am well, *spasibo*,' Coss replied and the conversation switched languages as fast as George's life had now changed.

'Come upstairs and we can talk. There is a lot to say. You can stay here tonight and Bill, your driver, will take you to *La Gavroche* this evening.' George nodded a curt, passing acknowledgement to his inconspicuous driver, showing the disdain so carefully instilled at Oxford.

It seemed that everyone knew about his life. He had only met Jane Sutton about three hours ago and their next meeting – or was it a date? – was already public knowledge. It seemed that nothing in his life was a secret. Bill (better known as Familiant) smiled a little at George's obvious confusion. *If only you really knew, young man. If only you really knew.*

On the first floor, above the library, was a large, high ceilinged and spacious flat. Coss had shown him around. The hall was so large George reckoned you could have a party for fifty in there alone. He had never been particularly interested in looking at other people's homes because he had never had a need to before, but this was fun. Maybe this was the kind of property he should aspire to with his new found wealth? Later he remembered a large lushly decorated lounge, four bedrooms, a large modern kitchen, a few bathrooms and a study.

'Grab yourself a drink from the fridge and let's go and talk,' said Coss. 'We have a lot to get through.'

They headed into the lounge, each with an orange juice in hand. 'Take a seat. Best you just let me talk and you can ask questions later. Okay?'

George nodded in agreement. So not all bankers wore suits, he mused. *Maybe I won't have to buy one after all.*

'I want to start with the Brotherhood of Saints Cyril and Methodius.'

This has just gone wacky, thought George, who was expecting an economics lecture.

'Ever heard of them?'

George shook his head and Coss continued. 'They were a small group in the Ukraine a hundred years ago or so. The were only together for a couple of years, and they had some interesting objectives which are kind of relevant today. What they wanted for the Ukraine were some of the things we take for granted – personal freedoms enshrined in justice. The books say they wanted four things. First, some human rights and abolition of serfdom. Second, the right of all Slavic countries to keep their national language and culture.' Coss counted the points off on his fingers as he went through them. 'Third, education for all. Finally, they wanted unification of all Slavs into a single country with Ukraine at its heart. You may think that with Mother Russia in charge they've got some of these. Well, education is kind of sorted. But the others aren't. We know all this about the Brotherhood from a couple of books that set out what they were all about. The first,' he was counting on his fingers again, 'was Ustav Slov'ians *Koho Tovarystva sv Kyryla i Metodiia. Holovni Ideï'.*

George translated out loud. '*The Statute of the Slavic Society of Saints Cyril and Methodius: Its Main Ideas*. And the other?' he asked.

'*Knyhy Bytiia ukraïns'koho Narod – The Books of the Genesis of the Ukrainian People*,' replied Coss, providing the translation this time.

'In the Ukraine mainly, but also Byelorussia and Poland, the spirit of the Brotherhood is alive again and if they have any success this time round then we have a large and highly industrialised free-trading block of what would be ex-Soviet states and—' he paused for effect, 'a lot of trading and profitable opportunities. Your job is to help us to help them.'

'Is that all?' said George with more than a hint of sarcasm. 'You want me to bring down the USSR so you can make some more money?'

Coss laughed hesitantly as George smiled.

George looked at Coss. He might dress like an Englander and he might talk like one, but he had a Russian name, and maybe no sense of humour. George didn't know what made him laugh; he clearly didn't understand the sarcasm as he continued his speech.

'Of course, not by yourself. There will be plenty of other pressure points, but this looks like a good and sensitive lead.'

'Okay,' George interrupted, getting slightly worried by what was required of him. 'What am I supposed to do? I'm not James Bond, you know?'

'Of course not. We will enrol you in Kiev University as a doctoral student. You will make contacts, collect information, process it, recommend investment decisions and let us act. As simple as that.'

'So you are paying me all this money to get my doctorate?' George asked, trying to hide his surprise. This suddenly sounded like something he could rather enjoy.

'If you put it that way, yes, but before we go on I must remind you of the confidentiality issues. All you can tell anyone is that you have decided to continue your studies in Kiev. Nothing about us, this place, me or Lord Ridley. And 'no one', I'm afraid, includes

Anna Kowalski. If you must say anything, all you can say is that you have inherited a small amount of money from an aunt – I'm sure you can be creative there – and have decided to continue your studies elsewhere. If Anna or anyone else asks, all you will say is that you met a junior official from the bank who was passing on some information about opportunities for continuing education in the Ukraine on behalf of the Chairman who had it given to him. Do you understand that, George?'

George didn't know what he understood any more.

'Your salary will be paid into two accounts. The first part will be enough to finance your studies and have a bit of fun. The balance will be paid into a second account which you will only be able to access when you have completed the project. If you break the confidentiality, you will never get the funds and – from our part – it is totally deniable. The auditors will never find it. Is that clear?'

For the third or fourth time in as many hours, George wasn't sure that anything was clear. He shrugged. 'You'd better carry on.'

For the next couple of hours, Coss and George talked some more but basically worked hard to compile his application for Kiev University.

'Hey, why "Coss"?' George suddenly asked.

'Sorry, don't understand, why what?'

'I mean why are you called Coss?' George explained.

'Oh, it's been around a long time. I am Ukrainian so my friends here called me Nikolay the Cossack and that got shortened to Coss. You see I have a real interest in this. I have a good friend who is still in the Ukraine and I hope you will meet her. Her name is Vera Safarova. We are nearly done now. What do you know about Ukraine? It's got a rich history.'

'Not a lot,' said George. 'Fill me in.'

'We're a pretty innovative bunch of folk. We were the first to ride horses about six thousand years ago and because our balls were getting pretty cold while riding, we then invented trousers. We have the oldest houses and cooking ovens ever found; the oldest map was found in the Ukraine. We used mammoth heads as drums and we washed our hair with soap before the Romans and maybe we invented wine. Certainly we impressed the Greeks by drinking it full strength while they added water. And two and a half thousand years ago we had tents that we used as saunas, and we smoked 'grass' to get high. Oh, and finally we invented a small bow which we could use while riding. You probably know it better as Cupid's bow. So what do we have, George? Very clean horsemen firing arrows while wearing pants, who had maps to know where they were going, who, having cooked their food, had a bit of singsong with their wine before going off for a sauna to smoke a joint and think about who they were in love with.'

George laughed. He was relaxing and liking Coss more and more. He was starting to look forward to his future, too. He looked at his watch and it was nearly six. Damn, he thought, I need to call Anna.

'Hey, Coss. Remind me again what I'm allowed to say to Anna about why I'm staying here tonight?'

'Well, you could tell her you have a date later with Jane, or alternatively that we have some more stuff to do tomorrow.'

'Thanks, not a great help. Is there a phone here I can use?'

'Sure thing, right there in the hall,' Coss said as he pointed towards the door. 'Direct line as well. This is a private residence.'

George walked out, closing the door behind him. He was not at all sure what he would say to Anna and he certainly didn't want Coss hearing.

'*Lapushka, privet? Kak dela?*' George said as a breathless Anna picked up the phone.

'I'm well, darling. I've had a good day, but tell me what happened? How did it go? Come on, I've been waiting all day for you to phone. Why didn't you phone earlier? Have you got a job?' Anna asked.

As always – too many questions at once. She asked so many questions that he felt the need to respond with just as much information. But this time it involved lying. He'd never really lied to her before, and he wondered if the end could really ever justify the means.

He was *only* lying to her because he believed the outcome in three years' time would mean that he would be able to marry and look after her, but was it *right* to lie in the first place?

'*Lapushka*, it's been an interesting day. Wow. I've been so busy. I'm sorry, darling, but I have to stay down here overnight. I've been offered a scholarship to do a doctorate– isn't that wonderful –and I have to get through all the paperwork a.s.a.p. It's got to be done by midday tomorrow. Only problem is that this position… it's in Kiev. It *is* wonderful, though, isn't it? We will be Doctor and Doctor someday.'

He wasn't sure if it was the tone of her voice or the delay, but he knew she was disappointed. There was an uncomfortable silence.

'Why Kiev?' she finally said flatly.

'Okay, maybe I should take you through this slowly. I need and I want you to understand before I fully commit, although I have very little time. We will talk more tomorrow, *lapushka*. I haven't made any commitment yet.'

He didn't like lying but what else could he do? And the conversation wasn't going too well, even though he tried to assure her they could talk about everything before any decisions got made and that everything would be okay. In the end, she agreed; they would talk more when he got back.

George felt angry when he put the phone down, only he wasn't sure whether he was angry with himself, or with Anna's lack of understanding.

'Everything okay?' Coss asked as George returned to the lounge.

'No, not really.'

'Never mind, George. You have an evening with Jane to look forward to. Don't know how you did it. I have been trying for, well, longer than you. Need a shower?' asked Coss.

'Yes, I think I do,' he said as he walked out to where he remembered there was bathroom.

The car arrived just before seven-thirty. Bill, still in dark glasses, opened the rear door and George slid in, looking not too happy.

'Meeting a beautiful girl for dinner in one of London's best restaurants and you look a little miserable, sir, if I may say so? Everything all right?' the driver asked.

'Yes, Bill, thanks. It's been a busy day and I think I may have upset someone I like very much.'

'I wouldn't worry, sir. I'm sure everything will turn out okay. I was asked to tell you that the chocolates and roses are with the compliments of Lord Ridley and that he will cover the restaurant bill, so no need to worry about that.'

George had totally forgotten about the flowers. At least someone was thinking straight. I suppose that's how you become Chairman, George thought. The last twelve hours had been a roller-coaster – more ups and downs than the Himalayas.

'You're right, Bill. Beautiful girl. Great restaurant, and London. I will enjoy myself. And, of course, many thanks for sorting out the flowers and chocolates. Now, take me to my date please!'

Unseen by George, the driver smiled again.

A tired but excited George got back to Oxford in the late afternoon the following day after he and Coss had finished off what Coss had insisted was the last of paperwork.

'But just for the moment,' Coss had added.

Coss had asked him how he had described his new job and absence to Anna. He seemed to think that it was a good cover and nodded acceptance. For some reason it pleased George to get Coss's approval. George got another lecture on secrecy and was asked to be available sometime in a month or so for some more 'orientation' sessions and to plan to leave for Kiev in late September. He could even afford a taxi back home in Oxford after Coss had refunded him his expenses plus a little bit extra. Anna wasn't there to meet him, but a note was.

In college. Back later.

So things weren't going to get any easier. He needed a shower because he hadn't changed his clothes for twenty-four hours. He thought maybe it was good that Anna was out so he could get ready quietly and plan what he had to say. So far he had rationalised along the lines of: I love Anna, but I am lying to her; but I am lying to her for her *own* good. Surely there is honour in that? If I were to kill someone in order to protect her from being attacked that would be honourable. A lie is minor compared to murder, so there might be some moral foundation for this.

But the big lie, of course was the work he was doing and the amount of money he was going to be paid. In fact, he wasn't lying about all of the work. He *was* going to be at Kiev University studying for a doctorate. So really it was just an omission. He simply wasn't telling her about the money and the extra services he was undertaking. Or the evening he spent with Jane.

Would she understand any of his logic, though? Maybe, George thought, this new development was good in another way – because it would be a test of whether she really loved him. If they stayed together during this upheaval then he would know they could survive anything together. He knew that *he* would pass the test and never give up on her.

He had arrived at the restaurant just before eight. Bill had made sure the timing was perfect. Around Sloane Square and they had turned left onto Lower Sloane Street and there was *La Gavroche*.

'*Oui, Monsieur. Vous avez réservé une table? Bon. Votre nom plaît, Monsieur?*'

It had occurred to him suddenly that he didn't know who had reserved the table. Should he say Lord Ridley and then – heaven forbid – they might think he was Lord Ridley? Or was it Jane Sutton?

'Cove. George Cove.'

'Thank you, sir. You are waiting for a guest, *oui*?'

'Yes. Should I wait here?'

'As you wish, sir, but we do have a small reception bar, to your right, behind you.'

George turned his head slightly and saw a small area with plush red seating. 'Thank you.'

As he sat down he suddenly felt a little incongruous with a single rose and a box of chocolates. At least whoever had bought them had ensured they were wrapped quite beautifully, so to the other diners the package could have been anything from perfume to a diamond necklace. As he looked at the other tables of waiting diners it occurred to him that most would be handing over diamonds as gifts. Somehow you could always tell money. Breeding and background were more difficult to discern, but money was easy. Take that group of four sitting around the table in the corner. It was a treat, probably a birthday, and George wondered how many months of saving had allowed them to eat here. What was it that made them stand out? Maybe it was the drinks on the table: a couple of gin and tonics and two glasses of white wine without an ice bucket in sight.

Just then, Jane was at the door and a waiter was pointing at George. She was beautiful. Her height and slimness was enhanced by a figure-hugging black dress cut to show off slim shoulders. She had a radiant smile and her blonde hair flowed free in loose curls. He glanced quickly at the rest of the room. He was not the only one there impressed by his companion. As eyes followed her to his table George rose to meet her. Should he shake her hand? She kissed him on the cheek.

'George, how wonderful to see you again. I have been so looking forward to this. Tell me, how has your day been?'

George thought it was just loud enough for everyone to hear. She was making him feel comfortable. She saw the presents and this time, and to his relief in almost *sotto voce*, she asked, 'Are these for me?'

'Of course.' It occurred to George that maybe she had ordered them, bought them and maybe even wrapped them. He would have to check with Bill later.

'Maybe I should open the present later when we are alone?' she said as a waiter appeared.

'Would mademoiselle and sir like a drink while they look at the menu?'

'Champagne?' George asked, looking at Jane.

'Of course. Always champagne.' At least his life in Oxford had led him to demand and expect the best. Those nights in the college wine cellars had paid off, although he was unsure that he could remember all the best vintages.

Menus arrived, food was chosen and after a while George and Jane were escorted to the restaurant as a waiter carried their drinks, returning to each their own glass. The food was superb and George understood why the Roux Brothers had earned their reputation. Conversation turned to laughter which at times was almost too loud for the church-like atmosphere.

George and Jane discovered they had a lot in common with each other. During their animated conversation, George thought about Anna and visualised her brooding in Oxford, and he felt a sudden but very short pang of guilt. Why should he be feeling guilty? He was only having dinner with a work colleague. Never mind that that colleague was beautiful and he was enjoying himself, and the flirting was *just* flirting. He was only being himself – charming George.

Jane noticed the moment's hesitation in his flow.

'Are you alright?'

'Yes. Fine. Sorry. I was just thinking of something Lord Ridley said. It's nothing. I was just thinking how wonderful it is to be here with you. This morning in Oxford and now I'm here with the most beautiful girl I've met. Jane, you are the most wonderful person. I wish the evening would last forever.'

Where the words had been hiding, George didn't know. He didn't know if they were true or if he was over-compensating for his guilt over Anna. He did want the evening to last longer to give him time to understand better what he had said. But it was time to go, and George suddenly realised he had no idea how to contact Bill or what to do. He couldn't put Jane on a tube train. Maybe a taxi, but to where? He needn't have worried. As he walked back out into the summer evening with Jane on his arm, both a little tipsy, there was his driver with the car door already open.

'Where would you like me to go, sir?' asked Bill as he slid into the driver's seat.

'George looked at Jane. He still didn't want to say goodnight just yet.

'Could you drive a little? It's such a nice night. Is that okay, Jane?'

She cuddled up close to him in the back of the car, their arms were intertwined and her head was on his shoulder.

'Perfect. Can we walk around St James' park? I do love the lake there.'

'Of course, miss,' said Bill and the car moved off.

Bill and the car waited as they walked around the lake with the background of Buckingham Palace haloed by a full moon which, as they walked and laughed and chased some ducks, cast soft moon shadows. Eventually it had to come to an end and George walked them back to Bill and the car.

'Where to now, sir?'

George mirrored the question to Jane. 'Where to now, Jane?'

'Great Smith Street, I hope, please George,' she said as she pulled him just a little closer.

She left before George woke up. He opened his eyes just a little and saw the mirror above the dressing table. Drawn in the same colour as Jane's lipstick was a big heart with a J and a G. He smiled, content, and decided to have ten minutes more sleep. Was last night a one off? It had to be. He would never see Jane again unless he went back to meet the Chairman, and that was highly unlikely. If he did, they'd probably just smile at each other, slightly embarrassed, and move on. It was obviously best not to say anything to Anna. After all, it certainly didn't *mean* anything, and the evening was already consigned to history, He and Jane would not meet again.

George had a shower and relaxed, waiting for Anna to come home. His mind drifted between what he was going to say about Kiev University, Lord Ridley, Coss and Jane. When Anna walked in, he was taken by surprise.

'So tell me,' she said as she walked into the kitchen. 'No, first let me go and have a shower,'.

George heard the coldness in her voice. It had taken a physical form and sat in the air as a hard barrier between them. He heard the shower running, then stop. Anna came into the living room in jeans and a T-shirt with a towel wrapped around her wet hair.

'So,' she said as she sat down opposite him, 'you'd better tell me everything.'

George suddenly felt angry again. Why did he have to explain? He'd taken some big decisions with their joint future in mind and now – what? She didn't trust him? He managed to push his tryst with Jane into another part of his mind.

'*Lapushka.*' Despite the atmosphere, he tried to adopt a conciliatory tone. 'I have done this for us. The British economy can't get better and jobs aren't going to be easy to get. This is a really good scholarship and we will still be able to see each other because I will be back often, and you will be busy with your work. You have to trust me. I'm doing this for us. I had no time in London to think or speak to you. It had to be done there and then – or else I would have lost the chance completely. In fact, I don't even know that I've got it yet. *Lapushka*, trust me.'

George told the rest of the story, carefully censoring certain bits to preserve his secrets. Anna listened and didn't interrupt. Actually, George wasn't sure at if she was listening at all. He saw that all she was doing was waiting for the chance to have her say, and when he had finished she did.

'I do trust you, but you should have asked me, talked to me – or something. If we are together, as an couple, then we need to decide these things *together*. Don't just do whatever you want. So… what are you going to do? I need to sort my own life out, too, you know. I was talking about it with Aleksandra today.'

She sat back. She didn't want a conversation. Just facts.

'I have said yes, Anna, and I said yes for *us*. I couldn't call you and I had to make a decision. We will know if I've been successful in a month.' George reached to scratch his nose and remembered Pinocchio. 'I did this for us and I do need you to trust me. Tell me about your plans now.'

'Later, when I have worked them through more with Aleksandra. I need an early night, George. We will talk about it again tomorrow. First I'm going to get some supper,' she said and headed towards the kitchen.

Sometimes, George thought, you can look back on your life and only from a distance see the real start of something or the beginning of the end. Tonight, he thought, might well be judged later as the beginning of the end. Was that what he wanted? Hell, no! Just a week ago he was ready to ask her to marry him, but then, he thought, maybe another three years to *really* see if they were perfect for each other would not be so bad after all.

CHAPTER XI

SUMMER OF 1973

George returned to Oxford, but it didn't mean that Coss was short of things to do. Over six months, Aleksandra and Vera Safarova had had infrequent but regular correspondence, all at an academic level, which was all the bureaucracies allowed. Aleksandra had thanked her for her paper which she said was helpful and moved her thinking forward. Vera had replied with the offer of any other help.

In February, Aleksandra wrote:

Dear Mrs Safarova

Thank you for your last letter and I agree with your conclusions as they support my own data. We will incorporate your thoughts into our developments and approach.

I have a very talented young student in Oxford, George Cove, a fluent Russian speaker, who is looking for an appointment in the Soviet Union to continue his studies. Maybe I could steer him your way? He has been part of my research programme and fully understands these issues. In fact he was a co-author on the paper I presented in Kiev.

I was hoping you might be his supervisor and we could see if he could qualify with his doctorate from Kiev.

I hope this is not too much of an imposition on you.

Yours sincerely
Aleksandra Ponomarenko

The bait was taken early and through a series of formal letters and responses, all with Coss's help, the arrangements were made. George's acceptance at Kiev was the last piece of the jigsaw to fall into place. Coss now had to make it work. He counted out the tasks. Formal acceptance by the university was hard enough, but getting the visa was going to be harder. It was his job to make sure these things happened. By late June, everything was in order, and he needed more time with George.

In Kiev, Vera was making the local arrangements. Among other things, she had to ensure that her academic colleagues were at one with her proposal. She had to get State approval and the academic support was crucial. She was excited at the prospect of building closer relations with Aleksandra.

'This is what we should all be doing. If academia builds bridges with the West, then maybe we can start to lead our politicians. It will only be a small step but every long march has to start somewhere,' she told Professor Stanislas Ziemkiewicz from Warsaw, who was visiting Kiev. 'I am going to be supervisor to a British student from Oxford, assuming we can get the university and visas sorted.'

'A very fine idea,' Stanislas said. 'Academia needs to be free of these stupid political boundaries. If the right student applied I would take them on immediately.' Vera passed this on to Aleksandra, who spoke to Familiant, who said, 'A wonderful idea. Make it happen will you please, *Sashunia*?'

While Coss was working, there was increasing and palpable tension between Anna and George. It was odd, George thought, but the spontaneity with which they had done things together before had now gone. He wondered if could you do the same things spontaneously? That was an oxymoron, but somehow it was true. Before, a shout down the hall of 'Let's go for a walk by the river' would have been greeted with fun and enthusiasm but now, more often than not, one or other of them was busy and answered *'Later'*. Previously they always had time for each other and their time together was their first priority. Now they were not each other's most important concern. Anna was working closely with Aleksandra.

She told George over a supper, 'She has some ideas of how we can take the research forward. She won't tell me until they are clearer but it does sound exciting.' Increasingly George noticed now she only became animated when she talked about her work and Aleksandra.

Meanwhile George had thrown himself into learning and improving his Ukrainian. He wasn't sure why. He knew it might be useful if he ever got to meet any of those nationalist to be able to speak their national tongue. But he wondered how many of them could speak Ukrainian? So strong was the Russian influence that Ukrainian, as a language, had almost stopped being taught. George wondered if they were like the Welsh and Scottish Nationalists in the Britain, fighting for an ambiguous cause, or if they would ever become more radical like the Irish IRA? Only time and a little more knowledge would tell.

On a different level, he also knew he had to find something to keep him busy. Anna was away in both body and soul. Their lovemaking was less frequent. He needed to be occupied to stop thinking about his future or their future, and increasingly – and far too often – Jane Sutton. Was its Anna's increasing distance from him, or the distance from Jane that made him think so often of her? He didn't know but he had to find out.

'Coss, this is George. How are things panning out? I was thinking of coming to London and thought I should drop in and see you. Any chance I could use that flat while there? Just for a couple of nights?'

'Hi, George. No problem on either front. Good idea because there are a couple of things we need to go over. When were you thinking of coming?' Coss's laconic tone gave the impression of always seeming to have all the time in the world and never being rushed.

'What about today?' replied George.

'Sure thing. I will stay until you get here.'

George replaced the phone into its cradle and killed the line. He picked it up and redialled. 'Lord Ridley's office, please. Miss Jane Sutton.'

He packed quickly and had one final thing to do: write a note to Anna.

Lapushka—Been called back to London urgently. Sorry.
Will call you tomorrow. G xxxx

George was on the train, reflecting on the impulse to go to London and the speed with which Jane had accepted his invitation. Meanwhile, Anna was with Aleksandra in her rooms.

'Anna, I have an idea which I hope you don't mind I've taken forward just a little to see if it is possible. It means I have been talking to someone about you. Like I say, I hope you don't mind,' Aleksandra said as they sat with papers sprawled across a large working table.

'I shouldn't think so. I trust you to keep my confidences.'

'No, it's not like that, Anna. I would never tell anyone about your personal life and the problems with George. I really don't know what has got into him. He was so different when we were all working together. Have you managed to find out any more about Kiev?' said Aleksandra. It was, she thought, unfair of Familiant and Lord Ridley to put her in this position. Only this morning she had been on the phone with Familiant who had briefed her fully on the latest position. She even knew what poor Anna didn't at that moment. George wasn't at home studying more Ukrainian as Anna thought, but was on a train arriving at Paddington station and probably looking forward to a couple of nights with Miss Jane Sutton rather than thinking about Anna.

'Anna, have I ever spoken to you about Stanislas Ziemkiewicz?'

Anna reflected. 'No, you haven't talked about him but I have read a couple of his papers. He's a professor in Warsaw specialising in fuel economics. Had some very interesting theories around the potential impact of major fuel price spikes and the relationship with the J curve. Why?'

Anna's capacity to read and retain information still impressed Aleksandra. One day, she thought, when she added the ability to interpret and conclude, she would be a very, very good academic. She turned to face Anna and looked straight into her eyes. She wanted to judge her reaction to what was coming next.

'Professor Ziemkiewicz has suggested that we share your supervision. I have agreed, subject, of course, to your views. Personally, I think it is a wonderful idea that will be of great benefit to all of us. What do you think, Anna?'

'I hadn't heard that he was coming to Oxford. I think it is a great idea for me, anyway.' There was a bounce and enthusiasm in Anna's voice that had been missing for a few weeks.

'Well, that is one of the issues. He isn't coming to Oxford. The idea is that you go to Warsaw as a visiting research assistant alternating between the two universities. Is that still so good?'

'Even better,' said Anna. 'Even better. But can it be arranged? I mean, behind the Iron Curtain and with my past?' The edge was coming off her voice.

'That I don't know, Anna, but if you are keen we can see what can be done. I do know some people. Anyway back to work.'

And that was what they did, but without Anna's normal high levels of concentration.

Coss had said that it was all nearly finally fixed and George should still plan for a departure around the end of September. Jane arrived home an hour after George arrived in London and just after George and Coss had finished their conversation.

Anna arrived home excited, wanting to say that she, too, had started to see some resolution to their problems. All she found was a note and disappointment. She went to the bedroom, took out a suitcase, packed some clothes and left a note of her own.

PART II

1973–1986

ENGAGEMENT

CHAPTER XII

AUTUMN 1973

Vera Safarova had been working through the options and felt she had built a bond with Aleksandra even if, sadly, this was only through a series of academically focused letters that were the most communication possible given continual State oversight. Her contact last year with Richard Walder had simply renewed an infrequent but longstanding relationship.

At a previous conference they had managed to avoid prying eyes and to spend an hour or two enjoying vodka and conversation. In another life, Vera thought, or maybe another country, they might have managed to do more and have a more intimate relationship. Through the drink and the chatter there had been a core of flirting, and once, as he made a point, he clasped her hands a little too tightly and for too long to be merely emphasising his words.

Like Aleksandra, Vera was originally from Byelorussia, brought up by an aunt after being separated from her parents just after the war, but she had graduated from the university in Kiev. It was there that she had met her soon-to-be-husband, Timur, who was in the Russian Army. Vera had continued her career as an academic while Timur had carried on soldiering. With their separate careers and Timur often based away from Kiev, their lives had slowly drifted apart. They had their first child, a boy, two years ago, conceived on one of the few nights they had spent together that year. She thought they still loved each other but the pressures of work had made separation almost inevitable. Timur lived much of his life in the army camp, a place that she detested because it represented all she now despised.

The conversation with Walder had drifted and diverged into political areas. He had asked what freedom was. Where did state freedom and personal freedom merge and diverge? These were questions she had thought about deeply for much of her thinking life, but they were questions that she and Timur had hardly debated and when they did, they never found a resolution. Timur was in the Army; he saw no contradictions.

But Vera thought about freedom a great deal. She lived in an oppressed State. She couldn't travel without a permit and she had to live within laws she didn't understand. The State Security ensured that she obeyed. She had to go to Party meetings and pledge allegiance to a system she fundamentally disagreed with. She explained this to Walder, who sat passively, simply listening.

'The opposite of freedom,' she said, 'is submission. I understand that there are some sexual practices where men and women freely allow themselves to be dominated. It may be right for them but it is not for me and it's certainly not right for a State to keep its people in submission. Even talking like this can cause me great problems. It is wrong that I can be punished for saying such things.'

Walder just nodded, unsure how to react.

'Slaves, through history, have been bought and sold,' she said. 'Slaves are used by masters to build their own wealth, and here in the Ukraine don't we see that the State masters have privileges that are not there for the masses? They have their communist dogmas of sharing for all the people yet still they have a better life. They have the *dachau* and cars and drivers while the people live in small tenement blocks. Do you know, Walder, there are some people who are naturally very dominant who gain pleasure by giving and causing pain? Sometimes in countries these people become despotic leaders, of which, of course, Hitler was a horrible example. But this is an extreme and it doesn't mean that every leader is a pain-loving dominant, and whatever their intentions, they cause pain, whatever their objectives are when they start and whatever they might think of themselves.

'Look around you. Can't you see the pain in the eyes of the people? By saying nothing and doing nothing we have chosen to be submissive to these dominant people. It doesn't matter if it's between two people in a private life or the State and the population; in any of these relationships the cornerstone is trust and I have to ask, can we trust our leaders? If we can't trust them, then we can't allow ourselves to be submissive, and I have to tell you, Walder, we can't trust them. Trust comes first. You can always love the one you trust but you can't always trust the one you love.

'We all love our country and if we could trust our leaders to love us and the country as much as we do then really we would have freedom. Based on love and trust, freedom and submission can be the same. If freedom is the same as shared and reciprocated love, and if a loving submission is that ability to give oneself in love and trust, then isn't a true submissive relationship really the ultimate statement of freedom? They are one and the same.'

Walder looked at her. He heard the words but he didn't really comprehend. This life Vera was talking about was so alien to anything he knew.

'But I am boring you, Walder,' she said. 'I am sorry. I sometimes get carried away, but there are people that feel as I do and really do not see this as the way forward for our countries, and, Walder, if you know these people in your country, please tell them there are those of us here who want to see change. If you know people, then tell them about Saints Cyril and Methodius. They will understand.'

Walder didn't understand and he didn't know anyone, but it seemed important.

When he got back to his hotel he had to write down the names of the two obscure saints for fear of forgetting them, and when he got back to London he had to contact someone who might explain to him what it all meant, so he wrote to the only person he knew at the time who spoke any Russian and might understand – Julia Candish at Oxford.

She replied promptly, saying she knew nothing about them but would do some research and get back to him. In fact, she did know about them, and the brotherhood, and it wasn't long before she was on the phone to Familiant explaining the significance.

'Richard,' Familiant said in a phone call to Walder. 'Julia Candish asked me to call you. I'm not sure if what you have heard is particularly important or relevant but we may as well dot the I's and cross the T's. Could I ask you a favour? To get a message to Vera? Are you going to the Chernobyl conference?'

Walder had assumed the 'us' was a shadowy branch of government, but was afraid to ask. Had he asked, a shadowy branch of government would have been the answer he received.

'I am not going to get myself into any sort of intrigue or problem am I?'

'No, of course not. Just the normal correspondence between academics,' Familiant replied. 'You will be just doing your duty.'

And so had started a very simple exchange of letters with Vera and a request to give Aleksandra a copy of her recent paper including some extra information not normally available. All he had to do was collect it and give it to Familiant. The need for a cover story about Familiant did raise some concerns but actually Walder had started to find it all rather exciting.

Vera was smiling to herself as she fed her son, Timofei, his tea. She had not meant to tell Walder all she did and, as she reflected on their conversation, she knew it was reckless but it had delivered results and George would soon be here as a permanent route for their views to be shared and promulgated. It also looked as if Stanislas Ziemkiewicz would have similar access. It was one thing, she thought, to have contact and access but it would make her life more difficult. They would have to be more careful in every respect. They had moved into a new phase which was more dangerous. The young Timofei looked up at his mum. He wanted more to eat. His eyes were wide and naïve; innocence was in the eyes of a child.

'I'm doing this for you and all your friends, Timofei. I promise, though, that I will still be there to see you as a young man. I promise you that. I promise you a better world. I am one mother who will never leave you.'

During the last two months as summer faded, George drifted between Oxford and London. Many times he tried to have a conversation with Anna but failed. The few times they met, the conversation was either stilted or loud because they argued. In London he now had a key to the flat in Great Smith Street and Jane spent many nights there. He and Coss had become good friends and often went for a drink at the pub around the corner in Stratton Street. Finally, in early September, he had moved out totally from Oxford and was packed for his flight to Kiev.

He wondered whether Lord Ridley knew of his relationship with Jane. He tried to ask her once but she just laughed it off and said, 'Of course not. He would be very upset.'

George feigned surprise but decided not to follow it up. He had already thought about it and decided he might not like the answer. At best, he thought, Lord Ridley might just condone their relationship. He was scared he might actually be encouraging it.

The time came for George to leave for Kiev. Two nights before his departure date, he and Coss went on a tour of London that led to a headache, and on his final farewell evening with Jane they were both upset at his parting. George even had to hold back some tears. Jane failed and her mascara ran onto her cheeks. At one moment George thought of Anna and how this was the way they should have said goodbye. He wondered what she was doing that night. Probably alone and certainly unaware.

Jane said she'd managed to take the day off work so she could come to the airport to say goodbye. Coss stood on the steps of the Great Smith Street flat giving final instructions as the car pulled up.

'Good morning, sir. Good to see you again. And you, miss, as well. I gather we are going to Heathrow this morning?' said the driver as he put the luggage in the boot.

'Yes, Bill. Heathrow. Going for a little trip,' said George.

Anna was unaware that George was leaving that day. She had been consoling herself in her new work and was far from sure of her feelings. She knew that by walking out she had been hasty, but retreat and a change of mind was not in her character. Once a decision had been made it was irreversible. George had often teased her that she was the most stubborn person he had ever met. They had just made love and she was teasing him as they lay naked on the bed.

'Do you really love me, George?' she had asked as she put her head on his chest.

'Of course I do, *lapushka*. You need never ask; you only need to see how I dote on you.'

'Why do you love me, George? You could have any woman you want. I see all the girls looking at you.'

George hated these questions. He loved her face and her body, but these were not the reasons he loved her. He loved the sound of her voice, and each word she said, however mundane, was still like poetry to his ears.

'There are a thousand reasons why I love you, *lapushka*. Why don't you ask me every day for a thousand days and I will tell you them all and, by then, I will recognise another thousand? But if you make me choose one today, other than your beauty, it is because you are such a proud person who has ideals and standards. I love your certainty and assurance.'

'I'm certain I love you,' she whispered. 'I wonder, is it always so good to be certain and sure?'

'Arrogance, I've heard described,' said George, 'as misplaced confidence, and stubbornness is misplaced confidence. When the world changes round you and you stick to your guns it'll hurt you much more than a loss of face. Pride comes before the fall, but, *lapushka*, there are a thousand things you love about me. Is one my lovemaking?' He pulled her closer to kiss her gently.

Today Anna reflected that maybe her stubbornness was hurting her more than anything he could have done.

'There's no weakness in admitting that you have changed your view because the world has changed,' he had said. 'There's a bigger weakness in not adapting and changing as the world changes around you.'

Maybe this was one of those situations, Anna thought. As they finished their time at Oxford could she have ever expected that they would both have stayed working in the same place? The world had changed and had she been too proud and stubborn? Well, he had upset her. He hadn't phoned to let her know what was going on and then he asked her to *trust* him and all he could do was leave notes!

If he really loved her, one day he would show it and this was a good lesson for him. He would learn his lesson. But had she done so much that he could no longer make a loving gesture? It was strange, she thought, when he had finally left for London they probably still loved each other. Now someday soon he would be on his way to Kiev and they hadn't even said goodbye. She hadn't even held him one last time. This wasn't fair. They had been happy. The tears started to run slowly down her cheeks as Anna reached inside her bag for a tissue. Instead she found his last note which she had been carrying and refused to throw away. Rereading it only made the tears flow more freely.

Boryspil airport,-thirty kilometres to the east of Kiev, was very unlike Heathrow, George thought. Heathrow was the world's largest and most sophisticated airport, matched perhaps only by Chicago's O'Hare. Heathrow was an international airport. George looked at the rudimentary departure board. International meant Moscow and that was the way he had arrived in Kiev.

There was no metro into Kiev and he had too much luggage to take the bus, which he thought would be rather more dangerous than the flight he had taken on a Russian airline. Moscow to Kiev was not a long flight and Coss had booked him into a business class seat at the front of the plane. No sooner was the plane off the ground than it seemed to George everyone was smoking and the air-conditioning could not cope. Smoke seemed to fill the cabin, and as the slightly plump and overly stern stewardess stated their services, George was soon to learn his first lesson about life in the Slavic states. His first course for breakfast was a choice of vodkas or any other drink he fancied as a tray of alcohol was placed in front of him. He just hoped that the pilot wasn't sharing the same meal, although he assumed he too was smoking.

Having rejected the idea of the bus, he took a taxi into the centre of Kiev. He held on tight to the door handle in a back seat and tried to wedge himself into a corner. The taxi screamed through a dodgem of old and unrepaired cars on poor roads. He was now very unsure whether the taxi, bus or flight was the biggest risk to his life.

Earlier from London, Coss had tried to make a four-week booking at the Lybid Hotel while George found a flat to rent, but as with all communications into the Ukraine, it was slow and uncertain. Coss couldn't even be sure his letter had arrived. The letter had arrived but that didn't mean that a room had been allocated or anything agreed, and so George spent more than an hour trying to check in.

While he waited, he picked up a brochure lying uninvitingly on the concierge's desk. This stated that there were three brothers – Princes Kyi, Chshek, and Khoriv – and a sister, Princess Lybid. Kiev was named after Prince Kyi and the seventeen-storey hotel, built in 1970, was named after his sister. Reading that took just a minute of his time. He sampled some of the other literature and felt none the wiser. This place really wasn't set up for tourists. He must remember to get a map, he thought. Maybe he should go for a walk while the hotel tried to find and allocate him a room, but he decided it was better to stay close to his passport and belongings. He had four days of sightseeing before he was due to report to the university and there was no need to try and cram it all into the first hour. Better to relax and get a feel for the place.

His room was Russian standard, even though the hotel had only been built for three years. It was functional rather than luxurious. The mattress was hard and the sheets clean, but more yellow than white. George decided a regular supply of hot water was a prerequisite for any room calling itself a bathroom and on that basis the facilities here fell short of his definition. The room decoration was bland, but at least the carpet hadn't yet been worn out. The stale smell of strong Russian cigarettes permeated everywhere. In the corridor sat the epitome of everyone's view of a Russian *babushka*. Sitting on a high-backed chair close to the lift was a rotund and impassive old lady dressed in catholic black, with a black head scarf; George had been pre-warned by Coss. An early attempt by George to engage her in conversation was greeted by nothing more than a blank stare.

'She is not there to help you,' Coss had said. 'She will watch everything that goes on and report back to the State police. If you bring any woman back to your room,' he had added with a smile, 'a policeman will know well before Jane.'

It was on the second day that the room phone rang and the operator said he had a call. 'George? *Privet*. This is Vera Safarova.

How are you?'

'I am well, Madam Safarova. Thank you for calling, and I am enjoying my first days in Kiev. It is a very beautiful city. It is good of you to call.'

'My pleasure, George. I was wondering, if you haven't arranged anything else, if you would like to join me for supper tonight at my home? I can come and collect you if that would help.'

George could not have been happier. He knew no one else in Kiev and he had already generated a real respect for travelling salesmen who spent every week night in a new hotel, alone in a room, by themselves. How dispiriting could that be? But then, maybe the stories of travelling salesmen were true and they weren't always by themselves. He had heard they often shared their lonely days with either a woman or a bottle. No wonder their marriages were so difficult and Alcoholics Anonymous was attended by so many salesmen. But he had no inclination to drink, and the memories of Jane and Anna were still too strong for him to even contemplate a relationship or search out a new companion. Then he remembered, even if he was so inclined, the *babushka* would soon put an end to that. He had only been here two days and already the evenings had started to drag.

'I would be delighted, absolutely delighted. What time would you like me to be there? I am sure I can try and get a taxi. Do you want to give me an address?'

Vera told him where she lived and George realised he still hadn't bought a map and didn't really know anything about Kiev other than a small circular area around the Lybid Hotel. That had to be rectified quickly. He wrote the address down and asked Vera, 'How long will the taxi take?'

Vera laughed. 'Anything from thirty minutes to an hour. It depends how much vodka the driver has drunk.' That didn't fill George with any confidence.

George knew it was customary for a guest to take a small present for the host, but there was nowhere for him to buy anything. He hoped Vera would understand. The journey took as long as Vera predicted and again it was as frightening as his first ride from the airport.

Vera lived, liked many Ukrainians, in an apartment block. It was a nondescript five-storey block among many other similar blocks, each presumably housing the same thirty apartments. The strong smell of cooking was at every turn as he worked his way up badly lit stairs to the third floor and Vera's apartment. There was the smell of cooking vegetables, probably borsch, from every kitchen. The corridor was badly decorated and the need for paint was evident everywhere as bare plaster broke through. Bare boards showed through worn-out lino. Not every light worked and at times George had to feel his way up the stairwell. He wondered if regular life like this existed anywhere in Great Britain.

Before he had left London, Coss had pulled together a briefing pack for George, which included information about Vera, who was to be his supervisor. It wasn't much to go on but it meant that George already knew a little about his hostess. However, he wanted to ask all the questions again. He wanted to understand her personally, and not through other people's recollections. As he walked through the door he had his first surprise and he realised his briefing was missing a lot of detail. That was understandable because Coss just couldn't have known. The lounge door opened straight onto the communal corridor and, as Vera opened it, he was surprised when a small boy, with the speed of a bullet, ran straight towards George's midriff.

'Timofei, behave!' Vera shouted as she reached out and stopped his headlong charge. Holding tightly onto a squirming Timofei, under her left arm, Vera offered her other hand which George took.

'I am sorry. Whenever there is a knock at the door he hopes it is his father,' she said.

As George entered the flat he was surprised how small it was: a kitchen and small lounge with a single bedroom. Even George and Anna had had more space and more corners to hide away in and be alone. As he left the Lybid, he'd assumed that as a senior academic she would live as well as she would have done in Oxford.

This was his second lesson of what life under communism meant. This flat was not large and this was not luxury.

'Timofei, this is George. He is a friend of ours.'

Timofei didn't look as though he believed it at all.

'George, do you mind if we spend a few minutes getting him to sleep so we can eat and talk without interruption? He is all ready for bed.'

Children were new to George, and while his natural and first reaction was to tell her just to lock him in the room, he hardly knew Vera and so he decided not to share his views on child-rearing. Instead he simply agreed. 'Of course,' he said.

Timofei calmed quickly and from the bedroom he heard Vera's quiet singsong of goodnights. It wasn't too long before she reappeared. The flat was quiet.

'Come and talk to me while I finish making supper and I will teach you a little about Ukrainian culture. The things you can't learn at university,' she said.

George followed Vera into a tiny kitchen; it was so small that, as Vera reached out for a sharp knife, George had to pirouette adroitly to avoid being cut.

'Gosh, it's small in here,' said George involuntarily, speaking his thoughts. 'I'm sorry, I didn't mean to say that. It's just that I was thinking it and it slipped out.'

Not a great start, he thought. I must concentrate. Vera turned to him. At least she's smiling, George thought.

'You are right, George, but this is normal and we are really quite lucky to have even this. Of course, we don't really have much choice. I am sure we are going to talk about this subject many more times over the next few years,' she said. 'And, George, you do have to be careful what you say and where you say it if you want to stay here for three years!'

'Does Timofei sleep in the same room as you?' he asked.

'At the moment, yes,' Vera answered, and when Timur is home we move him into the lounge when we go to bed. I am not sure what we will do when he is older. We haven't thought that far ahead.'

George again side-stepped Vera as she reached out, grabbed a jar and took a pinch of what he assumed was pepper and heavily seasoned and basted a sizzling joint of meat that she took out of the oven.

'So let me tell you about Ukrainian women' she continued. 'I am sure this is a subject of real interest to a handsome young man like yourself.'

Maybe directness was a Slavic trait. That was how Anna would have started a conversation: straight to the point and no messing around. George looked closely at Vera. She was as beautiful as her file said. Tall and elegant but dressed simply in a skirt, blouse and cardigan to repel the oncoming winter which George had already started to feel as he walked out in the evenings.

'Ukrainian women are the most beautiful in the world, except of course for the Byelorussians, which is where I come from.' There was a humorous glint in her eye which immediately appealed to George. She was teasing him and he liked the attention.

'We make the best wives. We are beautiful, we love to cook, we love to make a home and we love…' she paused. 'Well, we just love making love.'

'Are we talking about Ukrainian or Byelorussian women now?' George teased her back.

'George, that is for you to find out,' she said.

'I can see that you are beautiful and a temptress.' Was he really talking to his supervisor like this? 'So maybe for now you should just tell me about the food?'

As she was dicing a pile of herbs into fine shreds, Vera said, 'Traditional Ukrainian cuisine is very aromatic and we use lots and lots of herbs and spices like garlic, parsley, dill, mint and mustard. You will get bread with most meals and – let me tell you – it is the best bread you will ever taste, and you'd better get used to vodka rather soon. It comes with most meals.'

'What are you cooking tonight?' George asked.

'Well, over the next three years you will eat a lot of borsch so I thought I would treat you to something quite different. Anyway, borsch is best at the heart of the winter. We are going to have a hussar roast. It's a roast meat but with a stuffing. See, it has already been soaked in vodka. You will like it, George. I promise you that. We can leave it cooking now for another hour and have a drink and talk a little while we wait.'

They returned to the lounge and George sat down. Immediately, Vera realised she had forgotten to bring the bottle and glasses in and returned to the kitchen, leaving George to look at the room. The two small sofas were comfortable but worn. The décor brought back memories of his own childhood. It was neat and clean but out of date. The walls were covered with pictures or icons and all the shelves had bits and pieces on them. It was far too cluttered for George's taste. He had already decided that when he had all the money promised to him, his place in London would have a very minimalist feel to it. It would be nothing like this. Vera returned not just with a drink but with what to George looked like another whole meal in itself – dill pickles, raw carrots, bread, and what to George's untrained eye looked like pancakes.

'What are these?' he said.

'*Syrnyky*,' said Vera. 'Ukrainian *syrnyky*, or cottage cheese fritters. They are a traditional Ukrainian dish. We have them sometimes for breakfast and sometimes lunch but I like them with a drink. You see, George, unlike where you come from, drinking to us also means eating. We can't drink without eating.' She poured him a vodka shot.

'Now let's eat a little and drink a little and talk. This is how every Ukrainian likes to live.'

CHAPTER XIII

OCTOBER 1973

That first night Vera talked passionately about her views on freedom, but mentioned nothing about The Brotherhood of Saints Cyril and Methodius. George remembered Coss's words about the real purpose of his visit but he didn't want to (and didn't know how to) raise the matter. He wanted to hear Vera out, and at her pace; after all, he had plenty of time, at least three years he hoped.

Over the next couple of weeks they met at the university to talk about his work there. He was required to teach a little but also work on his thesis. Vera was every bit as good a supervisor as Aleksandra and so similar in her ways, he noticed. In fact at times he thought she looked a little like Aleksandra.

Vera was older than George and the other people he worked closely with, but he enjoyed being in her company. Jamila, Anna, Aleksandra, Jane and now Vera; some companions and all friends. He tried to list men who had the same status in his life. Only Coss came near to being a real friend and he was hardly a close friend. He thought about this and realised that he much preferred being in the company of women than men. It wasn't a sexual issue, rather it was that men together don't build the same level of trust and intimacy that he reached with women, and now here was not just a beautiful woman but also a woman who challenged his intellect. Maybe the brain is the most erogenous of all the organs, he thought.

Then suddenly there was so much to talk about. George had his portable shortwave radio which he listened to every night. He had only been in the Ukraine for a few days but already it had become his routine to catch up on what was happening throughout the world, courtesy of the BBC World Service from Bush House in London. The radio schedule started to become a way of life. He knew when there would be news in English and when there would be music, both *modern* and classical. He enjoyed his Saturday morning ritual of a run for exercise, breakfast for substance, and the World Service to feed his mind. He also discovered that he could pick up Radio Luxembourg and listen to the very latest music. Even if the news suddenly seemed parochial when heard from across the miles, and the music they played was rarely to his taste, he was comforted by the sense of *belonging* somewhere, knowing the real world was out there and he could return to it when he wanted. Then the news took on a truly global perspective.

It's October the Sixth and this is the BBC World Service from Bush House, London. Today Egypt and Syria attacked Israel, who it would seem were totally unprepared.

The news shocked him and George had felt the need to speak to Vera, not just for reassurance but also for the impact on his work. His thesis was all about the economics of energy, and surely this would have an impact? How would the USSR react, and what did it mean for the new Chernobyl power plant being built? Suddenly he felt alone and lost. It was one thing to be at home in Britain when these things happened, but now he was an alien in a foreign land.

'What do you think will happen?' George asked Vera, again sitting in her living room.

'I'm not sure we know,' Vera answered as she poured him a vodka shot. 'It depends who wins, but we can be sure we are entering a new era. Your thesis may be changing as we talk.' She paused for a moment in thought before continuing.

'One way or the other, something will happen to oil and energy prices. We will be on the Arab side. That is what Russia has decided. They have decided that Zionism is some big capitalist plot. The Jews suffered badly throughout all the USSR… but then we all suffer one way or another. It's no different for us. We are just like the Jews – we have a state and a place to live, but it's worse for the Ukrainian people because they really don't have an identity and soon it will all be gone. I don't know how many generations it will take but we really do need to do something.'

George was listening carefully. Where was this conversation going? He suddenly felt out of his depth.

'Why, Vera? I don't understand what this all means.'

'I think, George, I need to let you meet some friends of mine. I am sure they will help you understand better. It's better you meet some of our people. Real Ukrainians, who care.' Vera let the subject drop as she offered George some more *syrnyky* with pickles.

Over the following weeks, George and Vera met frequently at the university. The news of war from Israel was of less importance to George than its effect on the world's economies; after all, that was now really his job. OPEC, otherwise known as the Organization of the Petroleum Exporting Countries, had increased the price of oil and cut its supply. For a moment it seemed as if the USSR and America were going to square-up against each other, with the terrible consequences that would bring, but it was averted by the ceasefire of October 25.

George concentrated on his work. Russia was a net exporter of oil and the price rose dramatically. A seventeen per cent increase went through, which the West couldn't afford and a reduction in demand would be needed, which takes time. Russia would have more foreign currency to spend on wheat and other products. Whatever the embargos said, trade was trade and somehow it would happen. The West would also need more foreign exchange to buy oil at the new prices. There was going to be increased business. George was sure that Lord Ridley would have his own analysts working on this, but a paper from him, giving the Ukrainian perspective, would surely be appreciated.

This wasn't the first of his reports back home, but somehow George felt it might be among the more important. He was a novice political analyst but somehow he felt that there was a shift. Aleksandra would understand, and he thought for a moment of Anna. He reminded himself he was doing this not just for himself, but for Anna as well.

'I am doing this for you, Anna,' he said out loud to reinforce the thought. This time, he knew for sure it was a lie and he didn't feel an iota of guilt. He had spent more time with Jane this year than with Anna, and when he closed his eyes at night it was Jane – Jane with her long legs and flowing hair – who always came to his mind. He hated the idea of having to choose between them. But then, he thought, that would probably never be *his* decision.

CHAPTER XIV

AUTUMN 1973

While George was working his way into a new life and a new set of cultures and values, Anna and Aleksandra were spending more time together developing the structure of their work together for the next few years. Doctor Anna Kowalski. It had a resonance she wanted to hear, but working for a doctorate was going to be nothing like as easy as she had hoped. At times she felt she knew so much about her subject but then she sat with Aleksandra and realised how little it really was. They hadn't even decided on the detailed area of research, although they had narrowed the areas down. Like George, they had decided that energy economics was the broad topic.

Aleksandra said a decision could wait because first Anna had to think about research methods. She had to learn how to do research and until then they could keep talking about the details. She noticed that Anna was, as ever, throwing herself into her studies with an energy that was surprising even to Aleksandra. And Aleksandra was settling in to her life, too, spending more time in Oxford. Her work hadn't changed much but she enjoyed getting out of London.

On many evenings when Aleksandra was staying in Oxford they would meet for supper. They avoided eating in College whenever they could. It was stuffy and oppressive and reminded both of them too much of the privileges they had, which they were silently avowed to fight against. Instead they would find a small bistro and sit in a corner talking. A candle stuck in an old wine bottle hardly produced enough light to read the papers that would inevitably be spread across the table. It caused them to sit close. Anna would often turn and look straight at Aleksandra when she developed a new line of thought. It was often a look of admiration. Outsiders may have construed another kind of relationship.

Anna was in awe of Aleksandra. Not just her academic skills

but also her whole life story and what she had endured. She heard the stories of the journey from Byelorussia. They talked about what it must be like to live today behind the Iron Curtain. Aleksandra was Anna's senior by seventeen years and she alone of the two knew what had brought them to this point.

Tonight they were at their favourite restaurant. Anna sat next to Aleksandra searching papers for a new fact or detail. Aleksandra was quiet, sitting slightly back on the wooden chair, looking at her. She saw the intensity that was Anna; a youthful enthusiasm that reminded her so much of herself. She remembered Familiant's words of a few days earlier, when he had called her and invited her to join him for dinner.

'So tell me, Aleksandra, how is your young charge?' It was such a complex question, she thought, but Familiant knew that. Anna was her student, friend, protégé even, and her responsibility for a higher and wider calling. Familiant didn't wait for an answer. That pleased Aleksandra as she had not yet managed to frame an adequate response.

'We need to get her more involved. She has been too much on the periphery.'

'Is she ready to go out into the field?' Familiant had asked in one of those throwaway comments he had so mastered. Never for Familiant the direct question asked with deep seriousness and purpose and full eye-to-eye contact.

What had he been doing when he asked that question? Aleksandra tried to remember. That was the core reason behind their meeting, and what had Familiant being doing? Cutting a slice of brie or tasting a new dessert wine? Familiant has also chosen a bistro for their supper – in so many ways like the one she and Anna now frequented. Finer food, perhaps. certainly more expensive, with vintage wine bottles as candlesticks, but less intimate. And where would she rather be?

'What do you mean "in the field"? She's not a James Bond spy,' Aleksandra had snapped back, angry, and, as she later understood, defensively, on Anna's behalf.

'I simply mean that we have invested a lot of time and energy into this young girl. She was useful in getting George up to speed, but now it is her time to start to pay back on our investment,' he replied with his normal nonchalance.

'How is George doing?' Aleksandra asked, wanting time to think about Anna and her role.

'Rather well, actually. Ridley says that much of what he is sending through is more insightful than even George realises. Of course he hasn't actually sent through anything much more than Ridley is getting from other sources, but then again he is young and has only been there a short time. "Great promise" was the quote, I think. So, yes, rather well.'

Aleksandra had only picked at the bones of what Familiant was saying. She was still thinking about how to answer the Anna question. As she emerged from her thoughts she thought she saw a look of self-satisfaction on Familiant's face. It was normally impassive. She must have been wrong.

'Stanislas Ziemkiewicz. Do you remember who he is, Bill?' Aleksandra asked.

'Of course. Polish. Warsaw. Professor who was willing to take graduates. You thinking that we ought to send her there? That would bring her awfully close to George, though. Do we want that proximity?'

'Yes, we should send her. Stanislas has a good reputation and is supposed to be close to the Polish Brotherhood, and, no, she won't meet George. At the moment he won't get visas to get across the border and being out of Oxford might take her mind off him.'

'So does she still think about him?' Familiant asked.

'I'm not sure. Sometimes I think she works so hard just to put him out of her mind, and other times I think she is just driven and hasn't even noticed he has gone. I will try and find out before I set up the Stanislas meeting.'

'Good,' said Familiant, 'that sounds perfect. I think having her in Poland may prove useful.'

Aleksandra's thoughts returned to the present in the dimly lit bistro two days after that meeting. She looked across at Anna.

'Anna,' she said, 'Stanislas Ziemkiewicz has been asking after you. Remember we talked about him?'

'Really? That's exciting. I remember you said he might want me to work with him in Warsaw. Is that possible?'

'I think it is,' said Aleksandra, stopping Anna from compiling a list of citations and references. 'Do you really want to go there? I mean, what would George think?'

'I don't think that matters now.' A seriousness settled on her face.

'Do you want to talk about it?'

'He has chosen his own path, and although he said he was doing it for us, I don't believe him. We tried, and when he had to make a choice he made it for himself. I don't believe he didn't have time to talk to me. I have made my decision and there is no going back—'

Aleksandra interrupted her. 'But what if things change? Nothing can be so permanent, can it?'

'Aleksandra, it *can* be that permanent. I have made my decision. Now tell me more about Stanislas.'

Aleksandra stared at Anna, a stare returned without a blink. She thought of herself and thought how pride would have affected her, how she would have reacted. She wondered if Anna meant all she was saying. Could she really have such ambivalence towards George? It might take a long time for her to know. Maybe never. For now, the subject was closed.

CHAPTER XV

DECEMBER 1973

Christmas was coming closer and the weather was significantly colder. George had a decision to make: should he stay in the Ukraine or try to get back to the England? Events finally left him with no choice. He was working hard and needed a break, but leaving would mean he would have to go through all his visa applications again. He couldn't face that, and nor would Lord Ridley, so Christmas was to be spent in Kiev.

His days were spent at the university, lunchtimes eating *plov* and evenings often with Vera. Friends, real or minor, were hard to find. He was treated politely but with suspicion when he suggested to fellow students meeting for vodka or evenings out. Without a doubt, he was not yet seen as the best person to be seen with, or to be thought of as a close friend. It was not necessarily because they disliked or mistrusted him but he was not Ukrainian and therefore a subject of interest to the Security Police. The suspicion of him as a foreigner was obvious.

He had started to make contacts and friends through music. Students were students everywhere around the world and – although officially banned – British bands like the Beatles had cult status among the university. Running a few years behind England and the USA, Beatlemania was rife. Haircuts matched the pictures on album covers, and wherever he went people asked him if he knew them personally, or had met them, or had heard them play live. It became hard to continually say no, so his stories of life in England included more and more tales of personal meetings and intimate knowledge of the famous four. In one note to Coss, George asked him whether he could get Beatle albums smuggled into Kiev. Coss could see no way of doing so, but he did manage to send tape-recordings which were easier to disguise, which George traded for new friendships.

He looked at the students and saw a difference between them

and their elders. The old had a cause, but were cautious and careful, understanding that the State-delivered threats could easily be implemented. They had the collective memories of Hungary and Prague to reinforce their worries. The young, however, were rebellious, buying western music in black markets while putting themselves at risk of arrest. They had no focus for their discontent other than the normal teenage targets of their parents and elders. The new generations couldn't join the dots to see how to rebel. George thought about this. If they had a focus they could be the army of the Brotherhood. He checked as best he could and it was the same in Poland and Byelorussia, and even Russia. Western music was driving the spilt of the students from states all across the USSR. He wondered if the Brotherhood had seen this opportunity and knew how to mobilise the young? He decided to speak to Vera and write a note to Lord Ridley. As foreigner he had to be careful. This was a lesson that Vera was always giving. But if the State was watching him, it had become a simple exercise. There were only a few restaurants or bars he ever visited. With those, the university and Vera's flat, his boundaries were well defined.

The war in Israel had finished and it seemed to George that Russia might be the big winner. Oil prices had escalated and Russia, with its huge reserves, had – almost overnight – become significantly more wealthy, while the economies of the West, and Great Britain in particular, were heading downwards alarmingly quickly.

'Thank God,' George said to Vera as they sat in her living room. 'Thank God I didn't stay in England and try and find a job there. There isn't a job for anyone, and it will get worse.'

George now had a licence to buy alcohol, and the vodka he had brought with him was outside on the window ledge getting colder. Far better than any fridge, he realised. This was Ukrainian vodka, cheap by any standards he knew, but expensive here. He was starting to become a connoisseur of vodkas. Of all of them he found black vodka the most difficult to accept as it reminded him of black ink. He had tried vodka with different fruit flavours.

He had tried the cheapest, which was really close to fire water, and the most expensive, which was smooth but lost the very essence of what vodka should be. Vera watched as he topped up their drinks. A slight viscosity was essential. It must be the oils that give it the taste. He passed Vera her glass. She ate a *blini*, or *mlyntsi* as she called them in Ukrainian, and downed the vodka in one. George, brought up on sipping whisky and tasting wines at Oxford, still drank his slowly.

'So coming here was good for you, George?' Vera asked.

'For many reasons, Vera,' he said while still taking a small sip of his vodka and waving a gherkin, to Vera's amusement, as his hands followed his words. 'I would never have met you and Timofei, nor, of course, tasted such great vodka.'

The twinkle in his eye as he spoke, the easy smile and the relaxed delivery made Vera think about her lovers. If only she was younger, or he was older. What a perfect partner he would be. She thought of Timur, still away being a soldier, defending a land and ideal she no longer understood. What would sex and life be like with George? He was such a boy. Not much over twenty and brought up in that soft world in England. By now in the Ukraine he would be a real man; strong and rugged. But why shouldn't she seduce him? She was only just over thirty. *Only* thirty. What would life be like with George as a lover? As she said these words to herself it seemed like a lifetime had already passed. Timofei was already two years old and had become a firm friend of George. She was twenty when she had met Timur and he was twenty-two. She hadn't thought about it before, but both these men who were now so central to her life were the same age when she'd met them.

Timur had just finished university; with little else to do and to avoid being conscripted into some distant unit, he joined the army straight away so that he could be closer to Vera. They had assumed in the regular army he would be better able to control his career and hence where he was posted, but he was wrong and that decision had meant a life apart for most of the time. Already that tummy-churning love had diluted to simple affection. She no longer waited expectantly for his letters or cleaned the flat obsessively when he was due home for leave. She couldn't live in the barracks and her work was important, but she had Timofei and he was now her life.

George was still talking and she turned to him. 'Sorry, I was a million miles away,' she said.

'A million miles from here, or England and its green and pleasant lands?' he said. She shrugged in confusion.

'Never England,' she said. 'I don't think that is a solution… Oh, that wasn't a real question, was it. Someday I will understand you better, I promise.'

George smiled. 'Well, we can't afford oil now and this new chap Arthur Scargill is taking the coal fields out. And there are rumours that Prime Minister Heath is going to have to announce reduced working hours to save energy. Just working three days a week! It's soon going to be a real mess. I think I am far better off here. It's a pity about Christmas, though. It's going to upset Ma and Pa not having the family together, but that can't be helped.'

Vera looked at him. 'Then you will have Christmas with us. In fact you will have two.'

'Why's that?' George asked.

'We celebrate Christmas on January sixth, twelve days after yours on the twenty-fifth of December. Of course, "celebrate" is probably not the right word as we have to be a little careful. The communist doctrine doesn't approve or accept religion. That may be their downfall someday. We are still a deeply religious nation. Just like the Poles.'

Despite the vodka, George was still alert and he saw the chance he'd been waiting for. 'Can I ask you a question, Vera? A personal question. You may not want to answer.'

Vera looked carefully at him and paused. 'Of course, George. But not too personal. You know all women like to keep some secrets.'

George ignored her slightly flirtatious look. 'Can you tell me anything about the Brotherhood of Saints Cyril and Methodius? It's just that talking about Christmas made me think of religion and saints. Are they real or is it all fairy tale?'

George didn't know what to expect. Maybe Vera would stiffen and give him a stare and maybe even throw him out, but instead she relaxed into her chair and smiled.

'My Grigorski,' she said, using his Russian name for the first time, to George's surprise. 'You haven't asked a personal question at all. All you have asked me is do I think they still exist?'

He didn't know if he was being teased. He had asked that question to give her a way out of answering and all she had done was return his ploy and decided not to answer.

'I really don't know,' she said. 'They were real, but the ninth century was a long time ago. There are always rumours, but it is a bit like a fairy tale. We all want fairy tales to be real. Don't we?'

George had failed and he would have to tell Lord Ridley he had failed. This line was closed, for the moment at least.

'But, George, let's start to plan Christmas! You can help me choose some presents.'

Two days later, George had just finished giving a tutorial and his undergraduate students were collecting their bags and leaving, when Vera arrived at his desk.

'It's just started to snow,' she told him. 'We should go for a walk and start that present hunt. Get your coat. It is really cold outside.'

They left the university and walked carefully as there was already a thin dusting of snow over the icy patches. Vera put her arm in his and pulled him close as they walked side by side across the park. As they walked, her head was almost on his shoulder.

'The Brotherhood of Saints Cyril and Methodius. You should not talk about it where people may be listening. I think my flat is safe but one can never be sure. You will have to be more careful if you are to survive, young Grigorski.'

George turned to her with shock showing on his face. He hadn't thought that *they*, whoever they were, might be listening. He wanted to say sorry and apologise but that didn't seem to be enough. With a shrug he took the lesson from his teacher.

'Yes, they are real and yes, they do exist, but not as an organisation you would recognise. Think of it like "flower power" where you come from.'

George didn't feel like interrupting and explaining that flower power was really in California and never arrived properly in Oxford. But he understood. Flower power was about an attitude towards freedom and independence of spirit and action and a fight against oppression and bureaucracy. It was, he thought, an apt analogy.

'And so we never have meetings and we don't wear badges. Each one of us knows one or two other members, but we never know the whole. In fact, I don't know how many we might be. I am sure there are many, many, across all the Soviet states who think like me. There must be many, even in Russia itself, but it is probably here and in Poland where the feelings are strongest. We have so much history. We cannot let it go.'

She led him to a bench and they sat. Collars pulled high, coats pulled tight and close together, she talked on.

'What do you know about us Ukrainians? Did you know we are the centre of all civilisations?'

Fully remembering what Coss had said, George turned and looked at her.

'You're pulling my leg, Vera. What do you mean?'

'Do you know much about our history?' she asked.

'I know you are a very proud people with a long history. When I was with Coss in London he told me all about inventing riding and trousers and some stuff about smoking dope, but I'm not sure I believed him.'

George pulled Vera a little closer to try and stay warmer.

'If Coss told you the story then I know *exactly* what he said,' she said with her head resting on George's shoulder. 'In fact, I told it to him many times. I am glad it stuck.'

George sat straighter and looked at Vera. 'You know Coss? Amazing! How is that?'

'Coss and I are old friends but he escaped from here when he was a young man to try and find his father—' She paused momentarily 'Now *his* father is someone you would want to talk to.'

'Why?' asked George.

'Because if there was ever someone who wanted freedom for the Ukraine, then *he* was the man. And Coss wanted to emulate him, to be like him, and that is why he had to leave. The State was starting to harry him and we feared for him. He believes in the Ukraine and the people of the Ukraine.'

'Where is his father now?' George asked with trepidation.

'He died – but Coss has taken on his mantle,' she replied earnestly. 'Coss wants to see Ukraine free for his father. He wants to finish his father's work.'

George could see the pride she had in her country and the reasons why it was all so important. The conversation had a taken on a level of seriousness and intensity that George hadn't experienced before when talking together. He sensed it was not about the Ukraine alone. This was a very personal fight. Somehow, he felt the death of Coss's father was related to the Brotherhood. It wasn't the time to explore the minutiae. There would be a right time, and maybe that would be with Coss.

They sat quietly for a moment or two. The snow was starting to settle on their heads, whitening their hair and making them look a little like an old couple sitting on a park bench waiting out their years.

'But we should talk about the Brotherhood. After all, it's why you are here,' Vera finally said.

They sat and she was close. He enjoyed her warmth, although he knew it was mainly so that she could whisper in his ear.

'We don't want the past; we want to be able to determine our future. We want to build a future around the Ukrainian people and our culture. We don't want to be ruled by the Soviets and be their slaves in some great collective. They have moved so many Russians into the Ukraine it is diluting our spirits. They say it is to run the new industries being built here, and we do need people to run those industries, but do we *want* them? Is that the route we would have chosen if we could have made the choice ourselves? We don't know. We have never had that choice.'

George was listening as hard as he could. He needed to remember it all.

'This is not about armed struggle. We are not those sorts of people, but we need to find actions and deeds which have an economic effect and change perceptions. We need to be prepared for when the time is right.

'However sometimes it all seems so futile. We are few, we are limited in the things we can do and the power of the State is very strong, but if we don't do anything, nothing will happen.

'We saw what happened in Czechoslovakia in 1968. So close, yet so far away. It will happen here. We know it will. I see hope in my students' eyes. It is not a patriotic hope but a sense of rebellion. Have you seen how they have taken to western pop music? And have you seen how they dress? They will fight for freedom. Maybe not as Ukrainian nationalists in the way the older folk see it, but they will rise up and fight someday and we need to be ready to support them.'

George turned to look at her. The Brotherhood had seen the opportunity, he supposed. As she spoke and told him of these things there was a sadness he hadn't detected before, but he also saw resolve.

'Was the Brotherhood responsible for the Spring Uprising in Czechoslovakia?' he asked.

'I don't know that the Brotherhood stretches as far as Czechoslovakia, but those people were the same as us. They have the same ideas and hopes. If they had been in the Ukraine they would be part of the Brotherhood.'

'And,' began George, unsure how far he could go, 'does the Brotherhood stretch into Poland, Byelorussia and all the other satellites?'

'We're not an organisation, George. You need to understand that, but the same hopes and fears are in all those countries. We are all as one. We are all united. But we are never *together*.'

Enough, thought George. They should move on. 'Let's go and look for presents.'

However oppressive the political regime, Christmas in a country with a Christian background is still special … even if it is on the wrong day, George thought.

Vera, Timur and Timofei had been to church, they had feasted, and now they were all sitting around seeing the day to an end. Friends had come and gone and George was the last to leave. Timofei had fallen asleep on a chair; Vera was cleaning the kitchen while Timur and George talked.

Timur had been able to take leave and was home for just one week. At first he was standoffish and maybe even hostile to George. He had seen how easy Timofei had been with George and realised that he must have been a frequent visitor, but Vera had soothed his concerns by laughing off George's age and his almost naïve ways.

In bed, a few nights previously, she had told Timur, 'He looks eighteen, is clumsy, and hardly a man like a Ukrainian. Like you. Why should I be interested in him? He is a student away from home and it is good for me to be supporting him, and some day he may be useful to us.' Who this 'us' actually meant was never discussed. Timur reached across and pulled Vera closer to him. Ten minutes later he was asleep while Vera lay awake, frustrated about everything in her world.

George pulled himself more upright in his chair. Under the toll of vodka and mountains of food he had slumped dangerously low in the seat.

'Timur, are you allowed to tell me where you are stationed and what you do?'

It was an innocent question because he really was unsure whether Timur was allowed to say anything. If George was unsure at that moment, the vodka had muted Timur's concerns.

'Not really, but there is nothing special about what we do. I suppose I can tell you. I am in Lugansk in the East near the Russian border, but it could be anywhere. I am part of the Russian Red Army and I go where they tell me.'

Timur slugged another vodka. Maybe Timur's speech was slurred but George couldn't tell as his hearing was definitely impaired by alcohol.

Timor had more to say. 'There are still troops, many of them on the German border, but we also now have to look to internals –

these *dissidents* as they are known. Andrei Sakharov. *Bliad*! Look at those Czechs!'

'What would you do if these dissidents were here in Kiev, in the Ukraine? Would you shoot them like the Czechs?'

The words had sort of tumbled out of George's mouth and arrived before he had time to think of what he was saying, but Timur had also had too much to drink to think of any offence.

'I am part of the Soviet army.'

Enough said, thought George and he felt no need to say any more. But as he drifted back into his chair he thought about his walk with Vera. She would be one of those dissidents. Would Timur shoot at her? He probably would.

CHAPTER XVI

EARLY 1974

If the Michaelmas term had been busy for Anna, then the Hilary term was going to be no less hard. With Hilary about to start, the university was trying to work out how to deal with the new three-day week rules that had been introduced on the first day of January, but Anna and Aleksandra thought it was just a mild inconvenience and worked on as normal. The plan was for Anna to leave for Poland at the end of the term to work with Professor Ziemkiewicz through the summer. Anna thought the arrangements were being made by Aleksandra. However it was 'Nick the Cossack' who was at the centre of affairs and confident of completing all the paperwork on time.

Jane Sutton sat in Lord Ridley's office still, reading the reports coming in from George. With each one was a personal message to her. She had missed him – rather more than she had realised she would. She hadn't found a new boyfriend since their summer fling, as she found herself comparing each new suitor unfavourably. George had promised to come back soon and see her, but he hadn't. Idle, easy words for someone so far away, but then again she had seen the briefing on his visa problems. Jane also had mild pangs about Anna potentially being so close to George in Poland, for that information had also crossed her desk, but then, she thought, Warsaw and Kiev were as far apart for them as Oxford and Kiev. They would never get Anna across the borders.

Jane had other issues to deal with for the time being. Like everyone in England at that time, the affairs of the State were more important than the affairs of the heart. It was cold and Scargill was providing the only hot air with his words of revolution. Fuel was expensive and there was little hope.

'Miss Sutton,' Lord Ridley called to her. 'Familiant and I need to meet. Fix the details will you? For later this week.'

Aleksandra didn't have the same luxury of a personal assistant and had to make her own arrangements to get to London for the meeting.

Familiant sat in his office, feet on the desk and eyes closed. This operation had been ongoing for six years now, without taking into account all the preparation and preplanning. Maybe eight years, he thought. It was a long play. He always knew it would be, but how much longer would it last? At least as long again, and probably much, much longer.

His passion to fight communism, wherever it arose, was still all-consuming and there was no time limit; it would last as long as he did. He needed to be sure that all was going as planned. He hadn't envisaged that the fight might come so close to his office with the Trotskyist-inspired industrial unrest now so evident in England. Damn that man, Scargill.

So where had Familiant got to? His two 'children', unwittingly, had been recruited. He still thought of them as children. His children. They had been educated as he wanted and imbued with all the right skills. Anna was soon to be dispatched to Poland, and George was well established in the Ukraine and already providing good information. He had his assets in the right place.

The Arab war and the massive increase in the price of oil had been a surprise, but it was a scenario that had been considered. It had increased the wealth of the Soviet Union, which was not good, and soon they would have a network of nuclear energy reactors that would allow them to export even more oil and so give them the potential to increase their influence around the world. Again, that was not good. So the threat was not just *still* there but was, for Familiant, even greater. His thoughts wandered. He wondered whether God had these decisions to make. Was the world predestined and did He make all these decisions long ago, when He created all the world, or do we really have free will to determine good and evil, good against bad?

Familiant intended to push Anna and George harder and use them more aggressively, not just for gathering information, but to be catalysts for change. He knew how to play his pieces. Now he needed the commitment of the team. They would all still have a part to play, and he needed unanimity.

Miss Shaw came in and he opened his eyes and swung his feet off the desk.

'Aleksandra has arrived,' she said.

Arriving in Familiant's office, Aleksandra was surprised to be told when greeted by Familiant that Lord Ridley, Candish and Beck were also coming. Had she known, they could all have travelled down from Oxford together. Why all of us? she wondered. She thought Professor Beck had been out of things for some time. As she settled into her chair, Miss Shaw arrived with tea and Jaffa Cakes. That was reassuring. Within minutes, everyone else had arrived.

'The world is a very different place today from how it was when we started all this,' Familiant said, addressing no one in particular. 'We may have a bigger threat over here with this Scargill chap and all the unions. The question is, do we carry on, or pull them out? Your views, please.'

It was a big question and Aleksandra understood why everyone had been called together. Candish and Beck were mainly silent on the subject but happy that they had been included, and pleased still to be thought of as part of the team. Well, they thought, they did understand George and Anna from their years together, so perhaps they could contribute.

Lord Ridley took the lead and gave a balanced view of the local threat while only addressing the question tangentially.

'The communist enemy within our shores is basically known. They wield direct economic power but the majority of the people are apathetic about their principles. They are agitators. Heath will be thrown out as Prime Minister and Wilson will be back sometime soon. Now we are in the European Community this little dispute becomes a wider issue, but at the core, I suggest that eventually they will be defeated and a traditional government with democratic ideals will be elected.'

'On the other hand,' he continued, 'what's happening in the Soviet Union is still a major cause for concern. We don't know enough and we don't have good intelligence. Brezhnev may have seemed to relax things, but from a very hard line, and it's not an open economy or democracy in any way we would understand. The satellite states are still being oppressed and being used as colonies providing for the Russian people. The five-year planning approach is still causing huge inefficiencies, and the new wealth of the Soviet Bloc can still be channelled into military activity.'

Aleksandra noticed Familiant had started taking down notes but stopped midway through Ridley's words. His eyes were half closed and he seemed to be staring at some unseen spot on the ceiling. She looked up to see what had drawn his attention, but saw nothing.

'Thank you, Richard,' he said, returning his gaze to the table. 'Aleksandra,' he continued, without really looking at her, 'this should be your specialist topic. What do you think?'.

It was her special area but she also had the lives of two young people to think about. 'Lord Ridley is right in all he says. Simply, our main enemy is still the one behind the Iron Curtain.' She wondered for a moment whether 'enemy' was the right word and thought back to her own escape to England.

'But maybe our only concern should be for the welfare of George and Anna. Anna is fine as she has had no contact yet, and from what I understand George is in no danger. As we are fighting a regime that oppresses the individual, then maybe we should look after the welfare of the individuals we are using. If we follow the same route as them, then are we any better than them? The safety of Anna and George is paramount.'

There were nods of agreement around the room.

'I agree,' said Familiant, 'but they are both still very safe and we can remove them if there are any signs of a problem. Isn't that right, Lord Ridley?'

'Of course,' he said.

Everyone looked satisfied with this answer, but Aleksandra felt duped. She didn't believe him and knew deep down that he would manipulate them all to get his way.

'Good,' Familiant said. 'Now, given what we have just

discussed, I have to ask the remaining question: Are they better used against Scargill and his like? I can't see how that can be, mind you, but we need to carry on. We have invested too much already to back down now. But I would like your confirmation.'

Aleksandra was surprised by what had become a rhetorical question. Familiant had both asked and answered his own question. Was this a sign that he really felt Scargill was a bigger threat than the USSR? No, he would never think that; he was just making sure he had covered all objections.

This was Familiant manipulating again, she thought.

'Thank you all,' said Familiant. 'Agreed, then, that we continue. Richard, can we have a few more minutes?'

With that, Miss Shaw magically appeared to clean away the crockery; a sign for all to leave.

'Richard,' Familiant said when they were alone, 'I agree with all that was said, but there is more. This is a serious threat to our nation and it's within our borders. Someone has to act. We understand that things are being influenced by the Soviet Union. We need to think how best to use Cove and Kowalski. I'm not sure what they can do, but can you think about this matter?'

CHAPTER XVII

SPRING 1974

Whether in Oxford or Kiev, the onset of spring saw new plans being made. Anna was excited and George was working hard. For Anna, Coss had provided all the papers and planned her route into Poland, which was to be through Sweden. She arrived in Warsaw in early May to be greeted by Professor Stanislas Ziemkiewicz who had arranged all her accommodation. They spent the first evening having supper together while Stanislas regaled Anna with stories about his beloved Poland.

'In 1970,' he said, 'Gomulka raised all the prices to try and recover the economy. As a people, and all as one, we didn't like it. There were riots and protests and many died. It was also the end of Gomulka, and with that Ukrainian Brezhnev's support. Gierek came to power as the new First Secretary.'

As she knew all this, Anna wasn't listening as carefully as she should. Instead she was intently studying Stanislas. He was a small man and overweight. He must be in his fifties, she thought. With a round and happy face and twinkling eyes, he had an uncombed mop of white hair and nearly circular, dark horn-rimmed glasses. He would be perfect dressed up as Father Christmas or Saint Nicholas. Or, she thought, maybe he looked more like a panda.

Stanislas was waving his hand to support his words. 'Gierek borrowed from America and Western Europe. He borrowed a lot and used the money to import things for us to buy and life did become better. But he had over-mortgaged us. What is going to happen now with the oil crisis I don't know, and I don't know who does, but I do know we are in debt. Massively in debt. And I tell you this, Anna, if the lesson of 1970 is not learnt then there will again be unrest and this will be an interesting time in Poland's history. But as you know, it is always an interesting time in Poland's history... Welcome to Poland.' He raised his glass to toast her.

'*Mam przyjemność być tutaj.*' Anna raised her glass and they clinked glasses. 'I am pleased to be here.'

Anna soon learned Stanislas could talk without interruption and with very little prompting, and when supper finished he was still telling stories. Anna didn't mind, though; she liked to listen and was simply happy to finally be in Poland.

But already, on this her first night, she knew it was going to be completely different from her evenings with Aleksandra. Of course, this was just their first meeting, but Stanislas could never be more than avuncular, while Aleksandra was a good friend, and far more besides. Aleksandra had shown her all her possibilities and potential. It wasn't Oxford, the university, that had made her, it was Aleksandra. Stanislas' passion was Poland and she had seen how he would draw her into his arguments. We are formed, she thought, by the individuals, the people that touch our lives; Stanislas will form me in different ways, but it is to Aleksandra that I will always owe my greatest debt.

'Goodnight, Professor,' she said as they went their separate ways on leaving the restaurant. 'I will see you tomorrow.'

Anna settled into her life in Warsaw easily and well. She was uncomplicated and undemanding and therefore easy to get on with, but most of all she was interested in everything that was said to her, as she felt she was retrieving her past and heritage. She wondered what her father would say if he was here. Of course she had spoken to him before she left, and there were almost tears when she said she was going to Warsaw. He had sat her down on the sofa in the living room of their small house and had gone through the family photograph album with her again. He showed her pictures of all his brothers who had died in the war and, where he could, he pointed out every living relative, giving her what he thought might be their addresses so she could to go and visit them. His excitement had doubled Anna's, but the idea also made him sad because he had never been able to return to his home.

Anna made new friends quickly among both the students and the faculty. Soon she was being invited to suppers and parties.

The students, she decided, were in fixed groups. One group was of the social students who were either all about sport or drinking. Another group was at university to work and that alone was their focus. A third group was interested in the world and how to change it; this was the political group and Anna joined as soon as she could. Being in Poland changed Anna and it changed her quickly. She thought about her father and how he had suffered by being excluded from his homeland. He had left his home and his family to fight against the great German oppressor and he had lost his land, his home, and his family, not to Hitler but to Communism and Moscow. Her father had suffered because of Lenin and Stalin and she was starting to feel that she now had the chance of some retribution for him.

As students throughout the world in different eras, there were late nights in backstreet cafés with fierce political debates. At first Anna was reticent and stood back. She didn't know why. Maybe it was because she felt privileged with her Oxford background, she considered, but she learnt quickly and soon had her own strong views, and felt better able to express them.

As the weeks turned into months, two of the students became her closest friends. Dominik Bajbak and Gita Truskowsk had been a couple since just before they came to Warsaw and university. They now lived together and Anna had spent many an evening in their single-room flat. She liked their company and also their passion for Poland. With them she felt that she had come home. But unlike them, Anna didn't drink very much and so she declined the ready supply of vodka, but she always took a Kruger lager. She, like George, was noting the propensity of the Slavic people, men and women, to drink.

'Anna,' said Gita, 'we are going to go up to Gdansk next weekend. Would you come with us? We need to speak to the shipyard workers there and understand how they feel about what is happening. Every day it gets worse for everyone. We want to know what they feel and how they will react. We want to know how we can all work together as one.'

Anna was unsure. It wasn't because she didn't want to go, but because of the conversation that had taken place that evening. After a long day at the university she had, as was becoming more frequent, walked back to their flat to eat with them. On the way she had stopped off to buy the beer she alone was drinking and some dark bread and sausage. Not uncommonly there were other students there when she arrived. It seemed that supper had started sometime earlier and one of the vodka bottles was already almost empty. Voices were loud and strident as issues were debated – never hostile but always vibrant. Anna took time to get up to speed, listening and eating from the plates of food spread across the table. It was while she was biting into a mouthful of sausage and pickle that she heard Gita's words.

'We have a responsibility. We are the future and we should make our future. I say we, the students, should be the voice of the opposition. At a minimum we should report honestly and tell all Poles – and then the rest of the world – what is happening. At least we should start to lead and become a real opposition. We can't let Gierek do to us what Gomulka did. There will be riots and there will be more deaths. If there are deaths, they need to have a purpose.'

Anna looked around the room. There were nods of agreement. The feelings had become more militant and their frustrations were turning words into actions. There was no dissention and the conversation quickly moved on to how to make Gita's ideals real. It was settled by an initial agreement to start an underground newspaper or at least to distribute and post flyers. The trip to Gdansk would involve meeting the shipyard workers to get material for the first edition of their new newspaper. Anna was worried, though. She was here to develop her research and not become a political activist for change. Yet already she felt that Poland was also her problem.

'Yes, of course,' she said. 'I would love to come with you.'

The journey to Gdansk was easier than Anna had imagined. Three hundred kilometres north of Warsaw the train ran smoothly, as always, on *Polskie Koleje Państwowe*, the state-run railway. Dominik and Gita were excited. This was a new experience for them and they didn't know what they would find. Journalism was new and the risks unimagined.

Gdansk was an industrial city dominated by the ship-building works on the Baltic Sea. If it hadn't been summer it would have been drab, heavy and oppressive. They sat in a small bar, which Dominik had previously arranged, waiting to meet the workers. The motley crew of young idealists drinking beer looked incongruous in the rough bar, and even more so when they were joined by four men from the shipyard.

'Hello. My name is Mieszko Duda and these are my colleagues, Wojciech, Władysław, and Lech Wałęsa. We all work in the Lenin Ship Works. Why do you think we should be meeting?'

Gita talked with passion. She cajoled and entreated cooperation and the shipyard workers all listened intently – not just politely.

'Four years ago,' Mieszko said, 'we went on strike at Gdansk because of Gomulka, and we changed him. It got better, but, like you, we see the old times coming back. The workers need to form into unions to resist the power of the State. We need solidarity. We need to be together. We are a brotherhood.'

Anna was happy again to watch and listen as Gita and Mieszko carried on talking on behalf of both sides. They were all very similar to each other, these men. They were all big men, working men, who carried more than families – they drove societies. Among them, Lech stood out the most. He didn't speak for them, but he was a leader. He must have been about thirty, with broad shoulders and a worn, aged look made older by his large droopy moustache. The others would turn to him to validate what they said and he nodded acceptance and let them continue.

Mieszko turned towards Anna. 'Tell me who you are? Everyone else has a view. What do you think? Where do you fit into this?' he asked, looking directly at her. She also felt the stare of Wałęsa on her.

'Oh,' she said. 'I am Anna Kowalski and I am working here on a student secondment for six months. I am from Oxford in England. I'm not sure I have a valid view.'

'Everyone has a view, Anna, and yours is just as good as anyone else's. Maybe next time we meet you will tell us?'

'I hope there is a next time,' Anna said.

CHAPTER XVIII

EARLY SUMMER 1974

Vera kept a private line open to Aleksandra to share inform-ation on George's progress.

'Academically he is doing well but he hasn't been included in the university social life,' Aleksandra briefed Lord Ridley and Familiant, as the three of them lunched at Familiant's club. She continued. 'Anna, on the other hand, has become totally immersed into the life and culture of Warsaw, almost to the detriment of her work. I never believed that was possible. She has been to Gdansk and met a number of the worker leaders including the union leader Lech Wałęsa; by all accounts he is a very interesting man. The fact is that George is working harder than Anna and has become close to Vera, but he is not so well integrated into the university or social life.'

Her tone was factual and carried none of the emotion she felt. She was worried about both of them for different reasons, but Familiant didn't notice. Anna was a passionate person, and Aleksandra knew that her emotions might lead to problems as she would fight against all enemies, perceived or real. And George simply needed more than Vera in his life. He needed to be part of a group. She knew Lord Ridley and Familiant saw nothing wrong with him not integrating. They would have been surprised if it had been different. That was what they would expect of an Englishman abroad. So they saw nothing wrong and so would take no action.

'Let's deal with Poland first,' Familiant said. 'That has turned into an interesting area and faster than I had hoped. We need to support Wałęsa all we can and Anna is our route to do that. I need her to stay there.'

'But what about her degree?' Aleksandra saw the tide had turned and she needed to be Anna's supporter.

'Aleksandra,' Familiant said in an unusually gentle tone, trying his best to show understanding and compassion. It didn't come easily to him, however, but by speaking softly and looking straight into her eyes he thought he might succeed. Aleksandra knew him too well for that; she knew that this was not really him and she knew it was a device to persuade, and she knew she would lose the argument.

'Aleksandra,' he said again. 'We started this for a cause and for a reason, which was not to educate and support two children. They would have done perfectly well in life without us, but we gave them advantages, which they still enjoy, and for those advantages they will receive unseen rewards. Even if they don't know they work for us, it doesn't matter. Anna will get her degree but it may take a little longer than you had hoped. No. She is needed by us, right now, to stay in Poland. Please make sure that happens.'

Aleksandra didn't respond. Instead she posed a question. 'Can I ask why we are supporting someone who wants to introduce trade unions into Poland while at the same time trying to crush someone in Britain who is exerting the authority of trade unions?'

They all knew the answer but she felt the need to exploit the irony of the situation.

'And so to George,' Familiant said. He simply ignored Aleksandra's interruption and continued on his own path. 'I am much concerned about this Chernobyl nuclear power plant that's being built. It's the first of many. It changes the energy economics and hence the political balance. We can't stop it being built, but there will come a time when we won't it to be operated. The oil crisis has changed the dynamics.

'Aleksandra, talk to Vera, please. I'm sure you are worried about George's social life, and if George is to have a social life in the Ukraine we should make sure that that it has some relevance to Chernobyl. You might suggest that she introduces him to...'

Familiant stopped and searched the papers in his case. He pulled out what looked like a standard memo.

'Ah, yes. Here we are. Get Vera to introduce him to someone called Petric Hudolei. I think that may have real benefits for everyone. I always like mixing business and pleasure. I am sure, Aleksandra, this will satisfy your concerns as well.'

Aleksandra took out her notebook and wrote down the name. There was nothing further from the truth, she thought; your business is your pleasure, Mr Bill Familiant.

As Familiant and Lord Ridley continued to talk about the support they could give Anna, Aleksandra watched, hardly listening. Did she like what was she was doing? Had it gone too far? She was now no longer sure. She believed in the cause but did the means justify the end?

'So we are agreed then,' said Familiant. 'Through Anna we will provide limited financial support to the students. We will provide them with an outlet to the West for their stories. We can't do much more there. With George, Vera will make the introduction to Hudolei.'

'Now, Richard, what about a grappa? Any preference?'

The first of Aleksandra's tasks was the more difficult. Stanislas was due to arrive in England for a conference soon and she would talk to him there. She would seek both his counsel and his support. One more person would know what was happening. That worried her, but she put it on hold for the moment. Her second task was easier. When Vera read the message she sent, she read between the lines without difficulty and invited George around for supper. She then phoned Petric and also invited him and Liliya. A few more calls to other friends and the supper party was arranged. She understood perfectly what was wanted.

The door was unlocked when George arrived for supper. He had spent many evenings at Vera's and, rather than taking a present for his hostess, he had taken to buying and bringing a small present for Timofei who always now jumped up into his arms when he came through the door. George and Timofei were the greatest of friends. Often the young boy would sit on George's lap while stories were read to him. Timofei loved the small presents and rewarded George with a deep affection. Sometimes, when Vera was cooking supper, George put Timofei to bed. Other times when she was cooking, Vera would put the pans down for a while and watch them playing in the lounge. George might be nothing like the Ukrainian man she had described to Timur but, although ten years younger and half as strong, he was a better man. He was a better father to Timofei than Timur, and not just because he was with him more. He balanced his manliness with gentleness and compassion beyond anything Timur was capable of mustering, but more than that – much more – he hardly drank. Vera had never seen him drunk and she wished she could say the same for Timur.

With a present and food in one hand and Timofei in the other, George staggered into the kitchen. Vera was fussing with the food. Several men were standing in the tiny kitchen, talking, with vodka or beer in hand. Vera took Timofei from George and gave George a drink as she led him towards the group of talking men, and whispered in his ear. 'George, you wanted to meet some members of the Brotherhood. Be careful what you say, but all these people share the same view.'

She introduced Petric first. 'Petric, meet a friend of mine. This is George from England. He is studying here at Kiev. He is one of my brightest students.' George was thrust into their group and pleasantries were exchanged. 'How are you?' 'How long have you been here?' 'Do you like Kiev?'

Quickly George was assimilated into the group, and the conversation returned to politics. George listened and said little. There was not much he could add, and even less he could say. After a while some moved either to eat or fill their glasses, leaving Petric and George alone.

'Vera said we should meet,' Petric said. "She said you are an interesting young man with good connections in England.' This was more forward than George had expected and it took him aback, but he learnt quickly that Petric was a direct and forceful character.

'Our country is being overrun by the Soviets. We are feed stock for them. We supply the scientists and the leaders. Did you know Brezhnev was Ukrainian?' His head turned and he spat his disgust. One finger of his right strong hand stabbed at George as he made his points. George was more worried about the prospect of the vodka being thrown over him than the intellectual force of the argument.

George didn't know whether this obvious show of passion was normal for Petric, or whether he had simply drunk too much, but the rhetoric didn't abate until, abruptly, he said, 'Enough of politics. We will have plenty of time later for that later. Now I want you to meet my family. I came with them. I am sure they must still be here.'

Petric put his arm round George's shoulder and led him into the lounge. As they walked, George looked around the small group and thought, whatever nationality we are, we were all very much the same. As a teenager he had watched parties at his parents' house, more genteel and less vocal. At university there were parties and they all started with the men together near the drink and the food and the women together talking about something well beyond his comprehension. If people are so much the same, why do we spend so much time fighting wars? A rhetorical question, maybe, George thought, but it was people who made love and countries that made war.

'George, I want you to meet Alina and Liliya, my wife and daughter.'

As George stood in front of them, a cascade of thoughts flashed through his head: the companions of his youth, then Jamila, then others, and even Anna. Liliya was all of them in one. She was tall, as many Ukrainian women were. He was used to that. She had long fair hair and green eyes that were both perceptive and penetrating, yet soft and accommodating. The essence of Russian women. She was simply dressed in a skirt and blouse, but cut well to show a thin elegance. I hope her voice isn't squeaky, was the first thought that crossed his mind. Why did he suddenly think that? I hope she is clever, he followed up with quickly. Then his mind wandered back to his time in England and before Oxford.

What was her name? It was so long ago now. Tracy, possibly? He remembered being a teenager, with a girl he thought at the time was the most beautiful that God had ever created and he thought he had loved her at the time, but she must have struck some sort of pact with the devil because whatever He had given her in beauty she had traded away in brains; the relationship could never have lasted. I do hope Liliya matches both beauty and brains.

'George, I am very pleased to meet you,' Liliya said as she shook his hand. She spoke in English with a tone that was like music to George.

He replied in Russian. '*Dobryy vecher, kak dela?*'

Petric and Alina watched them as Liliya took his hand. They had seen what George and Liliya didn't know.

'Husband,' she whispered in his ear, 'I think we might be seeing much more of George.'

Vera was also watching and had seen the same. How did Aleksandra know? she thought. In one instant, George had gone from being an outsider and clumsy onlooker to being at the very heart of the Ukrainian Brotherhood.

CHAPTER XIX

LATE SUMMER 1974

That summer George and Liliya were together constantly. She worked in Kiev and rented a room with friends. At weekends they would either stay in Kiev or go to her parents' house north of the town and walk in the countryside. Some nights George would try and help Alina and Liliya cook. Although this was appreciated, his major contribution was his conversation which far exceeded his culinary skills. On other evenings he would be shuffled out of the kitchen and would sit talking to Petric.

Petric was one of the engineers of the Ukraine, educated in both Kiev and Leningrad, far to the north in Russia and at the head of the Gulf of Finland on the Baltic Sea. His expertise was in control systems. His work was designing the control systems for the new nuclear power station being built in Chernobyl.

'It is safe,' he said, 'except when someone decides to make it unsafe.' It was as much out of personal interest – not Lord Ridley's request – that George kept asking questions.

'When will it be finished? How much energy will be delivered?' George's questions were endless. Petric seemed not to flinch at any of them, and was open and relaxed in his answers. George suspected that he should have been more circumspect.

By late summer, George was deeply in love with Liliya and it seemed that she loved him every bit as much.

Through Petric and his friends, he had developed an intimate knowledge of Chernobyl and other aspects of the Soviet energy policy. Nothing was written down but he kept hold of odd drawings Petric made to illustrate one part or another of the design. He knew he was being trusted by his new friends, but was unsure why, but he knew his love for Liliya meant more, and that his membership of the Brotherhood and his friends could test him fully and he would not fail.

It was now nearly a year since he arrived in Kiev and he had to return to England for at least a month. That was part of the visa conditions.

'Liliya, come with me and I will show you everything,' he said one evening as they sat in his flat.

'*Zaya*, you know I would if I could, but it can't be. I will never get permission to leave,' she said, moving closer and running her hands through his hair. It had been on one of their walks that she had named him Zaya as they had seen young rabbits playing in a field. 'You are just like them,' she said. 'Playful and fluffy. I shall call you my little rabbit. My *zaya*.'

'Rabbits have another reputation,' George said, pulling her closer.

'Of course, that is another good reason to call you my *zaya*,' she said as they lay down entwined in the field under the bright summer sun.

When George finally arrived at Heathrow – alone –and returned to London he thought of all that had happened in the past year, from the day in Oxford when he had first said yes to Lord Ridley, to his new life in Kiev as part of a family. At one time, he thought, it would have been Anna who came to meet him as he returned. Later he assumed Jane would be the one at the arrivals gate, but his letters to her had become infrequent, initially because it took so long to get a reply and then, unless he waited, their messages always crossed in the post and their conversations became unsynchronised. Later, as he became more involved with Liliya, he didn't know what to say to Jane. All his news was about Liliya and he didn't want to share it, but more than that, it seemed to him that writing to Jane was some kind of betrayal of Liliya. Now he was back, all he could think about was returning to Liliya. His life had moved on a lot. So instead, as he stepped into the arrival area, the voice he heard was that of Coss, Nikolay the Cossack.

'George, how very good to see you. Had a good trip back? Here, let me help you with those,' he said, grabbing some of George's luggage. 'Let's get back to Great Smith Street. You can have a shower. We can have a drink and later you can tell me all about Ukraine. Sounds exciting, from what you have sent through.'

'Now that sounds fine by me,' George said, releasing his grip on his suitcase. 'Just want to make sure I have the chance to see Lord Ridley. I do have things I need to say to him.'

'No problem. It's already done. Do you think he would let you come back and not have a personal debrief? Now think about a bit of a holiday and some R&R for the moment.'

As their car headed into London they talked about everything except the Ukraine and George's life. The football World Cup that had finished in Germany a month ago was regularly revisited, with George wanting to know exactly what had happened. He was still wondering how Scotland had qualified and England couldn't, and how Poland managed to finish third. Finally, though, he felt he had to say what was actually on his mind.

'Does Jane still work at Wollacott?'

Coss was brief in his reply. 'Of course.'

It was more than a week before George saw Lord Ridley. He spent the time with his parents, telling them all about his life overseas. His mother asked about his friends but he took the coward's way out and said nothing about Liliya, but mothers being what they are, he was sure his line about 'spending lots of time with new friends' had already been reinterpreted.

He arrived at Wollacott with none of the diffidence of his first visit. He was excited at the meeting but apprehensive about seeing Jane. There was a lot of explaining to do.

It was a coincidence of timing that just as George stood up to go into Lord Ridley's office so Jane arrived back in the office. She was laughing, accompanied by an older man who she clearly knew well. She kissed him on the cheek.

Then she smiled at George and said, 'How wonderful to see you again. You look so well.' She skipped across the room and gave him a hug and a quick kiss.

'Daddy, this is George,' she said, turning to the older man.

'Pleased to meet you, young man. I have heard a lot about you.'

'I think Lord Ridley is ready for you if you would like to go in now,' Jane said.

Both men turned to the office door, a little to George's embarrassment, as he had assumed that Jane was talking to him alone.

'It's okay, George. Daddy is joining you in the meeting with Lord Ridley,' Jane said as she opened the door and ushered them through.

'Lord Ridley, George is here with Mr Familiant for your next meeting. I will bring in tea in a moment.'

No day at Wollacott was easy for George, he decided. On his first day he had been tested and now he was being set another test. Jane Sutton and this Mr Familiant were daughter and father; he gave no more than a passing thought to their unmatching surnames. What is important, he thought, is that Jane's father knows about my job – he must do! Otherwise Lord Ridley wouldn't have him here. Unless Ridley has no intention of even mentioning his work in the Ukraine.

The experience of the previous year had made George far wiser and he knew that time would resolve all these things; for now, the best approach was to go with the flow.

All the same, as he stood next to Jane's father, he had a niggling feeling they had met before, but there was so much else to take in that he quickly dismissed the thought.

'George. My, my, you do look well.' Lord Ridley moved from behind his desk and strode towards George, hand outstretched. George took it as he introduced Familiant.

'Let me introduce you. George, this is Mr Familiant who, shall we say, is one of the bank's key investment partners, particularly in the Eastern bloc. I thought it would be a good idea if he heard of your work first hand.'

Familiant took George's hand. 'Richard and I were talking about you just last week and I must say, George, we think you have done remarkably well in such a short time,' he said, nodding his approval in Lord Ridley's direction.

'Now, George, come and sit here,' said Lord Ridley, pointing at a seat at the conference table.

Lord Ridley and Familiant sat opposite him.

'Now, we need to understand everything. Not just the hard facts but your feelings and observations. Investment decisions are made as much on sentiment as on data. You will learn that over time.'

Jane arrived with a tray of tea and George noticed the contented look from Familiant as she put a friendly arm on his shoulder. George talked for much more than an hour, all the time asking Lord Ridley whether he wanted more detail or a summary.

'No, George, this is just fine. Keep going just as you are.'

George kept talking, adding his opinions to the detail as Familiant took occasional notes on a small pad that he took from his jacket pocket. Occasionally he would rummage back through the pages as if checking his memory from other events. Otherwise Familiant said nothing. Most of the detail was saved for Chernobyl and his meetings with Petric and his friends.

'Maybe when you get back to the flat you could write these into a report for me? There's a lot of detail there,' Lord Ridley asked and Familiant nodded.

'Now tell me, George,' said Familiant. These were pretty much the first words he had said in over an hour. 'What is your relationship with Liliya?'

George was thrown. He had not mentioned Liliya at all and had deliberately made sure that his personal life was kept apart from everything else. After all, it was his personal life and not Familiant's. Was this a father feeling angry because his daughter had been dumped? And how did he know about her anyway?

Lord Ridley saw George's confusion. It had been anticipated, and he and Familiant had spent a long time discussing it. They decided George had to stay in the Ukraine and what better way to gain his commitment than through a woman? Jane had taken him away from Anna and now she was the one stumbling block that might keep him from going back there.

'Love can be bought, Richard,' Familiant had said earlier, some time before George had arrived, 'and so love can be sold. Jane Sutton became more involved with him than we had anticipated. The lad has charisma and she saw his future. Now we have to convince him that there is no future with her. We must confront the issue and separate them. First we need to establish with George that I approve of Liliya and disapprove of his relationship with Sutton. I need to be in a position where my approval is important to him. We need to make sure that Sutton is compliant. How much did we pay her the first time?'

'I can check,' answered Lord Ridley. 'It was significant.'

'Good. Then make this payment doubly significant and I need to be at the briefing with George. I need to hear about Chernobyl directly.'

For a couple of hours of make believe – taking on a new father for the afternoon – Jane was given a bonus of one year's salary. She had also been paid the previous year earlier to befriend George, but not to make love to him or fall in love with him. She had been paid – and she knew deep down precisely what that made her. But she didn't feel like that. As George's letters had become more and more infrequent, her interest in him hardly diminished at all, but she read the reports and worked out that he would be over there for some time still. She tried to hold on to her wish to be there 'just for George', but she was a young woman, with exactly the same needs as a young man, and after a while she started dating again, generally with little enthusiasm. As time went on, her head told her it was not going to work. One day, she thought she would write to him about that.

Then she found out he was coming into the office. She accepted the payment from Lord Ridley because it did not affect what she'd decided long ago – to tell George there could be no relationship between them, and that was what her head clearly said, but when he walked into the office that afternoon her heart had a different opinion. Her doubts resurfaced, but she pulled herself together. She'd taken on the job and continued to go through with it to the letter.

Lord Ridley turned to George and was about to speak when Familiant interrupted.

'George, Jane is my daughter from my first marriage. Obviously she prefers to take her mother's name, but we are still close and Richard very kindly gave her a job here, which – I might add – I believe she does rather well.'

Lord Ridley nodded.

'Lord Ridley and I have been in business together for some time and we are particularly interested in the progress you are making. Understanding the energy policies is helping us make both operational and strategic decisions. When you have finished your contract in a few years' time, you will be a wealthy young man. *We* will have made you wealthy.'

With these words, Familiant leaned across the table and added an edge to his voice. Staring straight at George, he said again, '*I* will have made you wealthy.'

He sat back and continued more quietly. 'I know what young men do when they are away. They dip their wick whenever they can, and I know what wealthy young men do. They do it more often.'

George had to hide a smirk at the phrase used by Familiant. Why couldn't he just say they fuck everything? Why suddenly become so prim? It must be a generational thing, he thought, but anyway, he wasn't 'dipping his wick' and that started to rile him. He wasn't like Familiant obviously thought. But Familiant carried on.

'Jane doesn't need your wealth. I have provided for that, and I don't want her sitting here waiting for something that may not happen. I want her to live her life in the here and now. I can't say I approve or disapprove of you generally, but I do need to know about your relationship with that Ukrainian peasant. So I ask you again, what is your relationship with Liliya?'

George was now angry. Familiant and Lord Ridley knew they had gambled, but it was only a small wager that could easily be recovered. George wasn't angry at being forbidden to see Jane. After all, he had reached that conclusion himself, but calling Liliya a *peasant* was an insult he couldn't accept. In his anger the words flowed.

'I will answer your question directly. Liliya is not a peasant. She is educated and speaks near-perfect English. Being brought up in Kiev does not make her a peasant. Liliya is beautiful, she is my lover, she is my best friend, and soon she will be my wife.'

Even George was surprised by his words. He had never said these things even to himself. But as he defended her, he knew the truth: soon she will be my wife.

'I'm sorry if this causes Jane any issues. I had fully intended to tell her all of this myself, but now I will take your advice on what I should say.'

Familiant looked at him, his face still set impassively. 'In my experience, the truth is always the best way to advance,' he said. 'I suggest you have a few quiet minutes before I take her out for supper tonight.'

But those few quiet minutes with Jane didn't take place, and Lord Ridley and Familiant were amused that George had fallen for the same trap they had once set for Anna and Jamila. Oh, the innocence of youthful love, so impracticable.

Aleksandra was meeting with Stanislas Ziemkiewicz in her rooms at Oxford. Over his teacup, he was setting out in animated detail the differences between the universities of Warsaw and Oxford. The comparison wasn't fair as Oxford excelled in every regard, Stanislas admitted – except in one area. The faculty in Warsaw was far, far better, he argued. Aleksandra smiled. The usual academic rivalry, she thought. She had spoken with Familiant in detail and agreed what she could say.

'I need your help a little, Stanislas, but before that, how is Anna getting on?'

'A wonderful girl and very popular and very talented.'

'I need your advice on something. You see, I was wondering if Anna may gain more by staying in Poland under your supervision than she would here, and there may, of course, be benefits for you having – shall we say – access to some of our resources if they were channelled through Anna.'

Stanislas looked strangely at Aleksandra, who worried that she might have misread the situation and his position. How do I retreat from this? she thought.

'My dear Aleksandra,' he said. 'We have not known each other for long and you must know I like to speak plainly...' Aleksandra was now really worried and felt like she was shrinking as she sunk deep into her chair.

Stanislas continued. 'I must admit I really didn't understand what you said or, more importantly, what you *meant*. So let me say plainly what I think you meant. Among my students there is a deep concern over the state of Poland. There is a great resolve to address the situation. These thoughts are shared not just by the students but widely across my people, hardened and tempered from the revolution of 1970. Also I know Anna went with Gita and Dominik to Gdansk and met up with the shipyard workers including Lech Wałęsa – a very strong man by the way – and I applaud what they are trying to do, and if now you are offering direct support, possibly financial, to the cause of the Brotherhood...' He paused and considered his next words. 'I assume you have heard enough to know of the Brotherhood of Saints Cyril and Methodius?'

Aleksandra nodded.

'Then in that case we accept your offer and I agree that having Anna in Warsaw for a longer period would be beneficial to us both. Is that what you had in mind, Aleksandra?'

She was unsure what to say at the directness of his words. She thought for a moment and decided to follow Stanislas and be direct and straightforward this time.

'Well then, let's get to the practical details,' said Aleksandra. 'You will keep Anna in Warsaw for at least another year and preferably longer. We are unsure how or if we can get significant funds to support you, but we are still considering that. We will make sure any appropriate information that can be published is disseminated in the West. If there is more we can do, we will, but we will not put Anna in any danger. Can we agree on that?'

It was Stanislas' turn to nod in agreement. Aleksandra now had work to do with Anna but she knew it wouldn't be too difficult.

Anna had travelled with Stanislas and had been in Oxford for a week, meeting up with old friends. Now all three were to meet at their favoured bistro. The previous night she and Aleksandra had met for a glass of wine; Aleksandra had been overwhelmed by Anna's descriptions and passion for Poland. She could almost hear Anna pleading to be allowed and helped to stay there.

This evening, Stanislas was first at the bistro. Anna arrived soon after and it was as if they were back in Warsaw. They were so deep in conversation that when Aleksandra arrived she had problems even getting a word in to greet them. The food was simple, the wine rustic, and the conversation robust. Anna's commitment to a cause pervaded all she said that night. When Aleksandra asked casually, 'Anna, Stanislas was wondering if you wanted to stay under his supervision for another year? I am not sure that you want to stay, but we have agreed to ask you.'

The smile that spread across Anna's face was as wide as any Aleksandra had ever seen, and she knew the answer.

'Can I go back straight away?' Anna asked both Aleksandra and Stanislas.

'We will see,' said Aleksandra. 'And as soon as we can get all the paper work done – well, yes, of course.'

George and Anna left London within a day of each other. Both arrived back rejuvenated and happy to be back in foreign countries which they now called home. Gita and Dominik met Anna, and Liliya was at the airport to greet George.

Since his meeting with Familiant and Lord Ridley, George had been dwelling on his words to them. 'Liliya is beautiful, she is my lover, she is my best friend and soon she will be my wife.' It took him huge restraint to avoid dropping to his knees at the airport and asking her right then to marry him.

That night at home in their flat, Liliya was standing at the sink washing the dishes after supper, a colourful apron tied around her waist. George came up behind her, put his arms round her waist, and pulled her tight towards him.

'I love you,' he said. '*Ya tebya lyublyu, ya tebya lyublyu.*' He spoke first in Russian and then repeated himself in a Ukrainian dialect.

She turned, wiping her wet hands on her apron and looked at him.

'I love you, too, Mr Cove,' she said.

'Liliya, will you marry me and live happily with me for ever and ever?' It had been easier to say than he had ever imagined. Fleetingly he remembered that he had once rehearsed those very lines on Magdalen Bridge on a May morning in Oxford to be said to Anna sometime later. I wonder where she is, he thought. I hope she is happy.

Seconds passed and Liliya hadn't answered.

'Will you marry me, Liliya?'

'I think you should ask my father.' she said with a shine of happiness in her eyes.

'But I want to marry you – not him! And he's married already!'

'You should ask my father if he will allow me to be married to you.' She paused. Her English was good but the sarcasm had missed its target.

'If he asks me what I think, I will say…' Again she paused and turned away to put some dried plates back on the shelves, then skipped across the kitchen and looked flirtingly back at George.

'And what will Liliya say if her father asks what she thinks?' George asked.

He was sure he knew the answer but he wanted to hear it said out loud. He could see her happiness in each and every step, and in her smile, but he wanted to hear the words all the same.

'And if Father asks his Liliya if she wants to marry that foreigner who speaks Russian like a native and Ukrainian like a peasant, she will say…' She paused again and looked at him. She was across the room, ten small paces away. She looked down at her shoes, then at her nails, and then arms stretched wide, she ran at George and threw her arms around his neck, swinging them both off balance. She kissed him and then she kissed him again.

'Liliya will say "Papa, please Papa, please Papa say yes. I love him so much".'

They decided to spend the weekend with Petric and Alina so that George could speak to him after lunch on Sunday, when they agreed Petric would be at his most mellow. By then, his efforts of the previous week in England would have worn away and the labours of the next week would not yet have been contemplated. They agreed that Liliya would help Alina make the food to ensure it was good and filling, and George would make sure that Petric had plenty to drink.

'Then he is like a pussycat,' Liliya had said. 'You will ask him and he will look stern. He will ask to see me and I will look so happy, and then he will say yes. I know he will say yes.'

George was happy and during the week it was difficult to concentrate on his now mundane work at the university. As he sat at his desk, he quietly thanked Familiant for making the decision so easy. If he hadn't provoked him it would never have been this simple. As he was reviewing more energy data, trying to reason out a pattern from the jumble of numbers, Vera walked in.

'The cat has the cream – or so it would seem,' she said.

'What do you mean?' George turned his chair to face her standing in the door.

'George, it is obvious to everyone. You have a smile a mile wide and haven't done a scrap of work. You are just sitting there. If anyone ever looked like they were in love, it is you. What are you going to do about it?'

'Vera, I am not sure I should say. I need to speak to Petric first,' said George.

'My, George, that is wonderful news! Is Liliya happy? Of course she is. A Ukrainian wedding. Unnerving for the groom but you will enjoy it. So much laughter, so much fun. What shall I wear?' Vera could hardly stop talking and didn't notice that George's hand was raised.

'Did I say a wedding? Where did you get that from?' he said.

'Don't be shy and coy with me, George. I know and I promise not to tell.'

George acquiesced at the assurance and after a persistent prompting he told her all the details of the night in the kitchen when Liliya had said yes.

Vera didn't totally keep her promise, however. Within forty-eight hours, through Aleksandra, Familiant was sitting in London with a contented half smile as Miss Shaw brought him his tea.

'A job well done brings great satisfaction, Miss Shaw,' he said. 'We are right into the heart of Chernobyl. A job well done.'

Petric and Alina were in the garden when George and Liliya arrived, walking while holding hands. It was a difficult time for George. Liliya joined her mother in the kitchen which left George and Petric together in the garden. It had been agreed that he wasn't to raise the subject of marriage until after they had all eaten. The chat could be light and idle, but George wanted to use the time to impress on Petric that he was worthy of his daughter. They talked about Petric's work and the new power station. Petric explained with considerable passion about the control systems he was designing, taking George into technical areas where he was soon lost, but George listened patiently.

He thought it was like listening to someone who was in love talking about their lover. You felt their desire and passion. You knew a little through your own experience about what they might be feeling, but you could never understand exactly how they felt because everyone was in love in a different way. That was the joy and happiness of love, he thought. We all know, but really we never know. In Petric he saw a deep love for his project at Chernobyl, and George listened patiently to his outpourings of love.

George tried to explain to Petric the work he was doing and how the new nuclear power stations might shift the world's energy and economic balance. Too much nuclear power across Russia combined with their new oil-derived wealth could free up foreign exchange and allow Russia to follow a more aggressive political agenda; George wasn't sure how that would affect the relationship of the Ukraine within the USSR.

Petric stopped and looked at George.

'Tell me more. I want to know,' he said.

George was reluctant as he tried to keep the atmosphere light with the task ahead, but Petric was persistent and George set out to explain simply and quickly the work he was doing and the theory he was being asked to research by Lord Ridley. In fact he had received a short note from Coss outlining the area, saying that Lord Ridley wanted his explorations to focus on an understanding of how a network of Russian nuclear power stations would affect global trade. Global trade was built on political stability and that was where George had started the project.

'Maybe we should sit down on another evening to go through it all,' George said. 'It's complex and today is meant to be a rest day. Now tell me again, when will the station open and be on-line?'

He really didn't want to get into a discussion on energy macro-economic theory with so many other things on his mind and much to George's relief, Petric was happy to keep talking until Liliya called from the kitchen that lunch was ready.

'We are at interesting time in our country,' Petric said. 'If we, and I mean myself and my older friends, don't do something, we may lose our culture forever. I am not sure what we can do but we do need to give the new generations a focus and a cause.

'There is an old story from the Eastern border where the boundaries are always changing. An old man waited for his son to return with the news of the latest congress to decide such matters. "Are we in Russia or Ukraine?" he asked when his son returned. "Ukraine," the son replied. "Good," said the father, "I couldn't stand another of those harsh Russian winters".

He laughed out loud and put his arms round George's shoulder and led him back inside. They sat at the table where there was the usual spread of fresh food salads and bread and plenty of meat, both chicken and beef, and, of course, drink. It wasn't a meal of many courses, order or structure but a buffet all laid out to be picked and selected from. Hands were everywhere as food was taken and passed. George had a *blini* in his hand as Petric filled his glass with vodka.

'A toast,' he said. 'A toast to a free and prosperous Ukraine, free from the hegemony of Russia.'

Glasses were raised and refilled. George knew Petric was committed but this was the most open defiance he had heard.

'A toast,' said Petric, 'to all those of the Brotherhood in Ukraine, Poland, Byelorussia or wherever who share these same beliefs.'

More refills were required.

'And now the most important of all the toasts today. A toast to the happy couple. A toast to Liliya and my new son-in-law.' George looked across at Liliya with stunned disbelief and a 'what do I do now?' look on his face. She looked back at him as if she was the reflection in a mirror. George started to try and say something but Liliya was first to manage a word.

'Papa, what do you mean?'

Petric rose and moved round the table to stand behind Alina. He put his hands on her shoulders in a sign of clear affection. He could also see both George and Liliya.

'My children,' he said. 'My darling princess, I have never seen you so happy. Your mother and I know you are deeply in love. We probably knew before you did.'

George thought he discerned a knowing look from mother to daughter. Alina was smiling and leaning her head towards Petric's arm.

'And today you made such a fuss to get everything so just right. We know why. So, George… are we going to go outside and ruin this food, or are you going to ask me right now?'

George knew this was his cue. He stood and walked round to Liliya and, as a mirror of Petric standing behind Alina, put his hands on Liliya's shoulders.

'Alina, Petric, I love Liliya and Liliya loves me.'

Liliya turned to look up at George, giving him a loving look in agreement.

'Will you accept me into your family as Liliya's husband?'

It was too much for Alina. She burst into tears and, pushing Petric aside, rushed to George and gave him a huge hug and kissed him on the cheeks. Liliya had stood and mother and daughter held each other, both crying for joy. Petric and George tried to remain stoical. Petric walked to George, hand outstretched.

'Of course, George, of course.' Liliya and Alina had half stopped their embrace to hear the words that sent them into another bout of tears and happiness.

It was a long, noisy, happy lunch that stretched well into the evening.

It had been easy to become engaged, George thought. Getting married turned out to be a lot more difficult, but Liliya and Alina had that under control. They were to be married in the spring. Meanwhile, work continued. George worked on his project which had become the core of his thesis. Vera was still his supervisor. Petric had taken him under his wing and taken it upon himself to make George as much a Ukrainian as he could.

'Good materials don't always make a good product,' he had said to George, 'but bad materials can't make anything good. We might turn you into something someday.'

George took that as a compliment, but wasn't altogether sure if he should. So George was taken to meet people. He wasn't always sure who they were. And always there was vodka. George had many talks with Petric about his economic theory and Petric was turning into a reasonably knowledgeable economist. At first he enjoyed these discussions and debates, but as time passed Petric's mood seemed to change whenever they talked about the impact of the new Chernobyl station.

'And you are saying, George, that Chernobyl will do no more than make the Russians stronger and the Ukrainians weaker,' was the tone of his standard question.

'No,' George would reply. 'Not necessarily. Ukraine will benefit from the lower energy costs and it will drive industrial growth because it is part of the USSR. The whole of the USSR will benefit while the West will have to respond.'

'I don't care about the West, but I do care about Ukraine.

You are saying that it will increase the power and control of the Russians over the USSR and Ukraine?'

'You are the politician, Petric, I am an economist, but I would guess you are right.'

These discussions left George tired and Petric's mood was always black. He would become quiet and serious in a way George hadn't remembered from their first meetings. After one long conversation with other members of the Brotherhood, when George had been especially lucid in his theory and predictions, Petric hadn't contacted him for over a week. Alina even phoned Liliya to ask if she knew what had happened because Petric had become quiet and introspective. George and Liliya talked about her father and agreed that it must be to do with his job and the increasing pressure he was facing, so George should keep off the subject and spend less time talking with Petri about his work. With that, his mood seemed to improve.

Vera was as excited about the wedding as George. George and Liliya now still spent many evenings with Vera, who was a good friend to both of them. She had her work and she had Timofei whom she doted on. But she didn't really have the one thing she wanted, which was Timur at home all the time.

'Of course,' she had said to George and Liliya one evening. 'I want a man here to take me out and open doors, and,' she looked at George, 'just like men, I need sex, but more, I need to be loved and cared for. I need hugs and kisses all the time. Maybe even more than that I need my best friend to be here. You will understand one day.'

'When is Timur coming back again?' George asked.

'He was here for Christmas and now it will be at least six weeks before he is home again. Timofei is growing and changing so quickly and yet he hardly knows his father. I love Timur but I don't know *how* I love him. You two still have that fire and passion in your love. People will tell you that it changes over time. It doesn't have to. It will, but only if you let it.'

George and Liliya felt uneasy at these deep confidences and as they moved the conversation away from Vera's thoughts on Timur,

Timofei bounded into the room and launched himself head first at George – his normal way of arriving in George's arms.

'Did I tell you that it has just been announced that there will be another symposium about Chernobyl?' Vera said. 'I got the details today. It won't be very academic but with the site opening in two years the bureaucrats are starting to make more noise. Do you want to go, George? I am sure I can get you an invitation and you might get Petric to see if he can get special permission to show you more. It is good to see what you research every day.'

'Of course,' said George. 'That sounds like a great idea. Will Liliya be able to come along?'

'Unlikely, but we can try,' said Vera.

Roughly at the same moment in Warsaw, Anna was having the same conversation with Stanislas, although arranging travel permits for her for the journey east into the Ukraine would be more difficult.

Over the months Anna had managed to arrange small sums of money to be transferred to Dominik and Gita. They didn't need much and what she gave them was significant in their terms. She didn't know the source, only that Aleksandra had managed to arrange a study bursary well beyond her requirements. She heard that news when she was in Oxford and Aleksandra had met her in her study.

'I am the bearer of more good news.' Aleksandra had said. 'As you are now staying in Poland you will need better financial support and I have managed to get you a grant.'

The amount offered was at least ten times what Anna felt she needed. She had become used to the frugal way of living as a university student in Warsaw and while Aleksandra continued talking Anna was already thinking of how the balance could be extended and put to better use.

'Are there any restrictions on how I use it?' she had asked. 'Do I need to produce invoices or anything like that?'

'None whatsoever. It's yours to do with as you wish. It is there to further your research and your studies.'

'Thank you. It will be a great help towards my costs,' she had replied with understatement.

Later Aleksandra phoned Familiant, and Coss was asked to make the arrangements for the funds transfer.

Meanwhile, Stanislas had received news of the upcoming conference and was already thinking that he might go. The message from Aleksandra pointing out that it could also be of benefit to Anna was a surprise. Anna's studies were progressing slowly and had Stanislas simply been her academic supervisor he might have been more upset than he was. He knew he was part of the reason she was behind in her academic schedule. He had introduced her to Dominik and Gita and he was actively encouraging her activities with the Brotherhood. Maybe, he thought, she didn't fully understand her role and part in all of this. For her, the cause was more simple and personal. It was her homeland and she wanted to explore something she hadn't previously had an opportunity to explore. She didn't see the wider picture. I hope one day she does, he thought.

Anna was giving most of her bursary to Dominik who used it mainly to buy paper and printing materials in order to distribute newsletters and pamphlets. Occasionally it was used to buy small freedoms from officials who needed more drink than they could afford.

'The blind do not see what is under their noses,' Dominik said. 'And if we buy them enough vodka then soon they are blind.'

Anna was also spending more and more time with Mieszko and Lech. Lech continued to be a charismatic man and leader; they had become charmed with each other. He liked her intellect and that she had managed to come back to Poland to be with 'her people,' as he would say. She liked his passion, his vigour and commitment. With Danuta, Lech's wife since 1968, they had spent many evenings together talking, with Anna as his student.

Mieszko and others were often guests and once, when they sat over a supper he said, 'Anna, you may have been brought up in England, and educated in England, but you are a Pole and this is your land. You can never stop being a Pole.'

Back in Kiev, George now had to find time both to fit in

preparing for the symposium and arranging a wedding, although it seemed to him his main role was to be consulted on everything and then ignored. The details were in the hands of Alina and Liliya. They quickly turned down and rejected the idea of a 'red wedding' offered by the 1972 Presidium of the Supreme Soviet of the Ukraine. It wasn't just the offer of State money – Petric gave short shrift to anything Russian. This was going to be as close as Petric could manage to a traditional Ukrainian wedding, but that was not made easy by the probable absence of George's family. No one seemed to be able to find a way to get them there. This had caused much pain and trouble to George, but far more so to his mother.

The problem was finally resolved by a promise of a ceremony sometime in the future – no one knew when – in England.

Petric was concerned because the groom's family normally played a big part in the ceremony and he didn't know how to cope with it. That problem was resolved when Alina took charge, and Petric, like George, was demoted to the simple role of a consultant to be ignored.

The wedding was to be in early May. George learnt from Alina one day when she asked his opinion about something that the whole event lasted for four days – from the Thursday until the Sunday. He decided that just being consulted was good enough for now. There was too much to arrange. The Chernobyl symposium was just three weeks before the wedding and he put his efforts into his preparation for that. There, at least, he was in control.

CHAPTER XX

APRIL 1975

The conference had been arranged quickly and there was no time for George to initiate the normal exchange of letters with Lord Ridley through the channels that had been established. It was all too immediate. George had to imagine what Lord Ridley, sitting at the Chairman's desk in Wollacott Bank, might be looking for. George wasn't presenting a paper, he was only an attendee, but he needed clarity on some of the key questions they wanted answered around the progress of the reactor build. This was what took his time.

Anna and Stanislas had set out for Chernobyl two days before George. They made their way down through Poland by train, across the western border of the Ukraine and headed east towards Chernobyl. For delegates from Byelorussia it was easier. Chernobyl was on their southern borders. Russians flew into Kiev for the one hundred and twenty-kilometre trip north to the wooded marshlands where the reactor was under construction. For most, bare and stern accommodation was provided in Pripyat, a new, small town built for the workers and their families.

It was Vera who saw Stanislas and Anna. She waved and called across the crowded foyer. It was Anna who saw George first. This was not expected. They had been apart for so long and their lives had moved in different directions. This was the first time they had met since their undergraduate days at Oxford.

Anna looked straight at George who was with a woman waving in her direction. George hadn't seen her. Did she want to see him now? She couldn't be sure. Yes, of course she wanted to speak to him, to find out what he was doing, to understand how he felt about her and his life, but she didn't want it here and now. She wanted it on *her* terms and that was why, she reasoned, she suddenly felt angry. It wasn't a burning anger, an anger that rips from the stomach, heating the mind to incomprehensible agitation and irrationality. It was an anger built on sadness. Anna was calm.

George followed the line of Vera's wave and first saw Stanislas. He looked to his left and saw Anna. At first he didn't recognise her; she looked older, more mature and prettier. It was some time since he had thought about her and it was shock to have to it all brought back so rawly to the surface. Long ago he had exorcised guilt, even at one point blaming her. She had pushed him away while he was doing his best to build a secure future for them, but since then, in the little time he had considered the matter, he had started to accept that his behaviour may not have been quite perfect.

On balance, though, he thought, this was a good piece of fortune. The conference was going to be interesting but not exciting and now there was the chance to catch up with Anna. He remembered the good times when they worked together and then closed their books and sat and talked; and talk would invariably then lead to more intimate moments. Maybe that might be the outcome this evening, too? But as quickly as the thought formed, he quashed it. The moment of self-denial made him feel quite proud.

Stanislas and Vera pushed through the crowd towards each other. Anna and George moved with them. Anna calming and subduing the diminishing anger she now felt, and George smiling at his moment of personal discipline.

'Hello, Anna. Are you well?' George asked formally as he took her hand.

'George, what a surprise. I'm fine. You?'

'I didn't know you two knew each other,' Stanislas said. 'What fun we'll have– time for a great party.'

Neither was sure about that. Their individual planning had not included this meeting and it demanded a reassessment. It was George who made the introductions.

'Vera, this is Anna. We were colleagues at Oxford and worked very closely with Aleksandra. I'm sure I've told you about her?'

Vera nodded. She remembered and she noted what *hadn't* been said.

Stanislas took Vera's arm. 'Come on,' he said. 'Let's all go and get some of this awful coffee,' and he marched off with Vera.

George and Anna followed obediently like a pair of pet poodles not sure of what else to do but follow their masters. The conversation was polite as they found their way through the crowd of dour dressed delegates following behind Stanislas and Vera. Vera turned briefly to catch a glimpse of George's agonies and guessed she knew what he must be feeling. That's when she realised. So this is why Aleksandra had encouraged us to be here.

Familiant had framed the meeting to Aleksandra some days previously: 'I promise you this, Aleksandra. It is not a test for either George or Anna, but we need to bring the Brotherhoods in Poland and Ukraine closer together. I am sure George and Anna can see this through.' Aleksandra had been deeply unsure. Not because of the need – she agreed that that they had to meet to exorcise the past and the demons – but because of the deep trauma it might cause both of them. She didn't want either of them to be hurt again.

It was Stanislas who insisted they all find seats next to each other in conference hall but, thankfully, George found that he and Anna were separated by several seats. Even so, he found it hard to concentrate. We have to talk, he said to himself. I have to tell her about Liliya. But why now and why today? It was surreal. The days programme crawled at a snail's pace and its content was lost to both of them; their heads swirling with some less than welcome thoughts.

When the day's exertions were over, Stanislas said, 'I am taking Vera to dinner tonight. We are old friends. Will you two be okay by yourselves? I am sure you will find something to talk about.'

George looked properly at Anna for the first time since their meeting in the foyer that morning. 'Dinner?' he asked.

'Sure,' she replied but obviously with very little enthusiasm and undeniable resentment in her voice. She was focusing on one thought alone: this was her work and she didn't want him interrupting it. She had looked forward to this day when she was independently showcasing her skills and talents and now she had to be in George's limelight as the experienced Ukraine expert, but she also had to deal with the varied potpourri of emotions he evoked, and now they were going to be alone over dinner! What was fate doing to her? Blast him, but what else was she going to do?

George walked slowly through the town later that evening, collecting his thoughts as he set out to meet Anna at her hotel. When they met in the foyer, their greeting was restrained but they sat, stayed and talked. The conversation was stilted.

'Are you well?' she said.

'I'm fine. You?' answered George.

'Good, thanks.'

'How long have you been in Poland?' George asked.

Then, either the alcohol or the passing of time eased and smoothed the atmosphere between them, and as their anger and guilt abated and they recognised aspects of the friendship they once shared. The conversation became more intimate and personal, but it was some time before they talked about their time in Oxford.

'Were you honest with me about how you got here?' Anna asked.

'Yes, I was, and at the time I really thought that I was doing what I did for us. I never knew why you left me,' George answered, remembering the secrecy he was still sworn to by Lord Ridley.

'I thought you had left me, George. You never let me understand. You were gone without trying to understand what I felt and how bad it was for me. If you had tried to understand then we would be married now. I know you were going to ask me.'

'I was. That's a life away now.' George remained focused and steeled himself; he had to tell Anna about Liliya.

'I have something to tell you, Anna. I'm getting married in three weeks' time.' He looked hard at her to try and sense her reaction. What did he expect? Would she be angry or sad? Would she leave or would she shout?

Anna thought for a moment, trying to absorb what she had heard. 'I am really pleased for you, George. Tell me all about her.'

Anna listened as George spoke, but she heard little as she tried to push aside any thoughts of what might have been. She had put George out of her mind through work and her new passion – her Poland. She thought she was over him. Now she was not so sure of her feelings. Hearing that he belonged to someone else made her sad – even jealous. Whose fault had it been anyway? His? Maybe hers. Probably both. If only they could start again today. She realised with great resentment that he still excited her and she was sure she could see that look in his eyes as well. The thought had flashed through her mind that they could become lovers again.

But not now. Not if he belonged to someone else. There was a battle between her Polish passion and fire and English reserve. In the end, it was the polite social norms of her Englishness that won.

'I am truly happy for you, George. I mean it. But…' and she paused and took a deep breath, 'but – I really hope this doesn't happen – if ever there is a problem, come and find me. Maybe only at first as a friend—'

Then her voice lowered. 'And maybe we can see if we can finish what we started.'

Even as she spoke she regretted the directness of her words but there might never be another chance. After all, it was fate that had brought them together. Not just once, but twice now. Could she rely on fate a third time? George looked at Anna intently. The same thoughts had gone through his head: Had he made the right decision leaving her all that time ago? Why did fate throw these challenges?

'I understand, Anna,' he said. 'We are where we are and that cannot be reversed, but to know that you are safe and well is important to me. We will stay in contact now we know where each other is. I am not going to tempt any of the fates that have treated me so well. Let's just agree to stay friends, shall we? To stay good friends.'

Anna knew what he meant by what he had said and she knew what he hadn't said. The atmosphere lightened up immediately.

'Of course we will,' she responded brightly. 'Now tell me about your work. How is the thesis coming along?'

George explained about it all and was in the middle of his

stories when inadvertently he said, 'I was with Petric and his friends from the Brotherhood and—'

'Did you say the *Brotherhood*?' Anna asked. 'What is the Brotherhood?'

George immediately regretted his slip and was unsure how to answer. He opened his mouth but there were no words.

'It's okay,' said Anna. 'I understand you may not be able to say anything, so let me tell you what I know. The Brotherhood of Saints Cyril and Methodius is Ukrainian in origin but has spread across many countries. I am a member in Poland. It's now my purpose, George. It's my purpose in life. Are you involved in the Ukraine?'

George hesitated, still unsure. But this was Anna – not a trap. The Anna he knew would never work for the State.

'I know many members and many are my friends. Yes, I know of the Brotherhood of Saints Cyril and Methodius. I am clearly not as involved as you but I am close.'

That was as far as he would go, and he was pleased he hadn't incriminated Liliya and Petric directly. He became uneasy suddenly; what if this wasn't the Anna he knew anymore? He was wary now, but the conversation moved on and as he heard more and more about her commitment, his concerns diminished.

'It's odd,' he said, suddenly changing the subject. 'It's odd that of all the people we could have met at Oxford and fallen in love with it, it was you and me. I mean, I know we could have met anywhere, but here we are now on parallel courses in life. Maybe that's why we met. God knew our lives were meant to be intertwined. Who can say what His plans were or are?'

He paused and looked out of the window of the hotel foyer. 'Anna, I did love you and I suppose you can't stop loving someone totally, but I love Liliya today. Don't make life difficult for either you or me. God will decide what happens, but don't stop being friends. That can last forever.'

Anna smiled gently as she got up from the sofa they'd been perched on for the last two hours.

'Shall we get something to eat now?'

Liliya noticed that George was subdued on his return to Kiev, but he soon picked up as he was thrown by Alina deep into the wedding arrangements. They only had a few common friends, and George knew he would be totally outnumbered, but there was the excitement of not knowing quite what would happen; that made all the effort not just worthwhile, but fun.

Had the wedding been in England he knew what the form would be: hire a morning suit from Moss Bros; maybe go on a stag night with some strippers; meet up with the best man on the morning of the wedding for some Dutch courage and a quick walk to the church; swap 'I will's and 'I do's; reception in a marquee; standard speeches; and a honeymoon somewhere in Europe, but this wedding was going to be different and at this moment he had no idea how different. Liliya had explained as much as she could about the process and protocol of this unique country wedding but it too much for George to absorb. While he was sure he could cope, he would have liked a best man to lean on. He didn't want a best man just to drink with the night before, but someone to give him courage and be on his side when the odds seemed stacked against him. However, this was the way it was going to be.

Just get on with it and live it, George, he said to himself. He had no choice.

It was Tuesday. Liliya had gone home to be with Petric and Alina and finish the last of the arrangements. George was at home reading when there was a knock at the door. Probably one of Liliya's friends with yet another present, he thought as he opened the door.

'I hope you have room here for a Cossack to kip for a night or two?'

'Coss! I have never been more happy to see you,' a very surprised George answered. 'Come in, come in! Sure, you can stay! But there is one condition – you will be my best man for all four days of my wedding. I'm getting married this week, you know, and I need my own supporter among all these aliens.'

'Done deal, my friend. And congratulations by the way! But only as long you make sure I meet all – and I mean all – the best looking and prettiest of your beautiful bride's friends?'

'Done deal. Now get yourself in here!'

Coss, wearing as always a T-shirt and jeans and very high Cuban-heeled boots, had travelled light with just a rucksack slung over his shoulders.

'Clearly not planning on staying long?' George asked 'Did you hear I was getting married?'

'Yes I did, my friend. I was chatting to Vera about visas and things and she mentioned it and I thought to myself that there is old George sitting in Kiev with no one on his side, and I thought it was about time I came to visit! So here I am.' Coss accepted the beer George was offering and took a big long swig from the bottle.

Two weeks earlier, Coss had been sitting with Lord Ridley in his office. 'Coss, I have just heard from Vera that the meeting with Anna went well. I don't think there will be any problems with the wedding, but get yourself out there and make sure there aren't any last-minute nerves. We might also want a direct route to that Petric Hudolei chap. See if you can make a contact there.'

'Of course, Lord Ridley. Do I let him know I am coming?'

'Think not.'

'Okay. I will look forward to the trip. Thank you.'

He left, smiling at Jane on the way out, and started to make the arrangements.

Coss now sat on the sofa in George's living room with his feet on the table. 'So, George. Where to tonight? I fancy seeing my way round this town.'

'Not sure, really' he said, his mind racing for an answer. 'I haven't had too many of those sorts of experiences yet. Not my sort of thing. I've heard of some places, though. I guess what we do is put our money together, start at the first bar, and see where the fates take us?'

'Sounds good to me,' said Coss, finishing the beer and standing up. 'Let's go.'

George was very grateful for Coss's company. It was only when they were out leaning on a bar that he realised what he had been missing. Whatever his thoughts about male friends there was something reassuring about having support with him.

The next morning, he wasn't so sure anymore. His head was heavy, his mind slow and his stomach a churning mess. It wasn't helped by Coss bouncing around, trying to make fried egg sandwiches.

'I assume that Vera has let you off for the week?' Coss shouted from the kitchen. 'What about the tourist bit this morning, then? And you can introduce me to the beautiful bride-to-be for lunch? Unless you are afraid I will make her change her mind and she will fall madly in love with me instead?'

'No fears there, Coss,' George said, lifting his head up from the pillow as he started to experiment with a vertical position. 'She's a one-man woman and I'm that man. Although she might suggest I change my friends when she sees the state you've got me into.'

Coss was more taken with Liliya than he thought he would be. She was as pretty as he had been told and as devoted to George as he had heard. He could see how her eyes lit up when she saw George, how she sat close to him, held his hand and the look of love on her face when he was speaking.

'I am the black sheep of his family of friends and I'm here to make sure that he stays sober right through to the end of the weekend,' Coss told Liliya.

'I don't believe a word of it! Not that you're not the black sheep – but that you will keep him sober. Coss the Cossack, I don't trust you with George at all.' Liliya was teasing him and Coss saw the laughter in her eyes.

'Then tell me the form. Where do you need him? What time? And what state should he be in?'

'George knows all those and, Coss, whatever state you are in, you will make sure he is sober.' Liliya was making her point clearly and Coss had picked it up.

'Okay, I get the point. George, you tell me all the details later.'

George was watching and listening as Liliya and Coss sparred and was he more sure than ever he was doing the right thing, and he had Coss's confirmation that she was beautiful. It somehow seemed important to get approval from a mate. She was confident and at ease in strange company and he knew she was intelligent, but, he thought, these are only attributes of a personality. They are not the person.

What I know is that I want to be here, with her. She is not just my lover – she's my friend. He smiled.

Coss saw him. 'Found the cream?' he asked.

'Maybe I have,' said George and he turned to Liliya. 'I love you.' He kissed her gently on the cheek before she stood up to leave, turning briefly to wave a goodbye.

Petric had determined that the wedding would be a Ukrainian one, so much as the State still allowed, and even with the absence of George's parents it would be a traditional wedding. When Petric heard that Coss had arrived, he decided that he could be both the best man and surrogate parents for George.

As George had first learnt and Coss half knew, this wedding was going to be a long affair, and, as both suspected, staying sober was going to be one of their hardest tasks.

'These people know how to party. Even I will have to pace myself,' Coss admitted, as they dressed for the evening's events. As was traditional in the Ukraine, the party had already begun for Liliya and her girlfriends that evening, but George and Coss had been excluded – as dictated by tradition.

'If you want to marry a virgin,' Coss had shouted to George who was in the kitchen preparing them a bite to eat, 'you need to break up that party. You know what girls are like when they get together. Maybe I should go along and see if I can help them?'

'You just stay here with me,' George replied, entering the lounge with two plates of food in his hands. 'I'm not having you anywhere near them. I can imagine the havoc you'll cause. There won't be one virgin left in Kiev if you get out there!'

It took some persuading, but Coss finally managed to get George to have a mini stag-night while the girls were having their own get-together. It was George who had to make sure his best man stayed something close to sober.

'Come on. Wake up,' Coss shouted the next morning. 'We have a wedding to go to.'

It was the first of the four days. George hadn't drunk as much as Coss but he was sure he felt worse. They took a taxi up to Petric and Alina's house, but stopped short of the house, when they saw Liliya and her friends along the road, coming back from a walk. Her friends were all staying at the house. Liliya kissed George and he then introduced Coss. Coss bowed deeply in front of each girl and kissed their hands.

'You will have to excuse him,' George said. 'The beer from last night has befuddled him.'

'You were drinking last night?' Liliya put her arm through George's as they walked into back to the house.

'Just a small one or two. You know I haven't seen Coss for a long time.'

' You will be staying in the village tonight, but we will have to find an extra bed for him.' Liliya looked at George and they both looked at Coss, who was heading back to the house with a girl on each arm.

'I wouldn't worry about that,' said George. 'I think he's making his own arrangements right now.'

Liliya dug her elbow into his ribs. 'Not with my friends and not at my wedding!' she said.

'What's the plan now?' George asked.

'Today we make the *korovai* bread which tomorrow we will give to all our friends. Tonight there is a special party for Mama and Papa to say goodbye to me. Normally it is just for our family but you are invited as well. We are being kind to our foreigner, and at the party we will make the *hiltse*; it's a tree we will put on the wedding table.'

They went into the house and Petric and Alina greeted them. It was a hive of activity.

'Come into the kitchen and help with the *korovai*,' Alina said. 'There will be plenty of time to catch up with Petric later.'

Alina grabbed George's arm and led him away. Petric shrugged as if to say that he couldn't stop this one. Food was everywhere. There was food for the evening – enough food, it seemed to George, to feed all the guests, not just for one night but for a whole week. He knew the Ukrainians knew how to throw a good party. And this was going to be a good party.

This was a time for Petric and Alina to be with Liliya. They sat at the top of the table. Grandparents were given the places of honour, followed by cousins, then their senior village friends and work colleagues. Sundry others came next, and finally came George and Coss, stuck down at the far end of the table. They didn't mind. They understood.

'You know what you have to do tomorrow?' Coss asked.

'Get married, I thought,' said George.

'No, before then. Have you worked out how much you will offer for the ransom first?'

George looked at Coss. This part of the arrangements hadn't been explained to him.

'Of course she wouldn't tell you about the ransom. You are supposed to know. It is a test of how much you love her and how much you think she is worth.'

'Okay. Explain,' said George. He knew something would go wrong and this just added to his fears. If he didn't know this – and it sounded quite important – what else might he be missing?

Coss explained. 'Normally we would be at your parents' house now, somewhere in the village. Clearly we can't do that, so we will have to find somewhere to hang out while they all get ready. Anyway, you will have to come here to get your bride. It's like the old days, I guess – grab her hair and take her back to your cave. But all these beautiful bridesmaids…' Coss swept his arm in the direction of four of Liliya's friends seated further up the table. 'By the way, do you have the phone number of that redhead?'

'Get back to the ransom, Coss, and no, I don't,' said George.

'Okay, okay. So they try and stop you taking your bride away, without you paying any ransom. If you had a lot of mates here we would all help you get away with it. Sometimes though, in some countries, it's her friends who steal her and you have to pay them a ransom to get her back. So you offer something valuable like money or jewellery for her. They may even get some man to dress up as Liliya with a veil, so you can't see his face. You realise it isn't her and you ask for your true love, and they ask for more money because she is so valuable, so then you offer some more. There will be a bit of haggling and then they hand her over to the you… actually the groom's family – which in this case is me – and then Liliya and I race off to the barn for a—'

George poked him in the ribs 'Hey! I've heard enough and I've got the gist. I'm sure the last part is not one of the traditions and we are not going to start a new one now.'

But Coss had stopped listening and was gesturing to the redhead to join them at their end of the table.

Coss turned back to George. 'And beware of pumpkins. If you are ever called a pumpkin or given one during all that negotiation it means they have turned down your offer. They are very hospitable and want to make sure you don't leave empty-handed. They give you a pumpkin instead of a bride.'

Coss kept George amused and finally managed to persuade the redhead to move. However, he failed in his attempts to get her to join him for the night, or even to give him her phone number.

'Another day I will get her number. Just make sure you two keep inviting me back. Do you hear that George?'

They had been allocated a bed in a neighbour's house and woke early. Coss, as ever, seemed to have no ill effects from the previous night.

'What will Liliya be doing now? Presumably, like in England. Dressing. Make-up, and a bag of nerves.' George was making nervous conversation with Coss as he shaved.

'Probably not,' said Coss. 'They will be thinking about *Blahoslovennia* now. We would be doing the same if your parents were here. I trust this is just nerves and you haven't lost all your marbles since you got here! Can't you remember anything? It is a blessing by your parents. Each family does it then it is done for both families.'

Both men were now dressed and ready, and George was grateful that Petric had allowed him to wear his suit and not Ukrainian traditional attire. He had long ago decided that embroidered breeches and a little frilly mini skirt would not suit him.

'I will perform *Blahoslovennia* for us here,' said Coss. He handed George an ice-cold vodka shot. 'Not the traditional blessing, but here it is. Good luck, old man. Have a happy life.' And with that they downed the shot.

'My God, that was good,' said Coss. 'Now let's go and ransom a bride.'

They walked up to Liliya's house and outside, waiting for them, was a line of her friends blocking their way and trying to look intimidating. Broad men and boys with arms folded and girls and women with their hands on their hips blocked the path.

'Don't worry,' said Coss. 'It's just meant to put you off.'

'It nearly has,' said George as they were jostled by the crowd.

'Got your strategy sorted, mate?' Coss was obviously finding this funnier than George. They pushed their way in, past the guard who followed them into what was now a busy lounge. Petric stood on one side of an empty chair trying to look severe and stern. Alina was on the other side of the chair, her face soft and clearly happy with life. More intimidating to George was the line of elderly relatives and female village folk dressed in black with their black head scarves. None could be thought of as thin, George thought, and all were scary. Worse still, there was a large pumpkin at Petric's feet.

'What can I do for you?' Petric's voice boomed and then echoed round the room, frightening those who were unprepared for its volume. George included. Coss nudged him in the ribs.

'I wish to make Liliya my princess,' George said, and Coss nodded his approval. A good start, Coss thought. George understands the history of the Ukrainian wedding is about the prince and his princess. Petric also nodded his approval.

'As I understand the ancient laws of Ukraine,' George began, 'when a man resorts to custom and takes someone's maiden or widow or divorced woman for his wife and wishes to live with her, he must pay three *hryvni* appropriation tax to the castle.'

This was a pittance and Coss looked down. This wasn't going well.

Petric rolled the pumpkin forward with his foot.

'But,' George continued, 'that was in the sixteenth century and money has increased in value. I believe this bride is worth two thousand *hryvni*.'

Petric didn't say anything. He put his hand on his chin to make as if he were thinking. He stuttered to start a word and thought better of it. Finally he said, 'Bring the bride.'

Amid gasps and laughter, a bride was presented to George and sat in the chair between Petric and Alina. Dressed in a white dress, whoever it was would have been better cast in a rugby team. Taller than George by many inches and heavier than possibly George and Coss combined, a veil covered what George was sure would be a very hairy beard. George played the game, which he had to admit was good fun.

'This is not the bride for whom I offered two thousand *hryvni*.' He turned away and stomped a foot.

'Then if you want a better bride you need to pay more, my prince,' said Petric.

'I would like *my* princess,' George replied and so the would-be bride was shooed away to stand at the side to watch while his friends poked, prodded and laughed at him. The veil was lifted and George was proved right; a shave was needed urgently.

Good play, thought Coss, and nicely pitched. Not too small to offend and not too large to conclude. Now it was George's turn to ponder and think. He waited just long enough.

'Mmmm,' he said. 'I will offer…' Again he paused. 'I will offer three thousand five hundred for the right bride this time. And I mean the *right* bride.' George tried to summon up a serious face but was not entirely successful.

'Bring the bride,' said Petric.

Liliya walked in slowly, her head slightly bowed. She sat in the now empty seat wearing a white dress as another concession to George's western idea of a wedding. On her head and over her veil she wore a traditional floral wreath. They were flowers she had collected yesterday. George knew everything he needed to know at that moment. Liliya was the woman for him. He had fallen in love in an instant, the moment he first saw her, and his love was sure.

'This is the bride I want,' said George.

'Good,' said Petric. 'And now a *mohorych*.' Everyone cheered as the drink that symbolised a deal had been struck was served.

George turned to Coss. 'Wow, thank God I don't have to go through that every day. Do you think Lord Ridley could be more scary?'

Coss smiled and nodded. 'And now for the shared *Blahoslovennia*' he said.

The *starosta* was an elderly man from the village. who had known both Petric and Alina for some time. He tapped on his glass and brought some quiet to the party. He pointed Petric and Alina towards one bench and George and Liliya to another, facing them. A *rushnvk* embroidered in red, the colour of life, the sun, fertility and health, was placed on the couple's lap.

At this point the *korovai* wedding bread was handed round and George broke off a piece for himself. He thought everyone was looking at him and Liliya, and he was right – but they were looking for a reason. Coss leaned over and spoke into his ear.

'They say whoever of the bride and groom takes the larger piece will be in charge in the marriage. You've just won that round.'

Silence again and the *starosta* faced the couple.

'As these two children stand before their own mother, before their own father, before their uncles, before their godparents, maybe they did not listen to one of you; I ask you to forgive them and bless them.'

George did a double take. Forgive me? he thought. They do take marriage seriously here. '*Bih sviatyi*,' the guests said three times. *May God forgive and bless you*, they meant, forgiving them for any sins, and blessing the marriage. The wedding would have been over at this point in the Ukrainian tradition but the State and the church had other ideas about how to proceed. There was a hiatus in the festivities as the main protagonists left for the civil marriage.

Liliya sat next to George as they drove to town. 'A few years ago the State laid down all the rules of the wedding. Where receptions could be, how many guests could attend, how the tables should be laid out and set. This wasn't accepted and they had to give way. Thank God we don't still have that now, George. It would be so dull.'

If the civil ceremony was a measure of how exciting the State could make a wedding, George was pleased that their involvement had diminished. With the church service yet to come on the next day, it was a quiet evening with a small family supper. Even though George and Liliya had now been married twice, once by the families and once by the State, George was again dispatched to his room at the neighbour's.

'Sunday is the big one,' said Coss. 'This is where the party gets into top gear. Are you sure you don't have the phone number of that redhead?'

'Yes.'

'Then sleep well.'

George stood next to Liliya at the back of the simple wooden framed church. Petric was seated in a pew at the front of the church; he didn't have to walk his daughter to the altar as he had already given Liliya to George at the *Blahoslovennia* the day before. Instead, George and Liliya had walked into the church together. George reflected on this symbol of equality between men and women. They were equal in God's eyes. Maybe these Ukrainians knew something not yet recognised in the West.

They started to walk down the aisle, George glancing at the pews on each side, trying to spot anyone he knew. He was warmed by the smiling face of Vera, standing arm in arm with Timur. Before they reached the altar, the priest stopped them and led them to a small lobby at the side of the church for what George thought might to be the actual wedding. Here they were blessed by the priest and wedding rings were exchanged. Then the couple were allowed to continue to the front of the church for the remainder of the ceremony.

During his time at Oxford, George had been to the college chapel just a few times, but he was always moved by the soaring notes of the sacred music. There was something about a choir in a church that thrilled like nothing else, and here today, in this church, the sounds lifted him and his sprits. Singing was in the Ukrainian soul and the service was filled with elevating music from the traditional female choir. Whenever there was a gap in the service, there was music. It quickly became hypnotic.

At the front of the church, George and Liliya were finally and properly married. Crowns of myrtle were placed on their heads as they recited their vows with their hands on the Gospels and the *rushnvk* wrapped around their hands. Then they were led by the priest around the tetrapod – the small altar – three times.

Liliya whispered to George as they walked. 'They call this the dance of Isaiah.'

George was no wiser. Then the priest said, 'These are your first steps as husband and wife, so it is only fitting that you walk around the symbol of Christ.'

This time George understood the wisdom of what was being said and what they were doing.

To finish the ceremony, George was left alone as the priest led Liliya to the icon of the Virgin Mary in the corner of the church. As the priest offered up prayers on her behalf, Liliya knelt in front of the statue and laid a bouquet of flowers. They were married and now it was time to party properly.

A room in the village had been hired for the reception and George and Liliya arrived to be met again by the *starosta* who offered them bread, salt, honey and wine, representing all the requirements for a life of happiness and prosperity. Petric clapped his hands for quiet and in his bellowing voice addressed all the guests to propose a toast to the newly wedded couple. In many ways George thought that this was very like other wedding receptions he'd been to in England.

There was drinking and singing and lots of laughter. Older relatives and guests danced with young children, and those of his age were dancing, talking and drinking. Men eyed the unattached women, knowing that all weddings made them romantic and maybe even willing to accept advances which might, on other days, be quickly rejected. One song predominated in the band's repertoire and was sung over and over again.

'What's with the song?' George asked Coss at a moment when his hand wasn't being shaken or his cheeks kissed by an unknown aunt. Coss was in the process of collecting a drink for the redhead he'd been stalking all weekend.

'It's *Mnohaya Lita*. Get used to it. You will hear it a lot.'

'But that means "many years"', said George. 'Why many years?'

'It used to be many *happy* years but it was decided that no song containing the word "happy" could truly call itself Ukrainian.' Coss smiled and returned to the redhead.

The party rolled on. Men had started to gather and chat at the bar. Coss and George were back and forth, collecting more drinks for guests.

'Coss, I am acting as barman here,' said George. 'I am being sent to collect drinks for every aunt and granny. Is this the life of a Ukrainian husband?'

While he was playing barman, the band played a range of songs, both modern and traditional. The Ukrainians loved to dance and the floor was always filled with the young and old, and then a new song began. The busy bar emptied and the dance floor overflowed.

'What's happening?' George asked Petric as he watched everyone form into a circle.

'This the *kolomeyka*,' Petric said, pulling George onto the dance floor. 'It's a traditional Ukrainian dance. Watch for all the leaps, kicks, and spins. If you don't look out you will be taken out.'

Everyone was dancing and George joined in. Under Liliya's tutelage he gave a passable imitation of a Ukrainian.

'*Lapushka*, this is the happiest day of my life, but each day with you will be even happier. I love you,' and they kissed. Liliya had her arms around George's neck in a deep embrace.

As they opened their eyes George lifted his head and saw that a circle of guests had formed around them. It was one of those moments when you think you are alone only to find out that the whole world is watching. George realised the music had finished; the silence was only broken by the applause, cheering and clapping of the guests.

The evening had come to a wonderful end. Finally it seemed to George that the wedding, the day and now the evening were over. After a final toast from Petric they could leave. George and Liliya were married. They were properly husband and wife.

CHAPTER XXI

SEPTEMBER 1975

George and Liliya settled easily into their new married life living in George's flat in Kiev. Coss returned to London leaving a trail of broken hearts and general chaos. His job had been done and he had made sure that George and Liliya got married. He did not report all the details of his trip to Lord Ridley, however – especially not his dalliance with the red-head.

A new academic year and a new term was starting and George and Vera were planning the next phase of his work. Vera was happy and had a spring in her step because Timur was coming back for a long holiday. She needed him home as much as Timofei did. She needed to reconnect and find her husband again. It had been a lonely time since George's wedding – the last time she had seen him. It had reminded her even more how much she needed her husband by her side.

Timur was due back this evening and Vera sat waiting calmly but eagerly. The knock on the door was loud. There was banging. She was unsure whether she should open it, so she opened it just a little and looked outside. There was Timur, half slumped and half leaning against the door frame. For a brief second she thought he might be ill, but the bottle in his hand told its own story. Another dream was shattered. The dream of a tall and elegant solider bringing her roses and love had gone and was replaced by this. She opened the door wide then, and turned away, letting him find his own way in. He stumbled after her. Still in his uniform, his tie was low round his neck and his jacket half buttoned and crumpled.

'*Lapushka*,' he tried to say but the words were a jumbled mess. 'Come here. I love you.'

Vera was in the kitchen, quietly crying.

'Come here, I said. Timur is home and he wants to see his Vera.'

Vera ignored him but again he shouted for her.

'I said come here.'

Vera turned to meet him.

'Oh, Timur, why couldn't you have come straight home? Why did you have to drink?' She wiped away a small falling tear with the back of her hand.

As a drunken man does, he tried to pull himself to full height but that just made him sway a little more. He moved towards her and then, with a teetering step forward, suddenly he lunged and grabbed and pulled her to him and tried to kiss her. He was drunk rough and unshaven and Vera resisted. With both hands on his chest she tried to push him away.

Drunk or not he was still stronger. Vera turned her head to one side to avoid his attempted kisses. With his left hand he pulled her hair to keep her still and with his right he slapped her hard across the face. Whether because of surprise, shock or pain, Vera stopped crying. Fear was etched deep on her face. But Timur couldn't and didn't want to see it.

Vera was bent forward and shuffled trying to stay upright as he pulled her by the hair to the bedroom. He threw her onto the bed and she looked at him, terrified. Her arms across her chest, her legs tight together, she lay just like a baby, curled up and crying.

'No, Timur. Please, no.'

She was almost inaudible through the tears which had returned. She tried to stop him lifting her skirt by pulling it down with both hands but that only made her vulnerable to another smack across the face. This was even harder than the first. The involuntary movement to feel her face just left her more helpless to his attack and with the submission of futility she allowed him to rip off her underwear.

The thrusts deep into her were painful and all the dreams of pleasure had gone. Time was its own dimension and Vera counted it off as her body was jerked and pummelled. Then it was finished. Timur rolled off her and was soon in a deep, snoring sleep. Timofei, a tiny and bewildered boy woken by the noise, turned from the door where he had been standing for a while and went back to his room.

At that moment, lying on the bed crying, she saw the terrible power that drink held. For much of her life she had talked of freedom and equality and she had reached a point where she was in control of her life; yet now, in those last minutes, she had become submissive and a serf to someone she thought she loved. The drink was his weakness and through the vodka she had finally seen the man he really was. All those unfounded jealousies he had felt about George had surfaced and were doubled and trebled by the drink.

She knew then that her life had changed forever. Because she loved Timur, she had turned from being strong and independent to weak and submissive. She thought love could be the most wonderful way to make two people stronger, but it could also be the way to destroy an individual. The rational step would be to grab her clothes, take Timofei in her arms, and leave. But love was not rational.

The bruises of her ordeal were evident for more than a week. Vera developed a series of excuses by way of an explanation. George and Liliya both questioned her hard, suspecting what had happened, but Vera said nothing. All she did was sit and think for many days afterwards. Would I still marry him today if I wasn't married? Probably not, she thought, but then again I don't know him now. Yet Timofei needs his father and if we were together all the time, maybe I would love him again.

Timur was home for four weeks and neither of them mentioned that first night. The strain on their relationship was clear, but over the days it diminished a little as Timur tried hard to be more attentive. Still he drank, though, and Vera stayed scared and wary that he would rape her again.

Then suddenly one evening he said, 'I may be transferred to Byelorussia soon. They have proper married quarters there. I want you to come with me.'

Vera looked at him. 'I need to think about that,' she said. 'I have so much going on here with the university.'

He nodded, but both knew that she had to think about whether she wanted to be with him at all. She didn't answer the question, even when Timur left. He had pushed her hard for an answer but she resisted.

'I need to talk to the university,' she said every time, stalling, and Timur reluctantly accepted this response.

In her heart she knew she would finally accede to his request and go with him. It's called the pain of love, she said to herself. Then, after Timur had been gone for a week, Vera's next worst fear became reality. The doctor confirmed what she suspected. She was pregnant.

That night George and Liliya had invited Vera and Timofei to supper. George was bouncing the young lad around, swinging him and hanging him by his legs. Timofei was yelping with delight at the games. Liliya and Vera sat on the couch talking.

'He wants me to go with him to Byelorussia. I am so unsure of what to do,' Vera said. She explained her thoughts, and in an academic, structured, logical way she set out all the pros and cons. But she left out two pieces of information – that she was pregnant and how the baby was conceived.

'If you can get a job at the University in Minsk then you should go. Timofei needs his father. All children need their fathers, and you need a husband who is with you all the time' Liliya said.

Vera wanted to tell Liliya everything, but it was all too painful. Of course, she was right. Children needed their father, and soon there would be two children who needed their father. But what do mothers need? Love, attention and understanding, she thought. She needed to tell Liliya; she needed to tell someone but then only as much as she could bear before the tears would fall.

'There is something more that I need to tell you. It's important,' Vera said.

'What's that?' George asked, holding Timofei by the ankles, hanging him upside down. Vera was surprised. She hadn't realised he had been following their conversation. 'More good or more bad?'

'Well, for me it is good but it may not be so for you, George,' Vera said. George landed Timofei safely on the ground and took more interest.

'Tell us,' he said.

Vera took a deep breath. 'Well, I agree with you, Liliya, that children need their father, and now it is not just Timofei who needs a father; it his new brother or sister.' Just saying it took a weight off her shoulders.

'What? You're pregnant?' Liliya almost shouted. It was loud enough to make Timofei turn towards her.

'What is pregnant, Mummy?' Timofei asked from the floor. He hadn't moved from where George had left him.

'Come here, my precious one.' Vera had her arms out and Timofei came and sat on her lap. 'It means that soon you will have a new brother or sister.'

'Do we go to the shops? Will Daddy come with us and choose?' The innocence and humour in Timofei's words made them all smile.

'No, darling. We don't go to the shops for a new baby. I will tell you all about it some later day,' Vera said, smoothing the young child's hair.

'So what is the bad news? I assume that was meant to be the good news?' George asked.

Vera looked at him. She was very, very fond of him and she had been instrumental in getting him to Kiev, but now he had Liliya, Alina and Petric. He would be okay.

'It means,' she said, 'that I will almost certainly move to Byelorussia to be with Timur and leave the university.'

'Well, I suppose we will survive,' said George a little glumly, 'but only if you promise to visit us… and if it's a boy you call him George.!'

'I promise the first, but if it's a boy then George is the last name I will call him. Timur is already jealous of you and what will Liliya think?'

'I would divorce George straight away if you called the baby George.' Liliya playfully pushed at George's shoulder.

George returned to playing with Timofei. Vera was his tutor, supervisor and mentor and the reason he was in Ukraine, but now he had his own family. It would be okay and he was happy for Vera. Very happy. Liliya and Vera talked on, about babies and about how she felt.

'Will Timur be pleased?' Liliya asked.

Vera hadn't really thought about him and how he would react.

'He will be pleased that we are all together and if it's another boy – who we won't call George,' Vera said, catching George's eye, 'I am sure he will be delighted. Yes, I am sure he will be very pleased.'

Aleksandra had written to George with the news in general. It was a gesture she felt compelled towards as she was instrumental in George being in Kiev. She had heard from Familiant that George was married and happy, but she feared that Vera's departure would make him uneasy. George read the letter to Liliya. Great Britain, Aleksandra said, was in a financial mess and Prime Minister Harold Wilson didn't seem to know how to cope. Inflation was over 20 per cent and wages were out of control.

'Sounds more like a communist-run state,' he suggested.

Liliya disagreed. 'No. They would never let it get that bad,' and she laughed.

Two other pieces of news reached George within days of each of other in June. Vera was now living with Timur in Slonim, a small village south of Minsk, in married quarters on the barracks. She had a baby at the end of May. The issue of the name hadn't arisen because it was a girl. She was named Kristina. George left Liliya to read all the details.

The second piece of news, from Poland, was less encouraging. This reached George through Coss. There had been riots in Gdansk. Facing even more economic hardships, the Government had again tried to raise food prices. Dominik, Gita and Anna were in Gdansk and, like many others, they were angry and determined to show their anger. George started to worry for Anna's safety. He had seen the passion she felt and he knew her stubbornness could cause her problems. For a time he had thought about writing to her, but could never find the right words. If he were to caution her, she would ignore him. If he wished her safe, she might see it, at worst, as a platitude and, at best, a sign that his thoughts for her were more than they were. In the end, out of both cowardice and procrastination, he did neither.

George had started taking a greater interest in Poland and what was going on there. He convinced himself it was because of the political situation, which he had to reflect in his studies, but he knew that it was really because of his worries about Anna. He wondered if this was wrong. He loved Liliya but still he worried about Anna. *Just because she was my companion and isn't any more is not a reason to abandon her.* He worried about his parents as well. It was an easy rationalisation for him.

In Gdansk, Anna was close to the heart of the problems. Dominik and Gita had been part of the group of students forming the Committee for Student Solidarity. This had pleased Familiant as he felt it was his contributions through Anna that had been pivotal. He was also happy with all the news and gossip finding its way back from George. Like a Field Marshall, he had it collated, referenced and used it in many ways in his campaign.

While he could hardly argue that everything was going well in the UK, the bureaucracy in Brezhnev's USSR was stifling their economy and the economic stagnation seemed to be permanent. Could they get an economic act together and exploit the new wealth?

He was unsure, but maybe the next leader could. It had been a long road for Familiant but each new piece of information reinforced his commitment.

'Remember, Miss Shaw,' he said as she came in with his tea, 'we are in this for the long haul.'

'Yes, sir,' she replied. 'The long haul.'

As was now often, Anna met with Mieszko, Wojciech, Władysław, and sometimes Lech Wałęsa, at the same café in Gdansk where they had first met. Alongside the student committee, another had been formed by writers and activists: the Committee for Defence of Workers – the *Komitet Obrony Robotników*. All were pushing for reform, but with little success, although it seemed as if defiance had started to form a face.

'Mieszko?' Anna asked. 'How do you think this will finish? Is it safe? I am worried for you and all your comrades.'

'We will be all right. There will be difficult times, but we have right on our side and we have the people as one. It will be all right.'

He reached out and touched Anna on the arm. 'Do not worry,' he said.

Anna was back in Warsaw when she heard the news that Lech Wałęsa had lost his job at the shipyard. She, like everyone else, knew it was because of his opinions and actions and not his lack of skill as an electrician.

Meanwhile both Dominik and Gita were regularly stopped and questioned by the police, but neither was arrested. Yet. Always they were stopped for small and petty things.

'A flat has been broken into. Did you see anything? Where were you?' one policeman had said. 'Can you come with us to the station while we check it out?'

No charges were ever laid but always there was the threat and always the disruption. Both of them occasionally suspected they were being watched. This made Anna both more fearful and more determined. She had to look out for herself and be more careful, but the passion for her people and her Poland had increased. She was even more determined than ever.

Dominik, Gita and Anna were in her room one evening. They talked and dreamed.

'What were your dreams before you came here, Anna?' Gita asked. Anna, as ever considered, took a moment to answer. She hadn't really thought about that before.

'I'm not sure I had dreams like that. I suppose I just assumed a simple progression from where I was. Oxford, doctorate, marriage, research, children, house, home, retire. It was nothing and everything. They were dreams, but really just expectations.

I knew each would be a struggle and with each I would be passionate, but they weren't dreams of doing or being anything.'

In an absent-minded way, Anna walked to the table to get some bread and sausage while she carried on talking. Dominik and Gita watched her.

'But now I have dreams which are not about me and what I will do. Replace Oxford with Warsaw and that old dream could stay unchanged. But now my dreams are abstract and hard to define. They are dreams about a way of life. Polish people with rights to have their own dreams and make them come true. Freedom to stand on a street corner and say what you believe to anyone who will listen. Does that sound silly?' She turned and looked at her friends questioningly.

The question continued to prey on her. Is it important to have dreams and be something? she thought. Maybe it is enough just to be; just to exist. Why do we all feel the need to achieve and climb some ladder? I'm sure cats and dogs or lizards and snakes don't have an urge to achieve anything; they are just happy to *'be'*, but I *need* to be doing this.

She let the thought drop as Dominik answered. 'No, of course it doesn't sound silly. That is what we feel as well. I find it odd that you reached this point so quickly, though.' He paused. 'Would you die for a cause?'

'That is unfair, Dominik,' Gita interrupted. 'None of us know the answer to that.'

'But he is right, Gita' Anna replied. 'We may not like the question but we have to face it. We may be arrested and who knows what charges they will trump up against us? What will we do then? Sell our souls and our friends or face the consequences? It's not an easy question and I'm sure I don't know the answer. I really don't know.'

The evening became sombre. Attempts to lighten it up failed as each of them returned repeatedly to that thought. Dominik and Gita left to walk home at midnight and the subject was never raised again.

There was good news in Poland later that month. The Government again capitulated and reinstated the old food prices. Spirits were raised and vodka was drunk. But everyone knew it wasn't the end or even the beginning of the end; it was the start of a long struggle. It was a struggle that Familiant was ready to sit out as he waited patiently for results.

CHAPTER XXII

FEBRUARY 1977

It was cold in Kiev with temperatures hardly ever getting above freezing. It was no warmer in Slonim. Vera had left for Byelorussia nearly a year ago, when she was still pregnant, and was spending her time with her children. Timofei had started a school. Although Kristina was only a baby her mother described her as an utterly adorable but wilful child. Unlike Timofei at that age, she wanted her way at all times.

In the Ukraine, in George's family, the real excitement was the opening of Chernobyl. The first reactor was due to come on-line later in the year. Petric was consumed by it and it was taking up all his time. He had just heard that he'd been accepted as a senior operator for the plant, so he had a job for a long time ahead. Meanwhile, George was concluding his thesis with his new supervisor and it was to be finished by the late summer, so his thoughts were turning to what would come next in his career. He had done everything that had been asked of him by Lord Ridley and had to face the prospect of doing a proper job at Wollacott, in England. The thought didn't raise much of a smile.

He and Liliya talked about what it would be like to live in England. She understood the opportunities and the future, but the thought of leaving her parents once even brought her to tears. George tended to back away from the issue, but now it had to be faced. England was so different from anything she knew. The attitudes and the ways of the people would be so alien to her. It might seem to be just another patch of land on the Earth, and one that looked quite similar to the Ukraine, but the land was defined by the people who lived there. George had seen changes and he didn't like all that he saw. Englishness was a set of values, he thought, known around the world; a set of values encapsulating fair play and democracy. But he had now seen these from a distance and – if they ever had existed – they were being eroded slowly but permanently. The United Kingdom was less united than ever before and the imperial red was rightly being erased of the map, but somehow, the people of England hadn't changed to the new order. Openness and honesty was being replaced by indifference, and indifference was driving incompetence. The old stayed imperial, and the young became lawless, and immigration was diluting any chance of a salvation.

He thought he was fortunate to have settled so well into the Ukraine, but then he wasn't really integrated. He was accepted and he was fortunate to be loved – loved deeply – by a small number of people, but Liliya would find it very difficult to be in England. She wouldn't understand the differences and the nuances, and each day, possibly forever, she would be an outsider. She would rant and rave at the behaviours and the lack of real morality and family values. Of course, it was different for Anna because she was already an insider. She loved the country she was in and she was fighting for her people. Liliya would never have that sense of belonging. She would always be a Ukrainian out of place in England.

George spent days sitting at his desk thinking about how he could make her life in England happier and always better. It would be a constant struggle and never easy, he thought.

All the same, she needed to have some experience of his homeland, and maybe even get married for a fourth time – this time for his parents, and so George and Coss had been working to see if Liliya could travel. Coss had consulted with Lord Ridley who had spoken with Familiant.

'I know what Aleksandra says.' Familiant jabbed his finger to emphasise his point to Lord Ridley. 'She will say he has done his job and that he and his wife should be allowed to settle back in England, and that he should be allowed to work here. That doesn't work for me – I mean, us. We need him *there* and we need him working more actively. It's all been a bit passive. We are supporting that woman in Poland but it is not enough. We should have done more to support Alexander Dubcek and Czechoslovakia in 1968. We were okay with Poland last year. But there will be more. We need to be more in control.' Familiant's voice was getting louder.

'I still worry about all this energy they have coming on-line and the impact on their foreign currency reserves. We need to make sure it is spent badly until we are ready. Brezhnev is being drawn into Afghanistan and, if we can keep him busy in the satellites, then we can stretch him. No. Cove needs to be kept in situ and he needs to become more active. Of course, we could arrange a visa for his wife, but I don't want to. I want him in the Ukraine and if we keep his wife there, he will stay.'

Familiant calmed a little as he questioned Lord Ridley. He sat back in his chair. 'Why don't we establish a research institute and make it active immediately? We could set it up in Oxford, nominate him as a visiting research fellow, and also get Aleksandra nominated there. That way he can get papers back to you. Make him a director of it and keep him in Kiev under its auspices? It gives him cover and a purpose, and also provides a better way of getting funds in. Do you think that will work?'

In the years that Lord Ridley had worked with Familiant he knew better than to answer that question. He knew that Familiant would have been pondering the subject for days and worked through every twist and turn and he would know that the idea was sound. But also he needed to do the same.

'First opinion? It should work. Let me dwell on it and I will get back to you.' Lord Ridley, patriot that he was, also had the bank and its reputation to think about. He really had to think about that.

So George's trip back to England was alone, just before the opening of Chernobyl, but he would be back in time to congratulate Petric and his comrades.

Liliya was staying with her parents while George was away. The disappointment of not being able to travel weighed heavily on them. George had memories of leaving Anna and wanted to find a way to make sure he was never in that position again. For Liliya, the disappointment was about not seeing Buckingham Palace,

Tower Bridge and – most of all – not meeting her new parents-in-law. She hadn't even considered that she and George might someday be apart.

'It will be a good break for me from all your washing,' she had said.

George saw no solace in that joke. 'I promise I will sort it all out. You will see my parents some other day. I promise you that. They are your parents as well now. Remember that.'

There was no Coss this time to meet him and he made his own way to Greta Smith Street, and finally the bank.

'Good morning, sir. Can I help you?'

'Well, Jane,. You can tell me how you are and how your father is?'

Jane smiled at George.

'Well, fine, sir. We are all well, thankin' you, sir,' she said in her Norfolk accent, remembering the bonus she had received to pretend who her father was.

'George, how good to see you again.' Lord Ridley waved George into his office.

'It's been a time since you were last here,' he said, showing George to a seat at the coffee table. 'You have done a good job and I hear, Dr Cove, your degree is nearly finished. Again, congratulations.'

George nodded a thank you and Lord Ridley continued.

'Getting straight to the point, if I may?' He didn't wait for an answer. 'You need to speak to Coss and he will sort out the financial position to date. I think we can say that the first piece of work has been completed. We would now like to offer you another employment.'

George had been waiting for this and had already made up his mind. He needed to be with Liliya and Liliya needed to be near her parents. He had no idea how he was going to make that happen. He was pleased that Lord Ridley had mentioned the money. At least that gave him some reserves but he was not going to take a job at Wollacott and become a London commuter. However, best to hear what Lord Ridley had to say first. George steeled himself. He remembered the first time he'd been here, how his life with Anna had been turned upside down. He resolved not to let that happen again.

'I really can't see you as a London commuter,' said Lord Ridley.

At least we agree on something, George thought. That's a good start. So where in the colonies are you going to send me, Lord R?

'This is my proposal, but it has some of the same conditions. I want you to stay in the Ukraine.'

The palpable look of relief on George's face was clear to Lord Ridley.

'I see you like that idea. I assume your wife will as well?'

'Very much, Sir,' said George. 'She will be very happy, but I'm not sure I see how. My work at the university is nearly done.'

'We are going to establish the Oxford Institute for Energy Economics. It can also be how you send your reports back me. It will be a real organisation and we have decided that the bank should contribute more to its future. It has been decided that it needs a new European Director for the Soviet States. We would like you to take that job and coordinate activities as far as it is possible with all the local restrictions, etcetera. It's a real job and you will have a lot to do. You can carry on publishing academically and I am sure you can negotiate some sort of arrangement with the university in Kiev to stay on as a bit of an academic in their faculty. In fact, keeping close connections with them will help you. We will have to put in place the normal confidentiality conditions again. Any issues in setting all this up will be at the Oxford end and not the bank. There is to be no connection with us, but I will see that you are well remunerated, of course. You will need to sort that out on this trip if you take me up on this offer. So...' Lord Ridley asked, leaning back in his chair, 'what do we think?'

'Not a difficult decision, Sir. Of course, yes. Do I fix everything with Coss?'

'Please, George, and good to see you again.' Lord Ridley stood, indicting the end of the conversation.

George rose and headed for the door, shook hands and walked out.

'All good, George?' Jane asked as he left.

'Excellent, thanks Jane. Just excellent,' he replied, and he was gone.

'Miss Sutton – please phone Familiant and tell him all is fixed and done with George,' Lord Ridley shouted from his office.

George thought about the time he'd left here to meet Jane and cheat on Anna. How different life was now. This time he was leaving and everything had worked out just the way he wanted. No, that was wrong. It was many times better than he could have wanted.

He turned out onto Cheapside and headed back towards Saint Paul's tube station. The headline on the *Evening Standard* stated that the Government was bailing out Leyland for another hundred million pounds. Two days before, the new Price Commission had started up.

There are many people here having a really tough time of it, George thought as he flicked through the newspaper, and here am I making life look easy.

'I really must be rather good,' he mumbled to no one in particular, and he stood straighter and seemed to grow another inch.

Although, he thought, transport was a lot easier here than in Kiev. Maybe the tube was dirty, old and noisy but it arrived and was always there.

Along the District line he exited at Westminster and had a pleasant walk around Parliament Square before heading down Victoria Street and to the flat in Great Smith Street.

Coss was there to meet him and, as always, was prepared with papers to complete and forms to fill in.

'Am I so predictable?' George asked. 'You knew what I was going to say.'

'That wasn't too difficult, George. Paid to live with your wife and keep her happy. Of course I knew what you would say, and as I knew what I had to do, I got my work done, so now we have lots of time to drink.'

George had been unable to get a message back to Liliya. He couldn't wait to get home and tell her all his news, but Coss had other plans and wouldn't let him leave until their tasks were all completed. There were papers to sign and he had to visit Oxford. It was a strange feeling – going back. The first time, he'd gone there as a new undergraduate. Now he was nearly a PhD and the Director of the Oxford Institute for Energy Economics. He liked the sound of that, but he soon discovered that finishing a degree was easier than setting up a new Institute.

'One day you may feel as though you are in charge – but not yet,' Aleksandra said as they had a light lunch. 'First, this is Oxford and this is part of Oxford University. They are all upset that the Vice Chancellor pushed it through without going through the Senate. However, or I should say, *whoever* pushed this through has some real influence.'

'Really?' asked George. 'Why is that?'

Aleksandra was cross that she couldn't tell George everything. She had argued hard with Familiant and he was adamant. 'No, Aleksandra,' Familiant had said. 'He cannot know. He must never know how much we have manipulated his life. He will stop working. Only tell him what he needs to know to keep him interested and committed.'

Aleksandra took a moment to respond to George's question. 'George, everyone wants a piece of this pie now,' she said. 'First they want to stop it, but when they see it can't be stopped and there might be a little prestige, and of course some money and funding, then they are there joining the party. They will all want to be involved. Now, let's see. Economics. Engineering. Slavic Studies and Modern Languages. Which other departments may want some oversight?'

She paused and leaned towards him. 'I tell you, George, if you want to see bureaucracies and intrigue running at their best, go to a university. You see, not only don't they have anything else to do, they are also clever. Have you ever read *The Masters* by Snow?'

George shook his head.

'Read it,' Aleksandra suggested, 'and then you will understand. Tomorrow there will be a meeting which you will have to attend. They will expect you to tell them all your plans for the Institute.

You just have to say it's too early and then sit back and listen. They will all give you more advice than you will ever need, but please, George, don't side with one or other of them. Stay out of their squabbles. Those will carry on long after you have gone.'

'Got it,' George said. 'Now can we eat?'

George was back in London, tired after being attentive to ten various and sundry academics.

'It was every bit as bad as Aleksandra said it would be,' he told Coss later. 'You wouldn't believe how they can talk, and they are supposed to be smart but there was hardly a logical argument between any of them. None of them had been near Kiev or the Soviet Union but each of them had an opinion on how I should start it all, and on how to run it. You wouldn't believe it. Really you wouldn't.'

'No good advice at all?' Coss was at the fridge getting a beer.

'You need to cut down on that, you know, Coss. Or if you don't, at least get one for me.'

George took the beer and continued talking.

'There was one who seemed to talk some sense. Professor Eunice something. She had all the data but didn't try and lecture me. At least she was an energy specialist and she owned up and said she wasn't a Soviet specialist.'

'Noted,' said Coss. 'But now we need to add the bits that Oxford didn't teach you. Take a seat, lad. We need to go through what Lord R wants from this Institute. After all, we know he is funding it all. It's quite simple really.'

They sat at the kitchen table and George took out his notebook.

'Right,' said Coss, counting off on his fingers. 'First, you don't tell anyone about Lord Ridley. Same rules as last time. Break the silence and the money goes.'

George didn't bother noting that down. That was obvious to him.

'Two, your territory is more than Ukraine. It's Poland, Byelorussia, Hungry, Czechoslovakia and even Romania and Bulgaria. You won't get into them all, but we need snippets about them all.'

'What about Russia itself?' asked George.

'We have that covered elsewhere, but of course we will take anything. Now, three. You must keep the Institute focused on Energy Economics. You have to stay legitimate but we need you to have a wider focus. As you well know there are political activists in all those countries. You know of the Brotherhood.'

George tried to hide his surprise. Now everyone is taking about the Brotherhood, he thought.

Coss carried on unabated. 'Don't worry, George, we know you know. Here's our issue. Trade balances will change if the activists really get their act together. Trade opportunities will increase. If we are going to maximise the bank's advantage we need to be first in. Being first in means knowing when and where things are happening. Get my drift?'

George nodded. That seemed pretty obvious, he thought. Smart guy, Lord R.

'And number four?' he asked.

'There is no number four, George. Anyway, not a formal number four. Just mine. Stay safe. I'd miss my drinking partner and after all those promises I made to Petric I have to keep you safe otherwise he would kill me.'

CHAPTER XXIII

1977

The start up at Chernobyl was a low-key affair. On 1st August, the first fuel was inserted into the reactor.

'We are twenty-five days ahead of schedule,' Petric told George a couple of weeks later. 'All the fuel is now in. Of course, this is only the first reactor and over the next few years there will be five more. But it is a start. In maybe just over a month we will be on the grid. It is exciting, George. I can't tell you how proud I am.'

But George could see for himself. Petric was bubbling and his excitement was evident; the technocrat proud of his work. George didn't want to burst the bubble but he had to ask.

'Petric, is it safe? I mean, nuclear reactions are big and dangerous if they get out of control. How do we know we can tame nature like this? Kiev, Liliya, Alina and me,' he pointed rather selfishly at himself, 'we are only a hundred kilometres away. What if something goes wrong?'

Petric looked comfortingly at George, and George saw his paternal nature.

'George that is my job to make sure there is no problem. It is the job of the controller to manage the reactor and shut it down if there is the smallest hint of a problem. I have Alina and Liliya and now you to take care of, and I hope one day soon a grandson?' Petric put his arm round George. 'It is safe. I give you my promise. This single reactor will supply ten per cent of the electricity of the Ukraine alone. It is important and it is safe.'

George let the subject be; he had other work to get on with. He understood what Coss had said. A network of nuclear reactors across the Soviet empire would change their financial situation. Make them more prosperous. That must be good, he thought. More money, more trade.

For George the days wore on. Being a director and not a student was not as much fun, as he thought it might be. He fought with bureaucracies in Kiev and Oxford. He had to get affiliated with the University of Kiev. The transition from verbal agreement to acceptable paper work was difficult, but made easier as he received his degree. Dr George Cove. The problems in Oxford were more intractable and made worse as he wasn't there to manage them. The load fell on Aleksandra and Coss, with support from Professor Eunice. Finally the word of the Vice Chancellor won through and all was agreed. Wollacott had to fund an additional Chair and promise five years of top-up funding. The deal had been struck.

But as the year drifted on, George became more relaxed in his new job. He soon realised he was hardly a director of anything and his work was really just as it had been when he was working on his doctorate. He was a researcher.

Often he thought of Anna in Poland. He had always been sure she would get her doctorate first. How times had changed, but Anna was now far less interested in her work and saw her role in life as supporting the activists in her country. She made the most she could of both the money being channelled through her and her time. She didn't think that she was under surveillance, but she was never sure.

'I'm sure they are so good that if they wanted to they could track us all the time,' she told Gita, 'but I suppose we would never know anyway. So I just carry on doing what I need to do, but try not to be too obvious. I'm not sure what else we can do.'

The fear was compounded because Lech was always being detained and harassed.

'It's so hard on Danuta and the children. They're all so worried,' Anna said. Her worries were not just about her safety but mainly how best to further her cause.

Aleksandra had written to her and told her about George's new job. It was Familiant who had written the important paragraphs saying that George's role now embraced Poland and hinting that he had access to money. It was just right. Not too much to make a clear offer, but allowing Anna to join up the dots and wonder how he could channel more in her direction, and so Anna persuaded

Stanislas to write to George, inviting him to visit him at the university. That was not difficult when Anna explained the reasons.

'Industry requires energy. He needs to know what the capital base is and how productive it is. He will have to come, if he is allowed.'

The possibility of the trip excited George. He hadn't managed to get out of the Ukraine yet but here was a chance. He wrote to Coss asking for help with permits and visas. He wanted Liliya to be able to travel as well. The network of universities and academia pulled together and George, with the support of Stanislas and Vera, planned a trip to Warsaw and Minsk. Yet again, sadly, Liliya was still not allowed to travel.

The tyranny of the State to control travel was, he thought, akin to apartheid in Southern Africa. Both stopped the free movement of people to associate with whoever they wanted. As a boy at school he had seen the demonstrations against the touring South African rugby team. There had been riots in Soweto and talk now of stopping sporting contacts. South Africa was becoming a pariah but we couldn't mobilise the same outcry for the injustice on Europe's borders. Why couldn't Liliya travel? The thought intensified his resolve.

Once more she showed a brave face and hid her disappointment as she loaded George with presents for Vera, Timofei and Kristina. George was relieved he was going to Byelorussia first. Carrying that lot around from Warsaw would have been torture.

'Please, George, don't drop them or lose them,' she said as George tried to pack a case. 'The blue wrappings are for Timofei and the pink for Kristina. The others are for Vera. Oh, George, let me do that. You are useless at packing.'

George sat at the end of the bed as Liliya folded his shirts and packed his case. He looked at her. Those fine lines and delicate hands. He would miss her madly while he was away, but there would be few moments when he would not be distracted by all the other planned activities, and then he would want to phone her and, even if he did get through, he knew it would seem like a platitude or a call out of obligation. What new words could he find to make the sentiment behind 'I miss you' as real as it was going to be?

With all those presents to carry, George decided to drive. He would go west and then north across into Byelorussia. It would be a long drive. Nearly six hundred kilometres and generally the roads were not good, but he could just make it in a day if he started early, so he did.

Liliya packed him a lunch and he left both excited and heavy hearted. Liliya waved him goodbye and then she packed to go and spend time with her parents.

The journey was as long as George feared and the roads were worse; badly lit, narrow and pot-holed. The border crossing was slow, even with his good papers, and so his ten-hour estimate was woefully short. It was mid-evening before he arrived.

He couldn't stay with Vera and Timur as they were in army barracks, so Vera had booked him into a small hotel – in fact the only hotel in Slonim. It reminded him of when he first arrived in Kiev. Byelorussia was poorer than Ukraine and Slonim was not the richest of the towns in Byelorussia, but the countryside on his journey was beautiful, wooded in places and green. It reminded him of parts of England. Maybe Nottinghamshire, he thought.

As he drove he remembered the stories he had heard of wartime resistance against the Germans that was fought around these very places. Twenty-two million allied soldiers had died in the war and twenty million of those were Soviets. He also knew that more than twenty-five per cent of Byelorussians, civilians or soldiers, had been killed in the war. Byelorussia had been hit hardest of all the Soviet states. The Germans had destroyed over two-thirds of the cities with less than a hundred unaffected. Nearly all the industry had been destroyed, with deaths and casualties of maybe nearly three million. He tried to imagine how that would have been felt in Britain. Only four hundred thousand British soldiers or civilians had died in the war, but more than six times that number of Byelorussians had died. It was this resolve in the Slavic people he admired and respected. These people knew suffering, he thought, and now he had to respect one more Byelorussian.

There she was, the *babushka*, dressed in black and as ever with a black head scarf, sitting and blocking his way in the corridor.

'*Kak dela*?' He didn't get a response. He hadn't expected one.

His room was basic but, after a long drive, comfortable. He was soon asleep.

The next day Vera brought the children to meet him in a small sparse restaurant in the town. Timofei was excited by the presents as much as at seeing George again.

'Of course he remembers you, George,' Vera said. 'He has been looking forward to seeing you. He keeps asking when Uncle George is coming. I assume that Liliya bought these presents? They are far too thoughtful for you.' She smiled.

'And this is Kristina?' George was holding the baby. 'I hear that she can be quite wilful.' George added to her baby sounds with '*Cooo shuuu co shu*.' The baby was quiet in his arms and looked straight at him with dark, wide eyes.

'When are you going to have children, George? You are very good with babies. I would say you are a natural.' Vera had a big grin across her face.

'Ask Alina and Petric,' George answered. 'They would have grandchildren tomorrow, but Liliya and I haven't talked about it yet. But enough of my fertility and vigour, how does the world look from here? Are you coming with me to Minsk tomorrow?'

Vera put Kristina back in her highchair and set Timofei at the table with a cake.

'Of course I'm coming with you. I am still a member of the university, but only as an associate fellow. Life is not good here for most of the people. It is a poor country, although Moscow supports us well. We have schools and good education but few luxuries. I sense the same deep pride in the people as you saw in Kiev, but not the organisation and structure to do anything about it. You see, George, the Russians in Moscow shipped so many of their own here, as they poured money and industry into the country, that our culture has been diminished. Do you remember what Khrushchev said?' she paused. 'Come on, George, you should know these things.' She was teasing him.

'Nope,' he said holding both hands up in defeat.

'The sooner we all start speaking Russian, he said, the faster we shall build communism. It was just more of Stalin's Sovietisation policy. What they did was pour money into the industrial sector and staff it with Russians. The language here is almost gone, along with the peasant class. The Byelorussian Soviet Socialist Republic is Russian and controlled by Moscow. This is not fertile ground for the Brotherhood. The old remember but they can do nothing. The young think of Moscow and the Beatles first before Minsk.'

'What of the university?' asked George. 'Surely the students there want some freedoms?'

Vera thought for a moment. 'No, I'm not sure they do. They see themselves as Russian. It will take a big event to make them start to think about who they are, and then maybe two generations. They are too grateful to Moscow for rebuilding their country, and for many Russia it is their homeland. The BSU is an oldish university. You would think there would be some heritage.'

'BSU?' George asked.

'Sorry, the Belarusian State University. It was founded in 1921, and the academic levels are high, but you will see that tomorrow. Of course, the West does get to the students through all that music. The Beatles are very popular as an underground movement. I think it's the same in Kiev, but it doesn't make them Byelorussian; it just alienates them from an old and dying leadership in Moscow.'

The next day they drove for three hours north to Minsk in Vera's old Volkswagen. Through the woods and pastures George noted churches of almost Calvinistic simplicity but his heart sank as they drove through the high-density housing suburbs of the city. England had done no better, he thought.

'They're called *mikrorayos*,' Vera said. 'They're the same all over the USSR.'

The centre of Minsk was a surprise to him as Vera saw in his face.

'After the war they didn't reconstruct Minsk, they just rebuilt it, and these big boulevards are all of the Soviet empire. They say that they are large enough to get the tanks into the middle of the town. It has become a real centre of science as well. Have you heard of the Minsk phenomenon?' Vera didn't wait for an answer and carried on. 'Moscow brought science and research centres here. They brought skilled people from all over the USSR and regenerated the city, and all that was turned into manufacturing. You have heard about the tractors and trucks made here? That's why there are so many non-Byelorussians here.'

George had already learnt more than he expected and he was drafting his report as she spoke.

Investment opportunities were good, but difficult to transfer funds in. Little chance of nationalist revolt and separation from Moscow.

Vera had arranged for George to meet the heads of three of the science and research faculties where, much to his embarrassment, he was received as a minor celebrity. He listened hard but learnt little more than Vera had already told him. He exploited his status as an Oxford representative and identified areas of research and contacts that he knew Lord Ridley could develop. As a sign of commitment, he suggested that some of their core research might be funded with small amounts of money. Deep down they all knew that the bureaucracies would never be able to arrange and manage such a transfer, but at least the offer gained him credits and potential contacts to call on later.

'Thanks, Vera,' George said as they drove back to Slonim. 'I enjoyed today. It's a fine university. So, now tell me how you are doing. What is life like for Vera and Timur in Slonim?'

Vera was deeply reluctant to talk about her life and George sensed much anguish and even unhappiness. Liliya would ask him for every detail of her friend but he knew that he would have hardly anything to say.

Vera had been animated as they drove to Minsk, and happy, but a dark cloud descended on her the nearer they got to Minsk. As she withdrew, George didn't push her again.

Their journey the next day was just over three hundred kilometres west to Warsaw, and George was upset that he had decided to drive. The Moscow to Warsaw train went through and stopped at Minsk. He could have had a relaxed and easy journey, but this way he at least saw the land and the people at work; this way he had a feeling for the countries he was visiting.

Stanislas had arranged a similar agenda for George in Warsaw; supper with him in the evening and time at the university the next day. He was happy and surprised when he saw Anna walk in with Stanislas. He didn't recognise the man with them. A solid man, a worker. A happy man. Anna threw her arms around George.

'George, how wonderful! You look so well.' She kissed him on the cheek. 'You know Stanislas.' They shook hands warmly. 'And this is Lech Wałęsa from Gdansk.'

That night Lech talked and George listened and he was rapt, drawn easily into Wałęsa's spell. His wasn't just rhetoric but words from the heart – words of passion, and while George listened, he watched Anna. He saw her passion and he knew that if ever he wanted her back he was always bound to lose her. This was her true love and real passion. No man would ever replace what she was feeling now. Although George understood exactly what Anna must be feeling, he resented that there wasn't a man like Lech or a cause of similar stature in the Ukraine. If ever there was a man for the time, it was Lech. Ukraine needed a man for their time, and George thought of Petric. Petric had the same passion for freedom for his people. Two men, so different in many ways, yet so much alike in others.

The supper lasted long into the evening and George had trouble waking the next morning, not so much from the vodka but the restless sleep. Right through the night his mind had chased every political, economic and business possibility. He asked Stanislas to keep the meetings short as he wanted to talk to him again. But the meetings could not be shortened as Stanislas and Anna introduced George to person after person who gave him increased hope that the Brotherhood, or as Lech had said to Anna 'the solidarity of the people', could make a difference.

When at last they were alone, George said, 'Stanislas, we need to see how we can better fund these activities. You find me the right investments and I will make sure that the money gets here.'

That was going to be the basis of his report to Lord Ridley when he returned home.

CHAPTER XXIV

1980

George was pleased that he had met Anna in Warsaw and seen her in her new and proper environment. He knew she was home and where she belonged and that made him feel really good.

The Institute was developing and the research papers it produced were not just received well academically, but were meant the Institute received private commissions from banks around Europe. There was also a steady stream of specialist and unique information channelled only to Lord Ridley through Coss. This information was not shared with anyone else and as a direct result Wollacott was prospering.

Familiant was also pleased. He was gaining intelligence and insight into the politics. The time was not ready but he could see the opportunity would soon arise. It would require just a little more patience and he had plenty of that particular virtue.

Financial support was now getting to Poland. Not maybe in the quantities George had hoped for, but sufficient to make a difference. Through George there was a link between the Brotherhoods in Poland and Ukraine; something that could not have happened in any other way.

Familiant was reading the latest reports from Poland. Written by George, they talked of deep unrest in Gdansk. Was this the moment? he thought. It might be summer, and the Olympics Games, which were being boycotted by the USA, were about to start in Moscow. The Russian invasion of Afghanistan in the previous year had already started to become both a political and economic strain. He could see the fault lines, and here we were, in the middle of 1980 and there had been another price rise in Poland. What would Wałęsa do now?

Familiant also wondered what Walesa would do. He didn't have to wait long to find out.

With an August sun on their backs, Dominik, Gita and Anna were in Gdansk drinking coffee.

'There is another strike at the Lenin shipyard,' said Dominik, addressing them all. 'And I think Lech is going to march with others. We should be with him, showing the brotherhood of the students. They have sacked Anna Walentinowicz, the crane driver. They can't do that. It's a simple political act. We cannot let it happen.'

'How many will there be? Will it be a big march?' Gita asked.

'I don't know, but we should go now and find out,' said Dominik, gathering up his cigarettes and standing. The others followed. '

After the protests in Warsaw and the strikes by the bus drivers and state taxi drivers, anything is now possible. I sense a new confidence in the people. I sense we are close.'

Gita's question was quickly answered. It *was* a big march.

'There must be twenty thousand people here,' said Anna as she looked on the crowds ahead of her. 'Not that I know what twenty thousand people look like.'

At first they were on the periphery, being funnelled into the heart of the march from side streets. The marchers were in good spirits. Some were chanting slogans and others holding banners. Anna, Gita and Dominik linked arms as they walked, sometimes having to stop as those ahead slowed. As they walked they sensed the size of the crowd, leaving the small side streets and entering the wider boulevards heading down to the sea.

They talked to those around them. There were shipyard workers, students, workers from other towns and students and those simply wanting a different Poland, all united in the cause.

The march turned towards the main gates of the shipyard. They were being pushed along by the wave of humanity. Police were pushing at the edges to keep them together. The chanting became louder and the banners denser, but despite the mounting tension and the fact that she felt she was being crushed at times, Anna felt calm. Dominik said he had heard that Lech was going to talk to them all and demand that Walentinowicz should get her job back. Anna was trying to remember if she had met her at one of their meetings.

Dominik, Gita and Anna were near the edge of the crowd when the march stopped. Ahead of them were the shipyard gates with a huge white sign facing them. It read *Stocznia Coanska – Gdansk Shipyard*. The crowd was pushing to get a better view, to see what was happening, and maybe to hear Walesa.

What happened next, happened quickly. Lech was climbing the gates to get into the shipyard to be among the strikers, and the crowd heaved forward cheering; the police were restless sensing trouble. People were pushing and trying to keep their feet. Others were cheering and willing Lech onwards. Like a sunset swarm of swallows, waves of energy moved the crowd. Anna felt the excitement and energy of the moment. She was exhilarated and shouted slogans with the masses. If her life had a climax then this was it. This was *the* moment for her.

As the general levels of excitement grew, so the police had become agitated. The captain in charge saw he was losing control. He couldn't stop Wałęsa, but he was afraid that the crowd would lose control and a riot could ensue. Worse, they may even manage to break down the gates; they were large and solid and it would take a monumental effort which would cause a crush and certainly injuries – even deaths, but what if they were opened from the inside? The thought filled him with fear. He had a family, and however much his heart was with Wałęsa and the crowd, he needed the job. If the crowd got out of control and there was a riot, he would lose his job and his pension.

If I can get the ring leaders out then I might regain control, he thought. He saw the three excited students on the edge and remembered them from a briefing. They must be pushing and urging all the others on otherwise they wouldn't have been on my briefing sheet, he concluded. He issued the order to arrest the three students.

Heading for Anna, Gita and Dominik, a group of ten uniformed and helmeted riot police tried to push their way into the crowd, which resisted and pushed back. Some people stood firm and blocked their path, while others just milled around making progress awkward. The captain watched and waved his men forward towards the three who were still unaware they were being targeted; their eyes were fixed firmly on Lech.

Why one of the policemen hit a marcher with his truncheon the captain later said he didn't know. He swung his truncheon at a protester, a glancing head blow with the worse of the injury on his shoulder. As the blow landed, he screamed with the pain. All around him, others turned. Whatever the initial provocation, the crowd split and ran in all directions within a localised area of panic. But, as some protestors pushed forward, other new, agitated workers pushed back against the surging throng. Through all this, the police did not lose their focus; they closed in on the students like rabbits in the headlights of a speeding car.

The three students turned to see what was happening as people pushed past them. It was Gita who realised, at the last second, that they were the target and shouted to the Anna and Dominik to run. The crowd around them offered no easy escape route. The crowd kept moving, people ran in panic in every direction, and the three students was separated. The police were close now, and Dominik saw a truncheon swing but he wasn't sure whether it hit Anna or Gita, or missed them completely. He thought he saw one of them fall, but the crowd closed in around them immediately and he had to get out.

Gita arrived at the café twenty minutes before Dominik.

'Have you seen Anna?' she asked him anxiously.

'No. But I'm sure she will be here soon. I think this day, August 14th, will be marked down as a special day in Polish history, Gita. Did you see Lech?' Dominik was still flushed with adrenalin.

'Dominik, I am worried about Anna. She should have been here by now. Can you be sure she is all right?'

Dominik took a deep breath. Much as he was on a high from the march, he actually shared some of Gita's concerns. Anna should have been with them. She should be back at the café.

'We will go and try to find her. Come on, Gita.'

Sitting in his room – this one was a proper office – at the university, George opened the letter from Stanislas. It had been three weeks since the Gdansk march and the strikers had won major concessions. George had heard much about the march and strikes in Poland on the BBC news and was reflecting whether anything similar was possible in Ukraine. He read the letter, then he sat back in his chair and cried, and he read the letter again.

Stanislas wrote of Anna's bravery, her courage and her intellect. He said how he had come to see her as a daughter and part of the family. He explained how much she had done for the freedom of the people of Poland and how she would always be remembered whenever anyone talked of the march at Gdansk, and he explained how, in the crowd, Anna had been crushed and had died of her injuries in hospital that night. Her friends Dominik and Gita had been with her at that moment.

'You idiot,' he shouted at the wall. 'Why did you have to go and do that? There is still so much I need to say to you.'

Again he reread the letter. However many times he read it, Anna was still dead. Stanislas wrote:

The shipyard workers have persuaded the authorities to erect a monument in memory of those who died during the 1970 police brutality. Today they will add Anna Kowalski to that scroll of martyrs to a great cause.

I know that Anna was very dear to you. She often talked to me about you and your days together in Oxford. My dear George, no one ever wants to have to write to a friend these words of sadness, but if Anna had to die for a reason and die for a cause, there is no better cause than to die freeing one's people.

It was mid-morning but George packed his bag, locked the office. and went home. There was no more he could manage to do that day.

'What's wrong?' Liliya asked, more out of surprise at the time of his return than any look on his face. He broke down crying on her shoulder and held her tight.

'Please don't ever leave me. Please,' he whispered, drying tears away with the back of his hand.

Confused, Liliya got him to sit down and slowly he told her all about Anna, from the first day they met in Aleksandra's room to the moment she died for freedom.

The letter from Stanislas to Aleksandra took rather longer to be delivered.

'You did this, you fucking bastard Bill Familiant! You and your fucking god-like mind games!'

For the second time in their relationship Aleksandra had pushed past Miss Shaw straight into his office and was waving the letter from Stanislas under Familiant's nose.

He took the letter, ignoring Aleksandra's shouting, and sat back to read. He also read the letter twice before he said anything.

'This is sad. Very, very sad. But she was there when the rift started to open. She – no, we – were a part of the opening. We supported them and we nourished them. We made this happen. This is a victory, Aleksandra. Don't you see? This is a victory.'

'Maybe it is a victory for Poland, but it is also the death of a poor innocent, intelligent girl who we placed there and brainwashed, and our part in this victory is just this big,' she said as she held up her hand, her thumb and finger pressed tight together.

'Just this big… What do you think you're achieving, Bill? This obsession of yours. Do you think you are the grand pawn master?'

Turning toward the door, she added, 'Your Queen has just been killed.'

She pushed past Miss Shaw who momentarily juggled the teacups on her tray, and was gone.

'Put this in Anna Kowalski's file,' Familiant said to Miss Shaw. 'And mark it "File closed. Deceased".' He handed over the letter and returned to the work on his desk.

George was not finding it easy to work, but he still had to file more reports. He wrote to Lord Ridley.

I understand that on the 31st August an agreement was signed at Gdansk by the strike committee and Mieczysław Jagielski on behalf of the Government. Among the concessions was the right of the workers to have their own independent trade union. It has been called the National Coordinating Committee of the Solidarność, or in English, Solidarity. Lech Wałęsa is the Chairman.

You might say that this is the first time that The Brotherhood of Saints Cyril and Methodius has taken any power or had any real authority. This is the start of the end for communism in the Soviet States.

CHAPTER XXV

SPRING 1985

Time settled George and, although Anna was a recurring thought, she was a less frequent intruder into his daily life. He continued to monitor the changes in Poland and occasionally muttered to himself 'At least you didn't die in vain.' But then he always had to correct himself – she had. She hadn't died for a cause; she had died with it. At that moment she was an innocent bystander of a cause.

Her commitment and her death had given him more purpose and he had aligned himself more closely with Petric and the other members of the Brotherhood. He supported their cause wholeheartedly and felt more willing to channel support to them. He didn't feel guilty that it was Lord Ridley's time and money he was spending, and if he had to rationalise it he knew his reports were now conveying more insight, commitment and political reflection for Lord Ridley's investment.

For their parts, Lord Ridley and Familiant were equally pleased with their asset, both feeling that they were getting more back than they had paid.

Since *that day* Aleksandra had hardly seen Familiant but was pleased that George, at least, seemed to be safe and out of harm's way. She was also pleased that the Institute was going well and gaining a solid reputation for academic and commercial work.

'Miss Shaw,' Familiant shouted. 'See when Lord Ridley is free for a lunch, would you? Thank you.'

'Maybe it is time for a final push, Richard,' he proposed, in his club in Pall Mall.

'Well, it's been an interesting five years,' Lord Ridley said as he pushed his dessert plate to one side and reached for his Muscat de Beaumes-de-Venise.

'Let's see. Well, Russia has clearly stagnated. We know that if it weren't for all the wheat we've been selling them, mainly from the

US I might add, all the way through the seventies, they'd be in a right pickle. Brezhnev has gone and he was old school. Andropov from the KGB has gone. It really depends what the new man, Mikhail Gorbachev, decides to do. He isn't old school. Maybe we should try and help him a little?

'They haven't been able to exploit the oil wealth as much as they wanted. Afghanistan was a huge financial drain on them, and staying in the arms race has cost them, and now, of course, China is looking a lot smarter and making them look east again. I'm surprised that the satellite countries haven't been much of a political strain. I thought Poland might have been a trigger, but Ukraine and the *'staans* are all solid. We are close but not yet there.' He paused. 'Maybe you are right, Bill. One more push might make the difference. Did you have anything in mind?'

Familiant tasted the dessert wine. 'Yes,' he said. 'I'm worried about Chernobyl and the effect that free energy will have on them. We get little revenue from the build and design, but we have a lot to lose when all the reactors are up and running. More reactors are coming onto the grid all the time. By August last year, Chernobyl had generated one hundred billion kilowatt hours of power. Four units are now on line there.'

'I'm not sure what we can do about that, though.' Lord Ridley leaned back in his chair waiting for the answer he knew Familiant had prepared.

'Oh, there is plenty we could do,' replied Familiant. 'And I suggest there is one thing in particular we *will* do. I suggest we make Chernobyl blow up. Boooom!' His hands went up in the air with the explosion of words.

Few things had ever surprised Lord Ridley, but this did and he had to rebalance himself on his chair.

'What? You are going to blow up Chernobyl?' He realised his voice was getting loud. He took a breath and slowed down.

'Bill, do you understand the devastation that will cause? It could be millions of lives and maybe even cost lives here in England if the wind blows the wrong way on the day that happens.

Are you serious? Are you going to send in the SAS? Even you don't have that authority. Do you? … Tell me you don't?'

Familiant took a sip of wine. He cleared some space in front of him by moving plates to one side and said, 'Economically, destroying Chernobyl would put their nuclear programme back and make them use their own oil and gas and not export it. It will put great strains on their economy. Hits the mark there. Then it will cause huge dissatisfaction in the Ukraine. It may be supplying power to the Ukraine, but it is imposed by the Russians. It will give more supporters to the Brotherhood. It will give them fertile soil to till, and finally it may finally stir something into the Byelorussians.'

He paused and lowered his voice, looking intently at Lord Ridley.

'I wasn't actually thinking of blowing it up with a mushroom cloud. Something rather smaller. More of a big accident is what I have in mind.'

Lord Ridley sat back in his chair and wondered if Familiant was insane. Maybe the means were sometimes justified by the end, but wasn't this one step too far? He was sure that somehow George would be involved, and George was funded by the bank. He *had* to have a view.

'Do we go through the details of your hare-brained scheme now, or do you want to leave me to try and guess?' Lord Ridley asked with thinly veiled exasperation.

'Now, I think,' Familiant answered as if he hadn't heard. 'So here's a map of the area.' And he drew on the linen table cloth with his knife.

CHAPTER XXVI

APRIL 1986

Lord Ridley didn't like the potential consequences but he had to accept the plan had merit and was easy to initiate. They had agreed that failure would leave no one vulnerable. Coss was briefed in part, just enough to start the whole plan, but – unintentionally and unknowingly – George had already been sowing the seeds for some time.

During the weekends, George and Petric sat in the garden and talked, while Liliya and Alina made food. They talked about the progress of the Brotherhood in Poland and the lack of progress in the Ukraine.

'Our cultural identity is being torn to shreds and we are no closer to self-determination than before,' moaned Petric. 'The Poles have taken as one to the cause, but we are still here, in the same place. There the Brotherhood has taken hold. There they have *solidarity*.'

'Have I told you about Anna, my friend from University, who died at Gdansk? George asked.

'Only a little, and Liliya has said a little. I was very sorry for your loss, George. She was really a heroine.'

'I doubt you know everything though Petric. She was working with the Brotherhood in Poland and was friends with the leaders. I spoke to her about it when we met at Chernobyl. They are the real heroes. They are the ones that would give their lives for the cause, and the Gdansk strikes and Wałęsa have united the country into one.'

George talked of heroes and martyrs and even asked about the sacrifices that the original members of the Brotherhood of Saints Cyril and Methodius had made. They talked for over an hour and Petric complained more about the lack of progress in the Ukraine.

'If only we had our own Gdansk and our own Wałęsa,' Petric bemoaned, 'then we would make real progress. Our progress is slow and each day we are being pulled further and deeper into the Russian sphere. I don't know what we can do. We need our own symbolic Gdansk. We need to make a statement of our own. We need to re-exert our own nationalistic statement.'

Petric went quiet and closed his eyes in meditative contemplation. Then he jumped up, a brief smile quivering on his lips, before returning to a more sombre position.

'But now it is time for food. Let's go in.'

As they walked to the house together, George was not at all surprised by the turn of this discussion; it was a dialogue they had had increasingly over the last few months, and each time Petric outwardly showed the frustration that his words portrayed.

'What is wrong, Papa?' Liliya asked at lunch. 'This is supposed to be a happy day. In England they call April 23rd St George's day. We are celebrating our own St George.'

'It is nothing, my princess. Just work. We are completing some routine tests at the plant in a couple of days. Last year they didn't go well. We have designed some new equipment and we need to test it. I am just thinking about them. No need to worry.'

'Okay, Papa,' Liliya said, reassured.

'Remember, I love you all,' said Petric. He was not eating and he looked at them all as he spoke. 'I love you all. And George…?' he continued, 'can I ask a favour of you?'

'Of course,' George replied.

'Alina hasn't seen her mother in a long time and because of work I haven't had time to take her to see her. You said that your workload was light at the moment; can you take any time off work and drive her there? It's a long way, I am afraid, but I have heard that Grandmother is not too well right now and with all these tests I can't get away.'

'Of course,' George replied. 'When did you have in mind?'

'Maybe in a couple of days, if you could. Maybe the evening of the twenty-fifth?'

'What is the hurry, Petric?' Alina was looking at him. 'We don't have to rush, George. Petric, we only talked about it last night.'

'I know, my darling,' Petric said as he took her hand. 'But she is unwell, and I thought if George was free we should get you there sooner. She is old, and Liliya can see her grandmother, too. I'm going to be working hard these next few days and weeks. It just seemed like the perfect time.'

'Where does she live?' George asked, embarrassed that he didn't know. He had only met her once, at the wedding.

'Odessa. About five hundred kilometres south. It will take about ten hours driving if that is okay?' Petric replied. George nodded.

'Well, if you are sure, George, that you can get time away, it would be really kind of you. Are you sure you will be okay, Petric?' Alina asked.

'I will be fine. You can all go and enjoy yourselves,' he said as lunch was finished and arrangements made to collect Alina in a couple of days.

'Is Petric okay?' George asked as he and Liliya headed back into Kiev. 'He was very subdued today. His mood was bleak when he talked to me before lunch.'

Petric sat pensively at his place in the control room. He was there even before Alina had left for Odessa. The tests were scheduled to last two or three days and he had planned to stay at the site for the duration. Day one had gone to plan and he had retired to his room early. He took his book, *Ustav Slov'ians'koho Tovarystva sv Kyryla i Metodiia. Holovni Ideï*, and started reading again about the early days of the Brotherhood and the sacrifices that had been made for freedom.

Petric was early for his shift at his console in the Chernobyl plant. The procedures were clear and he knew what was expected. It was just past midnight and he issued instructions to his team and started on his own tasks. He began getting ready to test how long the turbines would spin for and supply power to the main circulating pumps if there was a loss of the main electrical power supply. This was the test that had gone so badly the previous year when the power from the turbine ran down too rapidly.

He reread what was required by the operating manual, much

of which he had written. Then, deliberately, he ignored the instructions, first by disabling the automatic shutdown processes. There was no check on his actions as he put the station into a state of overload.

He waited ten minutes until an alarm sounded and the panic he predicted ensued. Dials were checked, switches turned, and levers pulled. The same story was being told everywhere. The reactor was now unstable even as they tried to shut it down. He had caused a dramatic power surge while the power rods were being inserted into the reactor. All the instruments showed the same and most were bouncing in the red danger area.

Petric knew what would happen. Hot fuel rods and cold water would increase the pressure. The reactor cover plate – all one thousand tonnes of it – was coming detached, jamming all the control rods. He knew now there was no way back. The first steam explosion would release all the radiation and the second, a couple of seconds later, would throw out fragments of the fuel channels and hot graphite. Petric knew what would happen and he had instigated it. Thank God my family is safe in Odessa, he thought. Cold water and hot rods would create steam at an enormous pressure. The reactor would crack and all the controls would become inoperative.

His thoughts remained completely focused. This is my moment and I will be seen as a hero of the Ukrainian people. My actions will show that we are not to be taken lightly and ruled by yet another foreign invader. This time The Brotherhood of Saints Cyril and Methodius will last and bring us independence. In Poland there was Wałęsa and in the Ukraine there will be Hudolei. This is the action of a Ukrainian hero. There was an explosion and then, quickly, another.

Nearly the last thought of engineer Petric Hudolei was of his noble act to stir and awaken Ukrainian consciousness to the tyranny of Soviet rule. Would he be remembered for his act as a hero? He was sure of that. The very last thought Petric had was of Alina and Liliya happy and smiling at the wedding. He died a very happy man.

PART III

2006

DÉNOUEMENT

CHAPTER XXVII

2006

Apart from George disappearing briefly to bring soft drinks and some cheeses and biscuits from the kitchen, he and Aleksandra had spent the whole day in the garden. She had told George everything she knew about Familiant and Lord Ridley, from the time before George's arrival at Oxford – his first meetings with Anna, his job, Liliya, and really, he thought, his whole life. Together they had put all the pieces into a whole.

George's face was ashen. 'Why now?' he asked. 'Why have you taken so long to tell me?'

Aleksandra was pensive. 'I could have done. I *should* have done. I'm sorry, George. I didn't want to upset you. I knew knowing would hurt you, but in the end my guilt became too strong. Will you forgive me?'

George didn't know what he felt. Maybe it would've have been better if he didn't know. What would he have done if the roles had been reversed? Probably nothing. He was too much of a liar and a coward, he decided.

'Of course I forgive you. You've shown courage I could never have summoned. Thank you, Aleksandra. Can you try to fill in some of the other pieces though?' he asked.

'Of course. Anything I know.'

'Tell me. Did you have a relationship with Familiant? I mean beyond a professional relationship? After all, you said he had started to call you *Sashunia*. Were you tempted?'

Aleksandra looked at him wistfully and was even more considered with her words. 'I can't remember exactly when it was, but you were in the Ukraine and it was before Anna died. Familiant and I had started meeting more often. He always had an excuse of a business or project reason, but as I look back many were spurious and the intent was clearly to spend more time with me. It had become normal for him to call me *Sashunia* and I got used to it; to be honest I was enjoying it. He was a very powerful man and I was flattered. He had promoted my career and made it possible for me to work as I wanted and where I wanted. He gave me enormous freedom and at first I also enjoyed the cloak and dagger stuff we were playing. He made my life more exciting, but I had given him little thought in that way, after all he was a surrogate, an extra father, to me.

'I think we'd just been to supper at *Gavvers*, though I can't be sure. That was the very popular Michel Roux bistro, although I'm sure he'd hardly call it a bistro. By the way, you know you have been there?'

George looked at her. 'Are you sure? I can't remember being there, but you have my life fully documented so you would probably know better than me.' His tone was distinctly barbed.

'That's unfair, George,' Aleksandra retorted. 'Familiant had your life taped. I didn't.'

'I'm sorry, Aleksandra. Go on, tell me about my trip to *Gavvers*,' he said.

'It's a minor diversion but *La Gavroche* moved to Upper Brook Street in '81 and *Gavvers* was the restaurant that stayed there. The premises were the same as where you and Jane ate that first night after you met Lord Ridley.'

'Mm,' he said dismissively. 'Let's put Jane to one side for the moment. I'm still interested in you and Familiant. So what happened?' George asked.

Aleksandra continued. 'We had dinner and talked about very little and nothing of any real importance, just some gossip, and then Familiant said, "*Sashunia*, there is something personal I want to tell you". "Go on," I said. "I'm all ears". Probably I was a bit frivolous. I didn't really expect anything of real importance – after all, he was a manipulator and I supposed it was just going to be another ploy. Or maybe I'd had a glass of wine too many. Anyway, he looked straight into my eyes. He'd never been so direct before and I found it just a little disconcerting. I remember putting down my knife and fork so I could concentrate, and he looked at me and said, "*Sashunia*, we have known each other for a long time – ever since Cove's father started all this, when he met your father in Germany".'

At the mention of his own father, George stiffened. He realised now – and for the first time – how fate had brought them all together. Where, he wondered, would he be now if his father had done just *one* thing different in his life before he had met Pavel Ponomarenko? If they had never met, or if his father had disliked him, then everything that happened would be null and void.

He reflected on the phenomenon. Life is so full of so many coincidences, both small and large, that we really had no control over what happens. From a random moment in time when our parents procreate to create us, our life is directed and controlled by fate. Had their lust been met a minute earlier or a minute later we may have been someone different. Miss a bus or catch a train. Say yes once when we might say no. Then the history of the whole world is altered.Everything that happened to us, George thought, was random, and we don't see the coincidence of seeing someone walking down the streets who we have never seen before, but that is just as likely as seeing someone we know. In this morass of global and seismic coincidences, was Familiant really in control of me? Was he really able to manipulate the world – our worlds – so fully?

'Stay with me, George,' Aleksandra said. She had seen George drift away into his own thoughts. 'Familiant looked at me and said, "I have always put my work ahead of my personal needs, but with you I find it very hard to keep those distinctions clear. You are very important to me and I would like to start a closer relationship. We share the same thoughts, we have the same values, we have the same intellect."

'You know, George, he was clumsy in his words and he really didn't understand how to talk through his heart. I'm sure that he really thought an affair could be conducted like business. All he had to do was issue an instruction and I would follow his request and start a personal relationship. But I knew him and I understood and I thought I could teach him how to feel something deeper and more fulfilling, so I went along with him. I didn't tease him about his ineptitudes or failings. I simply smiled and put my hand on his as it rested on the table. I thought I almost felt him recoil at even this very simple moment of intimacy.

'He tried to make small talk, and eventually I had to call the waiter for the bill. I said to him "Yes, let's see if we can start a relationship. Let's go to your flat now and talk about it." We found a taxi and sat in the back, not close as would-be lovers should, but at the sides, until we reached his flat in Mayfair. It was beautifully decorated and it suddenly occurred to me that I hadn't been there before. I doubted at that moment if anyone I knew had been there. I realised then what a lonely and solitary man Familiant was.

'He offered me a brandy, which I turned down, and he poured one for himself and sat on the sofa opposite me. George, you know me. I'm not a sexual person or a sexual predator and I was so unworldly in all these things but I knew that I knew so much more than him. I thought in a relationship he wanted sex. So I did what they do in the movies. I went and sat next to him, took the brandy balloon and put it on the table, undid his tie and turned him towards me and kissed him full and square on the lips. You know, George, he was nervous, as if sex frightened him, and his response was slow. But then I started to feel him melt. Every man has passion deep down.'

George saw Aleksandra stop as she composed herself and he felt the need to ask a question to keep her lucid. 'And this turned into an affair? You and Familiant? Was he a good lover?' he asked.

'No, George. He was not a good lover. He was impotent. We tried again a few more times but always with the same result. I'm sure he was a virgin until the day he died. We didn't talk about it and after a time our social meetings returned again to matters of business.

'I will never forgive him for his many flaws that so ruined you and killed Anna, but I will always feel sorry for him on that matter. Today we have drugs that would have helped and he would have lived a much more fulfilling and rounded life. You and Anna were his children and he invested so much into you that he lived your lives vicariously. In part you both were the solution to his impotence.'

George's self-esteem was plummeting downwards during this barrage of revelations, to a level it had never reached before. He had to know. 'Tell me, Aleksandra. Did you really like me or was it all a sham?'

'George. That is a silly question,' she answered. 'Of course I liked you. I liked you a lot. Anna and you became like my children. It was different to the way Familiant was using you. I came to love you both, but as we are being so honest, I will tell you that I was always much closer to Anna. In many ways much closer than you know.'

'Will you tell me?' asked George.

'Of course,' she said. 'I have already said that the very first meeting with Anna was always going to be easier than with you. You can understand that, can't you?'

George nodded and smiled, remembering the young undergraduate at Oxford. He must have been quite a challenge to them all. Aleksandra sipped at her drink and continued.

'At first it was work, but as I worked with you and Anna I came to really like you both. When Familiant came up with that trick with Jamila, I was pleased. You see, I wanted you to be together. I wanted you both to be happy and you were. So blissfully happy.'

'We were,' said George, 'but Familiant couldn't leave it like that. He had to move us on. Did he really think he had that right, Aleksandra? And what did you do to stop it?'

'Nothing really. Not very much, George. Nothing too much at all. At one stage, Familiant was even going to make you believe that you and Anna were related. I think he might have convinced you that you were brother and sister, but we talked him away from that. We really did try to stop his worse excesses.

'I'm so sorry I didn't do more, but we really thought we were doing the right thing and doing it for a much bigger cause. We thought, or I should say Familiant convinced us, that we could make a real difference. With hindsight we did make a difference, but not how we imagined when we started, but then again, maybe we did. Did you ever read that paper I wrote on catastrophe theory and economic development?'

George shook his head as Aleksandra continued.

'It started with a French mathematician called Rene Thom and was taken up at Warwick by Chris Zeeman. Thom said that in his theory there are only seven sorts of catastrophe. These aren't the earthquake and tsunami sort of catastrophes but mathematical models in something called bifurcation theory.'

She saw George raise an eyebrow as he feigned going to sleep and started snoring.

'No, listen to me,' she said, again taking on her role as tutor.

'Simply, small changes in what they call a splitting factor can make an equilibrium disappear and disappear smoothly or catastrophically. Imagine you have a dog cornered and you poke it with a stick. It will cower at first and then suddenly jump at you, teeth bared. It has changed its behaviour catastrophically. It can be the same in economics or even acts of war. Chris Zeeman had some great examples in times of war, of hawks changing to doves, and how the democratic wishes of the masses are not followed by their leaders. When they do change, they change catastrophically, jumping suddenly and immediately, often to a more extreme and opposite view that is viewed as capitulating. I was trying to use the theory to explain why we have sudden and sometimes catastrophic changes in stock prices and share values.'

'So?' said George.

'We could never have brought down Communism by ourselves. We were never going to be the main reason, but maybe we were the final straw that broke the camel's back. I think at the end Familiant knew we were minor players and not the leaders he had hoped for.'

'You were talking about your feelings toward Anna and me,' said George to remind her of the things he wanted to hear.

'Ah, yes,' Aleksandra said returning to the point. 'When you were gone, Anna and I worked very closely together and we became very close. At first I saw myself as her guardian but that was not enough. We became closer. First we were friends and then much more.'

'More? I don't understand,' said George.

'For a time we had a very close and intimate relationship, George. For a time we were lovers.'

George looked carefully at Aleksandra and started to see tears form.

'And so when Anna died you felt it very personally and not just professionally,' he said.

'I was devastated. I cried for days and withdrew as much as I could from the project and then spent all my time hating Familiant and worrying about you. But I had to stay involved to look after you as best I could.' She paused and dabbed her eyes with her fingers.

'I still miss Anna. For a time she was my life, but she had to go to Poland. It was for both our benefits. We stayed friends. We stayed very good friends, but we were never lovers again.'

George was unable to take in all that he was hearing. His life was being turned upside down and inside out. He now needed to understand every last bit of what had happened.

'How did Familiant react to Anna's and death and the explosion at Chernobyl? Did he feel he had achieved what he wanted?' George asked. 'Did the deaths affect him? Surely even *he* had a heart?'

'When I heard about Anna dying in Gdansk I knocked down the door of his office and gave him the letter I got from Stanislas, but he just read it and filed it and he never mentioned her again. But he was ecstatic about the changes in Poland and he tracked Wałęsa through every one of his steps from winning the Nobel Peace Prize in 1983 to becoming President. Familiant even quoted to us what they said from Stockholm: "Wałęsa belongs not only to Poland but to the whole world." We were still funding money through to Gita and Dominik, and whenever Familiant thought about Poland he thought of success, and then in 1986 Karol Józef Wojtyła made his day.'

'Karol Józef Wojtyła? I don't recognise the name. Am I supposed to know who he is?'

'You should,' said Aleksandra, 'but you may know him better as Pope John Paul II, the first Slavic or Polish Pope. When he became

Pope the people of Poland found a voice to their deep religious beliefs. With Solidarity, Lech Wałęsa and Pope John Paul II there was no going back, and Familiant knew it.'

'Don't tell me Familiant thought he had a hand in the Vatican's white smoke?'

The look from Aleksandra told him that she thought the question unworthy, even from George.

'So somehow he rationalised Anna's death?'

'He didn't have to rationalise it because in his mind her death was an accident that happened in Gdansk while she was out walking.'

'That is ludicrous,' George shouted. 'If Familiant hadn't started all this then she would never have been there and crushed or beaten by police. The line of culpability leads straight back to him and no one else. It was his *fault*.'

'He didn't see it like that,' Aleksandra said. 'He believed that all he did was to liberate what was already deep in her and allow her be who she really was. By the way, he would use the same arguments about you. Familiant would say that Anna was destined to be there and he had no part in her death,'

'Rubbish,' said George as he started to pace around the garden. 'So what excuse did he have for the explosion at Chernobyl? Did he manage to explain that away as well?'

'I'm afraid so, George, because he felt he had *right* on his side.'

'So now we are all blessed by God before we go to work.'

'Now you are being sarcastic, George,' Aleksandra said. 'No, it wasn't like that. He used the same argument again. He just helped Petric achieve his destiny. Although he was rather pleased that the fallout, and I'm not sure that is the best word, was not as bad as some of the worst estimates.'

'You mean he thought it could be worse? I can't believe that.'

'That is what he told me later, George. He said he had assumed Petric would somehow try to save the Ukraine from the worst of the disaster. He'd given up on Belarus. Your reports confirmed that. He was willing to see Belarus finished so they could start again, and if the winds had been more to the east, then Russia would have taken the brunt and that would have been all right as well. In fact, the explosion and the radiation was far less than he had calculated. So all in all, Chernobyl was almost perfect and it caused him no guilt at all.'

'The man was a monster, Aleksandra.' George settled back into his chair. 'Leaving aside what he did to Anna, to me, Liliya, Alina and all the other individuals, he was willing to risk a whole country. Why didn't you stop him, Aleksandra? Why didn't you stop him?'

Aleksandra just shrugged. 'I'm sorry, George. I didn't know how to stop him.'

'So I suppose when The Wall finally came down in 1989 he was like the cat with the cream? He had won and communism was defeated, and he was the hero. I assume he was waiting for his medals.'

'Well, I suppose he was, but you must remember by then I hardly saw him. I was appalled by what had happened and I was ashamed of my part in it, but I heard that when The Wall came down – and you have to remember it all happened very quickly – that basically he broke. I suppose he'd spent all that time wanting something so badly that when he got it, the purpose of his life was "taken away". I heard from Miss Shaw that he didn't come into the office for days on end, or he was late, and he neglected all his other cases. He retired two years later, and two years after that he was dead.'

'How did he die?' George asked.

'He just died, George. Miss Shaw said he no longer had a purpose to live.'

'And did he take Lord Ridley with him?' George asked. 'He was probably worse. At least Familiant had some moral resolve about communism, but Ridley was just interested in money and the bank. He had no morals.'

'You are so right, George. I never really liked him much. After Anna's death I never saw him, and I have no regrets about that. I don't know what happened to him but the bank goes on successfully to this day.'

'I suppose that I should close the loop totally,' said George. There was one more person I never understood, George mused, and wanted to know more.

'Jane upset me, Aleksandra. I thought she loved me. Well, maybe not *loved* but liked me a lot, and to find out now that she did it all for money… I have to believe what you say but… I don't want to. Why are you bringing me all this bad news? Is there no end to it?'

'Maybe I told the story too quickly, George. Jane wasn't all that I have said.' George turned to listen to Aleksandra.

'How?' he said. 'What haven't you told me?'

'She was paid to be friends with you, but nothing more. She was asked to sleep with you but she refused. She said no amount of money would make her do that.'

'But we did sleep together.'

'That really was Jane you slept with and she did like you. She liked you a lot and maybe even loved you. She decided to write to you and tell you everything she knew about Familiant, Ridley, and me, and her. In fact, she did write to you but you never got the letter.'

'What do you mean I never got the letter?' George asked.

'All her letters were sent to you via Coss and Coss opened them. Lord Ridley and Familiant decided that that one was not to be sent.'

The look of disbelief was etched on George's face. Aleksandra wondered if that revelation had been too much for him. George pulled himself together. 'So why was Jane still there when I came back? Surely they would have fired her?'

Aleksandra continued. 'They would have fired her and they would have had her for breach of confidences and all those sorts of things in her contract, but actually she was good at her job. So they took her to one side and said they'd developed some evidence that she'd stolen from the bank, fabricated of course, and unless she did as they said – with regard to you – they would make the evidence available to the police. To reinforce their message they paid her again every time you were in the office, and each time she took the money, the bigger the charges would be against her. She had no way out.'

It was getting dark and they had been talking all day. Both were tired and George was almost totally wiped out. He hadn't had time to take in what all this meant, being bombarded with information faster than he could process it. He wasn't sure if he could absorb it all.

'You'd better tell me everything, Aleksandra. Is there anything else? Please don't hold back on me now,' George said.

Aleksandra was just as tired as George, but she pulled together her last reserves of energy and continued.

'There is one more thing. Vera and Coss.'

'What about them?' George asked, his mind flashing back to his first meeting with Nikolay the Cossack.

'They are my brother and sister.'

'What?' exclaimed George. 'What was even the point of keeping that from me?!'

'I didn't keep it from you, George. I didn't know either. When my mother had to leave Belarus, Vera was still a baby and the journey was going to be hazardous, cold and dangerous. There was a real possibility that she – or we – would not survive, or that we would be caught before we crossed even a single border. Nikolay – Coss – just happened to be away in the Ukraine with our aunt in Kiev when it all got chaotic. I remember my mother screaming and pulling at her hair as she paced around the house. She didn't know what to do. It was an impossible situation. If we stayed, then we could all be killed when they realised that my father had crossed sides. If we left, it would be without Vera and Nikolay, as Vera was too young to travel and Nikolay would never get back in time.

'We had to leave in a few hours and she had to make a decision. Really there was no choice, so she tearfully gave Vera to a friend to take to join Nikolay in the Ukraine, and we left on our journey. What was meant to be freedom became a cage of despair for all time… You know the rest. They took my aunt's name of Safarova and lived in Kiev.'

'Hold on. Hold on a minute…' George whispered then cleared his throat. 'So Timofei and Kristina are your nephew and niece?' He looked at her with sadness and compassion.

'So, how did you find them? When did you know?' George found this almost incompressible.

'I first met Vera in 1971 but I didn't find out she was my sister – or Coss was my brother – until Familiant told me when I came back from Kiev. They couldn't tell me. He had known all along, of course, and then one day he thought that telling me would make everything better. It didn't, of course, but with Coss as your contact and Vera as your guide here in Kiev, I knew they would have your interest at heart. Now that *did* made me feel better. It made us *all* family. George, I really was looking out for you. You may not see that now, but I was.'

George looked at her and measured his sadness against Aleksandra's. They both had reason to grieve for lost lives.

'My God, this is all such a mess,' he whispered. 'And where are you now in your life, Aleksandra?'

'As the project wound down in the early nineties,' Aleksandra said, 'I had to decide what I would do. I got a number of offers from industry and from Government but I knew I was never going to be able to cope with them. I missed Anna. And you. I resented Familiant for what he had done and also for dying. I needed him to be there to shout at. So in the end I stayed at Oxford and accepted their offer of a fellowship and then a professorship. I have some sort of tenure, so there I now sit supervising some students, writing and occasionally lecturing, but I tell you, George, life has never been the same since the end of the project.'

Her face brightened up and she took a deep breath before continuing. 'Except my biggest joy is that Vera, Coss and myself are a real family again! We can travel, we can see each other and, of course, we have the internet. I re-live over and over the decision my mother made, and over the years I have seen the pain she must have suffered. Her children are together now and that makes her sacrifice worthwhile.'

They decided to turn in for the night, exhausted; wanting to be alone with their thoughts and feelings.

George had a restless night and was still confused when he met Aleksandra for breakfast the next day.

'A lot has changed since we first met, George,' she said, sipping at her lemon squash. 'Chernobyl changed everything. Yet nothing. It depends on how you look at history. Gorbachev would probably have done much the same anyway. A Polish Pope. The Wall has gone in Berlin, and Petric is not here to see his free and independent Ukraine. A lot has changed… Tell me what happened to you after that day? Can you do that, George, or is it still too raw even twenty years on?' Aleksandra asked.

'We were in Odessa with Alina's mother, who turned out not to be as unwell as we thought, just a small cold. We didn't complain as it's really pleasant down there and we ate and drank a little. Nothing was said in the news about the explosion for a couple of days. Then there was just a brief announcement on the news. It didn't seem too serious. Alina tried to phone Petric but there was no answer, but we weren't worried because we assumed he was just sorting out the mess. We got back to Alina and Petric's house a couple of days later, and within a few minutes Andriy, one of Petric's colleagues, and another member of the Brotherhood, came to the door. Andiry was shaken and as white as a sheet. He didn't know what to say and just looked at us. When he did manage to say what had happened, it all just splurted out in a rush. A jumble of words.

'We didn't know what to do or what to say. We were all speechless." George gulped and rubbed his clasped hands against his chin. 'Then Alina started screaming and then Liliya stated screaming. I didn't know what to do. I wanted to hold Liliya but she wanted to hold Alina and I was left just watching them with no one to comfort. And no one to comfort me.'

He paused again, and Aleksandra waited for him to go on.

'There wasn't a body to bury so there was no funeral. There was only a memorial service. It wasn't enough.' He shook his head from side to side. 'None of us –especially Liliya – ever really got any *closure*, but the worst was still to come. We assumed it was an accident and we had visions of Petric struggling and fighting to limit it. Even stop it, but then there was the accident investigation and we started to piece together the parts of the jigsaw. Then it dawned on us what really happened.

'I'm not sure what was worse – his death or knowing he'd caused it. We had to live with the disaster, death and destruction and take it personally; as if we'd done it ourselves, and, of course, Petric was never a hero of the Brotherhood, but we were so glad he was not vilified. The bureaucracy decided that admitting their systems were that flawed – that one person could cause such a monumental disaster – was even worse for public relations.'

George looked as though he were reliving every moment of the trauma and his speech had slowed to a snail's pace, but Aleksandra could see he needed to talk more. Maybe he had never said this to anyone before. He needed to cleanse his soul, she thought, so she pressed on.

'And do you still see Liliya?' she asked.

'We stayed together for another twelve years. Each day – from the moment we heard what had happened to Petric – we drifted further apart. We'd talked about children, but that was *before*. We never talked about them again. At first she was grieving for her father. Then she started blaming me for putting all those thoughts in his head. Then I started to believe I *had* killed him – and all those people, and from that point on, there was no way back. We divorced. We had nothing more to say to each other.'

Aleksandra filled his glass with more lemon squash. He drank it down in one and wiped his mouth with the back of his hand.

'I still see her occasionally. We're still friends of sort. We've never hated each other. I try and make sure she's well provided for. She felt the need to blame someone so she blamed me. That's all there is to it. She said I'd put thoughts into his head. I didn't, though. They were always there. I sometimes think I was an outlet for some of them. But, Aleksandra, please tell me… do you really believe all these things you have told me are true?'

'Yes, George. I think we have the whole picture now.'

'That means I have achieved nothing,' George said. 'I have been a puppet at the end of Familiant's strings. You do realise that, don't you, Aleksandra? Anything I have achieved was due to someone else. He killed Anna and he had me kill Petric. Am I responsible for all the deaths at Chernobyl?'

His head dropped into his hands, and he hunched over, elbows on his thighs. He was crying. Again. He cried when he'd heard of Anna's death. He cried when he'd heard of Petric's death. He cried when Liliya left him, but he'd overcome all of those. He was not sure he could see his way past this.

'Aleksandra,' he sighed, visibly pulling himself together, 'do you know what it was like at Chernobyl? In the Ukraine we were lucky. If you can call it lucky. Even in Odessa we might not have been safe if the winds had blown a different way. It was a hundred times bigger than Hiroshima and Nagasaki. Most of the radioactivity went north, into Belarus, and as far away as Norway. That slow death went right over Vera's – your sister's – head where Timofei and Kristina were playing in the streets, and they were just two of the three million children living in the contaminated areas. Not to mention all those soldiers and fire-fighters who are still dying young.

'So what will Timofei and Kristina think when they come to have children? Will their children be born deformed? What legacy have we left them? And all for the *greater good*? And Familiant's argument was that it would free the people of Belarus. Do you know their economy was ruined by Chernobyl? Their land is worthless for agriculture. The economic damage is measured in multiples of years' worth of production. Familiant delayed their freedom and left them in the hands of that dictator Alexander Lukashenko.'

The anger was beginning to show in his voice.

'Do you know, nearly half a million Belarusians were forced to leave their homes and move, and over two thousand villages and towns were razed to the ground? Is that the kind of progress he wanted? He was mad, Aleksandra! I tell you, the man thought he was an old-time crusader to the Holy Lands, a bringer of enlightenment.'

There was not much Aleksandra could say. She agreed with him, but she felt anything she could say would only make things worse. She decided to leave him alone and let him consider what she had said. She stood up from the table. She also wanted to be alone with her own thoughts.

'I will go to bed now, George. I need to go shopping in the morning, but we will talk more. Come and meet me and we can go to that café in the square? I have a real surprise for you, George. One you will like. You need some happiness. Shall we say mid-morning? Around eleven?'

'That would be nice,' he said without emotion. He didn't get up to see Aleksandra back indoors.

The warm summer evening had turned dark and chilly. George hadn't noticed just how chilly it had become as he sat in the garden. He went back to the house only to get a vodka – a trip he was to make several times that night. He was caught in deep, deep thought. He was still young, he thought. He could still do a thousand new things, but their success would be measured by his past achievements, and all those past achievements had been wiped clean away. They were nothing to do with him. Did that mean his life was now worthless? He couldn't take any credit for any achievement or any success. Every door had been opened for him even before he had begun to push at them.

When eventually he went to bed, sleep didn't come easily. He was still tired and his eyes bloodshot when he woke. They met as planned in the café.

Aleksandra said, 'Wait here, George darling. I just need to pop down to the shop next door.'

He ordered his favourite combination of coffee and a croissant and picked up a newspaper to start reading, but really he was in no mood to read or talk as he worked through parts of the conversations of the last two days. He saw Aleksandra come back.

She was talking to a young woman. Maybe in her late twenties, he thought. She had long brown hair and a pretty face which was slavonicly square and strong, with deep-coloured eyes. She was dressed in jeans and a white baggy shirt with no collar – probably her husband's or boyfriend's – which reminded him yet again how immaculately Aleksandra dressed. They both came to George's table.

'I want you to meet someone, George.' She looked at him. 'Do you recognise her?'

George looked at the younger woman. He was embarrassed. Clearly he was supposed to know her. Failure to do so was rude; to guess and get it wrong a bigger insult.

'I am sorry,' he said. 'I have had quite a busy few days and my mind is a little confused. Do we know each other?'

The women smiled at each other.

Aleksandra said, 'George, I would like you to meet Kristina Safarova.'

George looked hard at her. He could start to see Vera in her features.

'My God, then you must be Aleksandra's niece?' he said. 'The last time I saw you, well, you were a baby, and as I remember, your mother said you were a wilful little thing. Has that changed?'

She didn't reply. With something between a stammer and a stutter George managed to ask the obvious sociable questions and they chatted politely over their coffees.

'I came here two years ago,' Kristina answered. 'I'm a journalist at the *Fakty i Kommentarii*—'

'That's a scurrilous newspaper if ever I read one,' George interrupted.

Kristina smiled. 'And then Aleksandra told me you were here and I said I wanted to meet you, and here we are. My mother has told me so much about you.'

The three of them chatted about life in Kiev and how different it was from Slonim, but George stuck to the mundane. With all that he had heard from Aleksandra over the past two days, he couldn't face learning more about Vera and her life. He could get that news from Aleksandra anytime, and right now, he didn't need other things cluttering up his life. He had too much else to think about.

'I have to go,' he said. 'Aleksandra, are you coming back later?'

A waitress brought the bill and George paid. As he stood, so did Kristina.

'I must get back to the office as well. I have a story to finish,' she said.

The three of them walked to the door together.

'I go this way,' said George.

'And I go the other,' Kristina said.

They kissed on the cheek and turned to walk, and as they did Kristina ran her hand down George's back. It was fast, but seemed to ripple and catch every vertebra along the way. George felt a shiver. He turned but she was gone, walking off into the distance.

'Are you okay, George?' Aleksandra was looking at him concerned. 'You look as though you have just seen a ghost.'

'No, I have just felt one,' he said.

Aleksandra stayed for a whole week and every day they talked, going over details and history. Aleksandra had had years to reconcile herself and was now supporting George, forever reassuring him that he was no lesser a person because of the information he now had. She was worried for him because of the personal responsibility he was taking for Petric's actions. She had hoped that his new perspective would reduce his sense of guilt, but it had done the opposite. It took George a while to realise that in his anger he had failed to understand that Aleksandra was just as upset. Under her stoical mask she felt complicit and just as responsible for every action and every death.

It was their last night together and still George could not absorb the enormity of all he had heard.

'I *could* have stopped him,' she said over dinner.

'And maybe I should have realised that life could never be so simple and straightforward,' said George. 'If it hadn't been you and me, Aleksandra, he would have found others. You know, I'm sure he must have been running other projects. I can't believe that my paltry and trifling activities kept him busy all the time.'

It was true, but a cold comfort to both of them. The debate and conversation continued unabated as they sat together.

'Whatever Familiant did,' said George, 'it was me who lived every day of my life – not Familiant. It was me who fell in love, first with Anna, and then with Liliya – not Familiant. Imagine if Coss had taken me on a blind date and introduced me to Liliya and we had fallen in love, would I now be blaming Coss for all my troubles? Of course I wouldn't, but it isn't that simple, is it, Aleksandra? All along the way I was brainwashed. I was led down each path like that proverbial lamb to slaughter. I might have made decisions, but they were always in reaction to a situation Familiant had engineered.'

Aleksandra just listened and George carried on trying to reconcile and come to terms with 'his' life.

'Maybe about a year before Petric died, I was talking to him. He was a religious man in a communist country. He said that his God led him each and every day and he was working to God's will. He said God was leading him and that his destiny was determined and led by God. If I believed in his religion maybe I was no different, and all I was doing was following a path that was as predetermined as Petric's, but surely no God would have time to look over each and every one of the billions of his flock and guide each hand and each action? We must have some free will in all we do. There must be room for free will, even in a predetermined and predestined world?'

'There are too many thoughts, George,' Aleksandra said. 'You are still confused. In time it will become clearer and you will be reconciled. I promise you that.'

Aleksandra left to go to bed and George shouted after her, 'I do hope you are right because right now I have no idea what I feel.'

The thoughts continued bouncing around and reaching nowhere. At times he felt closer to resolution, but eventually tiredness, alcohol and the cold drove him indoors and to sleep.

George drove Aleksandra back to the airport the next morning.

'So what did you make of Kristina? Was it a nice surprise to see her again?' she asked.

George glanced at Aleksandra. He had been asking himself that same question. 'At first I thought she was more plain than pretty, but I liked the way she dresses,' he said.

Aleksandra stopped his words with a wave of her hand in the air. 'Typical man. You see the body before the mind. But don't go there, George. Please, I beg you. It will not end well.'

'Typical woman,' said George. 'You assume because I describe how she looks all I'm thinking about is sex. You know our clothes and our face describe our personality. They are our projection of ourselves. I was describing her to describe the person. Analysis 101, Aleksandra.' George grinned. Aleksandra gave George that 'I'll buy that this time but don't try it again' look.

George continued. 'She is a free spirit but still learning how to exercise that spirit. She is still *wilful*. I can see that. I liked her. I was thinking that I would like to meet her again. She can fill in the last part of the story for me. She can tell me about Vera and her life. It is important.'

'You must take care, George,' Aleksandra said. 'The things we have talked about over the last week need very careful thought and consideration. You know I will always be here for you, to listen to you, and please, George, be careful with how you approach my niece. Keep it simple and just talk and nothing more. It will not end well.'

George nodded. 'It goes both ways, Aleksandra. It's not easy for you either. We can be a small self-help group, and I *will* only chat with Kristina. After all, she is young enough to be my daughter.'

They waved goodbye as she showed her passport on departure.

The days of deep introspection didn't finish after Aleksandra was gone. George either ambled through Kiev or sat in his garden. He felt very lost and didn't really know who he was anymore – and he was beginning to doubt he ever did. Despite the trauma of

Chernobyl and Petric, he had, for the past few years, retained his self-esteem. Before this last month, he'd had a clear perception of what he'd done and what he'd achieved; the accounts showed a very positive and healthy balance in his favour. But suddenly, he thought, *all* the positives, *all* the assets had been removed, and who was Jane? Was she really available by night to the highest bidder? He *had* left Anna for her. At times it was difficult not to cry. At times it was hard to find the energy to cry.

Was everyone so easily bought with money or a fast route to satisfy their own personal ambitions? What about Vera, he thought? Surely she was his friend? That led him back to Kristina. He had promised to keep the contact social but that was easy; she would have no interest in him, whatever his own feelings. Now he had no feelings. He was numb, and she was young and she was free and she could fill in some of the gaps in his past.

Whatever his, or her, motives, he thought, George Cove could take a positive step forward in his own life. Now at least he knew that he was making a decision. There was no Familiant pushing him one way or the other. He could face the wind or blow with it. There was a rush of exhilaration at the thought of being free of all their pernicious influences. He would ask her to dinner.

He phoned the offices of the newspaper *Fakty i Kommentarii*. A voice answered.

'Kristina Safarova, please,' George said.

'*Privet.* Kristina. Who is this?' George was unprepared for such a quick reply. He had assumed he would have time to compose a question or even an answer. Here he was, a successful businessman being confused and flummoxed by a twenty-eight-year-old woman who he actually knew. He was nervous of her because he wanted to impress her. He noted his reaction.

'*Privet.* This is George. George Cove.' Just in case she had lots of Georges phoning her, he thought. 'How are you?'

'George, how wonderful that you phoned. I hoped you would,' she said.

'I was wondering if you'd like dinner tonight. I could pick you up at the office at, say, six?' He held his breath.

'No,' she said. Deflation. 'Meet me at Buddha Bar at nine-thirty.' Elation. 'Do you know where it is?'

'No,' George had to reply.

'It's okay,' Kristina said. 'It's on Kreschatik Street near the Khrechatik Hotel. You do know where that is, don't you?'

'That I do. I'll see you there at nine-thirty.'

'Bye' and she was gone.

George held the phone and looked at it, startled by the speed of the conversation. Her directness and openness had stirred an emotion so opposite from all the intrigue and plotting filling his mind. It put all he had done into a stark, and he thought somewhat sad, reality.

The Buddha Bar was, he presumed, as busy as if it had been a weekend, but it was Wednesday. He was pleased he had booked a table for dinner. He sat at the long bar on the high, red leather-backed seats, an untouched vodka shot on the bar in front of him. Around him were couples or groups of men. There were some single girls, each of whom's ambition presumably was to be with one of those men when she left. George wondered what the standard rate was nowadays, and then criticised himself for his presumption of every woman's intent.

The dress code was not jeans and George thought he had chosen wisely. A light-coloured suit and an open-necked white shirt. He thought he blended into the scene just right. Then, with reflection, he remembered a book he had read maybe some twenty-five years earlier about self-perception. Everyone has a different perspective on each event, depending on whether they are a player or an observer and these are all different depending on our preconceptions and prejudices. When we felt good we see ourselves as stronger and more elegant. I feel good, he decided, because I am meeting a younger and attractive woman. Maybe this is what the Chinese mean when they say that every old man needs a young mistress to keep his Yin strong? It builds the energy and keeps the man mentally virile.

But will Kristina see the same? Will she see an old man – a man like her uncle or father – or will she see a friend or maybe even a lover? All those others sitting in the bar looking at me now, what do they see? A lonely old man who is here to drink and just look hopefully and longingly at the girls. Or when Kristina arrives, will other people around them see a sugar daddy tempting a beautiful young woman with promises of untold riches in exchange for a night or two in his bed?

Given our perspective, we see each event as different. What if, he thought, all of this is an illusion? Just like the rest of my life. My role in everything I have done is all about perceptions. It depends on your perspective whether you judge me as good or evil, leader or led.

An instant of panic ensued, and George was not used to moments of panic. What if I don't recognise Kristina? After all, I've only seen her in jeans and a baggy shirt.

'This is what it is going to be like from now on,' he said in *sotto voce*. The couple next to him turned and stared at him – a man talking to himself. When I didn't know I had a safety net I could do anything, he thought. Now I know it's been removed and I can't do anything. He felt vulnerable and alone and, if he was honest, a little bit scared.

He turned to the bar to reach for his drink. He felt a hand run down his spine and he knew she had arrived. If ever there was a more welcome greeting he had not discovered it.

'*Privet*, George,' she said, and George stood to offer her the stool next to his.

'Hello. You look…' He stepped back to look at Kristina. 'You look beautiful.'

The jeans and baggy shirt had been replaced with a short beautifully cut black and white Mary Quant-style 1960s dress. She must have had heels on as she was now only just shorter than him. Her long hair, once loose, had been pulled back tight into a ponytail, showing both the strength and vulnerability in her face. Her make-up was minimal.

'You know,' George said, making sure she was seated, 'sometimes men have to lie when they meet a woman like this.'

'How is that?' She was smiling.

'Well,' said George, 'we have to say every woman is beautiful when we meet them, and sometimes we have to lie because, to be honest, they are not, but I can say honestly that tonight I told the truth. No fingers or toes crossed. You look beautiful. In fact, as I have been here for fifteen minutes already, I have seen every woman here and I would go as far as to say that there isn't one more beautiful.'

George was suddenly worried that he had gone too far and he didn't know why he had flirted with her. He thought momentarily of his promise to both Aleksandra and himself, but Kristina had stirred an emotion that at that moment freed him. He was stunned by the way Kristina looked and he had told the truth, but maybe that truth was a bit too much. After all, this wasn't a date. This was Kristina who he had known as a baby, but if she thought he had gone too far she didn't show it.

'I have booked a table. Do you want a drink there?' Kristina nodded.

Over a bottle of white wine and a sushi selection they talked about her job and life in Kiev. She asked what she had been like as a baby. George thought that was to remind him of his age and the relationship they had. She told him she didn't have a boyfriend and she wasn't married, and she also flirted with him. But the most that George remembered was that she touched his arm when she talked and she was passionate about everything. The contrast between who he was and what she was, was harsh, he thought.

She brought back memories of both Anna and Liliya. He loved each and they were the right women in his life at the right times, but his love for them had now been tainted by the memory of Familiant. He looked across at Kristina. Maybe it was time to find a pure love, he thought, a love where he was making the decisions for once. He looked again at Kristina. The dinner went too quickly and soon it was over.

'I have enjoyed this evening more than you can imagine,' George said. 'Can we meet again?'

'I would really like that as well,' she smiled.

I could get used to seeing that smile every day, George thought. 'When?' he asked.

'I will call you,' she said.

George had started the process of reconciliation and he decided it was going to be a long path back to being someone of his own – himself. The news of his past, he knew, had left him dreadfully vulnerable and now he felt incomplete.

He had lived a life of deceit and lies. In his business life, he was not immune from that behaviour, but he had been lied to and deceived on a scale and intensity no one could ever possibly comprehend. To be himself he needed to change and transform. But could he renovate and re-form his life totally to restore and make amends for his sins? The sense of guilt was overpowering and the words 'sins' and 'atonement' dominated all his thoughts.

He needed to be open and honest. Not just to himself but to everyone else as well. Can leopards change their spots? he thought. He didn't know, but he had to find out. If he didn't change he would never cope again. He might muddle through life but there would always be so many unanswered questions. Prime among these, he decided, after sorting and rationalising everything was: could he survive and be a whole person without his nanny, Familiant, looking after him? He needed to know.

In this period of deep retrospection, any thoughts of Kristina had slipped his mind. He hoped she had enjoyed dinner with him and he expected her to phone the next day. She didn't and he supposed that dinner was a passing moment of amusement for her. His ego was deflated but, with everything else on his mind, this was a minor blip. So when, a week later, she phoned, he was both surprised and happy. At last something to look forward to.

'I'm coming round for supper on Saturday,' she had said without enquiring whether George was free or even wanted her there.

'As you say, Saturday will be fine,' George replied, but the phone was already dead.

He was ready at seven, not knowing when or if she would arrive. He was already half convinced that she would forget and not arrive, a feeling reinforced through a modicum of ambivalence as he was very unsure of his feelings. At least he felt that this was the diversion he needed to give himself space from all the thinking. It was a new perspective on his life. He couldn't totally dissociate himself from his past – it would always be part of his life – but at least through Kristina he could find out more about what had happened, and each time he thought of her he felt that hand run down his back. Did she do that deliberately or was it just a reflex she had learnt somewhere?

He heard a car arrive around eight. He looked out to see a taxi and Kristina getting out. He opened the door. Her hair was again loose and she was wearing a simple short skirt.

'Come in and make yourself at home. Want a drink?' he asked. She took the red wine offered and they sat on the sofa and talked about the week.

'Excuse me. I need to finish making supper. Make yourself at home.' George went to the kitchen to finish the risotto. Not a great cook but more than adequate, this was one of his specialities. Moist and rich and served alongside a green salad of baby spinach, it had always been one of Liliya's favourites. Now was not a time to think of her, he thought. They ate as the sun was setting and George lit candles. It was a soft light.

'Which way is the bathroom?' Kristina asked. George pointed down the hall and he started to clean away dinner. He'd finished before she returned and was listening to an iPod selection played through the home cinema speakers. The sound quality was impressive and, immersed in the music, he hadn't noticed how long she'd been gone. Suddenly he wondered if he had poisoned her.

He heard her before he saw her – the click of heels on the tiled floor. She had been wearing flat shoes, he thought. He looked up. She was standing a few feet away from him, legs apart and arms by her side. Drawn initially by the sound on the tiles, he looked at her feet. She was now wearing black shoes with very high stilettos. As his eyes moved up he saw fishnet stockings, red satin panties and a black basque which pushed her breasts up and together, exposing her nipples. Her hair was again tied back tight and she wore bright red lipstick.

He dwelt on the sight. She was an enigma and beautiful.

'Stand,' she said. He didn't want to obey but he did. She blindfolded him and pushed him against the wall. She teased him as she undid his shirt. It ripped as she pulled at it. He wanted to see her but he couldn't. To remind him he had only that single memory, as she stood in front of him, locked in his mind and printed on his retinas. She treated him roughly. She tore at his clothes and when he was naked she dragged and pushed him to the bedroom. She threw him on the bed and sat astride him until both were satisfied.

He felt her stand but heard no sound of the stilettos. He took off the blindfold and saw her naked back as she headed into the bathroom. Not a word had been spoken.

'Do you have a spare toothbrush?' she shouted. 'Don't worry. I've found one.'

She returned to bed and fell asleep in his arms.

Kristina spent more time at George's, often the whole weekend. Nothing quite as dramatic as their first experience happened again, although she occasionally dressed up and took a dominant role in their lovemaking. After two months, George noticed she was now more often at his house than her flat. A month later she moved everything into his house.

'How did that happen?' he asked her. 'I never saw you move in and now you are here.' She just smiled at him. They had developed an order and routine that suited them both. Through Kristina, George had started to find himself and better understand who he really was. Everything in their lives revolved around each other and they had become almost inseparable. Simple chores had become pleasurable and George was again growing as a person. The doubts and fears generated through Aleksandra's visit were present but diminished as he fought his demons. His demons were all in his past and not the present, and Aleksandra's words of caution were far from his thoughts.

He tried to explain to Kristina what was happening, but for that she had to understand his past and George had found neither the words nor the courage for that conversation. He tried many times and decided that it was his past, and not her present. He would fight the battle quietly and alone while he rebuilt all that he was: his esteem, his morals and his courage.

Then one night, unexpectedly, Kristina didn't come home from work. George was worried. He phoned the office and he phoned her flat. No answer. He sat in the half light wondering what to do. It was too early to call the police. She must be out with friends. It will be okay. To chase and hound her showed jealousy, but he was jealous that someone else, maybe another lover, had her time and attention. However, jealousy talked of owning and controlling and he didn't want to do either of those. Ownership was Familiant's way; it was the way of the past. Kristina was not his possession. The rationality of the head did nothing to ease the pain of the heart.

As he sat there. missing her, some of the darkness she had lifted returned. Why was he so happy? Why now? And why was he so troubled now she was away? She had brought freshness to his perspective of himself. She was open and honest in a way that he had never realised was possible and he had found himself responding with the same virtues. His time with Kristina was already brief but she had changed him.

'Not true,' he said out aloud. 'She has *started* to change me.'

It was two days before Kristina reappeared at George's. She walked in looking tired. Her make-up, normally so immaculate, was slightly smeared and smudged.

'You bastard,' she shouted at him. 'It wasn't meant to be like this. It was only supposed to be fun. It was about sex and friends. I was never meant to fall in love with you. It can never last. You do understand that, George, don't you? It can never last.'

George didn't understand. 'I love you,' he said as he looked straight at her. 'I love you and love will defeat everything if it is a real love. Come here, *lapushka*.'

Reluctantly she almost pulled herself across the room and they hugged and kissed.

'You bastard, I love you. But why did you make me love you so much?' Kristina whispered as they stood like intertwined statues in the middle of the room with her head on his shoulder.

George never asked where she had been during those two days. Once, he knew somewhere in his past, he would have found a way to find out, but now it didn't seem important. Not because she was back, but because trust and love didn't demand explanations. That night was a watershed that changed their relationship forever. They had moved from lovers to friends and soon best friends.

George at last had found a freedom from his past and enjoyed making his own decisions. It was exhilarating. He often wondered what it would have been like if Aleksandra had never told him their story. Would he have died happy with his contribution to the world, or weighed down with guilt over the deaths at Chernobyl? Would he have ever realised his part in what Petric had done?

They were sitting on the sofa, reading, when George turned to her and said, 'I am trying to change. You do understand that, don't you?'

He had finally found the voice to talk with Kristina about his past.

'I'm not worried about what you were, but only what you are now,' she replied as she leant back onto him to be more comfortable, and get better light to see her book. George put an arm round her, but he put his book on his lap as he spoke.

'This is important. I am not the same person you first met and I will be a different person next year. I need you, princess, to help me through all this. I need you to guide me and be my inspiration. I don't think I could have got this far without you. Tell me you will never leave me.'

She stopped reading. '*Milie*,' she used the name she had started to call him. 'I have told you this will not last. It cannot last. I don't know when, but…' Her words faded away. George wanted to shout that it would last forever, but he felt her crying quietly in his arms and he said nothing more.

As lovers their relationship became stronger, and as friends they were inseparable. She would tease him to the point where he wanted to make love to her wherever they were. On his birthday they sat outside, almost alone, on the terrace of a quiet restaurant.

As Kristina returned from the toilet she came to him and whispered in his ear, 'These are for you, my *Milie*' and put her panties in his hand. George looked at them speechless. Then she sat opposite him, her heels on the chair and her short skirt pulled up. 'Can't you wait to get home?' she said. George was unsure whether to pay the bill quickly to get home or stay and enjoy her there.

Kristina had not learnt to drive and George took it on himself to be her teacher. She took to it easily and often they were out and George felt sufficiently confident to close his eyes and relax. He would make nonsensical stories to make her laugh and relax as they drove. He felt easy in her presence and he could see no other way but with her. He was proving to himself that even without Familiant he could manage his life successfully.

'We need each other, *lapushka*,' he said one day. 'I am your teacher. I can show you so much of life. And you are my teacher. You are showing me how to live with my life.'

She just looked at him and said nothing.

The one thing George still needed to complete his story was to know what her life had been like as she grew up in Byelorussia; he still found it hard to come to terms with its new name – Belarus. As it was so much a part of his past it was important, but Kristina seemed reluctant to talk about it. After supper one night they were sitting together when, unrequested, she started talking.

'My mother had a hard life,' she said quietly. 'We were living in army quarters, yet still Timur was often away. Either they were on manoeuvres or he was busy at work, but more often he was drinking with his friends. Sometimes I could see the fear in her eyes when she heard him come home. When she heard him in the corridor or thought he might be coming in she would send Timofei and myself off to bed and even tell us to pretend to be asleep. Timofei found it more difficult than me.

'One night when Timur came home drunk, Timofei faced up to him and told him to stay away and not hurt mother again. I don't know what made him do it. Against Timur, Timofei looked so tiny but he stood between them and faced Timur, who swatted him away with a slap around the face. Then Timur grabbed mother and pulled her into their room.

'Timofei had a black eye for days after that. But that night, Timofei and I just stood outside and heard him shout and mother scream. We didn't know what to do. There was nothing we could do. I don't think he hit Timofei again, but Timofei stayed well away from him. My mother lived her life in fear of father. He could change so quickly and he was always drinking. It wasn't a happy house.

'When I was about twelve, mother was so afraid that she took Timofei, left home, and found a flat in town. She said it was to save his life, but she left me alone. She said I had to stay as she could only manage to look after one of us. She cried. I screamed and shouted, but she left. She said one day I might understand how difficult it was for her, but I stayed in the barracks with Timur.'

George looked at Kristina. He wanted to press her further on why she had to stay but thought the better of it. He wanted to know if her father had looked after her well and how she had coped with his drinking. Did Kristina know all of her life history?

'You knew that your mother had a brother and sister?' he asked.

'Yes, I knew of Aleksandra and Coss but we had never met them. I think mother was ashamed and of course it wasn't as easy to travel then as it is now.'

'And,' asked George, 'did Vera ever tell you of the decision that her mother had to make when she and Aleksandra left for England?'

Kristina shook her head and George told her the story that he had been told just a few months earlier.

A tear rolled down Kristina's face as George told all he knew.

'Oh my God,' she said. 'Poor mother. She had to relive all that her mother went through. Oh my God.'

At that moment he felt a deep sorrow for her and held her just a little closer. He wanted to know more and wanted her to carry on talking.

'What was it like being a young girl growing up into maturity living among all those soldiers?'

'It was not easy. I was leered at by all of them when I walked home from school. They made me feel dirty with their rude words and insults, but Timur was their boss and so they knew it would not be good to upset me too much. It was much worse for other girls. Some were chased and one was caught. They never caught the soldier who raped her. It was awful.'

'Did you see your mother during this period when she left with Timofei?' George asked.

Kristina hesitated. 'No, not much' she said. 'I missed her and I thought she didn't love me. We still have problems and we don't speak too much.'

George was determined to ask all these questions while Kristina was talking. 'You would have been ten when the Chernobyl disaster happened. What was that like?'

'I was at school that day and I was walking home back to the barracks and I saw lots of trucks leaving and everyone running around. I didn't know what was happening. When I was close to the house, mother came running out to meet me and said I must get into the house straight away. She told me there had been an accident and we were not allowed to go outside. She stressed that she meant *not at all*. We weren't allowed to go to school and had to stay indoors all the time. I was too young to really understand what all the problems were. Now I realise Timofei understood more, but no one tried to explain any of it to me. The worst thing was that father had to leave and I could see how much it upset mother and how worried she was. Normally she didn't change when he went away – often she was happy to see him go – but this time she gave him a big hug and a kiss before he left and told him to come home safely.'

'And when Timur came back, was he all right?'

'I don't really know. I was too young,' Kristina said and George could see that all this was taking a lot out of her. She looked drained and her book was on the table. She poured a drink but only sipped at it. 'Maybe that was the problem between them. Maybe it was the accident?'

George shook his head. 'No, I think the problems went way back.' He thought about telling her of the day she was conceived but that would be too much pain, but he had to make a confession to her as an act of atonement.

'*Lapushka*, indirectly I was the cause of the Chernobyl accident.' George could find no other way to say it other than directly. That was what he did now.

'That's stupid,' she said. 'How could you have caused the accident?' George told her all about Petric. He didn't know what to expect, but if there was going to be any relationship between them she had to know everything from the beginning. There could be no lies and no deceit. He could see her confusion as she tried to take in and comprehend what he was saying.

'*Milie*, it wasn't you. It was two hundred years of history and fate that caused the accident. Don't ever think it was you.'

George held her and kissed her cheek and as he did, he thought that he had told another lie through omission. It wasn't fate. It was Familiant. If it was possible, he loved her even more at that moment and he wanted to know all about her.

'Did you enjoy university in Minsk? That must have been fun.'

'Yes, but I left early. I never did get a degree.'

'Why?' George asked. He was surprised. Kristina seemed such a well-focused and clear person that it seemed unthinkable she would drop out early.

'My life had been a turmoil. Living with Timur alone on the army camp. Mother coming and going. I wasn't really balanced or ready for that experience. I got the entrance exams quite easily but then I had the discipline of school to help me. When I was in Minsk I was alone and didn't have the structure. I dipped into all sorts of fringe things and I wasn't alone in that. We were a confused generation. Our very foundations of right and wrong were being ripped from underneath us. At school I was taught about Lenin and the great achievements of the USSR. I believed in what I was told. I knew of the imperialist West and their attempts to undermine the only true way forward, but with my friends we heard Western music and wanted to be like them. There was an underground of thinking that wanted a freedom. But we didn't know what that freedom was or what it meant, and then suddenly it all changed.

'It was easy for you in the West. In many ways you just won and life didn't change. For us it was monumental. The Berlin Wall came down and we could see what was happening in Germany, Russia and Poland, and even the Ukraine, but nothing was really happening in Belarus. It left us deflated; we were rebels with a cause and no way to express it. So I found my own way to express my individuality.'

'What sort of fringe things?' George asked.

'I got into fetishisms, mainly,' she said.

George tried to stay focused on Kristina and not be titillated by what he was hearing. He let her continue at her pace. He sensed that this was maybe the first time she'd talked about these things and there was a cathartic benefit. Better leave her to go at her own pace.

'Before you tell me what, can you tell me why?' he asked.

'I wasn't political and I wasn't into music but I needed to express myself to differentiate myself from the past. That's a fairly normal thing for teenagers everywhere. But really it was more important for us, George.' He noted the exasperation in her voice. 'And also,' she continued, 'my boyfriend at the time was already into these things. Well, first it was leather and motorbikes, and then it became sexual. Just part of the great exploration all teenagers go through. I lived with him and he was very dominant and explored my limits because I was submissive to him. I allowed him to tie me, beat me and whip me and all the time it satisfied a deep desire in me. I can't explain why, but it transcended anything sexual. Once to increase an orgasm, he nearly strangled me. I can still feel his hands round my neck. I was climaxing as I passed out and I think I nearly died. Sometimes I wonder if the lack of blood to my brain somehow damaged me forever. Some days I find it hard to concentrate. I suppose that being submissive came from watching mother and all she was taking, and I thought that was the right way.

'But then I felt a real anger grow inside me and I didn't want to be submissive to anyone and I switched. I wanted that control and I wanted to be in charge, and I found my true role as a dominant person. I think you need to have been submissive before you can be truly dominant. It is a big paradox, George.'

George was listening and he heard Vera's voice talking to him all those years ago about how the people were submissive to their leaders and how submission was a sign of love and trust and never to be misused. He remembered his life as a submissive to Familiant and realised demons come in all shapes for different people.

'Why a paradox?' he asked.

'Because I want to be loved and held and nurtured just like everyone else. I want to be treated as an equal in everything, yet still I find these dark thoughts from my past that require sexual submission and control. George, please help me understand and live with all these contradictions. I need a strong and wise man around me. If you can understand, we can grow together.'

George felt he could understand because they were both fighting the tyranny of their past lives and trying to reconcile their histories. He was also impressed by the ease with which she talked about areas he would find so sensitive.

Kristina continued. 'But after that experience, when I nearly died, it all became too much and I left university. For a time I went back to Slonim, but after Minsk it was too small, so I decided to come here and start my life again. The rest you know.'

George held her closely. He sensed she needed to be comforted and held. He didn't talk for a time.

'And after Chernobyl,' he said quietly, 'are you worried at all about having children? You know there are still problems – the number of child deformities has increased from the children who were affected?'

'You don't need to worry, darling,' she said. 'You are far too old to have children with me.'

George was unsure what she meant, but he didn't pursue that line.

'And how is Timofei these days? What is he doing now?'

'He's happy. He plays with computers and is engaged to a pretty girl called Olga.'

George felt the story was now complete and he knew all the pieces; he felt better. He hoped Kristina felt the same.

Two years after they began living together, Kristina was still working at the newspaper and her career was progressing quickly. She was as happy at work as she was at home. She travelled around the Ukraine and George also travelled on business. When he could, he would arrange to travel with her. Meeting her from a trip, when one or the other returned, was still special. They would cuddle and kiss and talk long into the night about who they had seen and where they had been.

It's the small, simple and silly things that often define a relationship. Kristina had gone away overnight on a story. George, alone in the house, went into the kitchen, cut a tomato into small pieces, popped them into a dish and poured in vinegar. This was a treat he had learnt from his granny that he was going to enjoy while Kristina was away. Just as he was about to eat, Kristina arrived – her story had been shelved.

'And what do you think you are doing, George?' she asked as he was spooning the tomato into his mouth. He was embarrassed and explained about his granny and her old kitchen when he had been very, very young. He knew he was practically drinking vinegar and how childish it looked.

'And what makes you think I don't do the same kind of things when you're away?' she teased him.

'You do?'

'Not with tomato, but I love the acid taste. Let me try.'

And thus another small bond had been formed, together with an agreement that nothing was ever to be taboo and no subject, wish or desire could not to be discussed.

Recently married, Olga was now pregnant with Timofei's child. George was pleased for them, but less happy at being made to tour baby shops with Kristina. She was determined that the new baby, whether a boy or a girl, should arrive in the world with nothing less than the best. George quickly learnt about prams and pushchairs, cots and bumpers. He was equipped with enough information to write a user's guide.

The pregnancy was being followed from a distance, but Kristina was determined to be the first visitor when her new niece or nephew was born. Once born, George knew it meant a quick tour of the shops to choose between blue and pink and then Kristina would be on the train. Blue was the colour and Kristina was off for two weeks.

George helped Kristina onto the train with all her luggage. They stood on the platform and George held her tight.

'You are my very, very best friend ever,' he said. 'Whatever happens, please don't ever stop being that.' He kissed her.

Kristina put her head on his shoulder and whispered in his ear. 'And whatever happens you will never be able to negotiate me out. I am your bestest friend.'

They found it hard to say goodbye but the guard's increasingly loud whistle forced her onto the train. Like a 1930's movie, George ran alongside the tracks, waving as the train left. He stood and watched the train move off into the distance.

They were so much as one, but still two individuals; the sum of the parts still larger than the whole. He stood until the train was long gone, watching part of him leave. Without her, he was diminished.

Skype, messengers and other modern technologies to communicate were no substitute for having Kristina next to him. He missed her badly and the news that she was coming home in a couple of days lifted his spirits. The traffic down to the station that afternoon was heavy, and no amount of looking at his watch could clear the jam. The train was bound to be late, so he would not be late, he rationalised.

But the train was on time, and he was late. Kristina was standing on the nearly empty platform, surrounded by luggage, waiting for him. The words of apology did not convey the frustration he felt. He was angry at himself for being late and he felt guilty for letting her down. Kristina did nothing to assuage his guilt and, after shouting at him on the platform, she said nothing at all on the journey home This was all so out of character for her. George tried again to say sorry, but Kristina would have none of it. That night, he went to bed alone while she sat up watching TV. George was asleep when she finally came to bed.

As always, time seemed to heal the wounds and life returned to a more even keel, although George felt there was still an underlying resentment and anger in Kristina. It was still there three weeks later. He asked her.

'*Lapushka*, I have said I am sorry. It wasn't my fault I was late. I am sorry. Can't we forget this?'

She did no more than shrug and say 'Whatever.'

They had never argued before but George was angry and he wanted to see this out, but Kristina wouldn't. She sat sulking, only becoming animated again when new pictures of the baby were sent to her. It was perverse, he thought. Here was the person who had taught him to be open and honest, but who was now unable to find words to express the thoughts torturing her soul. At night she would sit and say very little and she had started to drink too much. She tried to encourage George to follow her into an alcoholic oblivion but he rarely took her lead.

He had known that in love he could, and he would, give everything to her. She was his salvation; she had saved him. He would have given her not only his head and his heart, but also his body to do with as she wished. To George this was the truest and purest sign of his love. That paradox again. Russian women (even though she was Belarusian he still sometimes confused Slavic and Russian) needed strong men. To feel comfortable, therefore, she needs that strong guiding hand; but George was not that sort of leader. He led through intellect – not actions – and through her past she had adopted this persona of dominance. The conflicts must sometimes have ripped her apart. He felt she needed a sense of belonging and calm, but, then, what right did he have to say what she needed? But he knew what he needed. He now needed Kristina in a way he had never needed Anna, Jane or Liliya. He needed Kristina with him to guide him into his new life. Without her, his story would have no end.

'Why don't we also have a baby?' George said suddenly. He was unsure where the thought had come from. 'We should get married and we have a baby as well, just like Timofei and Olga.'

Kristina looked at him. Her face melted back to the calm that George had once known. He felt good again. This had been the issue. Before, Kristina had not wanted children but the arrival of her nephew had changed all her feelings. Now she wanted children and George had understood, and at that moment he also wanted them to be a *real* family. He felt happy.

'My *Milie*,' she said. 'You know I will never find a better man than you. I will never love anyone as much as you. On the train up to Minsk I sat next to a mother and father and child. Their child had abnormalities from birth; cerebral palsy, probably. They loved that child so much, but tell me is it fair to bring that child into the world? And then I saw my beautiful nephew. Healthy and bright. My darling, you are nearly thirty years older than me. I want my children to be healthy and bright like my nephew. Because of that Chernobyl thing, I am already at risk of having deformities in my children. Your age makes it more likely.'

She paused and gathered herself. Tears were rolling down her cheeks.

'I will never love anyone as much as you. You are my very, very best friend. I will never find a better friend. You are my lover, but my children need a father who will be there for them. I am sorry. I must go. I am sorry I must leave you.'

George watched her go to the bedroom and watched as she packed her clothes. There were no words he could find that would convey the loss he was suddenly feeling. There were no words that could be used to confront her arguments. She had decided. He too cried.

'I will come for my other things when you are away. I don't want to hurt you anymore,' and she left.

Within the week, she had taken all her clothes and belongings but George was left with her presence wherever he turned. The way she had organised the room – it was still her way. The crockery they bought together, he still used every day. She was with him as a ghost who haunted his every move. Day by day Kristina distanced herself from George and answered fewer of the regular telephone calls he made, but she never left his heart. George was still hoping he could win her back but with each passing day it seemed less likely. They met just once more.

George had lit candles everywhere in the room. 'I want to show you the difference between making love and sex,' he said. 'There is a difference. I didn't know that until I met you. You have shown me the way from the dark to the light.'

George stood Kristina opposite him and looked at her. Her eyes were soft and her smile comforting. He had two silk scarves and he blindfolded Kristina and put the other on himself. He reached out and placed his hands on her face. Like a blind man he ran his fingers round her face, feeling and learning every shape. She responded and did the same. He learned to see her again through touch and the sweet smell of her perfume. He felt her soft, long hair. He learnt the shape of her mouth.

As he undid the buttons on her shirt, his was falling to the floor. It was not rushed, but slow, and with their hands and lips they traversed every inch of each other's bodies. He was connecting at a primordial level with each sense, tingling at new levels. The warm summer air flushed their bodies as they knelt and then lay on the floor. With each climax, Kristina shouted out, 'I love you, *Milie.*'

George cried. 'Don't ever leave me,' he whispered.

But she did. There was no talk and Kristina dressed quickly. She was crying and she ran out of the door, and his life.

George took a bottle of vodka and sat in the garden. He remembered how he had done the same after Aleksandra's revelations. The turmoil he felt couldn't be resolved.

He knew now the feeling of true love. He had for the first time in his life made love properly with someone. Whatever he had felt for Liliya once, he now felt their love had been tainted because of Familiant – tainted because it had been *arranged* for them to meet and fall in love. This making love transcended any physical release. He had made love not just with his body but also with his soul. He had risen above earthly affairs and joined the gods for one brief passing moment.

But those same gods had taken it all away just as quickly.

When you have climbed Mount Everest, he thought, can there be any need to climb another mountain? When you have given your soul in love, how can you ever give it again?

The root of his failure was his own. He could have convinced Petric all those years ago to take a different course.

He could have changed the course of history … and where would he be now? Happy with Liliya probably.

But would he change all that for those wonderful, exciting, fulfilling, life-changing two years with Kristina?

He didn't know.

'I don't fucking know!' he shouted to the dark night-filled air. 'I don't fucking well know.'

PART IV

2008

FINALE

CHAPTER XXVIII

2008

Autumn turned to winter and Christmas was a blur of unfulfilled anniversaries and memories. Coss phoned George and suggested he came to England for a holiday, but he turned that down with a series of lame excuses. By then, he was turning down all invitations and was almost totally a recluse.

George spent his days asleep because he could not sleep at night. The darkness of the bedroom reminded him of his failures. He could not see success or hope in anything he had done. He had been led through his life as a puppet is led by the puppeteer. He was complicit in Anna's death and complicit in Petric's death, and the injury and heartbreak of many millions more at Chernobyl. And why? So that a man he had met once believed that a single person could destroy Communism and change the world. It would all have happened anyway, he thought. Lech Wałęsa would still have become President of Poland, but he might not have named a child Anna. Gorbachev would still have implemented Perestroika and the Berlin Wall would still have been demolished in 1989.

When he had cut the strings from his puppeteer he had done no better on his own. Familiant would have found a way to keep him and Kristina together. Familiant would have seen all was right.

In that moment, George saw the futility in life itself. We all believe we have a purpose, a cause and a rationale, but at its root there is no *reason*. We are here to survive and nothing more. Our right to happiness and satisfaction is a selfish right.

If anyone demands the right to be happy, he thought, it will be at someone else's expense.

George would pace round the room, invariably with a strong drink in his hand. He would talk to himself and even shout out – at no one.

'Familiant decided he wanted to rid the world of Communism and he used people any way he wanted, and George Cove went along with it because it suited what he wanted. And I wanted Jane, so I hurt Anna.'

It was dark again and the thoughts tumbled out like a broken jigsaw he couldn't put together. Kristina wanted children and the drive of her genes was stronger than her love. The primitive need to find the most suitable mate had been stronger. She had used George no differently than Familiant had, to reach out and take what she wanted. What was that book by Dawkins? *The Selfish Gene*, yes, that was it. And in that moment George saw a universal truth: happiness was a reward for his, for Anna's and for Kristina's selfish gene. Everyone had their own Familiant. He had needed Kristina to show him that, and with that thought, George passed out, the empty bottle falling noisily to the floor.

Coss had finally despaired of George and simply got on a plane to Kiev to confront his old friend. Just as he had for the wedding, he arrived unannounced with the same rucksack over his shoulder. Age had not affected Coss's enthusiasm and energy, nor his joy for life and living. He was an ageing hippy. George was far from happy to see him because he still needed to be alone, but Coss ridiculed that.

'What you need are your friends around you. You know we are not just for the good times and parties but for the bad times as well,' he said, as he hunted the house for a drink. 'Talk to me, old friend. I won't know all the answers. You have those in that shut-down head of yours, but you need to speak them. You need to get these things out in the open.'

George felt he knew better but Coss's exuberance won him round, first to one drink and then another, then George told Coss all his deepest fears and how he had been completely disorientated by everything Aleksandra had told him.

Even after clearing his mind, George still refused to go out and leave the house. He was sitting on the sofa as Coss brought more drinks in.

'And when I try to change to become something better and more worthwhile,' he said, 'to be honest and truthful to myself and the world, I lose the one person who was my salvation. She has left me and I really don't know why. I am a work in progress, Coss, and everything was stripped down to the components. I was relying on her to be there as I rebuilt myself.'

'Women,' Coss said. 'Haven't you learnt yet *never* to rely on them?'

George didn't take that bait. 'This isn't about women,' he said. 'This is about me and my failings. I have not lived a good life, and when I try to change, it is no better.'

Coss had stopped listening carefully to every word George said, as he had all the same arguments. Maybe Coss hoped it was just the drink and he would wake in the morning to find George jumping with the spring lambs. But he doubted it, and he was right. George's mood didn't improve much over the rest of the week that Coss was with him. If there was a light and a dark, then the world was still pitch black for George.

'I have to get back to London,' Coss said. 'But answer your bloody phone when I ring and we can always talk.'

When Coss left, George was sad to see him go. Although he didn't want him or anyone else around, he appreciated having someone close by him to listen and absorb his darker moments. Through those conversations with Coss, George finally reconciled himself to being without Kristina; but even with acceptance, he did not find any peace with himself. He still occasionally heard from Kristina in emails and the contact kept him level, with a modicum of composure, but darkness had come over his life and his days were spent trying to absorb and understand.

He didn't need a lover now, but when he needed Kristina most – as a friend, a real friend – she was gone. It was her birthday soon and George decided that at least he should send the person he still saw as his best friend some flowers. He arranged for them to be sent to her flat. The florist called at eight that night.

'I'm sorry, sir, but there is no one called Kristina Safarova living at that address.'

He checked the florist had the right address. Yes, it was the one that George had given her. George stared at the phone as it cut off.

The devastation was complete; his tiredness absolute. His despair was embracing and his brain numb. For a reason he didn't know, he cleaned the house. He washed the dishes and vacuumed the carpets and polished the surfaces. He did things he hadn't done for months. He had this deep, almost primeval need for everything around him to be clean and in order. He straightened the books on their shelves. Maybe, he thought, a shower would wake him from the nightmare.

'She has gone. She has moved. I don't know where she is!' He shouted out loud to the wall. 'Where are you, *lapushka*?'

There was an inevitability, as if each action was being remotely choreographed by an unseen hand. This time it wasn't Familiant. George even chuckled as he had that thought. Maybe Familiant was sitting up there still driving all this and he wanted to see the final act so he could close his book. Showered and dry, George took a clean shirt and dressed in his suit. He wore his college tie. A good link with the past, he thought. As he went through to the lounge he collected a sheet of writing paper and his pen and placed them on his desk with a bottle of vodka and a box of tablets.

A single letter for Coss, Aleksandra and Kristina, he thought. He started to write.

I am sorry but this life has become too much for me. Wherever I look I see no purpose in fighting for life anymore. Anything that was important to me has gone and now I am sorry, Kristina, I have ruined one more life – yours. All I ever wanted was to do good. But now even the fates have turned against me. It is not worth it anymore. The loneliness, the pain of failure for all my sins has driven me to this point. It is not worth it anymore. I go out and see couples hand in hand in love and people laughing and smiling, knowing that will never be me again. It is too much for me. I need to atone for all my sins. In different ways I love you all so very much.

He folded the sheet and placed it an envelope, wrote all three of their names on the front and propped it against a vase on his desk. He looked at the vodka and pills. And George thought about himself.

In Ukrainian, the word *proschannia* is used, often at a wedding, to describe forgiving someone of their offenses as well as bidding them farewell. Then the family members repeat '*Bih sviatyi*', may Holy God forgive and bless you – just the way it had been done at his and Liliya's wedding. The couple then bows to their parents and kisses their faces, hands, and feet. This blessing is performed three times. This ritual symbolizes forgiveness for any sins. George was thinking about his union with God.

How George didn't manage to kill himself he didn't know. He had drunk enough to lose reason but reason prevailed and the overriding argument had been the new and extra pain he would cause if he was successful. He had caused enough pain in his life and now was not the time to add to the burden. He would carry the burden for all of them by staying alive. He would find other ways for atonement.

He woke on the sofa, still dressed in his suit. It was around midday but time now had no meaning to him. His head ached from drink and dehydration, but getting up to drink water would only remove the pain and he needed the pain. He was meant to suffer and feel for his sins.

He spent the next few days in a half world of sleep, or crying, with sudden bursts of energy to undertake trivial and meaningless tasks. But to him the trivia was important. He spent hours reading the great philosophers on the justification of suicide – or the basis of a promise. He had promised Kristina that he would be faithful to her forever. He hadn't been under duress when she asked him the question. He remembered the moment. They had been in bed, lying in each other's arms. She had said to him, 'Will you love me forever?' His answer had been immediate and from the heart. 'To my dying day.' He had asked her the same question. 'And will you love me forever?' 'Forever,' she had said.

This wasn't a promise driven and engineered by Familiant. This was a promise he had made by himself and of his own free will. The promise was unconditional. It didn't depend on anything else. He hadn't said he would love her forever while she remained young and beautiful or until she started chewing her nails or even until she stopped loving him. How could he now break that promise? Yet maybe she was with someone else right now breaking that same promise?

He thought of Liliya and the day of their wedding. He had made that same vow to her and had broken it. But this was a promise he now felt compelled to keep. George was a changed man. George told the truth and he would forever keep all promises, and this had been a promise. He couldn't now change what he had said. If only he knew then all he had learnt now.

He knew he could never love anyone again. The promise was unequivocal and could never be broken. He didn't want to die, but he didn't want to live. To stay alive meant living with pain and so each night he would say a prayer asking a God he hardly knew to make sure he didn't wake up. A natural death was less painful to those he loved. The envelope was still propped up on his desk. No questions were ever resolved and the hurt continued.

The relief of sleep was rare and when it came it was often with the morning sun. The greater pain was being awake. Through exhaustion and the pressure of trying to resolve or even understand so many intractable problems, it finally became too much. He had not slept for two days. He had not left the house for two weeks. He was unshaven in dirty clothes and he had hardly eaten. George ran, he started to run quickly, he ran at the wall. He didn't know what he wanted to happen. He just wanted the pain – the continual pain in his head – to stop. He wanted the pall of blackness to disappear. He couldn't see any other way. Forward was only to more of the same, and there was no going back. George felt trapped in a time warp that had no exit. Despair and fear drove him hard, head first into the wall.

George didn't know how long he had been unconscious. There was dried blood over his eye and cheek, a bruise; the cut and a bump showed the point of impact. He lay on the sofa curled up in a fetal ball, tears streaming from bloodshot eyes. The area around his bruises hurt, but no more than the rest of his head. George finally accepted he needed help and he would have to drive through his pride. He had deteriorated over the months since Kristina left him to become a shell of a person weighed down by all the sins of his past. Whether they were his sins or Familiant's was now not the issue. The deaths and the pain were his and he had to live with them all. He needed forgiveness and he needed to atone and to do either he needed to be well. He phoned Kristina and hoped that she had not changed her number along with her address. She was now the only person he knew.

'Kristina,' he said through the tears. He could hear she was driving. 'I need help. You know from your past what it is like to have dark moments. Help me please, Kristina. I can't go on. I need help.'

There was silence. Had she not heard or was she thinking? Finally she said, 'I'm not sure what I can do, George. I don't think I can help you.' The phone went silent.

'You are my very, very best friend. You are my only friend. You are the one who said you would never negotiate me out. You are the only one who can help me. I want you to take me to a doctor or take me to a clinic. I need help!'

George was shouting at the phone, hoping somehow the message would travel on the ether or airwaves and arrive with her, but it never did.

George had no choices left other than to recover or to fade away. He collected all the alcohol he could find in his house and emptied it down the kitchen sink and wondered how he would survive without the support it was providing. He was a virtual recluse, hardly venturing outside. Sleep was still a luxury and food no more than a necessity, but he fought hard and fought alone to recover from his breakdown.

It was a long and painful struggle, with regular and often prolonged bouts of darkness, and when they came it was a darkness that enveloped him for many days. In those moments the need for atonement was the strongest. Hunger was a price to be paid for the pain it caused, and pain was the price to be paid for his sins. Debasement was the requirement and each chance was taken, but with the passing summer there were shafts of light and the darkness became mere shadows. The urge to die diminished, although the joy of living had not returned.

With time, from somewhere deep inside, he continued to find many new sources of strength and courage. Summer and the sun helped; he would often sit alone in his garden as his verve returned. He went through each of Aleksandra's words and tried to make sense of them. He thought through every moment and every day of his life with Kristina, and finally that peace he had searched for, in part at least, arrived.

Once in his past he had read himself his last rites and the letter still propped up on his desk was a continual reminder of that. Not a day had passed without thinking of Kristina who had come to represent the core and focus of all his past. Through Kristina, there was a fault line to Aleksandra, Vera, Anna and finally Familiant. *She* was the symbol of everything that had happened to him. Once, he had placed all his hopes in her, and when she left she took them all away. With time, tears and reserves of unknown strength he had learnt to manage the pain and stop it dominating everything. He had started his relationship with Kristina to change his life and gain control, but it was in *finishing* the relationship that he had developed and changed.

His perspective was different now, and now he looked at the world askew. For the first time, he understood what his independence might mean. He found a deep and fulfilling honesty, once missing. He had experienced such a profound love it transcended friendship and could never be ignored. In accepting the joy it gave, he had found in simplicity answers to the most complex questions.

Coss was relieved when George phoned him and asked if he wanted to come over for a holiday. He agreed without any expectation of a happy time, but for an old friend he would do anything. Coss was pleased when he saw George had come to the airport to meet him. The smile had returned.

'Reconciled yourself to the world, George?' he asked.

'Maybe a little.'

Coss managed to get George out to a restaurant or two, but was upset that he hardly drank these days.

'Holy days and holidays only,' George had replied.

'And any special companions?'

'I have friends, Coss, special friends, but no companions. Those days are gone. I loved Anna and maybe I loved Jane. I loved Liliya, and Kristina I loved in a way that was once in a life time. Whenever love ends we leave a piece of our heart in the relationship, and then, when we try to find enough pieces to mend the jigsaw of a broken heart, we have to search hard to find all the parts. Coss, I left so much with Kristina I have no more capacity to love. I have told her I will love her forever and that is a promise not to be broken.'

Coss held up his hand to stop George. 'No one is telling you to stop loving Kristina. It is right that you do keep your promise, but, George, you can rebuild and reconstruct your life. It's a wonder of the human spirit that we have the strength to recover, survive and flourish, and we do this by loving and being in love. Your heart *is* big enough to love again. Take your honesty and find a new companion, George. You *do* have the capacity to love again.'

They talked and they enjoyed being with each other, and George really understood what it meant to have friends. When Coss left he was pleased that his old friend was recovering.

PART V

NOW

CHAPTER XXIX

TODAY

It is another beautiful summer's day and George is sitting in the garden of his small farm in Lugansk in the east of the Ukraine, near the Russian border. The grass is as green as he ever remembered from his distant childhood days in England. As he looks from his chair he sees the lawn break into an orchard, with a small brook running away at its end. Even in this dry summer he hears the sound of the water running over the stones in the river. Birds dive down to drink or catch a fish. He doesn't know which.

He is in shirt sleeves and in front of him on the table is his laptop and he is reading articles on the screen. Even after all this time the disaster and turmoil of Chernobyl has had little effect. Nearly fifty per cent of Ukraine's energy needs are met by nuclear-generated energy. So in the end, he thought, nothing has changed and the Ukraine and Europe is just as it would have been. *You failed, Familiant,* he thought, but now George had a balance in his life and this passing thought no longer caused him anguish. He looked at his computer screen and started typing.

My life has been an adventure and I have been an adventurer.

You may find this hard to believe but, as I reflect, I am now and will forever be thankful to Familiant for the opportunities he created and I gratefully accepted. He wasn't a bad man, maybe just misguided. He thought he was in control, but the choices were always mine. He created the spaces and the opportunities for me to make all the decisions, which finally led me to a wonderful life of richness. Of course, at times there were moments of deep despair, but without him my life could have been so mundane.

I blame no one for anything and take full responsibility now, for how I move my life forward. Sometimes I was naïve, but that is how we all start on this long journey called life; maybe I believed I was wiser and cleverer than I really was, and maybe I believed my influence over Petric was more than I imagined. I now suspect – no, I know – that Petric would have followed the path he eventually chose even if he had never met me. I was not the only influence in his life and maybe, through Liliya, I was the one person who delayed him and slowed him down and came closest even to preventing the catastrophe.

Petric, like Familiant, was misguided, and his actions could never be condoned. But he was a fine man with much love in his heart, who cared passionately about his country, and in his way he achieved a greater benefit for mankind than he ever did for his beloved Ukraine. The focus and visibility on nuclear energy, so horribly surfacing again with the recent nuclear incident in Japan, was started by his reckless actions.

For Aleksandra, Vera and Coss I am pleased beyond a level I can describe. To see brothers and sisters reunited is a blessing, and to be part of that, through a cause that honours their father, is a privilege. If there is anything real in humanity then it is the sum of all these small and very personal stories.

Anna had a passion I could never have satisfied if we had married and stayed in Oxford. I saw it burn brightest when we met in Poland, and someday that – or some other cause – would finally have pulled us apart. She would never have been satisfied in a life without a strong cause to fight for and a driving rationale. I doubt that Familiant knew what she had, or why she was so special, but he knew she was singularly different and that is why he handpicked her to join his project.

I am sorry for Liliya and I am sorry that we drifted apart. It is by far my biggest regret. Liliya and I do still occasionally meet and, although we are now on different paths, we share the same roots, and I can happily say we are once more good friends. And without that odd conflagration of circumstances I would never have met Kristina.

Kristina was the blessing in my life. I freely admit that I loved her more than anyone else and more than I think anyone else could or will again. She was charismatic and enigmatic and as a friend, not just a lover, she pulled together all the strands of my life.

I still think of her every day but increasingly with fondness and not the deep regret that initially accompanied my every waking moment. Leaving me was a hard lesson but maybe for her it was ultimately more difficult, and in the long term I hope it is not more painful. And, as sometimes with old injuries, the pain of her absence remains and is continuous; sometimes it's fleeting and small and other times great. Initially I tried to move her totally out of my mind. I tried to blame her, and I tried to be angry with her, but these were all futile attempts at resolution as neither were what I truly felt, and so now I celebrate our time and our love and use it as a strength and support. Since that one time we last made love I have not met her and I do not even know where she is. I hope she is happy. In time, I hope, she will see that the value of our friendship was more important than our time together as lovers, and then we can return to a shared life of friendship. But she was the catalyst for me to change and for that I owe her the greatest debt, and someday, one day, I may be able to make full repayment.

All life's experiences have changed and forged me; that is the nature of experience, but only when we learn and reflect on them. When I first arrived in Oxford, I was an independent and free spirit, at ease with myself and the world around me. I thought I knew what I wanted from life and I was willing to take it, and I was carefree in the way I enjoyed myself, and now, finally, I have grown up and life has gone full circle. From child and back to child. I am again an individual and no longer part of anyone's system or plans. I am without allegiance, rancour or motive.

I have become the man foreshadowed by that boy I was at Oxford. I am at peace with myself and the world. With age and time I have reasserted my right to be an individual.

I am fortunate I have saved enough money, so generously provided by Lord Richard, that broadly I can always do whatever I want, although today I am happy to live a more simple and honest life. I do not crave for possessions. I do not conform. If you conform to anyone else's expectations then you become a slave to their aspirations. Your hope and drive become submissive to their ambitions. I spent too much time trying to be the image of others' ambitions; that was how Familiant ensnared me.

In my darker moments I thought there was a finite pool of happiness, a weighing scale that always balanced one person's happiness with another's sadness. For many, like Familiant and Kristina, that is clearly a rule, because they take what they need and want for their happiness at another's expense. Familiant and Lord Ridley seduced me with money and riches and I accepted them all. And I see it all so clearly now and sadly I see it happening day in and day out throughout the Western world. Greed has become the norm and the 'must have' culture is everywhere around us. New generations feel alienated in a way that is both depressing and worrying.

However, I see now that this greed for happiness is not a universal truth. I remember Vera's words about true love being a shared state of submission and dominance. A world in which we will give all we have to those we love. The one real sadness in my life is that when I had friends, I doubted them and denied them my presence. Friends are the core of a contented life. We all need them to laugh with and to console us. Friends are the foundation and the bedrock of a balanced life – even if, like lovers, at times they frustrate and annoy, but we should always stay with them. I was feckless with my friendships. So now I wonder about Jane and what she does. Even losing Jamila, Evie, Lynne and Francesca are passing regrets. I only wish that Anna was still here to read these words. Even this is not even an original thought, though; I am recalling the words of the thirteenth-century philosopher, Saint Thomas Aquinas: 'The happy man in this life needs friends'. Why do we so easily forget our history?

We are not defined in this life by our successes, but by the way we confront our fears and fight our demons. Now I am sure that life has no ultimate purpose. We are not meant to achieve great deeds and we are not on a higher or different level than other creatures. We do not have to strive to be successful because success is finally measured in many different ways. Birds, bees, dogs and cats find their purpose, and I presume contentment, from simple genetically driven activities. We, too, can be content in simple truths, friends and lovers. A contented life is about taking opportunities while sharing the happiness and joy you feel. Whether it's your God or your Familiant that creates the opening, a good life comes from taking each chance and making the most of what is given to you. There is no pre-destiny but only a guiding hand creating space and opportunity.

And as I now consider how close I once was to taking to my own life, I don't dwell on that moment but draw strength from the courage I found to fight back and change and become more comfortable and at peace.

I sit back and re-read what I've written, nodding to myself as a satisfied smile breaks across my face. I look up and see her walking down the path carrying a tray, dodging a child's climbing frame. She brings me a drink of lemon mint. She is beautiful and she puts her hands on my shoulders.

'Nearly finished?'

'I *am* finished,' I reply. 'My story is written and finally told.'

'Come in soon,' she says. 'The children want to say goodnight to their Papa.'

She turns and goes back into the house.

'Now I have finished, *lapushka*. I've written all that I know of my life. Thank you, SY. Thank you, AS.'

My final words. I close down the laptop and carry it back to the house to say goodnight to my children.

ABOUT THE AUTHOR

Gerry Cryer is a full-time writer who now lives in Surrey in England. He is also an actor, business mentor, innovator, coach, and one-time guitarist in the rock-covers band *Mid-Life Crisis*.

After a university career contemporary with a British Home Secretary and the Editor of a daily national newspaper (neither of whom he knew because they didn't play rugby), he embarked on a long and successful series of jobs in business management and consultancy, which others have kindly called a career.

In his story-telling, he provides insights into top-level machinations, negotiations and behind-the-scenes issues that the general public know nothing about. Combined with his experience of different cultures, having lived and worked in over twenty-five countries on three continents – Europe, the USA and the Middle East – he has a vast knowledge resource.

He has high emotional intelligence also, and is a tenacious observer of the human condition, which gives him a special talent for looking at the detail and minutiae and setting them in the context of the bigger picture, dissecting human behaviour into its component parts within the complex situations that modern society demands.

Gerry has the useful knack of staying relaxed and calm especially in a crisis, not least because of the motto he lives by: 'Expect the unexpected'. This has proved particularly useful as his natural inquisitiveness and sense of adventure have caused him to be at the centre of many a crisis.

The Masterful Manipulation of George Cove is Gerry's first novel, and his second, *Blah Blah* will be released before Xmas 2013. A third novel is currently in editing for publication in 2014.

AUTHOR'S NOTE

Most of the characters in this book are fictitious, thus any resemblance to real persons, living or dead, is purely coincidental. However, several well-known individuals from this particular period of history are mentioned in the story or have been drawn into it more substantially; their thoughts, words and actions came purely from my imagination.

There are friends in my life I have respected and lost, and now want to meet again. As a mark of respect, I have borrowed their names (but not their identities) and this is a sign that I would like to make contact again.

To discover more about Gerry Cryer and his books, visit:
www.gerrycryer.com